seeking vengeance

EDEN SUMMERS

Copyright © 2021 by Eden Summers

All rights reserved.

No part of this book may be reproduced in any form or by any electronic or mechanical means, including information storage and retrieval systems, without written permission from the author, except for the use of brief quotations in a book review.

This book is a work of fiction. The names, characters, places, and incidents are products of the writer's imagination or have been used fictitiously and are not to be construed as real. Any resemblance to persons, living or dead, actual events, locales or organizations is entirely coincidental.

The author acknowledges the trademarked status and trademark owners of various products referenced in this work of fiction, which have been used without permission. The publication/use of these trademarks is not authorized, associated with, or sponsored by the trademark owners.

I place a sweaty hand on the restaurant door, my fingers holding the slightest tremble of anticipation as skin meets glass.

I've waited two years for this.

No. It took two years to know I *needed* this.

The retaliation.

The validation of revenge.

Two years where I forced myself to believe I was a bigger person, when in reality I'm nothing but a carbon copy of the monsters I'm now determined to end.

I shift my fake glasses farther along my nose and push my way inside, the aroma of fresh basil sinking deep into my lungs.

I discovered Perfezione on my last excursion to Denver, my novice detective work leading me to this Italian masterpiece with immaculately polished china, pristine tablecloths, and sparkling chandeliers.

A last-minute no-show was the only reason I gained a reservation when I previously walked through these doors. And an insanely generous tip secured a seat for tonight.

This place doesn't do walk-ins. It does millionaires and prestige. High-class and pomposity.

I give my fake name to the maître d' and keep my expression impassive as a young, slim waitress escorts me to my table—the two-seater I requested in the far back corner, right next to the window.

She pulls out the chair closest to the wall, but that's not where I want to be. I decline the offer with a polite smile and reach for the opposite seat, descending into the padded cushion with my back to the room.

There's a beat of confusion in her expression. The slightest pause where she looks at me in judgment for picking this position instead of hers. "Is someone else joining you, Ms. Javernick?"

I give a subtle shake of my head, the strands of my fake blonde wig skimming my cheeks. "Not tonight. It's just me."

There's another pause. Another perplexed glimpse asking why I wouldn't want to stare at the restaurant's opulence instead of the plain cream wallpaper. Then she nods and increases the wattage of her beaming smile. "Can I get you something to drink?" She hands over a leather-bound menu and grabs my cloth napkin to delicately place it on my lap.

"White wine, please. Pinot Grigio if possible."

She inclines her head. "Of course."

I'm left alone, the hum of conversation brushing my ears and adrenaline warming my veins. But it's the intoxicating promise of vengeance that consumes my thoughts.

The past few months have been filled with one idea after the next, each potential strike against my enemy joining a long list of possibilities.

I've contemplated financial ruin, family destruction. I've even humored the idea of loss of life. Nothing is off-limits. Nothing can be if I want to sleep peacefully in the future. Because this isn't just revenge. It's also vindication. I need to earn back the respect of those I love.

My wine arrives while I scan the menu, my eyes reading the words despite my wild mind not letting them sink in. I'm too eager, my nervous energy ratcheting my pulse and feeding my vicious hunger.

I still have many questions to answer before I strike.

I haven't decided if I'll outsource the attack—physical or otherwise.

Mercenaries are an option, however trusting a stranger is an issue. I have the stomach to do it on my own, though. Murder won't haunt my conscience. I already have a vial of cyanide in my purse posing as cocaine, the poisonous powder awaiting an unwilling victim. It's the panic over a lengthy jail sentence that gives me pause.

Either way, I won't reignite a war in the middle of a five-star restaurant. Tonight is merely reconnaissance.

I'm two sips into my alcoholic relief when a skitter of awareness shimmies down my spine, awakening my nerves.

They're here.

I can't see them. Can't even hear them yet. But I know the Costa family has arrived.

I fight against the discomfort of having my back to the room and take another sip, making sure my shoulders appear relaxed as my waitress escorts them to the table behind me, just as I anticipated.

Goose bumps whisper along my arms, all the way to my nape. I feel naked, my little black dress suddenly nothing but a slip of material as the gentle breeze of the air conditioner kisses my exposed skin.

I'm hidden, though, unrecognizable beneath the colored contacts, fake glasses, and long-flowing blonde wig. Even if we do come face-to-face, I doubt they will recognize me.

I hold the wine glass to my lips and tilt my gaze to the window, discreetly watching them in the reflection as they sit at the round table, all of them exuding an air of snobbery.

There's Emmanuel Costa. His wife, Adena. The younger men I know to be his sons—Salvatore and Remy. Then closest to me is Abri, his viper of a daughter, whose back is parallel to mine.

"We will have to make this a quick meal," Salvatore mutters. "I have plans tonight."

"Plans with who?" his mother asks. "A woman? Have you met someone?"

I listen intently, hoping for the details of his rendezvous, my heart beating heavy against my ribs. Lovers provide vulnerabilities. I learned that lesson the hard way.

The waitress approaches in my periphery, her increased proximity dragging my attention from precious seconds of information. "Are you ready to order, ma'am?"

"Can I have a little more time?" I keep my voice low, hoping she'll allow me to drag out my stay for as long as possible. "If you could give me five more minutes that would be appreciated."

She nods, her smile forced as she saunters away.

I spare a second to properly read the menu, picking a few items before I return my attention to the window, my ear cocked toward Emmanuel's table as I drink in their secrets with each sip of wine.

"We need to tighten our distribution channels," Emmanuel advises in accented English. "We have weak links that will cost us greatly if they're not handled."

"They'll be handled," Remy replies. "They're always handled."

"Not always. There was the issue with border security two years ago—"

"And you've never let us forget it. Since then, everything has been tight. We take care of any cracks that surface."

It's clear they're not talking about distribution for items in their designer fashion label. When our worlds collided years ago, it had been because Emmanuel wanted to diversify from their clothing empire and force my brother into a partnership revolving around my family's drug trade.

I guess they paved their own way. Or found a sucker to swindle to show them the ropes.

"How about you, Abri?" Emmanuel asks. "Have you done what was asked of you?"

"If you mean, have I sowed the seed for you to blackmail your latest target, then the answer is no." Her voice is a velvety purr, the confident drawl holding the faintest undertone of resentment. "He's proving to be a hard man to deceive."

"Well, try harder. You don't have the luxury of—"

"Can we *please* leave the topic of business for later?" Adena asks. "I want to hear about more important things like when my children will bless me with grandbabies."

Someone sighs. There's a groan, too.

"I'm happy to be artificially inseminated, mother," Abri snips. "But it will become increasingly harder for me to extort and manipulate men if I have a child on my hip. And then what value would I have to you?"

"Don't start," Emmanuel mutters under his breath. "Your lack of gratitude is beginning to grate my last nerve."

"And being constantly leashed by my father has long since grated away all of mine."

Silence follows. Tense, palpable silence for several heartbeats.

I don't need to search for Abri's lethal glare through the reflection in the glass. I feel it.

Pretty little bitch can't cut the parental ties. What a shame.

"Control yourself." Salvatore snarls the warning. "You're starting to make a scene and—"

"Have you decided what you'd like to order?"

Shit. I clasp a hand to my throat, startled by the waitress's return. "I'm sorry." I swivel to meet her waiting gaze from the corner of my eye. "I'll have the beef carpaccio to start and then the corzetti. Thank you."

"My pleasure. How about more wine?"

I swallow over my increased pulse and glance at the puddle of liquid in my glass. "That sounds perfect."

"Great. I'll return right away." She beams.

I throw back the remaining alcohol as she walks away, needing the wine to smother the chastising voices in my head.

I'm slipping.

Faltering.

I'm better than this. Underhanded tactics are practically a birthright. I was born to scheme. To be devious and manipulative. The ability to drag the Costa family to its knees is in my genes and I plan to lean into those intrinsic skills to get this job done right.

Focus, Layla. Don't get distracted.

I've worked too hard to mess this up now. I've tracked their fashion label on the stock market since February. I have online notifications set up for each property in their portfolio. I have files on all their legitimate employees. I've done background checks and rummaged around many skeleton-filled closets.

They *will* get what they deserve.

And I *will* be the one to dish out their punishment.

"…Well, I just don't understand how the gardener can't keep on top of the bug infestation that's destroying the roses at the back of the property," Adena whines. "What are we paying him for if the blooms are constantly ruined?"

I sag into my seat as the discussion diverts into menial topics that are of no use. The five of them discuss the weather, of all things. Then cryptocurrency.

I grow impatient as my first meal arrives and their conversation moves to Salvatore's next car purchase—an Aston Martin that I hope he wraps around a pole.

When my main is served, they're murmuring about an upcoming vacation, the parents requesting the company of their adult kids while Salvatore, Remy, and Abri decline with varying lackluster excuses.

Salvatore will be at their fashion label's flagship warehouse, meeting with management. Remy can't join the sun, surf, and sand because contractors are scheduled to paint his bedroom. And Abri gives no more than an "I'm busy" as she continues to sulk.

I finish my meal without another morsel of insight into their illegal dealings. No names to investigate. No meetings or locations to stake out.

I order another drink and force down a plate of tiramisu to justify my extended time at the highly sought-after table. But it isn't long before the waitress brings my bill, subtly announcing her desire for me to leave.

Goddammit.

I've outstayed my welcome and I can't risk not gaining another reservation in the future. I have no choice but to tip big and make my way to the bar for another glass of wine.

I refuse to walk away until the Costas do. It doesn't matter that I'm now out of listening range. I can still watch through the mirror behind the wall lined with liquor bottles, hating every breath they dare to breathe.

I try to read their body language. Their straight shoulders and tight jaws. I attempt to decipher the reason behind the occasional scowls from the three siblings, but the distance between us slaughters the deeper levels of observation.

When they pay their check and stand, I gulp my last mouthful of wine and pull my purse strap over my shoulder as I slide from the stool.

They walk for the door, one after the other, Abri in the lead, Salvatore and Emmanuel at the back like the protecting wolves of the pack.

I wait until the old man is at the entry before I follow, my footsteps immediately halting when a bulky suit-clad man pushes back from the bar to block my path.

"Excuse me." I attempt to walk around him only to have him pivot into me, countering my move, his hulking body deliberately obstructing my escape.

Hard blue eyes meet mine as his lips thin. "Take a seat."

The bitter taste of panic soaks my tongue. "I'm sorry, I think you've mistaken me for someone else. I don't know you."

I do, however, recognize his vibe. The ruffled dark-blond hair and perfectly smooth skin do nothing to assuage the distinct edge of malice I've been surrounded by since birth.

"Sit," he growls.

Shit. Shit. *Shit.*

"I'm confused. Are you a member of staff?" I raise a brow, feigning ignorance. "Did I not leave a big enough tip?"

He steps closer, his upper lip curling as he leans threateningly close. "Sit before you make your intentions more obvious, and tell me exactly what you have planned."

2

————

LAYLA

Two years ago

I PACE THE CARPET OF THE SACRAMENTO HOTEL PENTHOUSE, EVERY limb trembling, every thought brittle and panicked.

They took my daughter.

Abducted my baby girl as she slept.

Right from my brother's home.

I can't stop shaking, can't cease the bile-inducing mania that hisses through my mind on a loop of building desperation.

The things they could be doing to her… The things they could've already done.

I fight against the bile clogging my throat and shove my hands through my hair, tug, tug, tugging, wishing the burn of the pulled strands could distract from the madness. It only adds to my onslaught.

"It's going to be okay." My sister, Keira, approaches with caution. "They're following the kids. Nobody will let them out of their sight."

They—my husband, Benji, his brother, Luca, our enforcer, Hunter, and his woman, Sarah. Then there's the Fed, Anissa, who seems to have worked her way under my brother's skin to steal a heart I never knew existed.

"Is that meant to make me feel better?" I glare. "Have you spared a thought as to what could've already been done to them? They were sedated, Keira. Their babysitter murdered."

My baby girl and my half brother, Tobias, who I've only just met.

Keira winces, stopping a few feet away as if scared to get within striking distance. "Maybe a sedative will help—"

"Fuck you and your sedatives."

They forced enough of those pills down my throat yesterday, giving me no choice but to sleep through my daughter's suffering. But I won't take any more, not even when the allure of escaping this nightmare calls my name.

"They've found Cole."

My head snaps to Decker on the sofa, my sister's partner raising his cell in front of him.

"Where?" I ask. "Are they still following the children?"

I rush toward him and snatch the phone.

Found Cole. We're out of town. Will keep you posted.

"Out of town where?" My hands ache from trembling. "I want to go. We should follow."

"I know as much as you do." Decker grabs the cell from me and slumps back into the sofa. "We're not going anywhere. Just try to relax and let them handle this."

Relax?

I fuse my molars. Clench my fists. Swallow.

I want to scream. To wail and sob and scratch the torturous emotions right out from beneath my ribs with my fingernails. They have no idea what this is like. They don't understand how torturous your own imagination can be when your nine-year-old daughter is in the hands of monsters.

I return to my pacing, walking back and forth while my legs grow heavy and my mind paints blood-filled images narrated by little girls' screams.

What if they've touched her? Raped her?

I shove a fist to my lips, demanding the howl clogging my throat to remain inside.

Emmanuel Costa has my daughter. A man who had ties to my now-deceased father.

Most people would grow comforted by the family history. But most people aren't spawned from the devil himself.

Luther Torian was a despicable man and the worst part was his ability to hide it for most of my life.

Minutes pass. Hours, too. Silence blankets the luxurious penthouse even though my ears continue to ring with haunted screams.

I can't handle this. I *can't.*

I need to do something. Anything.

I shake my hands at my sides and breathe deep, the oxygen only stirring the bile pooling at the back of my throat.

It's been too long. My little girl has been taken for almost forty-eight hours. More than enough time to emotionally scar her forever.

"Can you quit the pacing?" Decker mutters. "You're giving me a headache."

I pause, about to let out the torture congealing in my chest when the hotel door swings open and Penny rushes in, relief written all over her pretty face.

"What is it?" I run to her, gripping her upper arms before she can get a word out. "What happened?"

"Luca called. They're coming back." She smiles, the perfection reaching her dazzling eyes. "There was some sort of confrontation with the Costas, but we've got the kids."

Time stops.

My breathing, too.

My hands drop to my sides as I retreat a step, and for a moment, there's silence. Pure, euphoria-filled peace as I stare at her, anticipating the weight of my daughter returning to the security of my arms.

"And Cole?" Decker pushes from the sofa and limps forward.

"Him, too." Penny's expression infuses with more brilliance when she meets my gaze. Her cheeks are high. Her eyes are beaming. "It's over. Stella and Tobias are both okay. The Costas have fled. Our guys are making their way to the cars to drive here right now."

All the air leaves my lungs on a heave of relief but the shaking increases. My arms and legs tremble beyond my control as my pulse grows fractured and rampant.

She's coming back.

My little girl is coming home.

"Oh, God." Tears burn my eyes. Emotion sears my throat. "They got them back."

I don't care how it happened.

I'm sure I'll relive it with Stella as many times as she needs to put the tragic events behind her. I'll do whatever it takes to give her back a childhood that I've always endeavored to make normal even though she was born into a family of crime.

Keira walks to my side. Her arm wraps around my waist, a kiss presses to my cheek. "Everything is going to be okay." She leads me to the sofa and helps me to sit. "I'm going to get you a drink. Something to take the edge off. The more grounded you are when the kids return, the safer they'll feel."

I nod, placing my hands between my knees, rocking back and forth while she walks to the liquor trolley on the far side of the room.

My daughter is coming back to me.

All those who were taken are coming back—Stella, Tobias, Cole.

I never thought my loved ones would return. The relief doesn't seem real through the layers of certainty I'd piled upon their death. I'd been convinced karma had arrived, seeking payment for my mistakes. My many, *many* misdeeds.

"Here." Keira kneels before me, placing a scotch glass in my hands with what I assume is a finger of vodka. "Sip slowly and tell me if you want more."

"I just want to get out of here as soon as possible." There's a tremble in my voice. "I need to get Stella home."

"We will." Decker gives me a fleeting look, one that speaks of judgment despite his deep-seated relief at the good news. "If they're coming here it means we've got time to spare. Otherwise, they'd want to meet us at the airport to make a quick exit."

I ignore the silent guilty verdict he places on my shoulders and down the vodka, then push to my feet in search of more. I drink and pace, drink and pace until the penthouse door opens again, the tiny squeak of hinges and whoosh of displaced air assailing me with temperamental anticipation.

Anissa walks in first, the Fed's face a picture of exhaustion, followed closely by Hunter. I stand rooted to the floor as those placed in charge of my child's rescue pile into the room, Tobias shoving past Sarah's hip to make a mad dash for Penny.

My heart squeezes painfully at the sight of him. His red-rimmed eyes. His dirt-stained clothes.

They embrace in a mass of clinging hands and relieved gasps while I remain still, my relief fracturing as my brother enters the room with my daughter limp in his arms.

"*Oh, my God.*" I rush for them, my arms outstretched.

She's covered in blood. Her clothes. Hands. Arms. There are even marks on the normally smooth skin of her cheeks.

"She hasn't been hurt." Cole's tone lacks inflection, his face devoid of emotion. "It's not her blood."

"Then what hap—"

"She was upset. I needed to sedate her."

I hold his gaze, trying to siphon the information he's keeping from me as sorrow plants its seed in my belly, the roots burrowing deep.

He hands Stella to me, her slim body pliant in my arms, her face so incredibly pure despite the blood stains. Everything else ceases to exist except her. The friends and family fade from my consciousness. The whispered words and mumbled conversation don't breach my ears.

I sink to the plush carpet, unable to stop myself from squeezing Stella tight. I nuzzle my nose against her neck. Breathe the faint scent of her kiddie shampoo. She's at home in my arms, her face peaceful with sleep, her head seeming to instinctively nestle into me as the slightest whimper leaves her lips.

The aftermath of tears is evident on her face, her skin red and puffy around her eyes. She survived a war. She was thrown into one of the deepest, darkest pits of this world and made it out.

God, I'm grateful.

I rock her in my arms, just like I did when she was a newborn—forward, back, forward, back—while the room grows quiet.

I don't want to face our audience. Not yet. I need this moment with her. I need a lifetime of me and my daughter and nothing else. If only I didn't have so many gnawing, clawing questions that demand answers.

"What did they do to her?" I raise my gaze to Cole.

His cold eyes are already fixed on my face. "We can discuss it once the children are settled elsewhere."

"Why?" I frown, glancing from my brother, to Anissa, then Sarah and Hunter. All the people before me stare back without emotion. There's no jubilation. No celebration. Not even anger over what must have happened to claim victory. "What did they do to her?"

I drag my gaze farther to little Tobias who now stands at Penny's side, his arms around her hips, his tortured gaze on me.

There's no relief in his expression. Not even a glimpse of happiness at being returned to his family.

Something is wrong.

Something is very, *very* wrong.

"What the hell did they do?" I demand.

"Let me take her for a while." Penny steps forward.

"No." I cling tighter to the precious gift in my lap.

"Do it, Layla," Cole mutters. "Penny can take Tobias and Stella into my room." He jerks his head to the open door a few yards behind him. "This won't take long."

"*This*?" I haul myself to my feet, carrying my daughter with me.

"Just do it, for fuck's sake," Cole snaps. "*Now.*"

I balk at his viciousness, but I'm not surprised. I'd wondered how long it would take for his pity to wear off. I'd mistakenly thought I'd have more time. That maybe I could find my feet not just in this room, but in life, before he fed me the animosity I deserve.

I close my eyes, continuing to rock as I place a kiss to Stella's forehead. I can't let her go. I *never* want to let her go ever again.

"It's okay." Penny reaches for her, Tobias still at her side. "She's safe. I promise."

A garbled cry clogs my throat as I admit defeat and hand my daughter over. Releasing her soft body after everything she's been through is akin to being gutted. Neck to pelvis. Hip to hip.

Nausea comes back with a vengeance as Penny cradles Stella's limp form in her arms, carrying her to the bedroom with a subdued Tobias following close behind.

I watch every step. Every movement.

When the bedroom door closes behind them, I struggle against the impulse to collapse into a fit of hysterical tears. I don't have that luxury though. I never have. Torians don't show weakness. We're not allowed to falter.

"Tell me." I straighten my shoulders and suck in a measured breath as I turn to face everyone. Flakes of dry blood cover my top, the gore threatening to break me. "What the hell did those monsters do to her, Cole?"

My brother's expression wavers, the animosity fracturing to expose something that holds a hint of sympathy.

Oh, God.

I scan the faces of those by his sides. Anissa lowers her gaze to the carpet. Luca's eyes are bloodshot and glistening with unshed tears. Keira's are, too. She knows something I don't. Something that must have been shared while I was lost in the reunion with my precious baby girl.

"Tell me." I glance from one person to the next—Sarah, Hunter, Decker—seeking out my husband. I reach the end of the semi-circle of friends and family without catching sight of his dark eyes.

"Benji?" I trek my attention back the other way—Decker, Hunter, Sarah, Keira, Luca, Anissa, and finally, Cole. "Where is he?"

Cole's chin hitches as if he's stealing himself for an upcoming onslaught.

"Where is my husband?" Icy dread slithers down my spine, catching on every nerve.

He has to be parking the car. Packing our things. Checking out at reception.

Keira whimpers, decimating my wishful thinking.

"Where's Benji?" My voice fractures, emotion tightening my vocal cords. "Why isn't he here?"

"He's gone, Lay."

Cole's calm words steal the air from my chest in a massive upheaval, the oxygen stripping itself from my lungs with jagged claws.

"No." I shake my head.

My husband and I were guilty of horrible things. Of traitorous, treacherous acts. But he wouldn't have fled from his punishment. He wouldn't have left me and Stella behind.

"You forced him to run?" It's hard to get the question out. Even harder to understand him leaving without saying goodbye. "Where did he go?"

Luca lowers his attention to the carpet and sniffs with a hard swipe of his hand over his nose. His fingers are stained with remnants of blood. More faint splotches mark his dark shirt.

I shake my head again, fighting the whispers in my mind telling me that a hardened man like Luca wouldn't cry over his brother skipping town.

"No." I suck in gasps. One after another without relief. I'm suffocating. Drowning in the karma I knew would come my way.

"He's dead." Cole steps forward, his face bleak as he opens his arms and envelops me in his hold.

"No." I batter his chest. "You're lying. You're doing this to punish me."

How had I not noticed Benji didn't return? I hadn't spared him a thought. My focus had been on Stella. On our baby girl he went to rescue.

"They shot him. He couldn't be saved," Cole whispers the horror in my ear. "I'm sorry for your loss."

A sob escapes, my eyes searing with a firestorm of tears.

I heave for breath, for understanding, pummeling and scratching at my brother's suit-covered chest as my legs threaten to give out.

"Don't cry." He continues to hold me, but those words are nothing more than a formality. No warmth exudes from him—only sterility. "Don't cry, Layla," he whispers. "We both know tears are a privilege for those who lack guilt."

3
———

LAYLA

Present day

I CROSS MY HANDS ON THE BAR AND STARE AT THE GLOSS SCRATCHED from the wood, wishing the crevices held the insight to get me out of here.

"All I want is answers," the man mutters from the stool beside me.

"And I gave them to you. I like sitting near the window. Most people do."

"*Most* people don't eavesdrop on neighboring conversations the entire time. *Most* people would sit with their back to the wall, not the room. And *most* people wouldn't hang around until the exact moment the patrons behind them left."

My cheeks heat. No matter how hard I concentrate on measuring my breathing and remaining calm, my skin doesn't stop burning, potentially exposing my guilt.

"You'd want to start talking, sunshine." His endearment is far from kind. "Why are you here? Who do you work for?"

So much for being discreet. Turns out my presence held the blinding discretion of tractor beams. But still, I've done nothing wrong. I overheard a conversation. I haven't broken any laws.

"I have no idea what you're talking about." I slide from the stool. "And I'm done pandering to your paranoia. Like I told you, I have somewhere else I need to be."

The man follows, his shoulders broadening, yet again blocking my escape route. He doesn't look at me, though. He stares over my shoulder, those icy eyes focusing on something behind me.

"I can take it from here, Bishop." A voice etched with smooth superiority and graveled confidence brushes the back of my neck.

I swallow, my pulse thunderous.

There's no threat in the newcomer's tone. It's far less abrasive than his colleague's. Maybe it even holds a hint of humor. But since my father's schemes ruined my life, I'm not easily fooled by cadence and timbre.

Bishop glances from me to the unseen guy at my back, pausing a moment before inclining his head and swinging around to walk away. Just like that, the threatening ogre takes his leave, meaning whoever stands behind me is far more powerful.

"You can take what from here?" I turn, my pulse catching at the mischievous chocolate eyes that capture mine.

The handsome stranger grins, his smile subtle and exuding just the right amount of friendly flirtation. He wants me to feel at ease, and for the slightest second, I do, gently coaxed into his web of sex appeal.

Then intuition kicks in.

"You can take what from here?" I repeat.

His grin deepens, the slight flash of wicked intent catching me off guard. This guy is good. Manipulative. Everything about him is perfect. *Too* perfect. From the expensive designer suit, to the devilish graze of stubble along his chiseled jaw, all the way to his finger-tousled dark hair.

Charming yet destructive.

Attractive yet lethal.

"Join me for a drink." He doesn't wait for my response before he raises a finger to attract the attention of the bartender, ordering another Pinot Grigio and a scotch.

He's been watching me. Closely enough to know what I've been drinking.

"You look concerned, but there's no need to be," he adds. "I only asked Bishop to keep you inside until the Costas were well and truly gone."

Fuck. I've definitely been caught. The only question now is —by who?

"Did you also ask him to pepper me with accusations?" I raise my brows. "You didn't want to do it yourself?"

"Maybe I was too busy spying on our shared target."

I frown, in part due to how I can't stop staring at him, but mainly because of his explanation. He's admitting to spying on Emmanuel? To me? A stranger? "What is it with you two and this Costa family? I honestly have no idea what you're talking about."

"And I honestly know you're full of shit." His gaze holds mine, those playful dark eyes keeping me captive. "I never forget a beautiful woman. You were here a few weeks ago. In a flowing navy dress that plunged at the neckline and exposed an impressive amount of leg." He leans closer and adds with a conspiratorial whisper, "A word to the wise—maybe wear something that doesn't make you look like a goddess if you don't want to draw attention."

My throat tightens. I have to drag a hand to my neck to ease the building tension.

Not only is the blatant seduction entirely foreign after years of celibacy, but this man is right about the navy dress, meaning I wasn't caught tonight.

I failed weeks ago.

I drag my gaze from his knowing smirk and focus on the bartender. "Thank you, but I won't be needing another drink. I'm leaving."

"Tell me I'm wrong." The cocky stranger casually glides onto the stool in front of him. "You had your hair out, the same as it is tonight, the blonde strands hanging over your shoulders. And you wore the sexiest pair of two-inch pumps. They were white, if I'm not mistaken."

Cream, actually.

"I don't know what you're talking about." I keep my expression in check and return my attention to his.

Christ. That was a mistake.

His potent stare intensifies, his gaze starting a leisurely trek down my body. I feel his attention like a caress as he visually devours me, from my breasts to my hips all the way to my toes.

"I distinctly remember the shoes." His voice reclaims the hint of a low whisper. "Because I imagined what they would look like crossed behind the back of my neck."

I choke on thin air. "You're quite forward aren't you, Mr…?"

"Call me Matthew." He reaches for the scotch the bartender slides toward him and jerks his chin in thanks. "Don't forget that glass of wine."

My eyes widen. "No. Don't." I fix the young bartender with a scowl. "I'm not going to—"

"She'll drink it," Matthew answers with an unhinged level of superiority.

To any other woman, this boldness from an excessively attractive man might be endearing. Unfortunately, I've been down this cocky, charismatic road before.

He thinks he's catnip to my animalistic senses when in reality he's merely a ticking time bomb in a cover model package. I should know—I married someone exactly like him.

"Are you always this arrogant, Matthew?" I need to get out of here. I should storm for the door without a backward glance. What's this guy going to do? Tackle me to the floor in the middle of a busy restaurant?

"What's the difference between arrogance and confidence?"

"Excuse me?"

"Why do you call me arrogant and not confident?" His brows furrow as if he's truly perplexed and one hundred percent invested in my response while he takes another sip of scotch. "Because confidence is the self-assurance that comes from appreciating one's abilities and qualities. While arrogance is an exaggerated sense of one's importance and abilities. In which way have I been arrogant?"

That goddamn grin, for starters. The curve of those perfect lips wordlessly boasts how he could devour me in one sitting when that will never happen.

"For God knows what reason, you're flirting with me," I state flatly. "Not only that, you're giving me the distinct impression you think you could easily seduce me. Which, my friend, is an exaggerated sense of your abilities, which, in return, is your definition of arrogance."

His player smile doesn't waver as he drawls, "Are you sure it's not confidence?"

My pulse stutters. It's not so much the question, but the smooth way he asks. The superbly adept way he seasons his masculine tone with the tiniest glimpse of a dimple in his left cheek.

"Yes." I snatch the fresh glass of wine the bartender places on the counter and take a gulp. "I'm leaving. Good night."

His smooth chuckle haunts me. "But I don't even know your name. What am I going to write on our marriage license?"

Yet again, I'm caught off guard, all the pulse hammering and skin tingling colliding in a mass of hysteria that sends a shocked laugh bursting from my lips.

I can't remember ever being hit on like this. Being the wife to a notorious criminal, within an already infamous crime family, tends to keep men distanced. Even if I was experienced, I'm sure this guy would still leave me unsettled.

He's too damn good at this game.

"That right there." I point a finger at his chest. "Pure arrogance."

He takes another leisurely sip of scotch. "Is it, though? Really?"

I release another spontaneous chuckle, take a final gulp of wine before returning it to the bar, and then step back. "It was nice meeting you." It's an exaggeration, although, honestly, not a lie. I haven't enjoyed a heartfelt laugh in years. "It's too bad I'm not the woman you think I am."

I swivel on my toes and make for the door, my neck awakening with goose bumps as soon as I turn my back on his charm.

"Come on, *amore mio*," he calls after me, the Italian words spoken with a pristine accent. "We could help each other."

I don't stop.

"With the spying," he adds, louder, drawing the attention of four nearby women who hush their table conversation to stare at us with curiosity.

I halt, my feet rooted in place, not only because he's outing me in front of staff and strangers alike, but because he's potentially offering me something I want. Something I desperately need—a way forward with my Costa plans now that I've been discovered.

Footsteps approach behind me and I suck in a ragged breath when his warm hand comes to rest on the small of my back, his woodsy aftershave teasing my senses. "I have a room at the Lydell Hotel two doors down. They've got a great bar. Let's go there and talk."

4

LAYLA

Two years ago

THE SILENCE IS STIFLING AS MY HUSBAND'S CASKET IS LOWERED INTO the ground, the descent of the shining steel box seeming to steal the gossip from the mouths of those in attendance.

Stella nestles closer against my side, my daughter's tears soaking into the black material covering my hip, her lone sniffle sinking deep into my heart to stab at my composure.

I breathe it in. Her agony. Her suffering.

I take all the misery she releases into the world and make it my own because it's what I deserve.

Then, all too soon, the service is over.

Benji is buried. Gone. His all-encompassing life was summed up in a few paragraphs.

Tissues are shared, words of condolence are given out like cheap candy, and the whispered rumors that follow once the guests walk away brush against the outer edges of my hearing, poisoning me further.

The entire scene plays before me as if through a stranger's eyes, the depth of my grief barely felt over the strangling claws of guilt at my throat.

I killed my husband.

I may not have pulled the trigger, but I caused the lethal blow.

I stole happiness from those I love, replacing it with sorrow. And I'm not sure I can redeem myself to them, let alone forgive myself for the mistakes.

After the mourners leave the cemetery, Stella and I follow where my brother leads, Cole's hand guiding me from the crook of my arm until we're in his sports car. Nobody speaks. We barely breathe, the air around us now tainted by my callous decisions.

Once we reach his house I'm left to stand alone before the glass doors leading to the manicured gardens, a head full of unrelenting nightmares and a heart carved from jagged glass.

Stella and Tobias sit at the dining table, playing a subdued board game. Their similar ages have made them inseparable, which is nice. They're thankfully both young enough to be easily fed lies to cover up the truth of Benji's murder, but unfortunately, they're old enough to be scarred by my actions regardless of the cover story they were told.

The people I call family are on nearby sofas, discussing mundane things I can't fathom while my world collapses around me. I don't deserve to be a part of their lives anymore. . . At least, that's the way they've made me feel.

I don't belong here even though I'd beg until my last breath to stay.

I've never been so lost. So alone. Without support. Lacking grounding. I'm loathed by everyone, despite how they hide their contempt behind sympathetic glances and sad smiles.

I'm no longer trusted or appreciated. Well, except by my daughter, who knows nothing of my loathsome betrayal.

My perfect little girl will be forever haunted by my actions but, God willing, she will never learn I sold out my own brother to a father who based his moral code on the devil himself, which caused a chain reaction resulting in my husband's death.

A death that will forever weigh upon my shoulders.

Footsteps approach behind me and I stiffen, my lungs painfully tightening at the thought of company.

There's only one person it could be. The heavy steps. The willingness to reach out. My suspicions are confirmed when I see Cole in the reflection of the glass door, the faint touch of my brother's palm coming to rest on the back of my neck.

He doesn't speak. He doesn't have to. We both know words won't change what I did. Nothing will.

There's little comfort to provide a woman as pitiful and vile as me.

"Thank you for arranging the beautiful service. I think Benji would've been surprised at how many people attended." I pretend as if most of those who came to mourn didn't arrive merely to snoop. I'm well aware the majority only wanted to learn how a healthy, middle-aged man passed from a supposed heart attack.

"He was your husband," he states flatly. "He received a family burial."

"Even though you think he didn't deserve it," I whisper.

I can hear it in his voice. The thinly veiled resentment. The biting betrayal that still lingers.

"We both know he didn't. But this lifestyle is nothing if not a masquerade to the masses. We all do what needs to be done."

I wince, not only at the games that have to be played, but the ones I don't want to participate in.

I turn to face him, my pride in my throat, my heart on my sleeve. "I need to ask you for something." I have no right to request anything. I don't even deserve to maintain my place in this family. But… "No, not just ask." I shake my head. "I'm begging, Cole."

He straightens as his hand falls from my neck. "What is it?"

The request scorches my throat leaving scars in its wake. "Nobody here deserves to be put through any more destruction. Our father and I have already caused enough damage. We need to think of Tobias and Stella's future."

His brows pinch, as if he's waiting for me to inflict a verbal blow.

"I don't want you to chase revenge over what happened to Benji." I suck in a breath, strengthening myself against the increased judgment in his stare. "At least not now, while our wounds are still raw. I need you to promise there'll be no more bloodshed. That the danger surrounding the children won't intensify. Let the kids grow a little older first. Let them have some peace."

Those brows dig deeper, his silent opposition settling between us.

"I'm pleading for you and Luca to let this go." I clasp my hands in prayer, knowing Cole's the only one able to persuade my brother-in-law to put this tragedy behind us. Temporarily or not. "We all know I'm to blame for what happened. Nobody else. There's no reason to start a war."

His jaw ticks, his nostrils slightly flaring. "You're asking too much."

"*Please.*" I glance at Stella, needing him to agree for her sake. For the safety of everyone under this roof. If he retaliates toward the people who shot my husband, more of us could die. And I'll be responsible for those deaths, too. I won't be able to live with the increase in blame. I can barely breathe as it is. "Don't risk those we love because of my mistakes."

His eyes harden, the pity vanishing. "That's not how things work. We need to make it known that we don't accept—"

"*Please*, Cole." I grab his wrist. "I'm begging you. My daughter was already stolen from me once. I can't spend each day thinking it could happen again."

He keeps that hard stare on me, his judgment building.

"I'll do anything," I plead. "Whatever you ask, I'll do it. Just don't break this family more than it already is. Don't risk their lives like I did. *Please.* I'll never ask anything of you again."

His lip curls in a snarl as he switches his attention to the backyard.

For long moments there's silence between us, the murmur of conversation in the background becoming static when pitted against the punishing heartbeats in my ears.

"I don't want to put those kids at risk any more than you do." He addresses the glass, not meeting my gaze. "But if I don't retaliate I'll be seen as weak. We all will."

"By who?" I step closer. "Nobody knows what happened."

Spiteful eyes find mine, the palpable hostility daunting me. "*They* know."

They—the family who pulled the trigger. The people who held my daughter and Tobias hostage.

"And they got away with murder." I lower my voice, making

sure the children don't overhear. "They'll never make it public knowledge. We all know they made a mistake in targeting us. They learned their lesson. If you let this go, at least temporarily, nobody will find out what truly happened. Our enemies won't know how easy it was to bring us to our knees."

"And nobody would need to learn how much of a snake you've been," he hisses.

I snap rigid, every muscle pulled so tight the slightest touch could sever me in half. "That's not what this is about."

He scoffs. "It's just a bonus, right? If I sweep this under the rug, nobody will learn the part you played."

I crinkle my nose, willing the threat of tears away. I can't deny that hiding my crimes is also part of my plea. If Stella finds out about my actions I'll lose her, too.

I'll lose everything.

"I'm begging you." The words push their way through the bile rising at the back of my throat. "*Please*." The first tear falls, burning a trail down my cheek.

Cole follows the path of moisture with his gaze, the muscles in his jaw flexing as he clenches his teeth. "If I do this, you'll owe me. I'm not talking about a family-friendly debt either, Layla. You'll owe me like everyone else. And when it comes time to pay, you'll hate the price."

Fear trickles its way into my chest, adding to the hollow beat of my heart.

It's what I deserve. My penance.

I nod. "I understand."

His eyes narrow in scorn. "Well, then, sister, I'll think on it. But I'm not making any promises."

5

———

LAYLA

Present Day

I ATTEMPT TO CONVINCE MYSELF I'M NOT MAKING A MISTAKE AS WE walk side by side along the footpath toward the hotel. It isn't easy when his buddy follows behind us in the distance like an imminent threat.

"Ignore Bishop. Deep down, he's a puppy."

"He didn't act like a puppy when he interrogated me." He resembles the exact opposite actually. Broad and menacing. "Is he a bodyguard?"

"Of sorts."

That means Matthew is someone important. Or a target. I can't tell which.

I slow as we reach the hotel, my stomach filling with butterflies as the bellhop pulls open the towering glass door for us to proceed. "Who are you exactly?"

"We'll discuss that inside." Matthew returns his hand to the small of my back, adding slight pressure. "Don't worry. You'll be in public view at all times and can leave whenever you like. You've got nothing to fear from me."

I'm not stupid enough to believe him. I am, however, intrigued enough to continue inside, remaining close to him and his intoxicating aftershave as he escorts me to the bar and pulls out a seat near the window.

"This is your favorite type of place to sit, right?" he drawls. "Near the window with your back to the room."

I glare and sink into the cushioned leather. "Your thug already critiqued my choice of seating. I don't understand why it's such a big deal."

He shrugs and claims the chair across the table. "Most people feel more comfortable with their back to the wall. It's instinct. And when you add the way you stared into the glass reflection the entire time you were at the restaurant, your neck slightly craned, it made your intentions obvious to anyone watching close enough."

My face heats with the failure.

"Are you a scorned lover?" His question is almost a purr.

I ignore him. I battle to ignore the building butterflies in my stomach, too, their fluttering wings now born from something other than curiosity.

"Or maybe you're a reporter." He rests back in his seat, seeming to shelve the playboy charm for a more serious, business-type approach.

"No." I scan the room, looking from one couple to the next until my gaze lands on Bishop seated at the bar.

"Cop? Fed? DEA?" Matthew asks.

"DEA?" I raise a brow and return my attention to his, appreciating the first piece of validation he's given me. "I thought the Costas ran a reputable fashion label," I hedge, despite knowing the truth. "Why would the Drug Enforcement Agency be sniffing around?"

"I'm merely guessing." He shrugs. "You're not giving me a lot of feedback."

A waitress saunters toward us to place a tray on our table. "Excuse me for interrupting. The gentleman at the bar ordered these for you." She places a glass of scotch before my handsome companion and a wine within my reach. "Enjoy."

"Thank you." Matthew claims his drink, inclining it in toast to the waitress before she walks away.

I'm not as eager to grab my gift. The warm kiss of intoxication is already gently caressing my senses, and although it's becoming clear I'm not the master spy I'd hoped for, I'm not careless enough to be unaware of a potential threat hidden in the liquid.

"There's no obligation to drink the wine." Matthew stares at me over the rim of his glass. "But I assure you it isn't drugged."

His promise doesn't provide comfort. All it does is bring me closer to the edge of unease.

Normal, everyday people wouldn't accuse others of spying. They wouldn't contemplate spiking a drink or assume that others in their employ could be accused of doing the same.

So, either this man is like me—living within sinister circles—or he's badge-wearing scum. Neither option will have me spilling my secrets.

"Who are you, Matthew?" I cross my legs, attempting to appear in control. "Are *you* a cop? A Fed? DEA?"

That could explain Bishop. The burly guy might not be a body-guard, but instead, a partner. Then again, cops don't have the income for the expensive threads these men wear. So maybe something higher up the food chain.

"I'm a businessman." He takes a sip of scotch, his gaze never leaving mine. "With a vested interest in what the Costas are up to."

He's a force to be reckoned with as well. An enigma. He's got me intrigued. Cautious yet captivated. I want to learn everything there is to know about this man. And I have a sense he feels the same about me.

"You're in the fashion industry?" I could buy that. He's certainly dressed well enough. "You're obviously not local if you're staying in a hotel."

"I live in D.C. But no, I'm not on the fashion scene. I'm more on the hospitality side of things."

It's my turn to grin. "You're being very vague, Matthew."

"Me?" He snickers, smooth and deep. "I've told you where I live, the industry I work in, and what hotel I'm staying at. Yet all I've learned in return is your ability to bewitch me with that stunning dress."

My heart kicks, thumping and throbbing. His player game is on point, and I'm loath to admit it's chipping away at my defenses. It's been too long since I had a man's attention.

Since I had *any* attention.

I reach for the wine, throwing caution to the wind as the liquid coats my tongue, the taste far more exquisite than what I'd been served at the fancy restaurant.

"Don't worry, I'm a patient man." His gaze dips to my mouth and I can't stop my tongue from swiping out to moisten my lower lip. "I don't give up easily."

The thumping and throbbing increases, pounding in my ears.

"I'm going to settle on my first assumption." His smirk returns. "You're a scorned lover out for revenge. Or, better yet, you're an opportunist, trying to secure a wealthy future by winning over one of the Costa heirs."

He's goading me and that's okay. He's not the only one who can play games.

"Maybe." I cross my legs and the split in my dress parts, exposing skin all the way to the bottom of my hip. "Do you think I'd have much success?"

His attention lowers to my thigh, his nostrils flaring. "*Amore mio*, you could take down an entire empire with your beauty."

I press my lips together, unsure how to respond.

I'm thrumming. Buzzing. Brought to life.

Benji never looked at me this way. At least, not once we found out I was pregnant after what was meant to be a one-night stand. He'd been sentenced to a future of parenthood and criminal activity due to an unplanned conception, but not once did I blame him for the resentment he spent years trying to hide.

"Did I say something wrong?" Matthew asks.

I glance away to regain my composure.

My late husband deserves more from me than this. Even though our marriage was forced, we still grew to love each other. We might have even grown into one of those all-consuming romances if we weren't so much alike—both ignorant and stubborn in all the wrong places.

"No." I keep my gaze averted as I take another sip of wine. "You didn't say anything wrong."

"I've upset you, which only brings me back to the belief you're a scorned lover."

I sigh. "What makes you think that?"

"Your eyes. I can see the emotional toll of whatever they put you through. The pain runs deep."

I don't correct him. It's better if he thinks I'm brokenhearted over one of Emmanuel's sons than to dive into the sticky depths of the truth.

"How did they not recognize you?" There's genuine curiosity in his voice. "You do realize they had their own security duo watching from both sides of the room, right?"

No, I hadn't known.

Goddamnit.

"That's why I had Bishop intervene when you stood to leave," he adds. "Although the family were on their way out the door, one of their guards still watched the room."

My failure continues to compile, the pressure growing heavier.

"How did they not recognize you?" he repeats. "Surely no man could forget a body like yours."

I smile despite knowing he's buttering me up for information. "I had a slight disguise." I remove the glasses, placing them on the table between us, then the colored contacts, and finally start to unfasten my wig, letting my dark hair tumble free.

I ruffle the long strands between my fingers and spy my reflection in the window, making sure I'm somewhat respectable.

When Matthew doesn't comment, I return my attention to his, curious at what brought on his silence.

He stares, his attention intense. "I wouldn't have thought it possible, but I find this version even more stunning."

The rampant flutters in my belly rise to my chest. My throat. I swallow, hard, struggling to fight his seduction as I dump the wig on the table.

"You're gorgeous." He studies me.

My hair.

My eyes.

My mouth.

Wherever his attention strays, heat follows, scorching me from the inside out.

He scoots his chair to the side so the table no longer stands between us and leans forward, his elbows falling to his knees, his dark focus unwavering. "Spend the night with me."

He asks with such surprising simplicity.

No, it's a subtle demand, the underlying conviction holding a curious hint of what sounds like awe.

Declining is the only option. Yet, I still find myself pausing to daydream about what a different future could hold. The two of us forging a bond through a common goal of destruction. Him protecting me from my enemies. His hands on my body. His words even more evocative behind closed doors.

I shiver from the possibilities, the thrill touching every nerve.

"Say yes," he whispers. "And I promise to make those men a fading memory."

6

MATTHEW

She grins, the curve of lips the prelude to a rejection. "You don't even know my name."

"I don't need to."

I'll find out everything soon enough. Her name. Her intent.

"I could be anyone," she continues. "That doesn't concern you?"

That's exactly why I want to crawl on top of her, where I'm at my best. I'll learn her secrets through her body, and we'll both enjoy every second of it.

"I already know enough."

She's cunning. Determined. She may not be the best undercover agent, but she has potential. She's also holding out on me. I'm hungry to know what information is hidden behind those mesmerizing eyes.

"And would your friend join us?" she asks.

She's messing with me now. Playing.

I grin, appreciating her sass. "I'm sure he wouldn't decline the proposition."

She laughs, the sadness I glimpsed moments earlier disappearing with the flash of a perfect smile. "You're too much."

"Just wait until I start seducing you."

"You mean that's not what you've been trying to do since we met?"

"This has merely been conversation. If I were intent on seduction, you'd know about it."

Her laughter fades, but that smile settles in place, almost blinding in its humble simplicity. "I'm not so sure about that. I've never met a man who oozes seduction more than you do. I can't imagine how you could increase the severity."

Challenge accepted, amore mio.

I shove the table to the side and lunge forward, grabbing her chair legs around the outside of her calves. She squeals as I drag the furniture toward me, not stopping the progression until our knees bump.

"Holy hell." She clasps a hand to her throat while the other clings to the armrest, her eyes wide as she glances to the couple seated nearby who watch our exchange with interest. "You're making a scene."

I nudge my knee between hers, the material of her dress slipping farther apart to expose more of her legs, bare inches away from what I assume is tempting designer underwear.

I want to taste what's hidden beneath. To devour and sate us both. Even if what she's hiding is poison.

"Okay. I get it." She keeps frantically glancing at the nearby couple. "You can stop the performance now."

"Look at me." I splay my hands on her thighs, trailing my calloused palms higher and higher. "Don't worry about who's watching."

She squares her shoulders, gaining composure, but I can tell she's a skittish lamb. Hungry wolves can sense that type of thing and I'm goddamn starving.

"Look at me," I repeat, squeezing my fingers.

Slowly, she complies, her wild eyes meeting mine as she hisses, "What the hell are you doing?"

"Showing you the difference between conversation and seduction." I want to know which brother broke her—Salvatore or Remy. Then I want to crush every memory she holds of the son of a bitch. "Aren't you having fun?"

Her lips part, and I swear she's about to give an adamant denial until she snaps her mouth shut.

She wants me.

Wants *this.*

I could almost laugh at the absurdity. The serendipity. Who would've thought I'd find someone else at the same restaurant, spying on the same motherfuckers, on the very same night I was? *Twice.*

"You can't deny you're attracted to me." I lean closer, inhaling her sweet perfume. Jasmine and vanilla. "And there's no way I can do the same."

I slide my hand beneath her covered thigh.

She sucks in a breath. "We're in the middle of a bar filled with people. Do you have no shame?"

"Do you have no sense of adventure?" I counter with a grin. "Surely a woman of your beauty has done far more scandalous things than be admired in public."

The way she stiffens is a clear indicator she hasn't. *Fuck.* She isn't used to being wanted. Craved.

"This isn't admiration." She clears her throat, her shoulders remaining stiff. "This is a man attempting to get information."

"Can't it be both?"

For a second, she holds my gaze, tense and unyielding. I don't breathe. Don't move. It isn't until she huffs a derisive laugh, her mouth yet again forming that fucking tempting smile, that my pulse kicks back in again.

"Matthew, I apologize for misleading you, but I have no information to give. I wish I did, but I don't."

I don't believe her, and right now, I don't care. She's pretty when she lies. Pretty, tempting, and an increasingly more enjoyable challenge.

"Follow me to my room and let me show you a glimpse of your worth." I rub my thumbs in circles, trailing my touch higher along her inner thighs. "Let me treat you the way you deserve."

Her tongue snakes out to moisten her lower lip, her dazed eyes fixated on mine.

She's going to succumb.

Any second now, she'll announce her submission and let me claim victory.

"No, thank you." She blinks away the bewildered look and violently snaps her knees shut. "We're done here." She shoves back in her seat and stands, forcing my hands to fall into thin air. "Follow me and I call the cops."

With a snatch of her belongings from the table and a flick of her dark hair, she storms for the entry, passing Bishop at the bar who slides from his stool to stalk toward me.

"We're letting her go?" He glowers over his shoulder, watching her stride through the reception area, his focus predatory.

I should leave her alone. No matter what her connection is to the Costa family, she's nothing but a pawn in a vicious game. But I'm too fascinated to end this here. Too fucking intrigued. I have to learn her secrets.

"Follow her." I casually clap him on the back, downplaying the adrenaline-filled interest coursing through my veins. "I want her name and any other information you can dig up before sunrise. Don't let me down."

7

———————

MATTHEW

The fucker let me down.

Bishop allowed the woman to slip through his fingers.

He didn't get her name. Or her number. He didn't even catch the direction she went in because apparently she disappeared into thin air. Now all I have are lingering memories of ocean-blue eyes and hair dark as night to go with the semi hard-on I've had since our chance encounter.

I return to D.C. the following morning, unable to get her out of my head. I keep replaying our conversation on a loop, telling myself I need to search for hidden clues to her agenda only I get caught up on other things. Like the way her sass increased my pulse, or the ingenuity that made me determined to get to know her, or those damn inviting rebuffs to my advances that made this more about winning her over than gaining information.

I want to know what she's up to. And I want to know why. But most of all, I want to know how long it will take to get her beneath me. On *top* of me.

When evening comes, I make my way to my latest club acquisition to check on the staff who don't seem to appreciate the way their new boss runs things.

They're scared of me, too, which doesn't help.

The dark crevices of my reputation aren't well-known around here, but someone must've broken the silence.

37

"I've stocked all the bars." A short-skirted, slim-waisted, cleavage-bearing waitress stops beside me, her hopeful smile doused in deep red lipstick as she eyes the dancing crowd before us. "And noted all the liquor levels like you asked."

She's a brown-noser. There's always one. Even in a crowd of staff filled with animosity over my overbearing ways. They're the reason this club had been run into the ground. Them *and* the previous owner, who was too busy living the highlife in the Caribbean. But their failings are my gain.

I'll flip this club within a year and make a mint, all because they'd plummeted its value to begin with, allowing me to buy it for pennies.

"Your hard work is appreciated." I raise my voice above the loud music. "Are any of the staff continuing to have problems with the way I do things?"

Her wide blue eyes glance away and she shrugs. "Not really."

"Tell me who?"

She nibbles her lower lip. "Maybe Reece. I think because he managed this place for so long before you took over the transition is harder for him."

Then I guess Bishop and I need to have a chat with Reece.

"Thanks for the information." I walk away, skirting the dancing crowd three steps below, the thoughts of my Denver woman assailing me as soon as I'm left alone.

I haven't been able to concentrate since our chance encounter. Can't think straight, either.

If she's an ex-lover looking for payback for Remy or Salvatore, she may not know what her actions will instigate. The Costas aren't the type of people anyone should taunt. Not only are they vicious, but they're fucking stupid. It's a lethal combination.

I stop at the railing separating me from the bopping, booze-infested club-goers and grip the cold metal in both hands. It's not them I see, though. It's still her. The dark hair. The unfathomably deep blue eyes.

I need to find her. To touch more of her velvet-soft skin.

The brush of her thighs was enough to haunt my dreams. The jasmine and vanilla scent of her hair will live with me forever. All of her will. Never has a woman been so intriguing. Strong yet scared. Confident yet unsure.

A commotion starts on the dance floor before me. One man shoves another before my bouncers push from nearby walls to silently threaten their involvement. But it's not the shoving or the hired thugs that attract my attention.

It's the woman swaying her hips to the beat a few feet in front of me, her arms raised high, her dark hair cascading down her back.

For a second, I think it's her—*Denver*.

The figure matches. The lush hips, the slender waist.

It isn't until she turns that my fantasies take a nose-dive. Everything else about her is wrong. The lips uneven, the lower far bigger than the top, not precisely symmetrical. The face is round, too, not oval with high cheekbones and mysterious eyes.

My body doesn't care though. My blood pumps faster at the diluted comparison. My cock hardens, wanting relief from the obsession.

I watch her, pretending the swaying woman is mine, not taking my gaze off her as the flashing lights blink over her body.

Need pulses in my throat by the time our eyes meet. It's a simple travelling glance at first. A brief scan of her surroundings. Until she notices me staring. Then her intent snaps back to mine, her smile quick to form.

That's wrong, too.

The curve of lips doesn't dazzle or intrigue.

It's fucking disappointing. Almost deflating. But my cock doesn't get the memo because it's still in full-blown Denver mode.

My libido thinks she's here. *She's* the one dancing before me, her wild eyes intoxicating, her delicious body coaxing.

The woman continues to hold my gaze, her hips rolling, her arms moving above her head. I cling tighter to the banister, my knuckles aching, my throat drying.

I'm going to succumb.

After twenty-four hours obsessing about a mystery woman— living and breathing the questions that continuously slam my mind —I need relief.

I fucking deserve it.

I crook a finger at the dancer. Her mouth flattens for a shock-filled moment before she lowers her arms to her sides and saunters toward me.

The closer she gets, the paler the comparison, but I'm too far gone to divert this train wreck.

She stops on the lower level before me and calls out, "Did you want me?"

No, I want Denver.

"Yes." I rake my gaze over her, my pulse lessening with the new misgivings now apparent up close. The irises that are brown not blue. The bump on the bridge of her nose. "Care to join me in the VIP room?"

Her eyes widen, then she swings around, glancing toward her friends in the crowd. She waves them farewell without a thought to her safety and returns her focus to me with a grin. "Let's go." She hustles along the outside of the dance floor, up the three steps, then straight to my side.

Self-loathing is a constant companion as I lead her to the upper level filled with more dancing drinkers, then through the guarded doors to the quieter, exclusive part of the club.

But it's early on a Thursday night, so nobody with a glowing reputation has arrived yet.

It's just us, the bartender, and two couples who would've shed a couple hundred bucks for a once-in-a-lifetime experience that reeks of egotistical exclusivity.

I buy my companion a drink, pretend to listen to her life story, and flash my winning grin whenever I feel it's necessary. But I can't hold her gaze. She's nothing in comparison to Denver. Not with her over-the-top bubbly personality or her constant need to flick her hair as if she's involved in some fucking pathetic mating ritual.

Problem is, my dick won't cooperate. He's still all in, demanding something to numb the infatuation I hold for someone else.

"Have we met before?" The woman asks in a garbled rush. "Do we know each other? Because I'm sure I've seen you around. Your face is familiar. Handsome, too. You're like this quiet, mysterious type. It's so chill." She pauses for a breath and a sip of her cocktail, then giggles to herself. "This is surreal… But damn, I really need to pee."

She's fucking high—the frantic speech, the glazed eyes.

I'm fully aware I'm scraping the bottom of the barrel, and I still can't stop.

When she stands from our booth to go to the bathroom, I escort her, always a fucking gentleman. Then I wait in the hall, my shoulder leaned against the wall, my arms crossed.

These minutes alone, with the bass thumping beneath my feet from downstairs, and my hunger building for a stranger, only increase my impatience. My fucking addiction.

I have to find Denver.

The restaurant staff told me her reservation was made under the name Adley Javernick. A ghost. Someone who doesn't exist in Colorado or any of the surrounding states. Not even online.

She covered her tracks, which only reinforces my belief that she was spying for underhanded reasons.

I'll make Bishop return to Perfezione tomorrow. He can obtain the security videos from my friends in management. If I'm lucky, she may have fled our hotel rendezvous toward the restaurant, maybe caught a cab and been lax enough to use a credit card as payment.

"You waited for me?" The brunette saunters over from the bathroom, her lipstick reapplied.

"I did." I push from the wall, hating how much she's a poor substitute. Hating myself even more for moving forward regardless. "I thought we could use a little privacy."

I grab her hand and drag her into me. She giggles like a child and I slam my mouth to hers to shut her up. But this isn't Denver. The kiss is awkward, her lips taking too damn long to match my rhythm.

What I picture with my fantasy girl is far more brilliant.

Fated and perfect.

The only reason I keep my mouth fused to hers is the knowledge that I need something more than my own hand to gain relief from my suffering. Five fingers and a sweaty palm won't dislodge the woman commanding my thoughts. I'm not sure anything will.

I keep our lips meshed and drag her hips into me, settling her against my cock. She moans, the vibrations filtering along my tongue, into my chest.

I picture the most brilliant blue eyes. The lushest thighs. The sexiest coy smile.

With rough hands I spin her, making her face the wall. I guide her flush against the cool plaster, her long hair cascading over her back, the sight a hundred times easier to manipulate in my mind.

This is what I want. What I fantasized about on the jet home. The slim waist. Beautiful hair. Athletic legs. I close in against her, my mouth on her neck, my hard dick pressing against her ass.

"You've made me crazy," I growl into her ear. "Fucking mindless."

She giggles, the sound stifling the illusion. It goddamn slingshots me from fantasy to sickening reality, the hardness of my cock taking the brunt of the downfall.

"Shh." I clasp a hand over her mouth. "You don't want anyone walking around here to see us, do you?"

She whimpers in agreement and wiggles her ass against me.

"Good girl." I close my eyes, willing myself to see *her* again. To picture Denver. "From the moment I saw you, I knew I had to have you." I graze my teeth along her neck, delighting in her shiver. "So confident, yet so pure."

She whimpers again and this time the sound is masked by my palm.

"I'll make sure you never forget me." I hitch her skin-tight dress higher with my free hand, dragging the material over her thighs to her waist, then yank at the flimsy string of underwear until it breaks. "You're mine."

"Oh, wow. You're so dominant." She tilts her head away from my hold on her mouth, glancing at me over her shoulder. "When did you first notice me? Was it tonight or has this been going on for a while?"

"Quiet." I speak through clenched teeth. Through pure frustration. "Don't talk."

"But I need to know. I want to understand." Her words continue to run a mile a minute. "How long have you been obsessed with me?"

I squeeze my eyes shut. Clench my teeth. *Shit.*

My cock falls limp like a turncoat little bitch.

After dealing with a day-long half-mast dick, the fucker decides no flags will be flying tonight.

Fucking great.

"This was a mistake." I step back, my jaw tight with tension, my palms slick with sweat. I should've fought this shit out instead of trying to fuck it.

"No, it's not." She turns, her mound on display. "I want this. I *really* want this."

She's nothing like Denver. I don't know how I convinced myself otherwise. Her makeup is overstated. Her clothing cheap and tawdry. And that face. *Jesus.* What the hell was I thinking?

"Cover yourself and return to your friends." I right my jacket. "This isn't happening."

"But I want it to." She grabs my lapels, attempting to drag me into her. "I'm so horny."

I snatch her wrists. Tight. Her mouth gapes with the impact, her eyes wide. "I said, this isn't fucking happening." I shove her arms away. "So lower your goddamn dress and go find your friends."

She blinks. Slow. Stupid.

"Fucking walk," I growl.

She snaps rigid, her chin hitching a notch. "Fuck you." She glares as she scrambles to lower the hem of her dress. "You're crazy."

No argument there.

"You're a piece of shit, too." She raises her voice, no doubt attempting to bait me into an argument. "Fucking weirdo."

The bartender comes into view at the end of the hall, his eyes on me. "Everything all right, boss?"

"We need security." I start toward him.

"You wanted *me*, motherfucker," the woman rails. "*You* wanted *me*."

No, I wanted Denver.

This piece of fluff is nothing in comparison.

The bartender jerks his chin at me in understanding, then focuses on the woman as I continue walking away. "I think you need some fresh air."

"I don't need anything, you son of a bitch."

I don't listen to the rest of her plight. I get the fuck out of the VIP area, opening the door to the consuming noise of the lower level, then don't stop until I'm in my car.

THE DAYS PASS. The obsession doesn't.

I can't quit going over my time with her, rerunning our conversation, trying to work out her angle. If she's a scorned lover, why eavesdrop in a packed restaurant? Why risk being recognized?

I don't bother attempting to sate myself in another woman. Instead, I shuffle my tight schedule and fly back across the country.

I return to the Italian restaurant where the Costas have a weekly standing reservation and make my way through the staff entrance at the back. Emmanuel may have claimed his favorite seat in the house, but I'm the one who pays to watch every minute of his meals.

"You're back sooner than usual." The head chef shoots me a glance as he flips something in a sizzling frying pan. "I might be able to retire early if you keep this up."

"Maybe." I slip a folded stack of cash into his pocket as I pass and continue to the swinging doors leading to the dining area with Bishop at my back.

Usually, I don't have to make my presence known. I can sit in my rental from the street out front and eavesdrop on their conversation via earpiece thanks to the listening device under their table. But this time, I'm not here for them.

It's her I'm after. The woman who doesn't fucking show.

I'm forced to walk out of there like a chump while Bishop wordlessly questions my motives, his judgmental stare increasing my annoyance.

I repeat the trip the following Wednesday, my impatience building when dreams of blue eyes haunt me on the daily. It's not normal. Denver triggered something and I'm not sure how to shut that shit off. But again, she doesn't show.

By the third week, I'm agitated as fuck.

It's not often I lose, at least not since my teenage years, yet here I am. I lost Denver. Without a trace. She slipped through my fingers and I can't figure out why the hell it matters.

Was it the challenge of bedding her? The thrill of a common enemy?

"How many times are we going to do this?" Bishop asks from the driver's seat as we sit in the rental parked on the other side of the road from Perfezione's entry. "I fucking hate Denver."

"We both fucking hate Denver, but we'll do this as many times as necessary." Until I get answers. Closure. "If you have a problem with the working conditions, feel free to fuck off."

He huffs a low chuckle. "You know this is messed up, right? It can only lead to drama."

I don't respond, partly because I don't answer to him, but mostly because I'm robbed of speech as a familiar figure saunters along the sidewalk to push through the front doors of the restaurant, her beauty captivating as she speaks to the maître d'.

She wears an auburn wig this time. A white dress. The glasses remain perched on her nose while she draws my attention to her perfect mouth etched in more subtle lipstick.

She's pure temptation.

Still way too beautiful to blend.

"She's here." I meet Bishop's stare and push open my door. "This time, you better not lose sight of her if she runs."

8

MATTHEW

I STALK MY WAY ACROSS THE ROOM, NOT GIVING A SHIT WHO SEES ME AS I pull out the chair opposite hers and sit. "It's been a while, but finally, we meet again."

Her face pales as our eyes meet, those gorgeous blue depths widening. "Are you crazy?" She frantically glances over her shoulder at the bustling restaurant. "What the hell are you doing?"

My pulse quickens at her panic. It fucking vibrates with euphoria. I can't help a grin. "Costa's not coming."

She frowns. "What do you mean?"

"He's in Italy. There won't be a family dinner tonight."

She blinks, her shoulders losing their rigidity, her expression falling. "Well, there goes a wasted flight."

I disagree. I think her trip here is the best money she's ever spent.

I've already discovered she lives far enough away to have to fly here.

It's astounding, but seeing her again, after all those days fantasizing about her, it's hard to believe she's more alluring than my memories allowed. Her eyes more mesmerizing. Her lips more inviting.

She clears her throat and rests back into her chair, regaining confidence and composure. "If you knew they weren't coming, why are you here?"

"Isn't that obvious?" I rake my gaze along the parts of her I've missed during her absence—every single visible inch above the table. "I'm here for you."

Her brows rise. The color in her cheeks does, too, as a timid smile curves her mouth. "That's smooth. But I don't buy it."

"No?" I rest my elbows on the table and lean closer. "Do you mean to tell me this obsession isn't mutual?"

She laughs and my dick takes notice of the hypnotic sound.

So pretty.

So real.

I know she's here for underhanded reasons, that's always been clear, but there's a gentle innocence about her, too. A fucking purity that's so subtle it makes me ache.

"Nice try," she drawls. "Why are you really here?"

A waitress sidles up beside her, placing a glass of wine on the table. "Would you like a drink, sir?"

"Scotch. Thanks."

The young woman nods and leaves us to our wicked games.

I swear the entire world ceases to exist for a few moments as Denver and I stare at each other with equal amounts of superiority and suspense. The air between us vibrates. The sexual tension crackles.

I narrow my attention to her mouth, her lower lip now slightly pulled between her teeth. *Jesus.* She's a tease. "I apologize for scaring you when we first met."

"You didn't scare me." She reaches for her wine with casual confidence, and I'm sure it's to prove her point.

"Well, whatever I did to make you run, I apologize."

She sips from her glass, eying me over the rim. There are no words between us for long moments, only a heated stare that bubbles my blood.

I don't know who the fuck this woman is but she's beyond temptation.

"Do you have a new lover since Remy or Salvatore? Is that why you took off?" I want the truth. Every last detail. If there's another man in the picture, I need to know who to get rid of.

"No." She takes another sip, her gaze still linked to mine. On the surface she appears unfazed and calm. It's her thumb rubbing over her wedding finger that's a tell.

I focus on her hand. On the lone digit.

There was no ring weeks ago. I made sure of it. I don't usually waste time on taken women. Yet for her, I'd make all the exceptions in the world. I'll break every one of my rules just for a taste.

She places the glass on the table and lowers her hands to her lap, deliberately out of sight.

"I have a husband." Her murmured admission packs a punch.

Fuck. I don't ruin marriages. Yet here I am, already planning the downfall of the relationship this woman has with her spouse.

"I thought you were a scorned lover?" I keep my disappointment in check. "So is it safe to assume you cheated on your husband with Remy? Or is Salvatore more your type?"

The heat building in my veins demands I find out who she was with—the younger, more emotional prick or the older, more conniving asshole. But I can't push her either. My impatience won't withstand another one of her disappearing acts.

The slightest narrowing of her eyes is her only response.

"Does he know you don't wear your wedding ring? Or is that integral to your disguise?"

Her lips part, only to have the waitress return with my scotch. We're silent through the interruption. Neither of us move or speak until Denver reaches for her wine to take another sip.

I don't glance at her hand this time. I don't dare to take my gaze from hers. I want to read every hint she gives. To see all the facets she doesn't know are on display.

Once we're left alone she tilts her chin as if preparing to announce war, but instead, she says, "My husband died two years ago."

I straighten.

That explains a few things. Especially the subtle glimpses of pain I've witnessed a time or two.

I palm my glass. "I'm sorry to hear that."

"No, you're not." She gives a derisive laugh. "You've been trying to sleep with me from the moment we met. I bet the death of my husband is welcomed news."

I frown and clutch dramatically at my chest, pretending she's not entirely on the mark. "You don't think very highly of me, do you?"

"I haven't thought enough about you to bother making an assessment."

"Now who's lying?" I smirk and clasp my scotch. "At least I'm honest enough to admit my infatuation. When you did the Cinderella routine weeks ago, I went crazy trying to find you. There wasn't even a ruby slipper left behind for me to trace back to you. Not even a name."

Her lips twitch. "First of all, the ruby slipper was in *The Wizard of Oz*, and second, I vaguely recall you mentioning you didn't need my name."

Touché.

"I assure you I paid a hefty price for that mistake. I almost lost my mind not knowing how to find you."

Her lips kick even farther. Not quite a smile, yet enough to raise her cheeks and brighten her eyes.

"Well, don't hold out on me, *amore mio*. Tell me your name."

She contemplates me for a moment, probably wondering whether to lie while she takes another sip of alcohol.

"Layla," she gently murmurs.

Victory consumes me, rushing hot and fast through my veins.

She's telling the truth.

I'm not sure how I know, but I do.

"Do you have a surname, Layla?"

"Yes." She answers simply, without elaboration.

Fuck me, she's phenomenal. All sass and charm.

I can't help but snicker, and it's beyond rewarding when she follows suit, chuckling along with me.

"Okay, Layla. I don't need anything more than your given name."

She raises a taunting brow. "Good for you."

"Don't get me wrong, *amore mio*. I'm happy to delay the exchange of information, but you're going to eventually give me a few more details. I need to know the history of the future mother to my children."

More laughter tumbles from her lips. Whimsical, entrancing laughter. "You need to stop before I choke on your massive ego."

I'd love to give her something else to choke on. I can already picture it. *Feel* it. But I need to be cautious of her boundaries. I won't risk losing her again.

"Take off the wig." I gentle the demand. "Let me look at who you really are."

Her mirth tapers under seriousness. "Not here."

"Then we'll leave. I'll take you somewhere more subdued."

She pauses. Hesitates. "I haven't had dinner."

It's not a rejection. If anything, it's an open door of opportunity.

I pull my wallet from the inside pocket of my suit jacket and place some bills on the table. "Come on." I push from my seat and hold out a hand. "I'll find us somewhere more appropriate to eat."

9

———

LAYLA

M ATTHEW LEADS ME FROM THE RESTAURANT AND INTO THE CHILLED fall air, the sound of Denver's nighttime traffic bustling around us.

I shouldn't be doing this again. It's stupid.

Problem is, this sizzling chemistry is potent enough to deafen the thoughts of caution.

"Your friend isn't joining us tonight?" I shoot him a sideways glance as I take off my glasses and place them in my purse, my heart thudding harder when he looks my way.

"Bishop?" He returns his attention to the path ahead. "He's always around."

"He's here?" I spin, scanning the sidewalk behind us as we continue walking.

The ogre isn't visible. Not hiding in the entries to closed shopfronts. Not lingering in alleys.

"He has eyes on us from somewhere."

Apprehension tickles my neck as I pivot back around, Matthew slowing until I catch up to his side.

"Want me to tell him to take the night off, *amore mio*?"

Yes, is my instinctual response. But I don't want him too aware of my concern. He's playing me for information and I need to do the same, even though my usually hibernating libido is under the impression I'm here for different reasons.

I'd been shocked at the first sight of him tonight. Panicked. Yet

51

there'd been something more adamant that soon took over my emotions. Something that had nothing to do with fear and everything to do with the way his sinful gaze devoured me.

"I'll call him." He stops and pulls out his cell.

"No, wait." I reach for him, only to have him lock devilish eyes with me.

"It's okay. He doesn't need to hang around." He tilts his head away, connects a call, and raises the cell to his ear. "Take the night off. I'll see you in the morning."

I don't hear Bishop's reply.

"Yes. Don't let me find you tailing us." He lowers the cell and disconnects. Simple as that. No farewell. No apology for the dismissal.

He's smooth, his excessive level of charisma continuing to slip under my skin.

"You didn't have to do that." As long as we stay in public, I don't have anything to worry about. I can hold my own, maybe not in strength, but definitely with the defensive goodies in my bag. And tonight isn't going anywhere private. Racing pulse or not.

"Of course I did." He pockets the device and grabs my hand. "If you're uncomfortable, I'll always be obliged to do something about it."

My breathing hitches as he drags me into his side and continues our trek along the path. But it's not just his vow of obligation that leaves me shook. It's the possessive, comforting grip of his fingers. Both tag team to leave me speechless.

I've been deprived of male touch since Benji's death. And before that, hand holding wasn't a part of my life. Displays of affection didn't exist. In public *or* private.

Now, I can barely think through the warmth of a stranger's hold.

"It's through here." Matthew leads me to the mouth of an alley, the path subtly lit by a dubious string of twinkling lights attached between the towering buildings above.

I stop, my heels planted.

He continues forward, not noticing my hesitation until his arm is outstretched and I pull my hand away.

"What's wrong?" He turns to ask. "You don't trust me?"

I raise a brow, glancing from him to the darkened alley and back again. "Not in the slightest."

"Beautiful and smart. How the hell did I get so lucky?" He steps forward, once, twice, his casual approach not stopping until we're toe-to-toe, those deep dark eyes staring down at me as his palms take liberties by sliding over my hips. "What if I promise to remain respectful at all times? I'll only bite if you want me to."

"What if I tell you I have a gun in my purse," I lie, "and I'm willing to use it?"

He grins. "That works, too. But let's settle on going somewhere else. You decide the location."

He keeps saying all the right things. Making all the smooth moves to bring me one step closer to his honeytrap. But it's those eyes. The shades of rich earth and chocolate that make me contemplate stupid things... like following anywhere he leads.

"What's down there?" I jerk my chin at the alley that's far cleaner than any I've seen before. No garbage litters the asphalt. No graffiti. It's all looming bricks with no windows in sight.

"An Indonesian food truck. It's somewhat of a hidden treasure." His fingers begin to move, kneading the flesh of my hips. "They've got an online presence. You can search them on the map. I promise I don't plan to drag you into the shadows to have my wicked way with you." His grin increases, a tiny dimple peeking out beneath the rich stubble. "That comes later, once I've gained permission."

I shouldn't be endeared. I shouldn't be goddamn turned on either. And I definitely shouldn't want to press my lips to his to assuage my curiosity over his taste.

But I do want.

I want and need and crave more than I can ever remember feeling with Benji. The thought is enough to leave me cold with guilt.

I step back, dragging my attention from penetrating eyes to the alley. Four people walk toward us. Smiling, laughing, the noise echoing off the walls. There's nothing nefarious about them or their mood.

"Let's keep moving." Matthew reclaims my hand and continues along the sidewalk.

"No." I tug him, making demands of my own. I want to see this hidden treasure. "Take me to the Indonesian food."

"Are you sure?"

Nope. Not one little bit. But the hazardous impulse flowing through my veins makes me nod. "Yep."

"Whatever you wish, *amore mio*."

God, he kills me each time he uses the endearment. Even though it's glib, it still affects me—how easily he can confess love when I've been denied those words my entire life.

My father rarely professed the sentiment. My brother never will. And although I assumed it from my husband, I rarely heard the admission from him. It came maybe three times in the nine years of marriage.

Matthew is similar to the men I'm used to in a lot of ways—his confidence, his authority. It's the aspects that are shockingly unfamiliar that leave me hungered and achy.

He has soft undertones. A gentlemanly nature that lives in parallel with the sharp edge of wicked intent.

If only I wasn't questioning whether every single part of him was some well-constructed act.

"You're quiet." He strolls beside me under the twinkling lights, taking me further into isolation. "Everything okay?"

"You're guiding me down a darkened alley, without your bodyguard, while dressed in a designer suit. I think it's normal to fall quiet from contemplating how many times we're going to be mugged."

"It's safe. I'd never knowingly put you in danger. I promise. And while we're back on the topic of Bishop, he isn't a bodyguard. He's more of a business partner. At times, he's my driver. My confidant. My eyes and ears. He watches my back. But I also watch his."

His words trigger subdued alarm bells. They should be louder. Deafening. But the fact that he sounds like my brother washes off my back without leaving residue.

"Your job sounds hazardous for someone who works in hospitality." I shoot him a sideward glance.

"You've obviously never been on the receiving end of an influencer's tirade when their dirty martini isn't quite as dirty as they would've liked. Some of my staff expect danger money when certain people walk through the club doors."

I smile and return my attention to the foursome who continue to laugh and chat as they pass. "So you own a club?"

He shrugs. "A couple."

Yep. He's sounding more and more like Cole. The only difference is restaurants to clubs.

The reasons to turn on my heels and escape are compounding, yet these shoes won't pivot. My body refuses to walk anywhere apart from straight ahead.

"We're almost there." His thumb rubs gently over mine. "It's just around this corner."

I keep my hand in his, my palm tingling as we reach the end of the building.

"Here." He tugs me around the corner into the open space where I'm sure a building once stood. Now the area is claimed by a food truck draped in white twinkling lights with park benches scattered on top of bright green fake grass.

Office skyscrapers loom around the oasis, with more strings of lights crisscrossing overhead. It's humble. A hidden haven, just like he promised. With at least twenty people eating and drinking.

"What do you think?" Matthew stops to look at me, those confident eyes scrutinizing. "I found this place years ago. I swear nobody cooks quite like Reza."

"What I think is that you're doing a great job of keeping me on my toes. I never would've expected you to escort me from a Michelin-starred restaurant to a food truck. I'm not sure if I should be impressed or confused."

He smirks, dropping my hand to slide his palms around my waist. "If you want to be impressed, you should've taken the invitation to my hotel room. It's not too late to head there now."

I burn. White hot. His touch sears me.

I'm almost tempted to sell my soul for a few minutes of suit-clad privacy. But I can't. I won't.

I don't know this man, and even if I did—even if this was a regular date between people who didn't have deceitful similarities —my baggage is full.

I have a daughter, a dead husband, and a family who don't welcome outsiders. Ever.

"You're dreaming if you think I'll follow you to your room." I chuckle to dissuade the lust.

"Let's call it forecasting."

"I won't go back to your hotel, Matthew." I attempt to hold his gaze, yet the draw of his mouth steals my attention. "Not tonight."

"How could I change your mind?" He leans closer, the intoxicating scent of his smooth aftershave consuming my fractured breaths.

"You can't," I lie. "I barely know you."

His stubbled jaw grazes my cheek as he inches closer to my ear. "That's what I'm trying to resolve." His attention lowers. His lips brush my neck with a torturous glide of connection. "I want to know everything about you, Layla."

I shudder, my eyes closing of their own volition, my entire body enraptured by the rough resonance of his tone. "I don't enjoy one-night stands."

"One night would never be enough."

Oh, God. I want to succumb.

With everything I am, I itch to grasp these stomach-tingling feelings and ride them for as long as possible. Just one taste of happiness even if it isn't deserved.

"You live in D.C.," I whisper.

"Yes." He nuzzles the sensitive skin below my ear. "And you live where?"

"Somewhere farther away from you than Denver." Much, much farther. So unbelievably far that this questionable attraction isn't worth humoring. I pull back, stricken with unwanted reality, and retreat a step. "I don't have casual sex. You're wasting your time if that's what you're after."

"Stop thinking so little of me." He counters my withdrawal with a forward stride, his hand sliding behind my neck, the other tightening around my waist to haul me closer. "This might be about fucking, but that's not all it's about."

I want to believe him. The rapidly building wildfire rushing through my veins makes it impossible not to.

His mouth descends on mine, the softness contrasting with the possessive grip around my neck.

For a second I'm dumbstruck, my purse strap precariously hanging on the edge of my shoulder as he consumes me.

I haven't kissed in… forever. I also haven't been held with such possession. And I've never, ever been so alive with choking jitters.

His lips move, coaxing mine to do the same. I can't deny him. I'm enslaved to give him what he wants, conceding with the softest whimper. Our mouths dance as I claim his chest with my hands, my fingers tangling in the material of his silk shirt.

He parts my lips with a firm glide of his tongue and a low growl of appreciation, and I'm done for. My nerves awaken in response. Every pound of my pulse is deafening.

Then, all too soon, he breaks the connection, gradually leaning back to stare at me with hungry eyes.

"Waiting until you're ready will kill me," he murmurs. "But the torment will be worthwhile."

He turns, reclaiming my hand to lead my mindless ass toward the food truck, acting as if he didn't just sweep me off my feet with a decimating kiss. He seats me at an empty park bench and says something about ordering food. Then he's gone, leaving me to stare at his fine form from a few yards away.

I honestly don't know how I got here. How I could possibly have traveled halfway across the country with intentions of destruction that guided me to romance?

Minutes later, he slides a heaped plate of marinated chicken sticks into the middle of the bench and takes a seat opposite me. "I hope you like satay chicken. They may not be the least messy option, but they're the best thing on the menu."

"It looks delicious." My gaze remains riveted on him as I suck my lower lip.

The subtle tweak to his mouth makes it obvious he knows I'm talking about him. *God.* I have to look away to curb the lust. I'm out of my element here. Entirely ensnared.

"Hey." He slides his hand across the table and claims mine. "I feel the same way, okay?"

No, he doesn't. He couldn't. I'm caught up in feelings I've

never felt. For a man I barely know. In a situation that is rife with danger and subterfuge.

"I don't chase women," he adds. "And I definitely don't beg for their attention. I assure you, I'm equally caught off guard."

I don't look at him. His reciprocated emotions only make this seem all the more surreal. I'm in Denver for revenge. For destruction. Not indulgence.

"How about we change the subject?" His touch retreats. "Tell me why you're watching Costa."

I chill at the whiplash in conversation. Here I'd been stuck in visions of heated flesh and sweaty skin while he's had Emmanuel at the forefront of his mind the entire time. "Why are *you*?"

He grins. "I'm sensing trust issues."

What he's sensing is annoyance. I shouldn't have been stupid enough to let down my guard. Instead of exposing my emotions, I grab a chicken stick and force myself to eat.

"I still think one of them broke your heart," he continues. "What I can't figure out is if it was recent. Maybe this is a childhood grievance. That would explain why you were so close to them without fear of being recognized."

"You're partially correct," I concede, hoping the slight forward momentum will be enough to tide him over. It isn't a lie, either. I didn't need to be in soul-deep love with Benji to have my heart shattered when the Costas stole him from me. He wasn't merely a husband. He was a father to our gorgeous daughter. And a good father at that.

"Which one?" He wipes the back of his hand over his mouth. "Which brother is to blame?"

"Does it matter?"

He eyes me for a long moment. Staring. Scrutinizing. "I guess not."

"It's your turn now." I finish the chicken stick and reach for another. "Why do you spy on them?"

"They've screwed me over more than once, and I don't plan to let it happen again."

The hair on the back of my neck rises. "Business or personal?"

"Does it matter?" He mimics my previous reply.

Yes, it does.

He said he works in hospitality. He owns clubs. In the eyes of the naive world, Emmanuel Costa is nowhere near that line of work. But I know better. I'm well aware the ties likely to bind them are drugs.

"I've said something to scare you." He discards his bamboo skewer on the side of the plate and frowns. "What is it?"

"I'm *not* scared." I take another bite of chicken, acting casual even though the risks are rising. "Why do you keep asking that? Are people usually frightened of you? Is that why you assume I'm the same?"

He eyes me, his gaze never wavering.

I'm right.

He's feared.

Why?

The thought should be enough for me to join the tally of those who are fearful. It *should*. However, the tingle running down my spine is far from fear-based.

"You're not going to answer me?" I taunt. "Why is that, Matthew?"

His jaw ticks as he breathes deep, letting the air out slowly. "You're right. I guess it is a default."

"Are you going to tell me why?"

His stare narrows. It isn't in anger. The intensity is something else. Shame, maybe. "Designer suits and fancy restaurants haven't always been a baseline, *amore mio*. I've had hardships, and those dark times had me doing anything to claw my way to the light. But that's where I am now—in better days."

His honesty is unnerving. Invigorating. I'm not used to people being open with me. Not when the men who usually surround me hoard their secrets as if their lives depend on the truth remaining buried.

This conversation is a gift. An offering.

"Were those hardships caused by the Costas?" I ask.

He continues to stare, long heartbeats ticking by as his choco-late gaze builds bridges between us. "Some. Yes."

Another thrill skitters down my back, the tingles hitting every nerve, spreading through every muscle. He's giving me so much. Information. Insight. Maybe my trip here wasn't a waste after all.

"Now it's your turn." He rests his elbows on the bench, unshakable. "Tell me what knowledge you're seeking about them. Tell me what you already know. Better yet, tell me about *you*, and put those assholes to the back of your mind."

Guilt stabs between my ribs. Sharp and fast.

This business of secret spilling was always going to be one-sided. He can't know about me. Not the *real* me.

"I've learned a few things about them that isn't common knowledge." I dilute my admission, hoping to appease him with tidbits. "And not all of it makes sense. I'm aware Costa has four children, but he only acknowledges three of them. Their oldest son, Dane, is in hiding, for reasons unknown."

"It's Dante," he corrects. "And he's estranged, not in hiding."

My heart kicks with the insight. "You know about him?"

"Of course I do." There's the slightest edge of superiority to his tone. Or maybe it's disappointment that I haven't done thorough research. "They attempted to bury evidence of his existence years ago. But there are still clues if you look deep enough."

"I also know Emmanuel's wife comes from a long line of Italian mafia," I add, hoping to redeem myself.

I don't.

He doesn't react to the meatier morsel of information either, making me question if he's a master of schooling his expression, or if he knows all there is to know about my enemies.

"Were you aware of that, too?" I raise a brow.

"I was, but not many people are. They go to a lot of effort to keep that information from going public."

"They should've tried harder."

I'm boasting for no reason. Cole was the one who obtained the knowledge. Not me. I only had the good fortune of overhearing him relay the news to Hunter.

"You're quite the sleuth, aren't you?" His compliment is slight, even a touch sardonic, and yet my heart warms. My stomach tenses.

This isn't good.

I'm succumbing to him. It's ridiculous and uncalled for. Dangerous and entirely stupid. My siblings would despise the choices I'm making. The risks I'm taking. And they already hate me enough.

"I'm sorry, Matthew, but this was a mistake." I hitch my purse strap onto my shoulder and brace my palms on the table. "I should go."

"What? Why?" His brow snaps tight, concern taking over his entire face all the way to the thinning line of his tempting lips. "We just sat down."

"I know, but…" The squeeze in my stomach increases, the war between want and obligation waging inside me. I came here for revenge. For redemption. *Not* for a romantic rendezvous.

"But you don't want to share any more of your secrets," he finishes for me. "You've decided you've got what you want and now it's time to leave."

Yes… No… Maybe.

I can't tell him what he wants to know. I refuse to divulge who I am or why I'm really here.

He wouldn't look at me the same way if I did, and I want his devouring attention to stay with me forever.

"I have a lot more information to give, Layla."

My insides twist. Not only due to the potential intelligence I'm giving up, but because he wants me to stay. Nobody has ever wanted me to stay before.

"I know." I swallow and push to my feet. "Regardless, it's best if I leave."

"Why?" The question is growled with delicious determination. "At least give me the respect of telling me an honest answer."

Honesty is tough. It always has been. From my childhood years, when I had to lie to myself about how my family made money, to my adulthood, when those lies had to be fed to everyone else.

"I could lose myself in you, Matthew," I murmur with a sad smile. "I barely know you, yet I'm well aware I could fall head over heels and never recover. And that's not what we're here for."

"Says who?"

My heart flutters. "I need to go." I walk around the bench only to be stopped by his hand grasping my wrist.

"At least take my number."

I want to take more than that. So much more it kills me to deny us both.

"I'm no threat to you, Layla. I have to go back to D.C. tomorrow morning." He pushes to his feet to stand before me, not letting go of my wrist. "I don't even know your full name. I don't know where you live. But if I give you my number you can at least reach out if you change your mind."

I hesitate. Having a lifeline to him isn't something I need. It will only act as an opportunity to succumb in the future.

"It's just a number." He steps closer and reaches for my purse.

I don't stop him from retrieving my burner phone. I even reluctantly enter the pin code when he holds the device in front of me.

He messes about with the screen. Tapping. Swiping.

When he hands it back, I notice he's sent a text message, the sneaky bastard, not merely giving me his number, but taking mine in return.

"I want to see you again." He reclaims the possessive grip around my neck. "And I know you want to see me, too."

I do.

God, how I do.

I want to touch, and taste, and breathe in more of his phenomenal aftershave. To strip him naked and kiss every inch of his perfect skin. To learn all about him—who he is, where he's from, what he stands for.

Unfortunately, I have a job to do and there's no place for distractions.

"Goodbye, Matthew." I place a kiss to his cheek.

"For now," he growls, his hand falling to his side. "We'll meet again, Layla."

10

———

LAYLA

He messages me before I leave the alley—*I'm in suite 1309 of the Delcato if you change your mind.*

Fate is such a tempting bitch.

Of all the hotels in all of Denver, we have to share the same one. But I'm not going to give in. Instead, I catch the closest cab and make quick work of hiding in my hotel room before there's another chance of us crossing paths.

I send sweet messages to Stella to distract myself. When that isn't enough, I call my brother. I make up a lame story about enjoying an out-of-town shopping spree to keep him off my trail. Then I shower and spend the rest of the night staring at my suite door, trying to fight the instinct to go in search of a stranger's bed.

I toss and turn for hours. I even reach for my phone twice, debating whether or not to cave.

Thankfully, I pass out before I can succumb. The sun peeking through the curtains announces I made it through the torture to the other side. Waking up alone doesn't feel like a victory, though.

I order room service for breakfast, not willing to see Matthew in the restaurant before his flight. Then I head out to shop my blues away, knowing he would already be on his way home to D.C.

I purchase dress after dress. Shoes. Makeup. Books.

Thoughts of him follow me the entire time. I even fantasize that he watches me from a distance. Stalks. I imagine his attention

63

fixated on my body, and my skin shivers everywhere his make-believe gaze strays.

But he isn't here. I make sure of it by glancing over my shoulder like a paranoid bitch every few minutes.

When my cell vibrates with a call after lunch, so does my pulse, because his name is the one displayed on my screen.

"You messaged me straight away," I say in greeting. "Then call me the next day. I thought men weren't meant to show interest for weeks."

He laughs, and I close my eyes briefly to enjoy the sound. "If so, I've severely messed up because I ditched my meeting this morning and stayed in Denver, hoping you might change your mind about spending time with me."

My stomach free falls, giddy greed consuming me.

"Where are you?" he asks.

Anticipation swirls beneath my sternum, my heart thundering like a drum.

"Layla?" His voice drops to a purr. "Don't deny you spent all night thinking about me, because you already know I did the same damn thing."

The reciprocation kills me. It eats away at my caution and makes me want to run to him. Just for a taste. Just one more kiss.

"I'm shopping. The mall is about a ten-minute drive from the hotel." My pulse thrums with the admission.

"Mine or yours?"

"Ours. We stayed at the same place."

There's a beat of silence. I swear, I feel his disappointment roll through the connection. It hits me right in the throat, stilting my breath.

"Tell me where you are," he says. "I'll come find you."

If I give him my location I'm done for. There will be no more restraint. No more talking myself out of this. I'll give in to temptation despite the risks.

But this could be my last taste of happiness. The one quick gulp before I return to judgment and resentment.

"I'm at the Cherry Creek Shopping Center." My blood surges. My pulse, too.

"Give me an hour."

He disconnects, leaving me to second guess if this is the most stupid decision of my life. And I've made some pretty wretched ones in the past.

I have to force myself to continue shopping as a distraction, but all I do is walk aimlessly from store to store, not taking note of the clothes or shoes or sales because all I can think about is him. He's all I see.

Within ten minutes, I'm outside, needing fresh air to dilute the suffocating apprehension. The traffic makes things worse. All the hustle and bustle increases the noise inside my head.

This can't be a thing—me and him.

Catching up is only to feed my curiosity. To answer the myriad of unspoken questions.

I pass unseen people and shopfronts, trekking in circles, getting lost. It isn't until I'm standing at the mouth of an alley that I stop, my shopping bags limp at my sides as the looming walls remind me of the night before. How Matthew had shown me a slice of Denver I never knew existed. How his kiss made my soul ache.

This alley isn't the same, though. Garbage bags are piled against the building walls. There are no hanging lights or laughing friends to lull me further into daydreams. The contrast to last night's environment only acts as an added warning that maybe things won't be as sparkling and shiny with Matthew in the light of day. That maybe catching up with him again is a mistake.

I continue into the isolation, seeking clarity, and the farther I trek, the more conflicted I become.

Matthew is an indulgence I'm not allowed.

Not after I spied on Cole for my father. Not when I contributed to Benji's downfall and Stella's abduction. And especially not with all the things I did in an attempt to keep my transgressions secret.

Happiness isn't a part of my all-inclusive life package. Mine revolves around heartache, guilt, and regret. There are some bonus pride-filled moments that revolve around my daughter, but I don't get to upgrade until I make amends.

I stop halfway to the street ahead and rest my shoulder against the brickwork, placing my shopping bags on the ground at my feet. The emotional drain of two years weighs me down. No, it's been longer than that. The heaviness has been a growing constant since the day my father asked me to spy on Cole.

Now the pressure is unbearable.

Each breath is etched in pain. Each step is more grueling with all that piles on top of me.

I retrieve my cell from my purse, my heart hurting as I acknowledge the rendezvous with Matthew has to be cancelled.

If I see him again, I'll kiss him. And if I kiss him, I'll sleep with him. And if I sleep with him, I'll never be able to get him out of my system.

Would the hours of bliss be worth the future filled with torment?

I have less than thirty minutes to decide.

"Give me your purse."

I stiffen at the male demand coming from directly behind me.

"*Now.* Hurry the fuck up." Hard metal nudges the back of my skull. A gun.

I slowly raise my hands, my fingers trembling, my mind on Stella and if I'll ever see her again. "Take whatever you—"

He snatches at my purse strap, the aggressive yank tearing at my shoulder.

I scream, the noise adding to the deafening rush of my pulse in my ears. He yanks again, harder, pulling, wrenching my arm as the gun grates into my head.

"Stupid bitch." He shoves me toward the wall, the side of my face hitting brick.

My muscles slacken with the impact. My arms fall to my sides. I become fluid, slithering to the ground as he claims his prize and snatches at some of the shopping bags on the ground.

I'm too stunned to move. In too much pain to think.

He runs for the far end of the alley, the clap of his footsteps a dull clip over the noise in my head, his black cap shielding his face before he disappears around the corner.

I crumple onto the remaining shopping bags, my left cheek throbbing, the bone beneath having taken the brunt of the impact with the wall. My shoulder burns from the assault from the purse strap, too. But what flames hotter is my blood, the rage flowing through my veins turning volcanic at my stupidity.

Not only did I daydream myself down a secluded alley with my arms filled with brand-name shopping bags, but I didn't notice I'd become a target until that asshole had been right on top of me.

I can't even figure out if it was luck or idiocy that I didn't have my gun.

If my weapon had been stolen, I'd have to report this to the police, then Cole would find out and the reasons for my out-of-town trips would be unraveled.

I hadn't even attempted to protect myself.

I didn't have the instinct to fight. I'd stood there, statuesque. Still and fucking pathetic.

Cole would be ashamed of me. Yet again.

I press my head back against the cold brick and whimper. How am I going to get out of this without him finding out? I'll have to cancel my credit cards. And my cell... What the hell happened to it?

The device had been in my hand. Now it's gone. When did it go missing?

Oh, shit. The cyanide.

Bile creeps into the back of my mouth, threatening to spill onto my dirty blouse and scuffed jeans.

"Jesus fucking Christ." I rest against the wall, my cheek tight from swelling, my pulse pounding through the tender flesh.

Why do I keep failing like this? My life has become a compiling stack of misgivings. One stupid move after another. Over and over again.

I'm not worthy of my family's notoriety. I bring nothing but shame to our name.

My throat tightens with emotion.

All I ever wanted was to make them proud. To help build our empire. And instead, my every decision has worked against that goal. I'm a liability. The most despised part of what has always been a vicious environment.

"I'm worthless." I cover my face with my hands, my nails digging into my forehead. I want to scream. To claw and scratch until the internal voices subside. But they never will. It never does.

The bags beside me rustle, the rhythmic vibration coming from my cell.

I straighten, riffling through the purchases worth far more than anything in my purse, and find my phone, the pink casing now cracked in the top corner, the screen alight with Matthew's name.

I shouldn't answer. Of all the things I should be doing right now, speaking to him isn't one of them. Not when I have to figure out how to cancel my credit cards without Cole knowing, which is going to be goddamn hard when he's the main account holder.

But my fingers work of their own accord, numbly swiping the screen. I answer without a greeting and sniff to dislodge the tingle in my nose.

"Hello? Layla?" He pauses. "Are you there?"

It's sickening how those few words wash me in comfort. How a stranger can ease my suffering without even knowing it.

"Yeah." I clear the fragility from my voice. "I'm sorry, I'm going to need to cancel catching up with you."

"What's wrong?"

I squeeze my eyes shut. He cares. The passionate concern in his tone takes hold of me and grips tight.

I don't know why it matters. Why it affects me even in the slightest. Having my purse stolen is nothing in comparison to what life has dealt me. A throbbing face and sore shoulder aren't in the same league as the threats I've endured as the sister to a drug boss. Or the heartache of the lonely nights spent in a forced marriage.

It doesn't even hold a candle to the disgust that brought me to my knees when I found out my father was a sex trafficker.

This is nothing.

No-thing.

And still, frailty threatens to drag me under.

"Layla, talk to me," Matthew demands. "What's going on? What's wrong?"

"Nothing." I scowl, willing the inner voices to quieten. "I'm fine. I just… My bag was stolen and I'm flustered. I need a minute to think—"

"Where are you?" he repeats.

"It doesn't matter—"

"*It matters,*" he growls. "Tell me where you are."

I'm used to protection. I've been shielded from hideous threats all my life. But never before has someone's need to care for me hit this hard. Someone who barely knows me.

"Layla," he implores. "I'm on my way to you. Just tell me your exact location."

The disgust in my veins increases. The tightness in my throat, too. "Outside the mall. In an alley nearby."

"Give me a name, *amore mio*. Do you know what alley?"

I look for the street sign and find nothing. "I don't know. I can't see—"

"As soon as I hang up you need to text me a pin on your location. Can you do that?"

I nod through the frantic emotions.

"Can you do that for me, Layla?"

"Yes." My voice cracks.

"Okay... Good. Stay where you are. I'm on my way."

11

———

LAYLA

I'M SLUMPED AGAINST THE WALL, MY HEART AND THOUGHTS IN Chicago with Stella, when a black Lincoln Navigator pulls into the alley, the glossy vehicle stopping in front of me.

Matthew flings open the passenger door, and despite not wanting it to, my heart squeezes in relief. He jogs forward in another stylish suit, falls to his knees before me, and cups my face.

"Fucking hell." His eyes harden as they focus on my injured cheek. "They hit you?"

"No. I was shoved into the wall. I should've put my hands up to stop the impact but..." I shake my head within his gentle hold. "I guess I didn't have time. I don't know... I wasn't thinking straight."

"It's okay." His attention softens. "You're going to be fine."

I'm not so sure. Not with my sinister intentions now out in the world in the form of a tiny cyanide vial. But it's nice to hear the assurance, to have such a confident and compelling man almost demand my recovery.

"What did they take?" His thumb strokes my uninjured cheek as Bishop climbs from the driver's seat. "Did you call the police?"

"It was just my purse and a few things I purchased. The cops don't need to be involved." They can't be. I wouldn't even know how to start explaining my reasons for carrying poison if my bag was found. Although not illegal, cyanide is a controlled chemical

70

and I have no reason to have it, especially not on my person and concealed in a drug vial. "It's only a few credit cards and some cash."

"You sure?" His gaze narrows. "This is serious."

He has no idea.

I can't explain how I obtained the murderous powder. The name of my contact would only raise more red flags. Could I go to prison? Or worse, if the Costas find out I'm here, and why, will they then target my family again in retaliation?

The blood drains from my face in a rapid vacuum.

"Layla, it's going to be okay. Just talk to me. You look like you're about to faint."

What if someone were to think the vial of white powder was cocaine? What if they snorted it?

"I..." I fight against the overwhelming need to blurt my fears. "I had something in my bag."

Matthew's shoulders straighten, but his confident attention doesn't waver. "Something illegal?"

I nod.

"A weapon?" The question lacks condemnation. He holds no surprise. Not even disappointment.

"Of sorts... If it got into the wrong hands—" My stomach lurches.

"It's okay." He leans closer, demanding I believe him with his close proximity. "I'll take care of it."

"How? What could you possibly do?"

"I've got contacts. If the bag is found, nothing is going to be tied back to you." He releases my face and glances over his shoulder, sharing a silent communication with Bishop who stands a few feet away before returning his attention to me. "You're a single woman alone in a foreign city. You're entitled to have protection, whether it's illegal or not. And if someone is harmed..." He pauses, his tone gaining conviction before he finally says, "I'll take care of it, Layla. I promise you."

I believe him. Even though he assumes I had a gun. Even though the aftermath of mistakenly snorting cyanide could be far worse than a gunshot, my traitorous insides relax a little at his assurance.

"Let's get you out of here." He helps me to my feet, then sweeps me into his arms.

"I can walk." My protest is faint at best.

"I know you can. But this is the first opportunity I've had to prove myself to you, so let me take it."

I look away, not wanting him to witness the effect of his words.

If this had happened at home, and my friends or family had rescued me, I'd be dealing with chastisements and judgment. The fear from my loved ones wouldn't come through in kindness. Only criticism.

This is such a sweet balm to my nauseating idiocy.

Bishop opens the back door to the Lincoln and I'm bundled inside, gently slid into the middle seat before Matthew takes his place at my side.

I don't get a chance to pull on my seatbelt before he's lifting me again, dragging me onto his lap.

"What are you doing?" I whisper.

"Holding you." He wraps his arms around my waist, bundling me against his pristine suit. "You're shaking."

I am. I can't help it. Even my heart trembles.

This shouldn't be such a big deal. I've been through worse. But the shaking doesn't stop. Not when Bishop climbs back into the car with my bags. And not once we start moving, with me still on Matthew's lap, his tight hold acting as my seatbelt.

"Tell me you're okay," he murmurs.

My throat burns with adoration. With appreciation. I lean into him, my head against his shoulder, my heart yearning for more. "I am. It's only shock."

"You sure?"

I nod. "Positive."

We fall silent, the low hum of the radio filtering through the speakers, the luxury of his hold cocooning me. I should be strengthening my emotional walls against him, against all the weakness, but for just this once, I decide to let someone else take the lead. To quit pretending I'm a force to be reckoned with and simply succumb to Matthew's rescue.

We reach the hotel without another word, then the underground parking lot. Once the car stops near the elevator, my savior opens the door, then slides out from beneath me to haul me from the vehicle and back into his arms.

"This isn't necessary." I press a hand to his chest in another feeble objection.

"I know." He nuzzles his nose near my ear, his breath tickling my neck. "I'm still taking advantage until the shock wears off. God knows once you're strong enough you'll return to being the independent woman who doesn't want a piece of me."

I huff a faint laugh despite his false assumption.

I *do* want a piece. I want all the pieces.

"What about her room key?" Bishop asks through his lowered car window. "Should I get a new one from reception?"

"Mine should still be in my pocket." I double-check to make sure, finding the plastic card in my stained jeans.

"Regardless, she'll be staying in my room," Matthew adds. "Park the car and we'll meet you upstairs."

I don't argue. I'm smart enough to acknowledge I need company right now. I don't want to be out of these strong arms. I'd love to stay here forever, constantly protected by someone who doesn't despise me.

I keep those thoughts to myself as I'm carried to the elevator, the confined space taking us to one of the top floors, then escorted to a freshly made suite far bigger than mine. We bypass a compact kitchen. A spotless living room. Then continue down a hall.

"Where are you taking me?" My question becomes redundant as we enter a bedroom, Matthew's stride not faltering until I'm gently placed on a king-size bed.

"You can rest here." He presses a kiss to my forehead and backs toward the door, a dedicated knight in shining armor. "I'm going to get you a stiff drink to settle the adrenaline. I'll arrange an ice pack, too, and run you a bath. Want anything else?"

I'm lost for words. Speechless.

"Food? Water? A fresh change of clothes?" His gaze falls to one of the large dirt stains on the side of my jeans. "I could go to your room—"

"No. I don't need anything else." Only company. I don't want him to leave. I swing my legs off the bed, preparing to follow him, needing his proximity. "Apart from a dose of the shakes, honestly, I'm fine."

"Stay." His voice drops in a gentle warning as he pauses at the threshold. "You need to rest. Let me look after you. I'll be back soon."

I fight another protest, the isolation hitting hard as soon as he's gone. The minutes spent alone only give me time to relive what happened. The demand for my purse. The harsh shove. The painful collision with the wall. Then the panicked aftermath.

I kick off my shoes and wither into the pillows, trying to think what Cole would do in my situation.

The cyanide is a big deal.

I could easily say it was planted in my bag, but that's not what I'm worried about. My panic revolves around the potential of an innocent victim. Then again, in my brother's case, I'm sure he wouldn't spare a stranger's death a second thought.

He wouldn't care.

If only I were that heartless.

I roll to my side, pull out my cell, and do a mental catalogue of the personal items I lost. My identification was definitely in there—photo ID for the airport who sometimes need more than the digital license stored on my phone. Then maybe one bank card. An AMEX. The rest were loaded to my cell months ago.

Realistically, I could get away with putting a hold on one account. But Cole would still find out.

I groan and navigate to my bank's website, connecting a call to the correct department before I can talk myself out of it.

After providing every speck of personal detail known to man, I cancel the card and disconnect. The reordering of my license will have to wait for a time when I don't feel as though I've run a marathon.

Even the allure of nearby running bathwater doesn't ease my pulse. I'm still shaking, my limbs heavy.

I stare at the ceiling, fighting against the inner voices telling me how much trouble I'm going to face once I get home.

"You doing okay?" Matthew appears in the doorway, a scotch glass in his hand.

I am now. The mere sight of him brings overwhelming relief.

It has to be his commanding presence. The strong way he holds his shoulders. The chiseled angle of his jaw. And those eyes. *My God*. The intense way he looks at me makes me shiver.

"Layla?" He raises a brow.

He has to know the effect he has on me. It's obvious. He walks into a room and the chemical shift is unsettling.

He's always lured me in with the tease of escapism. And for once, I want to grasp the offering in both hands and leave the darkness of my world behind. If only for a few hours.

"I'm good." I drop my cell to the mattress and push from the bed. "Thanks for taking care of me." I walk toward him, my heartbeat excited although I'm still filled with hesitance.

He watches my approach with hungry eyes, the drink hanging limp in his hand, his arms strong and sure at his sides. "The bath is ready. It'll help calm the nerves."

"My nerves are calm." I don't stop until my toes brush the leather of his shoes.

I need to get lost in him. To lose sight not only of my failures but of myself. I don't want to be this person anymore. I want to be free.

"If anything, this morning's events have made me emboldened." I lean up on the pads of my feet, place my palms on his hard chest, and inch toward his mouth.

My tongue tingles as I get within a mere breath of his lips only to have him turn his cheek, rejecting my advance.

"Layla," he warns. "This is the adrenaline."

I stiffen in horror, mortified.

All the air leaves my lungs on a rapid vacuum of humiliation, the scent of his exquisitely perfect aftershave only increasing my suffering when I have to draw in my next breath.

I drop back to the soles of my feet and retreat with heated cheeks.

"Wait." He wraps an arm around my waist, holding me captive. "Don't get the wrong idea. I—"

"You brought me into your room." I push at his arm, attempting to break free. "You placed me on your bed."

"Because I want you to be comfortable. I need you to feel safe." He frowns and leans closer until we're almost nose to nose. "But don't get me wrong and think I'm not interested in you. I've made my feelings crystal clear. I want to fuck you within an inch of your life, *amore mio*. What I won't do, though, is cross the line when you're making decisions based on shock."

I blink rapidly at his explicit detail. At the completely sordid image that inspires wildfire in my belly.

His arm tightens around me. "You've barely returned any of my interest. You only came to me now because you're scared and need comfort. And I can give that to you. I just won't do it in a way that will fill you with regret later."

All his aggressive compassion only endeavors to increase my attraction.

"Are you listening, Layla?" He stares into my eyes, waiting. "My need for you defies sanity. But I won't have you unless your appetite for me will hang around after the adrenaline wears off."

"It will," I whisper. "It will hang around."

He keeps staring at me. Reading me. Then, with the flare of his nostrils and a barely audible growl, his mouth is on mine, setting me aflame.

I close my eyes, descending into a different type of darkness, this one born of passion and possession.

He devours me with harsh lips and a controlling hold. I can't get close enough. Not even when my nails are digging into his shirt and my tongue is tangled with his.

It's bliss and euphoria.

Compulsion and addiction.

I struggle to catch my breath, not wanting to pull away, not wanting this to end. I need everything from him. More than lips and hands.

Matthew leans back abruptly, as if it takes all the power in the world to separate us. He pants, his chest rising and falling, while I do the same.

"Drink." He raises the glass in front of me, his eyes glazed with lust, and retreats a step, shoving his free hand through his hair. "It will dull the insanity."

I hesitate, my engrained caution toward the alcohol holding me immobile for a split-second. Just long enough for him to frown.

He gives a breath of a scoff and lowers the offering back to his side. "So you want to share your body, but still don't trust I'll give you a drink that isn't spiked?" He sighs. "Take a bath. You'll feel better afterward."

"That's not it." Well, it is, but...

He retreats again and again, understanding and disappointment staring back at me. "It's okay. I get it. You barely know me."

"No, you don't get it. And how could you when you barely know me in return?" I accuse. "I've had excessive caution drummed into me all my life. I couldn't even accept drinks at my friends' birthday parties when I was a child." I follow after him. "Caution isn't just a tale my parents told me to encourage good behavior. Vigilance has always been something that kept me alive against the harshest threats."

He stills in the middle of the hall, his eyes narrowing. "What threats? Who are you, Layla?"

"I'm someone with a target on my back." I raise my chin with confidence. "And that's all I'm going to say about it."

His gaze remains narrowed, digging under my skin from the few feet of distance between us until finally he nods. "I've got enemies of my own. Enough to know you're worth the risk of more."

My traitorous heart squeezes.

He raises the glass to his lips, takes a gulp, swallows, then steps forward to hand it over again. "It's safe, okay?" He raises a brow, wordlessly asking if his display is enough to gain my trust.

"Thank you." I take the offering and bring it to my lips. The smooth scotch awakens a slight burn all the way down my throat. I don't stop drinking until I've consumed every last drop.

"You're welcome. Now, how about that bath?" He takes my hand, gently placing it in his. "You're still trembling."

"Did you ever think that maybe I tremble because of you?" I entwine our fingers and squeeze to mask my vulnerability. "You unsettle me."

The pad of his thumb sweeps across my wrist, back and forth, gently exquisite. "You unsettle me, too. Beyond anything I've ever experienced. Why do you think that is?"

I wish I knew.

It's clear this pull has something to do with the thrill of the unknown, only the more I learn, the more my attraction grows.

"Maybe there doesn't need to be a reason." I inch forward, reaching for him, tangling my fingers in his shirt, feeling the hard muscle beneath. "Maybe this is just a phase that hit us both at the same place at the same time."

"You're no phase, *amore mio.* I can guarantee that."

When he says those things—the endearing luscious words—I fall for them every time. My skin becomes awash with goose bumps. My breathing falters. Now is no different.

"What if that's all I can offer?" I tug him into me. "What if right now is all there is?"

"You said you don't do one-night stands."

"It's still daylight outside." I grin, undoing the buttons on my blouse, exposing the lace bra beneath.

"I already told you, once will never be enough. I meant it, Lay." He presses his forehead to mine, ignoring the skin I've put on display. "You need to go take that bath."

"Why?"

"So I'm forced to leave you alone."

I close my eyes, drowning in the closeness. In the pure affection that's entirely new to me. "And if I don't want to be left alone?"

A gentle groan rumbles in his throat. "Take the bath, Layla."

I nuzzle my nose against his. "I don't want to."

The groan builds, the sound increasing my thrill.

I slide my mouth over his, the connection featherlight. In an instant, he's all over me, stalking into me until I'm backed into the wall, the glass taken from my hand to be dropped to the carpeted floor with a heavy thud.

He steals my mouth. My decency.

I claw at him, yanking at his shirt, forcing him closer. He responds with a harsh grip of my ass, his fingers digging into my flesh, his groan changing to a growl.

"I need you," I murmur against his lips. "Now."

He ignores me, kissing, clutching, parting my knees with his own. I'm so ready for this. *Too* ready. It's almost embarrassing.

"Take the bath." He snakes his tongue over mine. "Walk away because I'm too weak to make the decision for you."

I can't. I wish I could. This isn't in the best interest of either of us. I know this. I know it with every fiber of my being. And still I can't move.

"Take it, Layla," he begs. "You're not ready to sleep with me yet."

"I'm not?"

His chuckle is faint. "No, *amore mio*. You're not."

My blood runs hot, my pulse pounding at the apex of my thighs. But I believe him. The warning slips through the lust haze to give me a good shake.

"Okay." I plaster a hand to his chest and force myself to retreat. "I'll take the bath."

"Good." He turns and stalks away, disappearing into what I assume is the bathroom.

I pause a second to regain my composure before I follow, entering the gleaming white room a few steps behind.

He stands in the middle of the tiled floor, staring at the tub already towered with bubbles, the fluffy clouds piled above the rim, a towel folded and waiting on the vanity along the back wall.

"You didn't need to do this for me." I move farther inside. "I could've run the water myself."

"I'm sure you could, but I like having someone to indulge." He shoots me a lackluster smirk, his attention skating over my cleavage to my stomach. "It's been years."

"A romantic? Don't worry, your secret is safe with me."

It was meant as a joke, but the seconds that follow become far deeper than that. Tense. I've fractured the lust by bringing us back to the real world.

We both have information we could use against each other. Ammunition. The repercussions potentially run deep.

"And yours with me," he promises and makes his way toward the hall. "I left a robe hanging on the back of the door. Take your time. Relax. Call out if you need anything."

"And if what I need is you?"

"Then maybe hold off for a while." He meets my gaze for a beat before returning his attention to the hall. "When we're finally together, it won't be fast. I assure you, Layla, you're going to want energy in reserve."

12

LAYLA

HE PULLS THE DOOR CLOSED IN HIS WAKE, LEAVING ME TO PICTURE exactly how long fucking him might take as I remove my clothes.

My shoulder protests the movement and once I'm naked, the angry red lines marking my body explain why. The purse strap had a free-for-all with my skin.

A quick glance in the mirror doesn't come without a pained breath, either. My left cheek is viciously swollen along the bone, the puffiness almost reaching my eye.

I force myself to turn away, shoving my concern about Cole finding out to the furthest reaches of my mind, and climb into the bath.

The warm water is quick to soothe me, the heat coating my exposed skin in a sheen of sweat as the bubbles cuddle my chest all the way to my neck.

It doesn't take long for the scotch to go to my head, numbing me perfectly, making the shaking stop. The silence will be my downfall, though.

The long stretch of quiet gives me too much time to picture this energetic sex Matthew alluded to. My imagination runs rampant with wild scenarios that aren't entirely my forte.

It's been a decade since I experienced passion. Even longer since I felt adored.

Benji and I made things work because of Stella and the family business. And we played our roles well. But below the surface, we were far from wedded bliss. We flatlined before our daughter was born. No romance. No energy. Little lust.

It wasn't long until I discovered my husband was cheating on me, and I was okay with that. I always thought he was owed a mistress or two for what he was forced to give up. Especially when I would quit sleeping with him for months on end.

I kept the knowledge to myself, too. I never betrayed him to Cole due to fear of the punishment that would follow. Or worse— the death sentence.

Maybe it was wrong to pretend I didn't know. Maybe Benji would've stopped if I asked. But I kept quiet for my own sake, too. Not just to keep my daughter's father alive, but because it was a relief to rely on strangers to fulfill a duty that was meant to be mine.

Not once did I feel gnawingly hungry for sex like I do now.

Not once in more than nine years of marriage.

"How are you doing in there?" Matthew asks from behind the closed door.

"I'm good." My chest fills with butterflies as I picture him in the darkened hall. "Do you want to come in?"

"You didn't lock the door?"

I bite my lower lip. No, I didn't. I thought about it, though. "Would the flimsy lock have stopped you from breaking in if you wanted to?"

If Matthew's intent was to hurt me, he could've done it many times already. He could've whisked me out of the city while I was disorientated from the incident in the alley. He could've kidnapped me that night at the food truck. He could've forced me to do anything from his sheer masculine power alone.

The knob turns, the door gradually inching open to expose the man I've been daydreaming about for these unending minutes. *No,* for the last three weeks.

He leans against the doorframe, his gaze taking me in with hunger. "I made you another drink." Another glass of scotch rests against his hip as those dark eyes devour me.

"Thank you." I tilt my head to the side when he remains in place. "Do I have to wait until I get out for you to give it to me?"

"That's probably for the best." His attention lowers to the bubbles. "It's not a good idea for me to get any closer."

I press my lips tight, holding in a smile.

God, I love the predatory lust in his gaze.

"Where's Bishop?" I raise my arm from beneath the water, slicing open a path of bubbles to guide a stray strand of hair behind my ear.

"Out."

"Out?" I hold in my delight at his gruff response.

"He's busy rescheduling my flights. *Again.*"

My heart pangs at the reminder of our limited time. "When do you leave?"

"Tonight."

I play with the bubbles, raking my fingers through them, spreading them one way, then back the other, attempting to tease him with the possibility of exposing what the thick cloud hides.

"That doesn't give us a lot of time." I keep swirling, decimating the foam further and further with each swipe.

"No," he murmurs. "It doesn't."

When he falls quiet, refusing to continue the conversation, my thoughts become more daring, my curiosity growing wings.

I raise my leg onto the side of the tub and shiver when his nostrils flare.

"Are you deliberately torturing me?" he growls.

My heart kicks. Wild and unrhythmic. "Torture you?"

He raises the scotch, downing the contents in one fell swoop before returning the glass to his side. "You know exactly what I'm talking about."

There's a warning in his voice. A delicious subtle threat.

My throat tightens. My chest, too. Everything is so painfully, invigoratingly restricted that I have to fight hard to maintain level breathing.

I raise my other leg, crossing both at the ankles against the rim of the tub. I shouldn't be doing this. Warning bells ring in the farthest recesses of my mind. If only they were loud enough to put a stop to the craziness. "Join me."

His jaw ticks. That's his only response. No movement. No words.

"Matthew?"

His features tighten, almost setting in a glower as he grates, "Be sure about this, Layla."

"I think I am," I lie. I'm not even partially certain. I'm running on instinct alone. No, not instinct—infatuation.

"Then I'm staying where I am." He crosses his arms over his chest, the glass moving to rest in the crook of his arm.

"Why is this—"

"I'm on the precipice here. I can only pretend to be a stand-up guy for so long, then I'm going to start pushing my own agenda. So don't play with me, *amore mio*."

My cheeks blaze as I retract my legs from the rim of the tub to sit up straight. "I wasn't..." I shake my head. "I'm not..." I don't know what to say.

"What?" he asks. "You're not what?"

"I wasn't playing. I like being held by you. I just never assumed the offer had to come with a predetermined conclusion."

"It does and it doesn't." He raises his chin as if stricken. "If at any time I did something you didn't appreciate, you'd only have to say the word and I'd stop. But that's where your problem is going to be. I'll make sure you appreciate everything I do. I'll make you want me, Layla. I'll push you further than you anticipate and I won't regret it."

I shiver. Head to toe. Every inch of skin sizzles with goose bumps.

I don't doubt him. He's already pushed my boundaries. I've accepted numerous open drinks. I climbed into the car of a stranger. I've left myself vulnerable to him.

These are all cardinal sins set out by my family since birth. Yet, I don't regret breaking them.

I want more.

"Join me," I whisper.

He leans over in a swoop, placing his glass on the tile before he deftly shucks his suit jacket to the floor. Then, with one button after another, he exposes me to a torso of carved muscles, his hard work ethic and determination etched into the peaks and curves of his chest.

"Something wrong?" He raises a brow as he drops his shirt to the floor.

"My imagination didn't do you justice."

He smirks, his strong hands latching onto his belt. He holds my gaze as he pulls the leather from the clasp, but I can't keep the connection—not when my cheeks flame hot.

I tilt my face away, stupidly bashful, the heat in my cheeks seeping down my neck.

My heart thunders at the continued clink of the belt buckle. In my periphery, I see him discard his suit pants to pile them on top of his shirt.

He snickers, the faint sound making me shiver. "What's wrong, Lay?"

I pull my legs to my chest and focus on the bubbles as he continues to undress, removing his socks, then his underwear.

"Don't tell me you're shy." He approaches, stopping directly over my shoulder, almost out of sight. "Another bashful flutter of those lashes and I'm done for."

I focus on levelling my breathing as I hug my thighs. "Not shy. Just respectful. It's rude to stare."

There's another muted snicker. "Let me make this clear—the things I've pictured us doing are far from respectful. Now scoot forward. Let me sit behind you."

I do as instructed, shuffling farther along the tub.

Every one of my nerves tingles as he climbs in, raising the water level along with the horizon of bubbles. The moment his legs slide around me, I tense, my nipples beading painfully. It's such a strange sensation, this hyper anticipation coated in brutal nervousness.

"Relax." His hands find my forearms under the water. "Lean back against me."

I don't know how. I'm frozen. All the overflowing confidence I had moments earlier has vanished, the traitorous bitch leaving me to fend for myself.

"It's okay." His voice is soft as he guides me to recline against him, his hands adding tender pressure on my shoulders. Then he falls quiet, not saying a word as I settle into him. There's only the gentle ebb and flow of his breathing and the thrilling hardness of his dick against my back.

"You're still shivering." He glides his fingers over my arms, gently teasing me below the surface. "The adrenaline is taking its time to wear off."

"It's not the adrenaline." I clear the discomfort from my throat while his touch climbs higher to my biceps, then farther.

He massages my shoulders, lightly kneading. "You've got no idea how much I appreciate knowing I have an effect on you." He nuzzles my neck, awakening the sensitive spot below my ear. "You're a hard nut to crack, Layla."

I tremble, the vibration skittering along my chest. "You poor thing. Did my restraint batter your excessive ego?"

"Like you wouldn't believe." The words hum against my skin before his lips follow with a brief kiss. "But don't worry. I'll turn the tables."

I hold in a smile, fully aware the tables have always been turned. Soon they may even be flipped.

"How's your cheek?" He scrapes his teeth over my shoulder, his hands continuing their gentle onslaught down and around my waist.

"Throbbing."

"Room service shouldn't take long to bring a bucket of ice. And the concierge is arranging a cooling pack."

"Thank you. But I shouldn't need all that. The swelling will go down soon." If it doesn't, Cole is going to be on the warpath.

"I ordered a bottle of champagne, too."

"Now *that* I would accept with open arms." I need to reclaim the confidence I had when he was standing in the doorway. I want the upper hand, not these flimsy, flaky responses.

His fingers move to my belly and I stiffen with the intimacy before I can stop myself. The low hum of his laughter only increases my tension. He's so incredibly sure of himself. So deliciously confident.

"Relax, Layla." He kisses my shoulder. "You're safe."

Safety isn't my concern. What I fear is disappointing him. Our connection felt different when he was struggling for restraint at the door. Now he's in his element, having already won this game of seduction, and I didn't even leave the starting blocks.

"Easier said than done." I struggle to loosen my muscles.

"Why?" His touch trails lower, along my abdomen, inching farther and farther toward the apex of my thighs, where I already feel his effects the most.

"You know exactly why." I'm unsettled. It's clear he has me tied in knots.

"How would I know? You've been successful in exposing very little about yourself." He places another kiss to my neck, the kindness followed by a rough scrape of teeth. "Am I moving too fast? Too slow?"

I don't know.

Nothing is certain anymore. There's only sensation, and it's taking me over like a drug.

"Maybe," I croak.

"Maybe too fast?" His touch continues to descend, gliding over the slim patch of curls at my pubic bone. "Or maybe too slow?"

I suck in a ragged breath, my pussy clenching as his fingertips divert farther down along the path where leg meets crotch. I shake my head, unable to answer, no longer even sure of the question.

"Too fast or too slow, Layla?" he murmurs.

I whimper, the blanket of bubbles doing nothing to stop my mind from visualizing what's happening below the surface. His strong hands consume my vision. The image of his lips on my skin makes me throb.

He adds pressure to my legs, parting them, exposing me beneath the water. "Want to know what I think?"

I breathe harder, clenching my eyes shut.

"I think your fragile little whimpers mean you're hungry for more but don't know how to ask for what you want," he rumbles under his breath. "I think you're throbbing, your body begging to be sated. I even think you might finally be realizing all the pleasure that could've been yours the first night we met if only you'd allowed it. How we could've been like this weeks ago."

He continues to speak against my skin, punishing me with wave upon wave of goose bumps as his fingers continue to sweep back and forth along the apex of my inner thighs.

"And just think, *amore mio*—I'm barely getting started."

I clench my molars. I'm going to moan. I feel the release build in my throat, determined to escape. There's so much tension. Too much. My body craves. My heart pounds.

"Tell me you want more," he teases against my neck.

"I want more." I respond too quickly. So damn fast my answer should be humiliating. But the embarrassment will have to wait until the aftermath. Right now, craving is all I know. Hunger entirely consumes me.

His fingers continue to creep, swiping closer and closer to my core. "How much more?"

Everything.

The moan escapes, my head falling back to rest against his shoulder.

"You can't say it?" he asks.

No. I've never asked for sexual favors before. Never even voiced my need.

"Please, Matthew," is all I can admit.

"It's okay. I won't make you say it. Not today." He sweeps those fingers closer. "But soon."

The threat shivers down my spine. The warning that I will one day have to admit my desires fills me with unstable excitement. I'm high. Euphoric. Entirely mindless with lust. I never knew this heightened state of hunger existed. This clawing, savage need.

"I enjoy seeing you like this." He continues the external sweep of his touch. "Worked up. Greedy. This is how I've felt since we met. My cock hard as stone, my thoughts always on you."

I shake my head. "You barely know me."

"That's the crazy part. I don't know a damn thing about you, and still, I'm infatuated."

Those fingers skirt the edge of my pussy. Back and forth. Up and down. Constantly teasing. I grasp his wrist, clinging tight. He has such inspiring control, such unwavering confidence.

I wiggle my hips, eager for this torture to end.

"Don't worry, I'm impatient, too." He kisses my jaw, my neck. "So fucking impatient, *amore mio*. But this is merely the beginning."

I'm about to force his hand where I need it the most when a knock sounds on the furthest reaches of my consciousness.

I freeze, blinking back to reality.

Matthew growls in frustration.

"What is it? What's wrong?" I brace to sit up, but he holds me down with those strong hands clamped around my crotch.

"It's only room service." He tilts his face away, calling a loud, *"Come in,"* toward the hall.

I tense further, ready to fling his hand off me so I can scramble for a towel.

"Stay." He keeps me held tight. "They'll be gone in a minute."

My pulse thunders as the suite door creaks open, the unmistakable rattle of a trolley quickly following.

"Sir?" a man calls. "Would you like me to leave your order in the living room?"

Matthew steels his hold, his legs tightening around me. "No, bring it to the bathroom."

13

———

MATTHEW

"Jesus Christ." She scrambles, wiggling and slushing water over the edge of the tub in an attempt to get out.

"It's okay," I purr in her ear. "Your modesty remains intact. You're completely covered by the bubbles."

"Matthew, please." Her hands snatch at my wrists.

"Breathe." I kiss her shoulder, the back of her neck. "*Relax.*"

We're barely getting started. And to be fair, I warned her. I told her she wasn't ready.

The rattle of the trolley continues down the hall, making her nails dig into my skin.

"I've got you," I whisper. "You can trust me."

The door is pushed wider by a kid barely in his twenties, his eyes bugging at the sight of us before quickly lowering to the tiled floor. "Umm. Where would you like your order, sir?"

Layla remains stiff against my chest, her fractured breathing brushing my ears.

"You can bring it over here." I relax my legs around her and loosen my hold on her thighs, gently running my fingertips in circles a bare inch from her pussy.

She flinches, her spine snapping rigid.

I grin into her hair, loving her unease, as the trolley is wheeled closer.

"Here?" The kid stops a foot away from the tub, his gaze cautiously flicking from me to Layla then back to the floor.

"Yeah, that's perfect." I trail my touch closer to her heat, over the smooth softness of flesh leading to her pussy, as I murmur against Layla's neck, "Would you like him to open the champagne?"

She moans and shakes her head. Fast. Fucking rigid.

It's a chore not to laugh.

I kiss her shoulder and tilt my hips, nudging my cock against her ass. "You sure? It will only take a second."

She remains quiet, her chest rising and falling in a rolling wave.

"Just open it." I meet the guy's gaze. "It'll save me having to get out of the water."

The kid nods and reaches for the bottle seated in a metal bucket, the slush of ice filling the energetic silence.

Layla's breathing quickens, the rapid cadence shifting to a gasp when my touch skims her pussy lips.

Her virginal jitters are a drug. The tension. The sharp nails piercing my skin. I close my eyes and press my face into her hair, focusing on those breaths, letting them fuel me as I trail a teasing swipe right down the middle of her sex.

She shifts against my cock, and I could groan from the exquisite friction.

I could fucking come.

I've imagined this for weeks. Pictured every scenario. Daydreamed a bucket list of sordid ideas. But they didn't live up to this. They weren't even close.

The *pop* of the champagne startles us both, the bath bubbles slushing against the upper curve of her breasts.

"Matthew," she whispers, her legs clenching.

"Mmm?" I inhale the floral scent of her shampoo. The sweetness. The purity.

She doesn't respond, not with words, only fractured inhales as she remains statuesque, not portraying the depravity going on below the surface.

"Would you like the bottle down there?" the kid asks. "Glasses, too?"

I tease a fingertip around Layla's opening, circling wider and wider. "What do you think, *amore mio*?" I edge deeper, gliding slowly inside her, that delicious pussy clamping down around me in an instant. "Do we need glasses?"

"No." The response is nothing more than a rushed breath while she shakes her head. "Nothing. We don't need anything."

"It sounds like we're all good here." I jerk my head at our guest. "If you check the pockets of my pants on the floor you'll find a tip." I sink my digit all the way inside her, making her shudder as I smirk into her hair.

"Ahh... Sure thing." He backtracks toward my clothes, chancing a glimpse at the beauty in my arms, before snapping his attention away. He rummages through my pants while I slowly twist my finger inside her. Teasing. Dragging out her pleasure.

Her fingers claw at me. Her core clenches. And those hips I love so much, they fucking jolt oh so slightly. Not once does she protest my advances. Her digging fingers are a pleading sign for more.

"Want me to get him to hang around?" I whisper in her ear.

She whimpers as the guy straightens from bending over to pull the clip of cash from my pants pocket, his attention returning to the bath.

"Excuse me, sir, how much would you like me to take?" He stares at Layla, his Adam's apple bobbing with an arduous swallow.

He envies what I have. And so he should. The woman in my arms is beyond compare. Not only in appearance. In class, too. In seduction, and sensuality, and above all else, the trust she's placed in me.

"That depends." I slide another finger inside the most perfect pussy, and her body rolls in the subtlest of waves, her back arching, her chest stretching. "What's the going price for discretion?"

His lips part, his skin turning a paler shade. "There is no price, sir. I would never—"

"Then take it all, my friend. Enjoy yourself."

"All of it?" He gapes. "Are you sure?"

I slide another finger inside her. "Positive. I'm always happy to reward loyalty."

The guy pauses a moment, watching as Layla's head rests back against my shoulder, her teeth buried in her lower lip as she nuzzles shyly into my neck.

I slowly pulse my digits, enjoying how he watches her. How he *wants* her.

She needs to bear witness to that. To how she's desired. Adored. This gorgeous woman may be confident in battle, but right here, gloriously naked and wanton, she seems far from empowered.

"Like what you see?" I ask.

The kid nods.

"She's beautiful, isn't she?" I want him to say it. To tell her how perfect she is. How revered.

"She's gorgeous," he murmurs.

Layla moans, the sound seeming born from pained modesty and heightened pleasure while she hides her face deeper against my neck.

I need her to know she's hungered for. Treasured.

"Matthew," she whispers against my skin. "Please ask him to leave."

My lungs restrict at her polite plea. The delicate cadence. The charm of her voice. "Of course. Anything for you." I nuzzle her hair, working my thumb over her clit as I meet the guy's gaze. "You can leave now."

He blinks. Once. Twice. "Yes, sir. Thank you, sir." He backtracks, stumbling to the hall, disappearing into the shadows, his footsteps retreating until the suite door squeaks closed in the distance.

"You okay?" I keep gliding my fingers inside her. Punishingly gradual. Torturing us both.

She doesn't respond. Not in words. She keeps those claws embedded in my wrist, her pussy clenching with each new slide of penetration.

"He wanted you," I utter against her ear. "Anyone who could see you like this would want you. You're so fucking beautiful."

She pants. Mewls. Scratches.

"You're breathtaking, Layla." I increase the pulse of my fingers. "So fucking breathtaking."

"Don't… stop." Her core clenches, her nails breaking through skin to bring the most gratifying burst of pain. *"Please."*

I plunge deeper inside her. Press harder against her clit. With my free hand, I grab a fistful of her hair, guiding her neck to the side so I can devour her throat.

"Matthew," she wheezes.

I kiss.

Lick.

Suck.

"This is just the beginning, *amore mio*." I feast on the flesh below her ear as she shudders in my arms. "Wait until I fuck you. Wait until my cock is buried so goddamn deep you can't remember what life was like before I was inside you."

Air leaves her lips on a rapid rush. Her pussy flutters around my fingers. She comes undone, grinding into my touch, one hand reaching behind my neck to tear at my hair.

She cries out in orgasm, riding me, fucking killing me in the best possible way as her back arches, her breasts breaching the surface to give me the perfect view of her ruby pebbled nipples.

She whimpers. Whispers my name.

Then finally, she collapses against my chest, the arm around my neck slithering back to her side.

I slide my digits from her core, but don't stop touching her. I trail my fingertips around her pussy lips, straight up her center, and over her clit, the leisurely path lasting long minutes as she regains level breathing.

"I can't believe that just happened." She retracts her claws and slumps farther against me, sinking lower until the water is at her neck.

"Did you enjoy that little bit of fun?"

"Little bit of fun?" She glances over her shoulder, eyes wide. "I've never done anything like that before... In front of someone, I mean... It was..."

I'm about to grin at her purity when she turns back away, the faintest glimpse of shame flashing in her gaze before her face is no longer in view.

"Hey." I grab her jaw in gentle fingers and guide her stricken expression to look at me again. "You didn't enjoy yourself?"

"I did." She swallows and licks her lips. "But I'm..." She shakes her head. "I don't know who that woman was. All I know is it wasn't me."

Shit.

I release her jaw and inch back, extricating my softening dick from her tailbone.

I told her I'd push.

I warned her this would happen. I warned us both. I thought that had been enough to prepare her.

"Forgive me." My apology is unwittingly growled, my tone laced in self-loathing.

"No." She turns her entire body toward me, a wave of water escaping the lip of the tub to patter to the tiles. She's trembling again, the swelling on her cheek now darker and beginning to bruise. "I didn't want you to stop. I just…"

Just what? I want to beg her to continue but she's skittish. One wrong push and she'll run. I can see it in her eyes.

"You don't need to explain. I'll give you privacy to get out on your own." I lean forward, poised to stand when her hands clamp down on mine.

"No. Don't go." She gives a bashful smile as she lowers her attention to my chest. "I'm sorry… I'm just shocked. That was the most thrilling thing I've ever done."

Her expression undoes me. The modesty that stands meekly in the shadows of a woman who seemed fearless last night.

"Tell me which part was thrilling, Layla." I settle back against the tub, relief pumping through my veins. "I want to know every little detail."

"All of it." Her teeth rake her lower lip, her attention still on my chest. "I'm making a fool of myself, aren't I?" She glances up through dark lashes. "I feel like a virginal teenager."

I reach out, gliding a stray strand of hair behind her ear, then gently brush my thumb over her damaged cheek. The bruising is deep, almost as deep as my anger toward the person who inflicted that pain.

"You're far from foolish." I guide my touch to her lower lip, grazing the soft flesh as I grin. "And don't worry. I like my women confident on the streets, and easily scandalized between the sheets."

Her laughter is instantaneous. Melodic.

Something about her finds a home inside me. Something that meshes without flaw.

I don't know how she came to be so perfect. But she is. Her courage and determination out in the real world is remarkable. Then the contrasting meekness once she's naked and vulnerable is enough to have me entirely hooked.

I envisaged her being a tigress in bed. Sure and poised and bold.

This modest kitten is far more detrimental to my composure.

"You're the devil." She holds my gaze, the bubbles licking over the tops of her breasts. "But do you know what?"

"What?"

Her face flushes as she whispers, "I'm starting to think I might really like you."

I snicker and push to my feet. Water and bubbles rush down my abdomen and thighs as she quickly glances away from my exposed dick. "Well, welcome to the party, *amore mio*. You arrived late, but I guess it's better than nothing."

14

LAYLA

I keep my gaze averted as he dries himself, my hands clinging to the rim of the tub, my heart wildly fluttering.

He likes me.

He actually likes me.

It's pathetic, but after a childhood when I was constantly watched by overbearing males who didn't allow boys near, then being forced to spend years with a man who found it hard to love me, all while being the daughter to a monster who used me for his devious games, the confounding exhilaration of someone actually liking me—*me*, Layla Hart—is such an incredible relief.

"You okay?" Matthew pulls on his suit pants in my periphery, then yanks at the zipper.

"I'm better than okay." I meet his gaze and the collision has his face falling.

"No, you're not." He frowns. "Something has upset you."

I shake my head and smile. It's a forced expression, but only due to the overwhelming whirlwind of sensation taking over my insides. "I'm perfect."

I really am.

For the first time in more than a decade something other than my daughter has brought joy to my life, and it's come in the form of a muscle-etched, stubble-ridden, gorgeous human whose eyes are currently scrutinizing mine.

"I'm going to give you space to clear your head." He snatches his shirt from the floor and slides his arms into the light material. "Have a glass of champagne. Call out if you need me."

"You don't want to stay?"

His grin returns. "I don't want to leave, but you need a moment to breathe. I'll come check on you soon."

He grabs his jacket and belt from the tile, and walks toward me, grabbing the ice bucket to place it closer. "Are you hungry? Is there anything else I can get for you?"

Just you.

Only you.

"Are you sure you don't want to stay?" The sound of my own fragility tightens my throat. I'm not going to be this woman—this needy, pathetic excuse for a full-blooded Torian. "Ignore me." I cringe. "I'll be out soon."

He leans down and kisses the top of my head, his fingers trailing along my shoulder in the briefest tease of contact. "I'll be waiting in the living room whenever you're ready."

He straightens and I feel the loss immediately. His steps toward the hall are torture. The isolation once he closes the door behind him is hell.

It takes all my self-control not to chase after him and finish what we started.

He didn't get a release.

He didn't ask for one, either.

Benji would never have let that happen. He didn't do selfless acts. Not in the bedroom. And—*shit*. I need to stop this. I have to quit comparing Matthew to my late husband because it always ends in guilt.

I'm not doing it anymore.

Benji is gone. And Matthew is only temporary.

I need to start enjoying this for what it is and leave the comparisons behind.

What I need is champagne.

I grab the bottle, pour myself a glass, and sip what has to be excessively expensive alcohol. And all the while, Matthew's touch haunts me like a ghost.

The memory of his lips on my neck.

The tingle from where his firm hands spread my thighs.

The more I drink, the more he fills my head. Not only sexually, but how he rescued me, too. The way he cradled me in the back of his car. The cadence in his words as he promised to look after me.

I push to my feet, wobble with the sudden shot vertical, then place my glass on the floor and grab a towel.

In less than two minutes I'm cocooned in a plush hotel robe, the champagne bottle in my hand along with the glasses as I pad to the end of the hall and find Matthew on the sofa.

He's hunched forward, elbows on knees, his back to me as he talks on his cell in snarled tones. "Tell him this is unacceptable. We had an agreement."

I wait there, not wanting to interrupt, not willing to get in the way of his work.

"I don't give a fuck," he snaps. "I think you know me well enough to understand I'm livid right now."

I stiffen at his vehemence, never having heard it before, and the glasses clink in my hand.

"I've gotta go." He straightens. "Layla is out of the bath."

I wince, wishing I'd been more discreet even though I refuse to be a snoop.

"She's doing well." Matthew glances at me over his shoulder, his annoyance nowhere in sight as he takes me in with appreciation. "The swelling is getting worse on her cheek, and there are marks on her arm, too. But she's strong."

My stomach warms with the compliment. With resurging lust and need, too.

I approach, placing the bottle and glasses on the table in front of him, remaining a foot away. I take him in while he leans back, relaxing into the sofa like a king atop his throne, one arm stretching along the headrest, an ankle crossing over his knee.

"Handle the situation, Bishop. Thoroughly." He rakes his gaze down the length of me, his eyes hungry. "I'll be ready to fly out at five." He disconnects the call and places the device on the far cushion. "You're flushed."

"It's the champagne," I lie.

It's definitely him. All him.

He leans forward, reaching out to grab the front of my robe to pull me closer. "I promised myself I'd give you space." He drags me down onto his lap, his hands fisting my lapels. "You're turning me into a liar."

I grin at our similarities and settle against his thighs, my palms finding his silk-covered pecs. "I don't want space."

"No, but you need it." His lips brush mine, once, twice, the kisses commanding but oh, so gentle. "Yesterday, you wanted nothing to do with me." He lowers his hands to seize my hips and guides me to move onto the cushion beside him.

"That's not true. I've wanted more from you since the moment we met. It's the complications that kept me away."

"And have those secretive complications changed since you were mugged?" He stands and stalks to the kitchen to grab a drinking glass from a cupboard, then fills it with water from the fridge. "I think I can answer for you in saying they haven't. The only difference from last night to today is a chemical imbalance brought on by shock." He returns, holding the chilled water out to me. "Drink. You can't live on alcohol alone."

Goddamnit, he's charming.

Big and broad and conniving. Yet sweet enough to cause cavities.

"Thank you." I stare up at him as I take his offering.

Maybe he's right. Maybe the fixation gnawing at my insides is only due to the scare I received. But even if it is, what does it matter? There's no future between us. There's only now, and I want to take advantage of our limited time.

"In answer to your question, no, the issues keeping me from being able to see you again haven't changed." I take a sip from the glass, not realizing how much I needed water until my throat throbs with the cool relief. "This is all we have. And I'm willing to take advantage of every minute if you are."

He moves to the armchair opposite me—the farthest seat in the living room—and sinks into the cream leather. "Minutes aren't what I'm after. A seized night every other Wednesday whenever I'm lucky to catch you at Perfezione won't be enough. I want more from you. Everything else is merely a provocation that won't satisfy."

I school my expression, not having anticipated the rejection. "Does that mean you want me to go back to my own room?"

"No." He scowls. "What I'm saying is that touching you—tasting you—only works as a taunt when I know I can't have everything. And I'm too old to torment myself that way."

Everything he says is a compliment.

I'm not sure if he's even aware of what he's doing. But his words act as a confidence booster. He tells me all the things I've dreamed of hearing. One after another, each perfectly constructed sentence making me crave him all the more.

"How old are you?" I ask, fighting the need to bite the inside of my mouth.

"Thirty-three. Old enough to no longer be satisfied with casual sex." He kicks his ankle back over his knee. Suave. Sophisticated. "What I want is a wife, *amore mio*. And children. Both of which I can easily picture with you."

"Excuse me?" I sputter, needing another sip of water to stop myself from choking.

"You heard me." He grins. "But my point is that fucking you isn't my only aim. Getting to know you is."

I swallow. Clear my throat. Swallow again.

Even if this didn't have to be temporary, I can't give him what he wants.

Dragging him into my world isn't an option. I already forced one man into the darkness that consumes my family. I refuse to do it again.

"Come back to D.C. with me tonight." He remains composed through the gentle demand. "Let us get to know one another. You'll have access to my jet to return home whenever you like. You'll be safe at all times."

My pulse increases as a lifetime of emotions batter down on me.

I can't withstand the yearning. The hope. There's happiness, and excitement, too. But they're all washed away with the tidal wave of guilt, heartache, and longing.

I'm not meant for happy things.

"I'm sorry, I can't." I place my water on the table, using the movement as an excuse to drag my gaze from his.

"Why?"

It's a simple question. If only the answer wasn't entirely complex and multi-layered.

There's my family. My lifestyle. The dangers and threats. Not to mention why I'm in Denver in the first place. But I can't tell him any of that. He can't know who I am.

"Why, Layla? Can't you give me that much? Is it your job? Do you have responsibilities to get back to?"

I wince, not wanting to lie to him. "It's a lot of things I can't explain."

"Can't or won't?" He sits forward, returning to his elbows-on-knees position, his attention bearing down on me. "I already know you're spying on the Costas. What else do you need to hide?"

If the question is a provocation to get me to look at him, it works. I meet his gaze, my pulse hammering in my throat, my heart squeezing with each rampant beat.

I want him to know me. *Truly* know me. But the knowledge wouldn't work in my favor.

"Talk to me," he demands. "You don't get to share your body then simply walk away."

If I don't simply walk away, you wind up dead.

I don't tell him that, though. I don't give him the truth that would stop this inquisition in its tracks.

Instead, I resign myself to giving him a different glimpse into my life. A slightly less confronting admission to get him to back off. "I have a daughter."

For a second, I don't think the news bothers him.

His confidence and sophistication remain in place. Then, gradually, as if being siphoned by the smallest filter, his forthright stare turns weak. Those dark eyes lose their intensity. His lips part.

The change is incremental. Entirely punishing in its lethargy. But it's there, the disappointment blinking back at me under midnight lashes.

"See? This is why I didn't want to say anything. *This—*" I indicate the disturbance and turmoil now surrounding us with a wave of my hand, "—is exactly why I wanted to remain anonymous."

And to think the existence of Stella is merely the tip of my complicated iceberg. He has no idea who he's trying to get involved with.

"I guess it's best if we part ways now." I push to my feet. "I appreciate everything you've done for me. I'll see myself out."

"No, you won't." He follows suit, bridging the distance around the coffee table in three determined steps to grab my robe-covered wrist. "You can't blame me for being caught off guard. I didn't expect you to be a mother. Not when there are no scars on your body. No stretch marks. Not even the barest hint of imperfection to indicate you carried and mothered a child. But that's all this is, Layla. Shock." He leans his face into mine, demanding I meet his pleading gaze. "Having a kid isn't a deal breaker for me."

Christ.

Who is this man? And what is he doing with my previously cemented conceptions of the opposite sex?

"Well, it is for me." I square my shoulders, steeling myself against his charm. "Nothing is more important to me than my daughter. Nothing ever will be." I twist my arm from his grip. "I still think it's best if I leave."

I hate the hesitance in my voice. I want him to stop me and I need him not to in the same breath. Before I can fall victim to my own weakness, I trek to the hall and into the bathroom to reclaim my clothes, wishing things didn't have to be this way.

My shoulder doesn't ache nearly as much when I pull on my stained blouse and jeans. It's my chest that takes the brunt of my pain.

The emotional toll of this romantic rendezvous gets to me, sinking deeper and deeper until I raise my gaze and find him standing in the bathroom doorway.

"Is she—" His question falls short, his brows pinched as he drags a rough hand over his mouth. "Is one of those assholes her father? Is that why you've got eyes on Remy and Salvatore? Did they turn you away once they found out?"

"*No.*" I glare, despising the thought of those men fathering any child, let alone mine. "My *husband* is Stella's father. She's almost eleven."

Matthew's features relax.

That's what he was worried about?

That's what caused the change in his demeanor?

I guess I can't blame him for thinking my enemy was my baby daddy when I've played along with his scorned lover assumption.

"My daughter has nothing to do with me being in Denver." I ignore the regret that accompanies the lie. I can't allow her to become more involved in this. "But she's one of the reasons we can't go beyond today. I'm a mother who lives on the opposite side of the country to you."

"Portland isn't more than a plane flight."

Panic descends in a blinding rush, stealing the breath from my lungs before I can rein it in. I stare at him, aghast, partially livid, entirely caught off guard. "I never told you where I was from."

I should've held my cards closer to my chest. Should've played along, pretending I hadn't noticed the insight I never gave. But out of all the time we've spent together, right here, right now is the only instance where I hadn't expected him to surprise me with deception.

Everything he's done for me today lulled me into lowering my guard.

"I overheard the tail end of your conversation with the bank." He raises his hands, offering surrender. "I was checking on you, and when I heard private information being shared I didn't hang around."

I want to believe him. The added squeeze of discomfort in my chest makes it obvious this isn't just personal, it's emotional. I've already been swept off my feet.

"What else did you hear?"

"Nothing." His hands fall to his sides. "You still have your anonymity for now."

I hold his gaze, trying to see any hidden deceit.

All that blinks back at me is sincerity. A cloying, agonizing seriousness that makes me want to blurt everything to him—my secrets, my failures. I need him to know the ins and outs of my life so he can find me lacking, because having him stare at me with adoration is a gift I don't deserve.

He moves forward, approaching with slow caution.

"Don't." I backtrack, needing more time to catalogue the seriousness of his newfound knowledge. "Give me space."

His jaw hitches as if I've struck him. "Why? Am I the enemy now?"

No, he's the exact opposite. He's the blessing I'm not entitled to. The warmth and happiness I haven't earned. At least, not yet.

"Why, Layla? Tell me."

I shake my head, attempting to fight how he's already come to mean something to me even though we remain strangers.

"Tell me." He continues up to me, his palms gently gliding over my biceps. "If you want me gone, I'm gone. I'm only staying in town for you." He leans his hips against mine, suffusing me with warmth. "Tell me what you want from me."

"I don't know," I whisper, backtracking farther, only endeavoring to drag him along with me.

"Then tell me what you don't want." He follows until I'm caged against the vanity.

"I don't want to do something I'll regret." I've already endured too much of that. I can't take any more.

"Like getting caught up with me?"

I close my eyes. Even behind clamped lids I see him. His intent. His hunger. "Like missing an opportunity to be with someone like you," I admit.

His grip tightens on my arms. "Then don't." He leans closer, the brush of his breath skating over my lips. "We'll find a way to make this work."

"It's not that simple."

"Make it simple." His voice becomes a growl. "Forget the complications."

"I have a daughter," I repeat into the darkened void.

"And where is she now?"

My heart squeezes. "At boarding school." Far from where I want her to be—under my roof, in my arms. I'd had no choice in her leaving at the start of the first semester a month ago.

Cole had made plans to send Tobias to the illustrious school in Chicago a year prior. What I didn't anticipate was my crippling eruption of grief when Stella begged to go with him.

"She doesn't live with me," I whisper.

I'd tried to talk her out of leaving for months. I'd pleaded, bribed, and coerced to the best of my abilities. But nothing I did persuaded her to change her mind, and I couldn't bring myself to make the decision for her. I'd already stripped enough from her life.

I also refused to take my concerns to Cole.

He granted my wish the day my husband was buried. He went against his usually unbreakable beliefs on retaliation and let those who pulled the trigger on Benji walk away scot-free.

I had no right to ask for more favors.

"That's why you can travel to Denver whenever you like?" Matthew asks.

I nod. My daughter's absence is why I'm here. For more reasons than one.

Within days of her leaving, I'd realized the innumerable sporting and craft distractions I'd scheduled to fill her time since her father's death were actually a benefit I'd also grown reliant upon.

I'd needed those long drives to baseball and the homework sessions to keep *me* occupied. To divert *my* thoughts. Because with her gone, my idle mind became a vicious mistress who demanded action.

"I'm here for a reason." I open my eyes, my inhale hitching at the deep brown that stares back at me. "I can't afford to be distracted."

It's clear in the tight set of his lips that he understands what I'm referencing.

I've spent every spare minute stalking my enemies since Stella moved away. Learning exactly how wonderful the Costas' world became since they murdered Benji.

I don't regret begging Cole not to retaliate. The years of peace were necessary to get my daughter and I back on our feet. But my spying made it clear it was now time to set things straight.

I need redemption, and they deserve to suffer.

"I don't want to be a distraction." Matthew lowers his hands to my waist, gripping me tight to raise me onto the counter. "The Costas aren't a family to be messed with, Layla. Snooping around isn't safe. I can fuck with them enough for us both. Just tell me which one of them to target and what you want done."

And with those admissions, I'd be handing over insight I'm not willing to give. He'd know I wasn't a scorned lover focused on a single family member. He'd be fully aware my thirst for revenge runs far deeper, my intentions more vicious than spying due to lover's heartbreak.

"Let me think on it," I lie.

I can't.

I won't.

I have to do this without him.

I spread my thighs, welcoming him between my legs, succumbing to the allure of his strength just for a moment. He has no clue *my* family are far more insidious than the Costas.

Dark folktales have been created about my brother. Worse were made with my father in mind.

It's a given in the criminal world. Ghost stories are brought to life from a slither of reality. Like the Butcher Boys of Baltimore.

The Dark Death in Dallas.

Freddy Fingers from Arizona.

My brother's enforcer—Hunter—has his own moniker, too, one I'm sure was built on fact.

But Emmanuel Costa is different. He isn't a blip on the underworld radar. And he sure as hell doesn't scare me.

"Think as long as you like." Matthew leans closer, brushing the tips of our noses, the intimate contact making me yearn for things I can't have. "There's no rush as long as I know you're mine."

His possessive words coil around me, strong and delicious. I eat them up despite knowing they're not meant for me. Not *made* for the type of person I am.

He wouldn't even think them if he knew who I was.

"You don't under—"

He cuts me off with a kiss, punishing and hard, before retreating. "I can make this work, Layla. Just tell me it's what you want."

It is.

God, how it is.

I want him and us and this.

I want fun and happiness and lust.

I crave all the things he's shown me and all those that wait in the wings. But—

"Stop thinking yourself out of this and tell me what I want to hear," he whispers against my lips. "I want you, *amore mio*. And I know you want me, too. Chemistry doesn't lie."

No, it doesn't. I'd never even known the power of attraction until we met. The strength of it. The delicate suffocation of sense and control.

I stare into those demanding eyes, hating how easy it would be to lead him on just for a few more moments of bliss.

He teases his mouth over mine, his tongue grazing my lips. "Tell me."

I whimper, too weak to withstand temptation. "I'm yours," I whisper.

For now.

Until the moment he leaves for D.C.

15

———

LAYLA

AFTER UNENDING KISSES UPON THE VANITY COUNTER THAT SEND MY blood racing, Matthew swoops me into his arms and returns me to the sofa.

He ignores my panted breaths, and the lust I know glistens in my eyes with every docile blink, and places distance between us like a devout gentleman, making sure I hold a cooling pack to my cheek for hours.

We talk. Laugh. And even though I don't want to, I fall, not just hard, but wholeheartedly, for a man I barely know.

He orders room service. We eat oysters and drink more champagne. He asks question after conversational question and listens to the answers with a level of interest most don't pay me. And he isn't intrusive.

He asks about my happiness.

He wants to know all the intricate details of my soul. From my favorite sounds, to the places in the world I love most, and every trivial piece of information in between.

He takes in the tidbits I share with unwavering focus, devouring the insight like I'm an anticipated book he's finally able to read. Not merely listening, but learning. Studying. He seems to take note of the cadence in my voice, and holds my gaze longer when I attempt to guard myself, waiting for me to expose the truth.

And I do. For the most part.

Everything I tell him is real. It just isn't deep.

I skate on the shallowest depths of my being, never truly letting him in even though I want to.

And although we don't kiss or claw at each other's clothes again, he has me in a constant state of thrumming tingles with his attention, his gaze raking over me with slow deliberation.

By late afternoon, I have a full belly and a body that has succumbed to adrenaline detox. Yawns come every other minute until Matthew demands I rest my head on a cushion he places on his lap.

We continue learning surface-level details about each other, neither of us asking the finer questions because we both know everything else is off-limits.

And our time together is still perfect.

I don't need to know his surname and he isn't getting mine. I don't ask about the darkness from his past, but I learn of his love for Switzerland and his hatred of hot weather.

He finger-combs my hair, his touch perfectly gentle for such a strong man, as I lay cuddled around his waist.

He makes sure I still have access to money to get home. That I have ID stored in my cell to be able to board a flight. He treats me like a treasure as my heart becomes full and my eyes grow heavy.

Sleep is inevitable. The adrenaline and alcohol knock my feet out from beneath me, and all I want is a nap. I just expected him to still be here when I woke.

Instead, the only thing left behind is a note on the coffee table in a now empty suite.

AMORE MIO,

I couldn't wake you for two reasons:

1. It seemed sacrilegious when you sleep like an angel.

2. I didn't want to give you closure by saying goodbye.

This isn't the end for us, even though I assume you've told yourself it would be. We will see each other again. I'll make sure of it.

M.

. . .

I'M SUCKER PUNCHED by the intense level of desperation and heartache that overwhelm me once I realize he's gone.

His presence lingers in the bedroom. His delicious scent clings to the sheets. And even after I leave his suite, I can't release myself from the hold he has on me.

I cancel the last remaining night on my reservation and return home to a place that doesn't feel the same as it had when I left.

I'm not the same.

The tingle in my chest inspired by Matthew's existence stays with me. I can still smell him. Can still feel the brush of his lips against mine.

But when Stella and Tobias come home Friday night, I put the infatuation to the back of my mind and dedicate the time to my daughter.

I thrive in our moments alone, because thanks to my brother, I only get to see her one weekend a month.

We watch movies and talk about boys. We eat popcorn, give each other mani-pedis, and make up for the distance usually placed between us.

As much as I hate her living in Chicago, it has become clear she's flourishing with the independence.

Maybe I am, too.

She didn't even notice the swelling on my cheek, the bruising now hidden beneath numerous compacted layers of foundation.

We spend two wonderful days together, made all the better by the sordid text messages Matthew sends me on the regular. He's become my dirty little secret. A treasure for me and me alone.

Each silenced vibration of my cell chips away at my resolve to keep things casual. I grow empowered by his determination, loving the way my confidence builds with his attention.

Our monthly family lunch on Sunday at Cole's house feels different, too. Usually I have a sense of underlying heartache whenever I'm surrounded by the perfect pigeon pairs. Everyone has a partner to rely on. Cole has Anissa. Then there's Hunt and Sarah, Keira and Decker, as well as Luca and Penny.

This time, there's no pain or jealousy.

I can't even wipe the subtle smile from my face as we all hug in greeting.

It feels like Matthew is here with me. Or maybe could be in the future.

I spend the meal daydreaming about what my perfect world would look like. How Matthew would take the seat by my side at upcoming dinners. How he'd understand who I was and where I came from without judgment or anger.

I deliberately skip past the introduction phase in my mind, knowing the first few months would be filled with paranoia and interrogation from Cole. But what came afterward would be bliss.

We'd cuddle on the sofa, unashamed of any public display of affection. We'd have each other's backs. And for once, I'd be the one to make everyone jealous because my relationship was enviable, not fake and devoid of emotion.

It isn't until Stella and Tobias leave the dinner table to escape into the backyard that my daydreaming stops.

Everyone else's hype and excitement over having the kids home disappears as if it were a facade. Keira, Penny, Sarah, and Anissa fall quiet. Cole, Hunter, Decker, and Luca's conversation becomes stilted, their responses turning sharp and gruff.

I missed the cause of the transition while in my imaginary state.

Something that must have been important.

I glance at each of them as I nibble on a bread stick, the hair on the back of my neck standing on end when more than one of them meet my gaze before quickly glancing away.

This is about me.

The tension seeping into the air is somehow my doing.

I discard the half-eaten bread stick onto my plate and pat the corner of my mouth with a cloth napkin. "I'll pack the dishwasher."

I push to my feet, preparing to cut and run. Nothing good can come from this vibe.

"Sit," Cole grates. "We've got things to discuss."

My stomach grows heavy. "Like what?" I reach for my sister's cutlery to my right, pretending I'm immune to the tension.

Anissa pastes on a friendly smile. "How have you been handling life without Stella?"

"I'm doing well." I fight a frown. It's no secret my brother's wife and I have had our share of trials over the years. We don't do feelings, which is why it's strange for her to ask. "Obviously, it's tough. But I'm handling it."

"You're glowing," Penny adds. "Have you met someone?"

My hand pauses in the middle of reaching for the dirty serving spoons. I'm caught at what to say and know it seems entirely forced when I chuckle a few seconds later. "I guess my new skincare regime is working. I have late-night online tutorials to thank for that."

"It's definitely working," she adds. "I've never seen you like this."

My heart pangs. Guilt follows.

She's never seen me like this because I've never felt like this. Not even while married.

"Is this new skincare regime the reason you cancelled your credit card?" Cole raises a taunting brow. "Have you been making purchases from a disreputable company? Were you scammed?"

He's playing with me. Mocking. The worst part is, nobody attempts to save me from his underlying recrimination. They all sit and stare, waiting for answers.

"I lost my purse." I hold my brother's gaze. "It's not a big deal."

"When you were out of town?" Keira asks.

"Yes," I grate. "While I was out of town."

I keep staring at Cole as his eyes narrow, the authority in his gaze raising my apprehension. I know this look. I know what comes along with it, too.

"You've met someone." Keira pushes from her chair and grabs my dirtied plate topped with cutlery. "That much is obvious. You walked in here with a bounce in your step and this subtle giddy smile." She starts for the kitchen. "I don't know what I've done to be blocked from the happiness in your life, Lay, but it hurts that you didn't share this with me."

I don't deny her observation.

I keep staring at my brother as crockery clutters into the sink. He's angry, but not like my sister. The tightening in his jaw lets me know he's positively fuming.

"What, Cole?" I sigh. "You told me months ago that it was time to move on. Are you retracting your approval now that you've seen me happy for once?"

"So it's true?" He leans back in his chair, crossing his arms over his suit-clad chest. "You've met a man?"

I raise my chin, unwilling to voice a response.

Despite daydreaming about romance, I didn't let myself truly believe there was a possibility of a relationship until now. Until the moment when my brother could destroy it for me.

"Is he the one who hit you?" he seethes.

All eyes remain on me, the weight of their scrutiny making me nauseous.

"No." I square my shoulders, raise my chin, and bite back an emotional response. I can't win this battle unless I focus. "He didn't hit me."

"Then who did?"

"I fell." I use all the conviction I have to continue holding his stare. "I tripped on the sidewalk and stumbled into a brick wall. It's no big deal."

Cole shoves aggressively from the table, the legs of his chair screeching across the tile. "Don't fucking lie to me." He leans forward, placing clenched fists on either side of his dinner plate.

I don't react. Don't move. One badly timed blink and he'll dig in his heels, demanding to know everything. Not only about Matthew, but about where we met, and why I was there.

He can't learn about Denver. If he finds out he'll put a stop to my plans, then I'll never be able to make amends or prove my loyalty to him.

"Cole," Anissa warns. "Calm down."

His nostrils flare as he glares. "Who is he? Tell me his name."

My heart lodges in my throat. "It wasn't him."

"*Bullshit.*"

I swallow, caught between wanting to scream and needing to crumple. "You think I'd be walking around with the giddy smile Keira mentioned if the man I was interested in hit me?"

"I don't know, Lay. Especially not when you married a man you didn't love and watched him fuck around on you for years."

My face drains of warmth, all the blood seeping from my cheeks.

He knew.

Of course he did. It was stupid to assume otherwise.

I guess it was even more idiotic to assume my brother would care enough to do something about my husband's indiscretions. But it's the humiliation that stings. They won't understand why I ignored the existence of Benji's mistresses. They'll assume I have no self-respect.

"Careful," Luca warns. "Benji isn't here to defend himself."

"This isn't about your brother," Cole snarls.

My pulse increases, pounding in my throat.

Usually I can understand Cole's protective nature. I don't always like it, but there has always been an understanding of why he is the way he is.

Now is different, though. This isn't merely protection. There's resentment in the mix. Disgust, too. Both byproducts that stem from the bad decisions I made in the past. Decisions he refuses to stop holding against me.

"Fine." I speak through clenched teeth. "I was mugged. That's why I needed to cancel the credit card. My purse was stolen and I got shoved into a wall. I'm not being abused. I haven't made any more bad choices. I was just in the wrong place at the wrong time."

Silence descends before the most out-of-place chuckle carries from outside as the kids remain oblivious to our argument.

"Why didn't you say something?" Hunter mutters. "If you're in a position where you're getting mugged, you need to—"

"*What?*" I fix my brother's enforcer with a scowl. "I need to do what, Hunter? Quit leaving the house? Lock myself inside? Go back to living a non-existent life just so you think I'm perfectly managed?"

"Watch your mouth," Cole warns.

"No. I won't." I glare. "I didn't tell you—I *couldn't* tell you—because I knew how you'd react. You always fly off the handle. You've spied on me like I'm a goddamn traitor since Benji died."

"You can't deny your track record of making smart decisions is lacking."

His verbal strike hacks at my confidence. "You're never going to let me forget my mistakes, are you?"

I never should've given my father information on Cole. I'd

naively thought I'd been looking out for my family because, back then, my brother was a hothead who enjoyed spilling the blood of anyone who glanced sideways at him.

There were whispers he'd start a drug war for frivolous reasons.

For pride. Or spite. Or even arrogance.

So I kept my father updated on his son. I gave him insight when he couldn't seek it for himself because he'd fled the country. And I convinced Benji to do the same.

It was for the family's safety.

For our future.

Back then, I hadn't known who my father was. *What* he was. I would've killed him myself if I'd known about the sex trafficking.

To me, he was the same man who'd always denied me attention.

Affection.

Love.

His request created the only bond I'd ever had with him. The one connection between us. So when he offered financial compensation for the information I'd already been giving freely, I didn't see it as a bribe. It was merely a strengthening of our building relationship.

At least, that was what I told myself until he proved otherwise.

The thickening tension builds.

The men at the table judge me with annoyance and disappointment. The women do the same with shame and embarrassment.

Every second, every blink, every sigh or noise of displeasure scampers under my skin, the toxicity finding a home inside me.

"I think we need to end this conversation before it gets out of hand." Sarah pushes from her chair and grabs the salad bowl. "I vote that the women clear the table and the men stack the dishwasher."

This is far from over.

Cole will keep hounding me. Will keep holding everything against me until I finally stand up to him.

"I'm not done." My eyes burn as I stare my brother down. "I've apologized over and over again. I've tried my best to make amends. I let you bug my house when you said you couldn't trust me. I allowed your guards to follow me—to invade my home and my privacy—because that's what you wanted, even though I despised having strange men in my home when Stella and I were at the height of our grief."

"And?"

I bite my tongue, caught between crying and screaming. "And I didn't protest when you deliberately sent Tobias to boarding school because you knew Stella would follow. She was all I had, Cole. The only thing to bring me happiness, and I let her go. All for you. I've done everything you've asked of me. But I won't allow you to dictate my life anymore."

"You won't allow me?" He raises a brow, his livid rage crackling below the surface.

Someone curses under their breath. Hunter or Decker. I'm not sure because I don't drag my gaze from the severity in my brother's eyes.

"Yes. I won't allow you." I stand my ground. "Everyone at this table has made mistakes. Every single one of them. Yet, two years later, their sins are forgiven and mine seem brand new. Why is that?"

"They're not blood," he snarls.

"They're not *blood*?" My voice rises without my consent, the tone filling with feminine emotion I despise as I swing an arm toward my sister in the kitchen. "Keira made mistakes, too. And don't get me started on your wife."

He flashes his teeth in a snarl. "Choose your words wisely, sister."

"I have. For *years*. I've done everything wisely, with extreme caution, always keeping everyone here at the forefront of my mind because I want to make up for what I did. For how I allowed my own father to manipulate me. But that's what it was, Cole—manipulation. Our father tricked me. *Used* me. Just like he used so many others. And yes, I know it's still my fault. And yes, I profited from it and have to live with my decisions for the rest of my life. But what I won't live with is you throwing it back in my face whenever the whim takes you." I sniff to kill the tingle in my nose. "I won't take the overbearing protectiveness anymore. I won't play along with you thinking you can decide where I go and what I do. Or that you need to know why I cancelled my credit card or how I got a goddamn bruise on my face. What I do now is my business."

Cole raises his chin, slow and deliberate, the anger receding as smug superiority takes its place. Then he inclines his head as if in agreement.

"That's it?" I frown. "You're not going to say anything?"

He gives a faint shrug. "You're doing me a favor."

That hurts.

Really hurts.

I want to hunch from the pain he slices through me, his rejection tearing open old wounds as my eyes burn like wildfire.

"Cole," Anissa pleads. "Don't say something you'll regret."

"I won't regret it, little fox." He keeps his gaze on me as he speaks to his wife. "As far as I see it, this is perfect timing. Layla no longer wants me to know her business, and I'm more than happy for her not to know mine."

There's an ominous ring in his tone. Something that alludes to a deeper meaning.

"You see, sister, I've wanted nothing more than to claim retribution against those who murdered my niece's father for years. But I held back because you begged. You fucking pleaded in the most pathetic display of weakness I've ever seen. So I gave you what you wanted. What *you* needed to move on, because I couldn't risk you jumping further off the rails. But with this new outlook on our relationship, I guess I'm no longer burdened by your wants and needs. I can take what I'm owed. What we're *all* owed."

I stiffen, my lungs tightening.

He's going to claim the retribution I've been trying so hard to achieve. He's going to take the only chance I have to right my wrongs.

I panic, wanting to backtrack but not knowing how. "What are you going to do?"

"I'm sure you'd love to know." He looks at me with self-righteous indignation. "Unfortunately, though, it's now clear we don't share that kind of information."

16

———

LAYLA

"YOU'RE NOT GOING TO TELL ME?" MY LIMBS QUAKE WITH FURY.

"You tell me yours. I'll tell you mine." Cole smirks, the curve of his lips sickening in its arrogance.

"Fuck you, you manipulative piece of shit." I shove at my place mat, the heavy material scooting forward to topple the salt and pepper shakers. "You're just like our father."

His eyes flare. I don't stick around to take more of his toxicity. I storm for the sofa, snatching the old purse I'd found at home to tug the strap over my shoulder.

"Layla, wait." Keira hustles toward me from the kitchen. "Don't go."

"I'm not staying." I continue to the sliding glass doors leading outside and yank them apart, plastering on a fake smile as the gentle breeze brushes my face. "Stella, it's time to leave, sweetheart."

She raises her gaze from her cell screen and snaps a glance toward Tobias sitting on the lounger beside her. "I'll see you at the airport?"

"Yeah." He jerks his chin and gives me a quick finger wave. "See you next time."

I should hug him goodbye. I should at least walk out there to speak to him properly, but I'm the shortest step away from my

118

breaking point. One inch in the wrong direction and I'll drop this temperamental bag of emotions and cause a scene.

A *far* bigger one.

I keep my sham of a smile in place for Stella's sake and wait patiently at the front door for her to say her farewells, my animosity bubbling below the surface.

Cole and I always disagree. We fight. It hurts. This isn't a first.

What derails me, though, is how I'd become used to the idea of me being the Costas' downfall. That I'd be the one to gain vengeance for my daughter being abducted and my husband's murder.

I wanted that accountability.

The atonement.

I need it.

I battle the panic of approaching failure as I escort Stella to my car parked out front and drive us both home. I don't allow her to see how my world is crumbling. How I've let her down again.

While she's busy packing for her return to school, I do the same, grabbing clothing and toiletries. I also arrange store-bought debit cards and stockpile cash for a longer-than-usual escape. And when it comes time to drop Stella at the airport, she has no idea a suitcase of my own is stashed in the trunk.

I kiss her goodbye in one heartbeat and stride my ass to a check-in counter to book a flight to D.C. in the next.

I don't spare more than a thought at not knowing Matthew's surname, or where he lives, or even works for that matter.

I fly across the country on impulse, arriving after nine at night with absolutely no clue where to go once I climb into a cab.

Layla: Tell me about these clubs of yours. What are their names?

My text to Matthew spits in the face of the anonymity we've tried to maintain. Our contact since Denver has been mostly seductive or complimentary, and my stomach twists with the possibility of him ignoring me entirely.

Matthew: Why, amore mio? Searching for skeletons?

I should be. By now, an extensive background check would've been done if Cole was involved. But I haven't snooped. Instead, I've fallen deeper, and allowed trust to blossom where skepticism should.

Layla: One day I might make a surprise visit. But I can't do that if I don't know where you work.

His reply is instantaneous—*Don't tease, woman.*

Layla: Me, tease? Never. Just tell me where you're likely to be if I arrive in D.C. unannounced.

He doesn't respond. Not for several long minutes that turn my stomach into a bile pit.

I glance out the cab window, my teeth gnawing my lower lip as I watch the illuminated skyline pass by.

This can't be a mistake. I won't let it be.

If I misjudged Matthew's interest I won't allow the rejection to sting. He may have wanted me here days ago, but those were his terms. His timeline. Now could be different. There may be another woman on his arm. And God knows we're far from claiming exclusivity.

If things don't work out, I'll take this as an endeavor to gain breathing room from my family. I'll indulge in spa treatments. Get my hair done. Dine in fancy restaurants.

Three dots appear in the text chat, the anticipation of his response forcing me to hold my breath.

Matthew: Mon-Tues, I'm usually on the coast. Wed-Thur, in Richmond. Fri-Sun, I'm in DC at Trend or The Mill.

I exhale in relief.

In appreciation.

He's opening up to me. *Trusting* me. And he's also in town.

Layla: You know what they say—all work and no play makes Matthew…

The dots appear again. This time, the reply comes quicker. *It makes Matthew preoccupied with work so he doesn't fall victim to thoughts of the woman he's obsessing over.*

I smile, big and bright enough for the lingering swelling in my injured cheek to make itself known.

Layla: Does this woman know about us?

I bite my lip, hoping for a flirtatious response.

Nothing comes.

I'm driven further and further into the heart of D.C. Closer and closer to the hotel I booked last minute, yet those three dots never reappear.

It's hard not to take it as a sign. Maybe he does have another woman. Maybe I'm the mistress this time.

I refuse to dwell once I'm delivered to the front doors of my accommodation and check into my room.

I change clothes, pulling on a tight black dress that leaves little to the imagination, before perfecting my makeup. The bruising on my face is now easily hidden, but that's no longer all I'm striving for. I don't merely want to cover up.

I want to slay.

When I'm as flawless as I'm going to get, I grab my purse and make my way toward the first club he mentioned—*Trend*.

I don't tell him I'm coming. I don't even message once I arrive at the front of the building to find an illuminated white script sign of the club's name elegantly placed above an entirely black brick wall, the lone door framed by two hulking bouncers.

This needs to be a surprise. Not only so I can judge if he's excited to see me. It's to cast aside any lingering concerns. I don't want him to have time to prepare or hide those skeletons.

If he has secrets, I need to know now, while I can still walk away with my head high.

"You can drop me off here." I unclasp my belt and pay the cab driver in cash before getting out.

I join the end of the small line of people waiting to get inside, show the ID stored on my cell when it's my turn, and then walk into the darkened entry, the carpet beneath me barely visible as loud music thunders from the dance floor up ahead.

I reach the main area without drama and stop at the railing that sets me apart from the dance floor a few steps below.

For a Sunday night, the interior is swarming with people bopping and drinking along to the techno beats.

The place is massive. A two-level rave fest with a glowing purple bar in the center of the ground floor with more along the side walls, and a glass-encased room upstairs.

I can't help being impressed. But it's not the hyped crowd or glistening bars that steal my attention. It's Matthew, who stands on the middle landing of the metal staircase leading to the upper level, both hands gripping the banister as he scrutinizes the crowd, the flash of lights making him look hardened and devilish.

My heart flutters.

He's wearing another stylish suit, his stubble now thick along his chiseled jaw. His hair falls around his eyes, framing the perfection, while his lips are pulled thin.

God, he's attractive.

My body reacts as if he were made for me. Born to the exact requirements that stoke my libido to its highest peak.

I don't know how it's possible to be this captivated. This magnetized. But I am.

All the way down to my curling toes.

He remains a statue of confidence before the crowd as a woman climbs the stairs toward him, her long, dark hair plaited over one shoulder, her attention intent as she sways her hips in a skirt that has to be giving those on the dance floor an indecent view.

My throat dries the closer she gets, my heart taking on a panicked rhythm.

She stops at his side, placing a hand on his arm, the touch seeming sexually familiar even from this distance.

Shit.

I step back, wanting to shrink into the shadows.

Matthew stands there without reaction, still eyeing the crowd as she inches into him, her breasts brushing his bicep as she speaks close to his ear.

They're together.

They have to be. A woman wouldn't approach a man with his current icy demeanor unless she had carnal confidence.

I retreat another step, apologizing as I bump into someone behind me. But I can't take my eyes off him. I can't quit staring at the approaching car wreck that will knock my feet out from beneath me.

I can already feel it. The impact of heartache. The collision of fantasy and reality.

I fell too hard, too fast.

I'm stupid for thinking our tryst had depth when even our conversations didn't.

I shake my head, attempting to dislodge the self-loathing as he continues to eye the crowd, the woman now leaning in to press her mouth to his neck.

I'm such an idiot. We've only spent one goddamn weekend together and a handful of texts, and here I am, shattered.

Matthew jerks back from the dark-haired woman and turns on her, a flash of overhead light illuminating a face filled with anger. He says something, his words unkind if the way she straightens and balks is any indication, while my pathetic ass clings to hope.

They're arguing.

Fighting.

He remains cold as he speaks, his confident posture unwavering until she raises a hand to slap his face.

I jostle with the impact more than he does, and blink in shock as she storms back down where she came from. I don't realize I'm panting until she disappears into the dancing crowd.

All the while, Matthew remains unfazed, pivoting back to grasp the railing like nothing happened.

I'm more stunned than he is, and I don't know whether I should leave or stay. The flighty flutter of my heart has no intention of letting me escape without answers. The brutal twist of my stomach makes me question if I want to learn the truth.

I'd thought of him as a gentleman. A sly, devious gentleman, but a gentleman all the same.

Now I'm not so sure.

And still, I crave.

Even after witnessing that drama, I can't stop wanting him. Can't stop making excuses for what just happened.

The woman obviously couldn't take no for an answer.

His body language had been clear. Hell, I could see his lack of interest and I'm ten yards away.

What unsettles me, though, is the difficulty in aligning this severely frosty man with the flirting and smoothness of the one I'm accustomed to. This side of Matthew doesn't fit the person I've been fantasizing about.

This guy is different.

I'm about to turn on my heel to rethink my options at the hotel when someone else climbs the stairs. A hulk of a man this time —Bishop.

The temperamental offsider leans in to say something to his friend and this time, there's an immediate reaction.

Matthew stiffens, his face pinching as his attention glides in a straight line right to where I stand. Those eyes take me in, holding me immobile while his harshness evaporates with a sly grin.

Goddamn. Gorgeous.

I swallow over the desert claiming my throat and curse my fluttering pulse.

He maneuvers around Bishop and descends the stairs to the ground floor. I can't see his face as he parts the dancing crowd like a warrior destined to decimate.

His eyes don't meet mine again until he's a breath from the few steps in front of me, his confident stride jumping them in one fell swoop to stop before me.

There are no words. No niceties.

He wraps a hand around my neck and hauls me in to steal my mouth with his.

I gasp against his lips. My doubts vanish. Self-control disappears.

I'm breathless, my mind spinning as he awakens my body with his kiss. Then, just as fast, he pulls away and instructs me to follow him.

He grabs my hand, leading me back to where he came from. Through the crowd, up the metal stairs, to the glass-encased room.

My palm is at home in his. The tight hold. The possession consuming.

He escorts me inside the soundproof area, the noise still loud but from chatting people this time, and takes me to the bar, the counter illuminated by a dark blue glow. Then he kisses me again, one hand clutching mine, the other tangling in the hair at my nape.

I lose myself in him. The concerns disappear, too.

Despite the crowd around us, it's only me and him. The two of us in our own little world.

"This is a nice surprise," he murmurs against my lips.

"Not as much of a surprise as I wanted." I keep my eyes closed, our noses touching. "Did Bishop see me arrive?"

"You're hard to miss. Especially in that phenomenal dress. How the hell do you keep knocking me off my feet?"

I meet his hungry gaze and fight a needy whimper.

He evokes so much animalistic ferocity it's agonizing. I'd give anything to be alone with him. One-on-one. Naked.

"You have the same effect," I admit, raising my hand to trail my fingers over the red mark on his left cheek. "Who was that woman?"

His expression doesn't falter. I don't catch the slightest glimpse of guilt. "Do you really want to know?"

Yes. *No.*

I sigh. "Unfortunately, I can't unsee what happened and my imagination isn't kind."

He straightens his shoulders. "Let me get you a drink first."

Shit. Is it that bad?

"Wine?" He raises a brow and steps away to walk around the bar. "Vodka? Maybe a cocktail?"

"Surprise me."

He smiles as if appreciating my trust, and begins making my concoction, swirling bottles, deftly adding shots while the bartenders ignore his liberties.

He needs to quit impressing me, otherwise I'll never return home.

Never ever.

He snatches a bottle of gin and pours the liquid into a tall glass, his gaze downcast. His confidence bolsters mine. I don't get it. In a new city, in an unknown club, I should be cautious and concerned. Instead, his presence empowers me, turning me into a wildcat, my claws barely hidden below the surface.

The only thing decreasing my self-assurance is that other woman. I'm not sure I want to hold his gaze while he tells me about her. I'll be a slave to my emotions. How I feel will be written all over my face. Then he'll know exactly how much power he has over me.

"Who was she?" I take the opportunity to have the unwanted discussion while he's occupied.

He grabs for the vodka, adding a nip of alcohol to the glass. "Obviously someone who doesn't appreciate my charm."

I swallow the dryness building in my throat. "Is that all you're going to give me?"

He looks up at me, stray strands of hair shading one eye. "She's someone I almost slept with." He holds my gaze for a beat, then returns his attention to the drink, adding juice, before stirring with a plastic swizzle.

I don't want to ask. It makes me nauseous thinking about it, but the question slips free. "Almost?"

"Yeah." He pours himself a scotch, then rounds the bar, placing my drink in front of me before raising his own to his lips. He holds my attention over the rim, his focus intense in its honesty. "Things got heated. But I didn't follow through."

Jealousy eats me from the inside out, the sharp teeth burrowing deep. "When?"

"A few weeks ago," he admits.

A few weeks?

After we'd met, but before we'd kissed.

"What else do you want to know?" His question isn't angered, or a taunt. He's offering genuine transparency and I'm no longer sure I want it.

"Do you like her?"

His mouth kicks up as he takes another sip. "Did it look like I like her?"

"It looked like she liked you up until the second before her hand slapped across your face."

He shrugs. "She wanted to finish what we started. I didn't."

His candor grates me. Will I be the next woman who wants more when he doesn't? Is my heart his next victim?

"You're judging me again," he drawls. "I thought we were past this."

I thought so, too. I really did. Now I'm not sure.

"Fine." He sighs, his brows pinching. "I guess you want the full story?"

I don't know. Part of me needs to understand how he could be unabashedly cruel. The other doesn't want any more knowledge of him with another woman.

He leans in, dominating my personal space and grazing the stubble of his cheek along my jaw, his lips near my ear. "The truth is, I got back to Washington after meeting you for the first time and I couldn't get your fucking phenomenal body out of my goddamn head."

I shudder. Hold my breath.

"I couldn't sleep," he continues in a seductive murmur. "Couldn't think straight. So I found someone to replace you. A woman with the same hair. A similar figure. A pretty face."

My skin erupts in goose bumps, my nipples beading for reasons unknown.

His nose nuzzles the sensitive skin below my ear as he says, "I wanted to fuck her while pretending it was you. But no fantasy could live up to the hype."

I shiver, every inch of me tingling.

"Less than an hour spent with you, Layla, and I was obsessed." His lips brush my neck, the graze of his stubble providing the most deliciously contrasting friction. "Seeing you again only heightened the infatuation."

My breathing labors. My core tightens. "But you didn't sleep with her?"

"No." His response is instant.

"Have you slept with anyone else since we met?" The need for answers is pathetic. I can't help it.

"No." He tastes my skin with a minuscule slide of his tongue. "And I won't."

I believe him.

I believe his words. His vibe. The hunger in his mouth as it delicately devours my neck.

Lust bubbles in my belly, seeping out through every nerve.

I don't understand this yearning. This desire. It's all-consuming. Mind-numbing.

I slide a hand around his neck, grazing my nails along his scalp to hold him close. "How long until we can get out of here?"

He snickers, the sound devilish enough to make my pussy clench. "As soon as you'd like."

17

___

LAYLA

HE LEADS ME BACK DOWNSTAIRS, MY HAND IN HIS, THEN THROUGH A staff door, along a shadowed hall, and out into a gated parking lot.

Matthew directs me to a black Roadster nestled between a line of sedans and compact vehicles, and opens the passenger-side door.

We're on the road within silent minutes, the blood pounding from my building libido the only sound.

"Are you having second thoughts?" He flashes me a look of concern.

It makes me want him more. "I'm right where I want to be."

His lips tweak in the slightest curve of approval before he concentrates on traffic. We head into the heart of the capital, not far from my hotel, and stop inside another parking lot, this one below a towering apartment complex.

He entwines our fingers as we walk to the elevator, my tongue tingling, my chest throbbing. I wait for him to maul me inside the enclosed space, but there's no voracious kissing session. He maintains his air of calm, not showing a hint of this obsession he spoke of, and takes me to the top level.

The penthouse.

I'd envisaged we would've been all over each other by now. Fingers clawing. Legs tangled.

It's the opposite. He's suave with his sickening patience,

opening his front door wide to allow me to take the first step into his perfectly appointed space.

I'm not sure what I expected—maybe a bachelor pad with sleazy art or clothes strewn on the floor? But that isn't what I stand in front of. This place is beautiful, the kitchen before me entirely spotless from the marble counters to the stainless-steel appliances, and all the way down the floor-to-ceiling wine fridge.

"Want another drink?" He closes the door behind me, then strides ahead.

"I'd love one." I'd love anything that might taper the rabid beat in my chest.

"Do you have a preference?" He opens a cupboard and pauses, waiting for my response.

"I'm easy. You decide."

He reaches inside for a glass and grins to himself, as if he can't wait to test just how easy I am with a million X-rated surprises.

I place my cell on the kitchen counter and turn in a slow circle, taking in the home that suits him without flaw. The furniture is commanding and elegant. All polished woods with white coverings, from the lounge setting in the adjoining room to the dining table a yard to my left.

Everything is immaculate. No clutter. Not even dust.

Eclectic art lines the walls. From abstract to surrealism and pop. The different pieces draw attention to what must be expensive taste.

"Your home is beautiful." I turn back to face him as he makes our drinks.

"*Our* home," he corrects without missing a beat.

I chuckle, and slowly sidestep toward the mail farther along the counter. "Are you like this with all your women?"

"*All* my women?" He pulls out a drawer, the clink of liquor bottles following the movement. "You say that as if I'm not obsessively picky with who gets to share my time."

"So I should be flattered?"

"Don't go twisting my words, *amore mio*. You're special. I think you know that."

Arrhythmia takes over, the fractured heartbeats overwhelming me. I focus on the three letters on the bench as he pours alcohol into the glasses, and read the name on the top line of the address.

Matthew Langston.

I let the syllables roll around in my head with slow lethargy and fight the compulsion to say *Layla Langston* out loud just to hear how it would sound.

I may not have slept with him yet, but this is moving fast.

I'm picturing my life here, in this penthouse, in his world. Away from the drama of my family and the complications that always follow them.

"Here." He rounds the island counter to hand me what looks like a glass of juice. "A screwdriver."

"Perfect." I take a sip and watch him do the same with his scotch.

For a few seconds we simply eye each other between subtle swallows of alcohol. No words. Only blazing attraction.

"I'm going to preface this next question by telling you I've never ended a work night on a better note," he murmurs. "But why are you here, Layla?" He places his glass on the counter and cocks his hip against the marble, his full attention remaining on me.

My throat tightens, not only with the way he reads me, but in contemplation of the truth.

He's opened the door to his life, allowing me free rein, and I'm still hesitant to unlock mine. Even just a little.

"You owe me a goodbye." I shrug.

He steps closer, the tips of his shoes nudging mine. "Well, you're going to be disappointed." He cages me against the counter, one hand on either side of my waist. "There are no more goodbyes for us."

I hold in a smirk. "Ever?"

"Ever." He leans in, but doesn't touch. I'm almost certain it's a strategy. To make me want what he holds back. "Is there anything else I can compensate you with?" The question is purred with the most sinister seduction.

He wants me to voice my desires. To ask for sex. "I'm sure we could find a suitable compromise."

His lips kick with a grin as he glides a gentle hand through my hair. "You captivate me. You're bold and fearless enough to fly across the country to see me. Yet hesitant and almost unsure when it comes to voicing how much you want to fuck me."

I suck in a shallow breath.

"You're a puzzle I need to solve." He slides his hands over my hips and lifts me onto the counter, just like he did in the hotel bathroom in Denver.

"And once you have me figured out?" I raise a brow. "What then?"

"I don't think that will happen. This is a rest-of-my-life type of task."

I laugh, my humor quickly smothered by his mouth swooping down on mine.

He kisses me with severity. With strength and conviction and lust. His lips are so damn commanding. His hands a steel-like grip at my waist.

When he pulls back, I'm panting, struggling to catch my breath… my thoughts.

"You think I'm kidding, *amore mio*," he whispers. "But this isn't a game. You mean something. *We're* meant to mean something."

"What if you're wrong?" My insecurities voice themselves before I can rein them in. "What then?"

He narrows his eyes, staring at me with fascination. "Then you can walk away without any animosity between us… But that's a future that isn't in the cards."

He makes everything seem so easy. So dreamy. And maybe that's what our world could be like—all rainbows and unicorns—if I were another person.

"We're adults, Layla," he continues. "I'll make sure you don't regret your time with me."

I want him to be right. *God*, how I want it.

I want to be protected. Not by an overbearing brother, but by an adoring, passionate lover. I want more of this giddy feeling in my stomach. I want freedom and happiness and a fresh slate.

"I think you might be right." I lock my legs around his, encouraging him to decimate the space between us, the hem of my dress rising to my crotch. "I want this."

He lowers his hold from the adamant force at my waist to the most delicious hold on my upper thighs. He keeps his hands there, his thumbs mere inches from where my body demands attention as he stares down at me, waiting.

"Do you want me to beg?" I ask.

"No. You never need to beg for anything." He digs his fingers into my flesh. "My hunger isn't a charitable donation you ever need to plead for. But I do want more of an assurance that this is what you want, because every other time I've had my hands on you it's felt like shock or intimidation has played a role."

I nod, even though the devil on my shoulder whispers I'm only here because I've fled my family and he was the only one I had to turn to. The only person I know who doesn't owe my brother favors.

"I'm here for you." It's still the truth. "All the other times I was, too. Even under duress I can make clear choices."

"Be sure, Layla. I'm playing for keeps."

"Are you trying to talk me out of this?"

"Never." His eyes glaze with lust, his nostrils flaring slightly before his mouth steals mine again.

It's a frenzy of lips and tongues and teeth. A wild dance of my snatching fingers at his collared shirt and his strong hands on my heated skin.

"It feels like a fucking lifetime since I had you naked." He reaches around the back of my dress, finding my zipper to drag it down. "I'm going to burn all your clothes."

He grabs the heaped material at my thighs and helps to pull the dress over my stomach, my shoulders, my head. "On second thought…" He leans back to take in my fire-red lingerie, a lone finger reaching out to trail along the tiny strap of silk circling my waist that holds up the even tinier V of lace at my crotch. "You can keep these… at least temporarily."

"You like?"

"That's a fucking understatement," he growls. "They look brand new. Tell me you bought them for me."

"I bought them for you," I whisper.

"*Jesus.*" The oath is groaned. "You're so goddamn obedient. Such a fucking treasure." He pushes farther between my legs, the hardness behind his zipper a mere inch from where I want it to be. "After all the things I've fantasized about doing to you, you'd think I'd know where to start." His fingers creep higher and higher until they're at the crotch of my panties.

I jolt at the briefest swipe of his thumb over my pussy as his lips approach mine.

"You missed me." He holds my gaze, staring deep into my eyes. "You're already soaked."

I bite my lip. Nod.

"What did you miss most?" He strokes his thumbs back and forth along the lace V, sending a mass of tingles through my clit.

I close my eyes and nuzzle his nose, working my fingers down his buttons, popping them one by one. "I missed the empowerment I feel when I'm around you. You increase my confidence."

"And you feel confident now?" he asks against my lips.

"Yeah. I do."

He kisses me, soft and gentle. Teasing and slow. "Okay then, *amore mio*. Show me."

18

MATTHEW

SHE ISN'T STARTLED BY MY REQUEST, YET SOMETHING LINGERS ON THE edges of her expression, spitting in the face of the confidence she claims to have.

I step back, readjusting the stiffness in my pants. "Strip for me."

Her chin lifts, as if in defense, but she holds my gaze and snakes her arms around her back, unclasping the see-through bra in silence. The straps loosen at her shoulders as she cups her breasts, guiding the material into her hands, then dropping it to the tile floor.

"Slow and steady doesn't always win the race, *amore mio*." I'm not sure she's aware of how much she's teasing me. But I'm dying here. The anticipation of sinking home between her thighs is fucking killing me.

"Do you use that endearment with everyone?" she purrs. "It means *my love* in Italian, right?"

"Right." I fight against the need to claim those perfect tits with my hands, my mouth, my cock. I want to cover them with my seed. Mark her like a fucking beast. "Would you prefer *tesoro mio?*" *My treasure.* "Or *bella mia?*" *My beauty.*

Her lips curve. "I'd prefer an honest endearment. One without the player charm."

"Then hear this, *sei tutto per me*." *You are my everything.*

She blinks back at me, lost for a moment, her hands gripping the edge of the marble counter.

"Want me to translate?" I lick my lower lip, itching to taste her, to plant my head between those thighs.

"No." Her response is breathy as she grabs my jacket and yanks me forward. "It's best if you keep quiet. You undo me in both languages, and I need to keep my wits about me."

I snicker as she drags me in for a kiss, one arm curling around my neck, the other working on her underwear as she jostles from side to side.

I help her, yanking the string of material down her smooth legs, letting it fall to my feet. She's exposed, her thighs spread, yet she holds me close, not allowing me the freedom to look my fill.

This attraction has a life of its own.

I was consumed by it from the first night we met when I'd been watching her from the restaurant kitchen, her expression filled with determination and strength as she spied on the Costa family dinner. Then, in a split-second, Bishop scared the confidence from her features, and the frail panic triggered regrets from my past.

She needed saving. And unlike those I failed in my youth, I refused to let her suffer.

"*Ho un debole per te.*" *I'm weak for you.*

Completely powerless.

I would fall to my knees for her. In lust. In protection. For no other reason than this maddening chemistry between us.

"Shh." She presses her mouth harder to mine, demanding silence as our chests brush.

I snicker, dragging my palm to the apex of her thighs, sliding my fingers over her mound as our tongues tangle. I'm worked up. Hard as stone. Determined as hell. "*Nessuno potrà mai computer con te.*"

She gasps. "Stop it. You're killing me."

"And not being inside you is killing me."

She whimpers and holds me tighter to her lips.

I glide my fingertips to her slit, finding her wet, making her hips roll. The growl of gratitude that vibrates in my throat is uncontainable.

I'd hoped she'd be like this—utterly perfect—and prayed she

wouldn't be in the same breath. There's no withstanding her. Not now. Maybe never.

I sink my fingers inside her, the walls of her pussy clamping down on me while she shudders.

"Matthew." Her voice is nothing more than a breathy plea. "You make me crazy."

She grinds into the curl of my fingers, kissing me harder, gripping tighter on my neck.

I need a fucking drink.

A time-out.

Something… anything to keep this from ending too fast. One blink and it will all be over.

"You have the same effect on me." I reluctantly remove my fingers from her heat, needing to savor this, and clench my fist as I pull back. Her juices dampen my palm, the exquisite texture tempting me to lick my own damn skin.

She stiffens with my retreat, panting, her brow furrowed. "What's wrong?"

Everything.

I don't just want to fuck her—I want to watch her. *See* her. *Know* her.

I raise my knuckles to the underside of her chin, tilting her face flush with mine. The scent of her sex lingers between us, the heady perfume filling my lungs.

Does it drug her the way it does me?

Is she drowning in lust, barely functional due to her need?

Those deep blue depths staring my way keep me grounded.

"*Nei tuoi occhi c'è il cielo.*" *Heaven is in your eyes.*

She licks her lower lip, her gaze lust drunk as her hands circle my wrist, guiding my knuckles higher. With a gentle touch, she unfolds my fist, and tilts her face to align my fingertips with her lips.

I hold my breath. Captivated.

Then she plunges fantasy into reality, gliding her mouth over my digits to suck them against the warmth of her tongue.

Fuck.

I feel the suction all the way to my dick. I picture it, too—her lips along my shaft, her tongue teasing the slit.

"You're destroying me," I grate, "in the best possible way."

She chuckles and pulls my fingers from her mouth with a pop. "Do you have protection?" She reaches for my belt, undoing the buckle.

I tense, already close enough to end this with one damn stroke. "In the bedroom."

"How far away is it?"

"Too far," I growl, smashing my lips to hers.

She begins to stroke me through the material of my pants, gentle and slow. "Are you clean?"

Sweet Jesus.

"I've never fucked without a condom." I clench my teeth to fight the pleasure, the delicious drag along my shaft driving me to madness.

She increases the pace. The severity. "Are you willing for me to be your first?"

"*Amore mio*, I'm willing for you to be my last."

She pulls back to meet my gaze, her eyes glistening in that sexually timid way of hers even though her palm circles my dick. "Don't say things you don't mean. It makes me hopeful."

"Are you asking for a commitment, Layla? Because I'll give it to you."

Her brows pull tight and she shakes her head. "I just want you. Just for tonight."

Tonight is only the start.

I lower my zipper, pull out my cock, and align it with the sweetest pussy known to man as she makes quick work of my jacket and shirt, shoving them off my shoulders to fall to the tile.

I grip her hip in one hand, digging my fingers deep, and guide the head of my dick to her slit, dragging it back and forth through her heat.

She closes her eyes, releasing a moan as she leans one hand against the counter, thrusting those breasts toward me.

Fuck, she's flawless.

Malleable. Eager. Yet with the slightest hint of innocence.

I increase the pace, rubbing back and forth, each graze of my cock making her back arch, her hips tilt.

So fucking incredible.

I lean forward, no longer able to resist those gorgeous tits, and suck a stiffened nipple into my mouth.

She moans, the feminine sound filling my ears, her fingers finding my hair. She pulls tight, causing pain to lash my scalp. The harder I suck, the stronger she pulls, until the burn running through my head is the best fucking thrill I've ever had.

I suck until she writhes. Until I can't concentrate on grinding her against my dick because I'm too fucking wound up from her whimpers and moans.

"You ready?" I growl.

She nods and shuffles closer to the edge of the marble, positioning herself right where she needs to be. I don't tease us a moment longer. I thrust home, sinking my shaft to the hilt as I palm her hips.

Those gorgeous eyes roll. Her head lolls back. She keeps those breasts in my face, and I latch on, sucking, grazing, as I pound a hard rhythm inside her.

"Oh, God." She tightens her legs around me. "This is going to be shamelessly quick... I've never..." Her pussy clamps tight around me. "Matthew..."

She scours my skull with her nails, but I don't stop the suction on her nipple. I ride out her orgasm, her pleasure filling my ears, sinking into my memories.

It takes all my restraint not to follow after her, not to spill my seed and make her mine. I wait her out, tensing every goddamn muscle until she's done riding the high.

"Good?" I ask.

"So good." She wraps her arms around my shoulders, nestling close. Chest to chest. Skin to skin. "I've never come so quick," she whispers in my ear. "Not even by myself."

Fuck.

The image of her touching herself is punishment of the most exquisite kind. Cruel and divine in one carnal visual.

"Lay down," I grate. "I want to see you stretched out before me."

She pauses a moment, then pulls away with a shy grin to rest against the marble, her hair splayed, her nipples hard.

I continue riding her, forcing myself not to blow as those tits bounce from my thrusts. *"Potrei guardarti tutto il giorno." I could look at you all day.*

It's no lie.

I could keep her like this forever. My masterpiece.

She groans, her hands reaching above her head for the other side of the counter.

I run a palm from her hip over the smooth planes of her waist, then between her breasts, learning all her curves. Committing them to memory. My other hand glides along her abdomen, my thumb finding her clit.

"Come sei bagnata." I groan. "So fucking wet…"

She gasps. Moans. Squeezes her core around me. "For the love of God…" She groans. "Stop talking."

"Non ti lascerò mai andare." I tweak a nipple, grazing a thumb over the pebbled peak as I place pressure on her clit. *"Vieni di nuovo per me.* Come for me again."

She shakes her head, her brows pinched as if in concern.

"You okay?" I slow even though it's torture, even though heaven is right there waiting to be conquered. "Talk to me."

"Nothing's wrong. I just…" She keeps shaking her head. "I've never come twice… and I'm… I can't believe I'm so close."

I despise her fucking husband, and whoever else she's slept with. But those assholes did me a favor. They made it easy for me to win her over. She'll never dare to walk away when I continue to treat her like a queen.

"Then come, *amore mio.* Let me watch you."

She blinks, dazed with lust. "I'm not used to being watched either."

"Well, get used to it. I'm going to witness you doing some filthy fucking things, Layla. And you'll enjoy every minute of it."

"Is that a promise?"

"It's a vow." I lean forward, replacing the hand at her breast with my lips. "Soon you won't recognize yourself."

"I already don't." There's a tremor in her voice as her fingers reclaim my hair. "You've changed me."

"You've changed me, too." I thrust harder, stoking us higher. The harder I suck her nipple, the more frantic her pace builds beneath me, the roll of her hips becoming fearless.

I groan against the flesh in my mouth and close my eyes to the bliss.

I'm beyond ready. A brief step from the finish line.

"Matthew…" Her breathing fluctuates, her chest rising and falling beneath me.

I beat back the need for relief, vowing not to come until she does, promising to reach the end together. *"Mi far stare bene."*

I fuck her savagely. Faster. Harder.

She tenses, her legs a vise around me. "I'm…"

I open my eyes and she's gaping, her lips trembling as she shudders.

I'm powerless to stop myself from following her this time. I come undone, spilling inside her, losing myself to the climax and promising myself this will be the first of many.

19

LAYLA

I LAY STREWN ACROSS HIS COUNTER, MY SKIN COATED IN A SHEEN OF sweat, my heart fluttering like a sail in a hurricane.

"I'll get you a cloth." He moves out from between my legs and grabs my hand to pull me into a sitting position. Then he walks around the counter to claim something from a drawer. The faucet turns on seconds later. In the next blink he's back in front of me, handing me a clean damp dish towel.

There's nothing smug in his expression. No egotistical victory. He gives me the offering with respect in his eyes and steps away, allowing me a modicum of privacy to clean up the sinful mess between my thighs as he rights his pants.

"Do you want to take a shower?" He shoots me a sideways glance and picks up his shirt and jacket from the floor. "Or would you like something to eat? There's a takeout place nearby that stays open late."

"I'd love a shower… if you don't mind."

He winces. "I want you to feel comfortable here. In my city. My home. My bed. Take whatever you need."

My stomach swells, doing a somersault of appreciation. So far, two out of three can't be bad.

I'm entirely comfortable in D.C., in his penthouse. And we may not have used his bed, but I think I took quite a few liberties to make myself feel at home on his kitchen counter.

My problem is the exact opposite of what he wants. I should be feeling cautious. Skeptical. Cole would want me to be entirely vigilant.

I've been none of those things.

Neither has Matthew.

"You barely know me." I scoot to my feet, ignoring the bite of self-consciousness now that he's righted his clothes and I'm wearing nothing but shiny red heels. "Aren't you worried I could be a gold-digger? Isn't that what you thought I might have been with Remy and Salvatore?"

"You're no gold-digger. And even though I might not know you as much as I'd like, I'm learning." He grins. "And thoroughly enjoying the lesson."

That swoopy, somersaulty thing takes over my belly again, then quickly fades into guilt. He has to be more wary. The thought of disappointing him when he learns the real me is punishing.

"There might come a time when you don't like what you learn." I give him a pointed look, trying to be his voice of reason. "Don't put me on a pedestal. I won't live up to the hype."

He inclines his head and gives a subtle nod. "Okay. Point taken. Neither of us are pillars of the community. But there's something in our chemistry, Layla. You feel it, too."

I do, and it's maddening in its potency. I don't think I could escape the clutches of this attraction even if I wanted to.

"Umm…" I tilt my head toward the hall on the right of the open living area, then do the same toward the darker one to the left. "Which way to the shower?" I point my ass to the counter and bend to unclasp the straps of my heels, leaving them on the tiles.

"Use my personal bathroom. To the left. Last door on the right. Want me to show you?"

"No. It's okay." I start walking, needing a few minutes of breathing space to regain my equilibrium. "I won't be long."

I pad onto the carpet of the hall, glancing into rooms as I pass, appreciating how every space is neat and tidy. Without flaw.

I stop at the threshold of his bedroom and flick on the light, taking a moment to let the sight sink in. It's another perfectly appointed room. Dark wooden furniture. Even darker bed coverings. Not one piece of strewn clothing or speck of dust in sight.

It doesn't take long for my stare to move beyond appraisal and into daydream territory. I picture us both on the king-size mattress, his body atop mine, his movements hard and rhythmic.

Then he has me bent over the chest of drawers. Or my naked breasts pressed to the glass doors leading to the balcony as he takes me from behind.

I need help.

I sidestep past the walk-in closet and move into the bathroom where I use the facilities and shower quickly. I should get back to my hotel. For anonymity's sake. To make sure I don't push the already fragile boundaries of my stupidity.

I dry myself with fast strokes of a clean, plush towel, discovering that some parts of me are already deliciously sore from his attention. Then I shuffle from the bathroom with the thick material wrapped around my chest.

Matthew sits waiting for me on the side of the bed, his feet on the floor, his elbows on knees. He glances up from under dark lashes, his chocolate eyes meeting mine with an expression I can't quite read.

"Feel like you've been catfished?" I ask, suddenly aware that this is the first time he's seen me without a mask of makeup.

He reaches out a hand, wordlessly beckoning me forward. My feet comply without my consent, bringing me right before him.

"You floor me with every new layer you expose." His fingers glide around my wrist, leading me between his open knees. "I'm not worthy of your attention."

I wither inside, my strategy for space disintegrating. I want to climb onto him and cuddle in his lap. To be his very own purring little kitten.

"Your cheek is still swollen." He reaches for my face, gently cupping my jaw, his thumb sweeping over the healing skin. "Does it hurt?"

What hurts is the destruction it caused.

The drama.

Then again, I wouldn't be here if I hadn't been mugged. I would've walked away from Matthew, possibly never seeing him again.

"I don't notice it most of the time." *Especially not when your hands are on me.*

He nods, continuing to stroke the bruising, stoking my sensuality with each pass. He drugs me with his touch, building an addiction that will require a multi-step program to achieve recovery.

"Tell me why you're really here," he murmurs.

I tense before I can stop myself.

"Don't lie to me, *amore mio.*"

I step back, fearful of his scrutiny while something inside me yearns for transparency.

His touch falls away with my retreat, but those eyes slay me with their questioning.

"You didn't come all this way to sleep with me," he continues. "Do you need information on the Costas? Did you decide to take my help?"

I wince for so many reasons.

For starters, he's wrong. I *did* come all this way to sleep with him, no matter how desperate and dysfunctional that sounds. It's deeper than that, though. Painfully deeper.

"No." I swallow and straighten my shoulders. "I didn't come here for information. This has nothing to do with them."

"Then why?" The question barely breaches my ears, the gentleness painfully coaxing.

Because I'm alone.

Because I had nobody else.

Because my family hate to love me, and love to hate me in equal measure.

I turn away, starting for the door. "I need to get my clothes."

"Your clothes are gone, Layla."

I swing back to face him, panicked. "Gone where?"

"I put them in a dry-cleaning bag and sent them down the laundry shoot." He reaches for something beside him, claiming a handful of dark material that almost matches the covers. "You can wear one of my robes."

He's trapped me. Not behind bars, but with nudity.

"You're judging me again," he warns.

"Because you're effectively holding me here until I can get my dress back."

His placid face hardens as he hunches over, elbows back on knees. "I have a room full of clothes if you're in a hurry to run. Take a sweatshirt. Take my whole fucking wardrobe. I'll have your clothes sent to your hotel first thing in the morning." He shoves to his feet. "Forgive me for thinking I was doing you a favor."

He stalks to the door, shoving the silk robe into my hand as he passes, then escapes into the hall.

Damn it.

I'm not used to this.

I have no familiarity with someone doing things for me out of kindness instead of strategy. The compliments are all new. The affection foreign.

My walls may be down where attraction is concerned, but I guess snap judgment is still my default defense mechanism.

I return the towel to the bathroom while feeling like a complete bitch, then shove my arms into the billowing robe, tying the sash around my waist.

I'm pushing away the best thing that's happened to me since Stella's birth and I don't know how to stop.

Vulnerability isn't an enjoyable sensation. It's caustic and cruel, its sharp teeth nipping at my heels. But denying the exposure means giving up on this connection. This passion. Even if it's temporary.

I pad back along the hall, finding him in the kitchen, one hand on the counter, the other on his scotch glass.

"Want me to arrange a driver?" He peers at me over the rim of his drink before taking a gulp. "You wouldn't have to wait long."

Do I go or stay?

He takes another mouthful, leaving the glass dry, then drops it down to the counter with a heavy thud. "You're not my fucking hostage," he mutters. "I'm not keeping you here."

"I know."

He frowns. "Do you?"

"Yes." I wince. "And I'm sorry. You caught me off guard."

He remains quiet as he watches me, unappeased.

"I felt stupid when you said I didn't travel all this way just to sleep with you, because the truth is I kinda did." My wince deepens. "But it's even more pathetic than that."

"What do you mean?" His expression softens.

My throat tightens with the resurfacing rage I harbor toward my brother. "I had a fight with my family and needed to get away. It's hard to admit I had nowhere else to go."

The confession hurts. Soul deep.

There's nobody else in my life. All I have is Stella, my innocent daughter, who I'll never burden with my troubles.

Matthew releases a long breath and wipes a rough hand down his face. He's tired of me already. Bored of my bullshit within an hour.

He doesn't say anything as he walks toward me, probably preparing to reintroduce me to the front door. I bite my lip as he approaches, each step leaving me more vulnerable in an already isolated world, until he stops before me.

His gaze rakes my face, a subtle frown pinching his brows as he conducts the appraisal. "Are you okay?"

I release a tight breath.

He's concerned about me? After I accused him of having bad intentions, he's still acting protective?

I blink through the sharp burn in my eyes and step back, needing to distance myself from the weakening effects of his patience and concern.

"Hey." He reaches out, grasping my fingers to drag me into his chest. "Tell me you're okay."

I hold in a whimper, the fragile sound built from overwhelming gratitude. I wither against him, lowering my head to his shoulder, wrapping my arms around his waist.

In his embrace, I'm good.

I'm sheltered.

I'm whole.

"I don't need you, Matthew," I whisper against his skin. "I'm not someone who can't take care of herself. I just…" I squeeze my eyes shut. "I'm not used to having someone care for me. Not like this."

"I understand." He kisses the top of my head. "I don't have anyone either."

I lean back, needing to see the truth in his expression. "What about your family?"

"I have a mentor. But apart from him, Bishop is all I have. All I trust."

He has it worse than I do, and now that I know of his isolation, I can see it. Loneliness is hidden beneath the confidence in his eyes.

"I have a feeling we're similar in a lot of ways," he continues. "Maybe that's why I'm drawn to you."

"And here I was thinking I'd captivated you with my body," I tease.

"That, too." He doesn't laugh—there's only the slightest upward curve to his mouth as he gives me a subdued kiss. When he pulls away, the humor is gone. "I want you to trust me."

"I'm trying."

"It doesn't come easily for me either." He kisses my nose. My forehead. The sweetest brushes of gentle lips. "We have to give it time."

I sigh, nestling back into his shoulder. "It sounds like your life is as messed up as mine."

"It was. But not anymore. I left it behind. You can, too."

I close my eyes, picturing this dream world of his. One without notoriety etched into my family name. A place where tables aren't turned on the daily and I don't have to constantly watch my back. A utopia where Stella would always be safe.

"Want to tell me about the fight?" he asks into my hair.

"It was about you."

The muscles of his chest stiffen. "You told your family about me?"

"No. But they guessed I'd met someone. Apparently, my face has a tell when I've received my first non-self-administered orgasm in years."

He snickers, deep and sinful in my ear. "If I'd known it'd been that long—"

"*Nope.*" My face heats as I snap a finger to his lips, silencing him. "We are *not* talking about my abstinence."

His grin presses into my fingertip, the glimpse of a dimple teasing me from his left cheek. "But understanding why you're confident in one moment and shy in the next is fucking cute."

"Stop it." My eyes flare. "There's nothing cute about being daunted by someone else's prowess."

He's right though.

So fucking right.

I guess I grew up being self-assured by my family's power. Of how to conquer and rule. But when it came to sexuality, my teachings came from a man who would've preferred never to have met me.

"You're daunted by me?" he teases.

I shove at his chest. "You know I am."

He sobers, the flirtatious vibe seeping away as silence builds.

"I don't want you to be daunted by me, *amore mio*." He grabs my hand, raising my knuckles to his lips. "You told me before that I made you feel empowered. That I gave you confidence."

"You do that, too." I shake my head. "I wish I could explain…"

I can't find the words. *No*, I can't find the honesty. The truth about how Benji made me question my desirability isn't something I'm willing to discuss.

"A man gave you these insecurities," he answers for me.

I glance away, unsettled by his insight.

"It's okay." He kisses my knuckles again. "I'll fix that for you. It won't take long and you'll realize the power you have over me with your body alone. I'd start a war for you."

The blush creeps down my neck, heating my breasts.

A war is what it would take for my brother to let me be with an outsider.

"Tell me the problems with your family," he adds. "Maybe I can fix that, too."

"*You* are the problem… Well, the assumption you're responsible for the bruising on my face, anyway. They think I'm shacking up with an abuser."

His face falls. "Why would they think that?"

"My past preferences, for a start."

"With one of the Costas? Did Remy or Salvatore hit you?"

I want to correct him. To set him straight once and for all and confirm that I had no sexual relationship with my enemies. But I can't expose that much of myself.

"It's a long story," I hedge. "Suffice to say I didn't appreciate their judgment, and they didn't welcome my anger. So when I delivered Stella to the airport, I caught the first flight to the only place I wanted to be."

"It'll blow over." He tugs me back into his chest, pressing his lips to my forehead, holding me close for long, silent moments. "I'm sure they'll be crawling back before you know it."

"Apologies aren't their strong suit." They can't even accept ones they're offered. "But you're right. It will blow over." Eventually.

I place my palms on his waist, running my fingers over his smooth skin. The quiet stretches, yet the emptiness is filled with comfort.

I lean into the ease of simply being with him. I breathe him in and close my eyes to enjoy his warmth. It isn't until a yawn takes over that his arms slowly fall to his sides.

"Do you want me to arrange a driver?" he murmurs into my hair. "I won't hold it against you if you leave."

The struggle of right against wrong and should against shouldn't whispers in my ears. But what I *want* is this. More moments like here and now. More me and him in our own little world, even if it's temporary.

I forced myself to stop feeling guilty about my life with Benji. Why can't I stop questioning every forward step with Matthew, too? Just for a little while. Only until he grows tired of my anonymity and starts searching for more. Then I could leave.

Why not dive deep until then?

"Lay?" His lips press to my temple. "Are you staying or going?"

I suck in a deep breath, hearing Cole's warnings in my head, battling against a life where I've been force-fed the line that I shouldn't get close to strangers.

I wrap my arms around him, sinking in to what feels right. What feels whole. "I'd like to stay."

20

———

LAYLA

"You sure?" The devil enters his voice. "You'll get more sleep at a hotel."

I graze my nails along his flesh, awakening goose bumps. "Sleep can be overrated."

He palms my chin. "It definitely will be tonight." He kisses me, soft and sweet and slow. Then incrementally, the connection changes. Soft builds into firm. Sweet shifts to wicked. Slow transforms to rabid.

We're back to being all hands and lips and gasps, and it feels like my decision to stay is paving a brighter future, not inching toward impending doom.

We're together all night, our bodies either entwined in passion, or collapsed in exhaustion. And in each moment, he treasures me. With his words. His touch. His gaze.

I can't take one breath without it catching in my chest, the air latching onto feelings that morph and build beyond my control.

When morning comes, I wake to his lips on my shoulder, his whispered words greeting me to a new day. But I drift back to sleep, cocooned in bliss between his sheets.

I don't know what time it is when I finally wake, the subtle noise in the living area keeping me conscious this time. I left my cell silenced in the kitchen knowing Cole would blow up my inbox as soon as he realized I fled Portland, and there's no bedside clock in this room.

Matthew is no longer beside me. I can't see him or smell his intoxicating aftershave. The only thing kissing the air is the faint hint of coffee, which is enough to drag me to my feet.

I contemplate walking out to him in my birthday suit, hips swaying, seductive smile in place. But I'm not that woman yet. After the obsessive adoration paid to my body last night, I'm a few steps closer to sexual confidence. I can sense it within reach—I'm just not quite there.

I grab the black robe strewn on the floor and cover myself as I pad from the room, already eager to place my mouth on Matthew's.

Too bad Matthew isn't the one sitting at the dining table. It's Bishop's scowling blue gaze that peers over the cell in his hands to look me up and down.

"Morning," he mutters.

"Morning." I cinch the gaping lapels higher around my chest as I glance over the open living area, searching for my life preserver.

"He's not here." Bishop slaps his cell on the table. "He had to go to the coast for business and didn't want to wake you."

"And he asked you to stay with me?"

"Apparently, I'm here to make up for my bad first impression by offering my services. I don't think he anticipated you sleeping away my entire day, though."

I focus on the microwave in the kitchen, squinting at the tiny numbers.

"It's almost twelve." There's a bitter growl to his tone. "And I've got more than your shit to take care of, so I'm going to need to know the name of your hotel."

My gaze snaps back to his. "Why?"

"To retrieve your things. You're staying here from now on, aren't you?"

"Yes," I whisper, raking a hand through my tangled hair. How the hell did I sleep until noon? "But you don't need to get my things." The contents of my suitcase are strewn across my suite— lingerie, toiletries. There's also a whole heap of cash in the safe. "Could you give me a ride instead?"

He holds my gaze, those severe eyes doing absolutely nothing to retract his first impression. "As long as you're not going to take up the other half of my day. Like I said, I've got shit to do." He pushes from his chair with a jerk of his chin toward a garment bag on the end of the table. "He said that was for you."

"My clothes." *Thank God.*

"Can you be ready in ten?" He stalks for the kitchen, entirely intimidating with his bulky frame beneath his suit. "I'll make you a coffee while I wait."

"Yeah. Okay. Thanks." I hustle for the table to grab the garment bag, then rush for Matthew's bedroom to get changed.

I pull on my now clean underwear, then shimmy into the dress, ignoring how I'm about to do the walk of shame into a five-star hotel, with a bruised face and tangled hair. Not to mention all the fresh marks now clinging to my body from Matthew's rough kisses and enticing, ruthless hold.

When I walk back into the kitchen, my heels clapping on the clean tiles, Bishop greets me with a huff and a travel mug in his outstretched hand.

"Ready?" He starts for the door before I answer.

"Let me get my phone." I hustle to snatch my cell from the counter and follow him, taking a sip of steamy heaven once I step over the threshold to the elevator.

The preview on the locked screen triggers my guilt—*eight messages and five missed calls.*

Cole will be responsible for most.

"Something wrong?" Bishop leans against the back wall, his legs crossed at the ankles.

"No. I'm fine." I unlock the screen and open the messages, skimming over the mass of capital letters and exclamation points from my brother without reading them, and focus on the text from Matthew.

Morning, amore mio. *I had an important meeting I couldn't postpone. But I've changed my plans to be home in time to take you to dinner. Be ready by 7. Don't miss me too much. I'll make up for my absence when I return.*

I grin, juggling the coffee in one hand with my cell in the other as I reply—*Afternoon. I don't think Bishop appreciated me sleeping in. What should I wear tonight?*

I lock the screen, ignoring the messages from my brother, and jostle when the elevator reaches the parking lot.

"You going to tell me the hotel?" Bishop strides into the cement jungle filled with six-figure cars, maintaining his glower of annoyance.

"Avarden Towers."

He shoves a hand into his pocket and the indicators of a nearby Lincoln Navigator flash to life. "Get in."

I bite my tongue against the deliberate dictatorship and climb into the passenger seat, biding my time until I can get my belongings and place distance between us. The ride is silent—nothing but city traffic and the barely heard hum of the radio.

It isn't until we're at the hotel and he follows me into my suite that his look of disdain gets to me.

"You don't like me very much, do you?" I grab my scattered underwear from the bed and place them in my suitcase, the silence stretching the air thin. "No comment?" I shoot him a look.

"Of course I like you," he drawls, heavy with sarcasm. "I love complications. They make my life more colorful."

"I have no intention of being a complication."

"Right… And what about your plans with the Costas?"

I pause, my hands filled with lingerie, my paranoia finally waking after the night of bliss. "I'm not here because of that. I don't want my time with Matthew to have anything to do with them."

He scoffs. "Does he know that?"

The superior undertones in his voice bug me. "Yes, he does."

"Then you're already well aware he won't stand to be left out of any plans you have. There's no way you can keep him in the dark."

Watch me.

I clamp my mouth shut, keeping my thoughts to myself.

"Look, Layla. I don't know you. But the fact you're in the same circles as the Costas is a sign you're bad news. I don't need more proof than that."

"You don't think that's hypocritical?" I storm for the bathroom and make quick work of snatching my makeup and toothbrush to shove into my toiletry bag.

"Regardless of if it is or isn't," he calls from the other room, "I think you know you're trouble. And Matthew's worked too hard to distance himself from that shit, changing every part of his life to keep his nose clean, to have you drag him back in."

His words hit home, squeezing at the parts of me already filled with remorse over the tryst I can't walk away from.

I hang my head and grip the counter, hating that he's right. Hating how he can sense the pandemonium that shadows me like a vengeful ghost. Hating even more that Matthew has slain unknown demons to correct his life and I'm threatening to revive them.

But I promised myself I'd lean into happiness despite the obstacles. That I'd take what I could while I could, until the first glimpses of drama surfaced. And this self-righteous asshole won't talk me out of it.

"I thought you were meant to be making up for a bad first impression." I clutch my toiletry bag under my elbow and force a smile as I saunter back into the main room.

"Yeah…" He shrugs. "Doesn't really seem like my thing, does it?"

I laugh. "I actually think you nailed your first impression. In hindsight you were authentic. You came across as a bully, and it's now clear that's exactly what you are."

"I'm no bully, sweetheart. I'm a loyal friend. There's a difference."

I continue to the bed, shove my toiletry bag into the suitcase, and swing around to face him, his attitude scraping against the nerves already made raw by my brother. "I'm here in D.C. for no other reason than to spend time with Matthew. What I do in Denver is my business. I don't want his help. Or yours, for that matter."

"You were never getting mine."

I fight a wince at how easily he loathes me without even knowing me. "Thanks for clearing that up."

"You're welcome." He drops his arms to his sides and pushes from the cabinet to stand tall. "You ready to leave?"

"I need to get a few things from the safe. Can you give me a minute?"

He gifts me with another appraising look, still finding me lacking. "I'll meet you at the car."

I FOLLOW A FEW MINUTES BEHIND, catching up to him in the parking lot.

We don't speak again. Not on the short drive back to Matthew's penthouse building. Not even when we ride the elevator. He keeps quiet, swinging open the penthouse door and holding it wide for me to proceed, then slamming it closed with him on the other side.

"Great," I mutter.

Without a key, I'm effectively caged in. Again. But I'm not going to go chasing Bishop about it.

I busy myself for the rest of the afternoon by getting changed, then familiarizing myself with the many rooms in Matthew's home. I open every door, careful not to snoop, but eager to learn more about him.

I admire the expensive artwork decorating the walls and the books on the shelves. I use the jacuzzi in his main bathroom and research his clubs online. I drink coffee on the balcony and text Stella to send her my love. And all the while, I fight against rerunning my conversation with Bishop this morning on a continuous loop.

Even here, away from my family and the mistakes of my past, I'm still the bad guy.

Bishop knows it.

I know it.

But as soon as Matthew returns that night, his grin subtle despite the unfiltered appreciation in his eyes, all my worries fade.

"Fuck, I missed you." He drags me into his chest, his mouth roughly claiming mine. "You look stunning."

I *feel* stunning.

I'm wearing white tailored pants and a mauve halter-neck top, yet he makes it seem like I'm dressed for a red-carpet event instead of dinner.

"I need to freshen up." He speaks against my lips between hungry kisses and scrapes of teeth. "Help me get undressed?"

I smile, my eyes closed, my heart in heaven.

He didn't just need help undressing. He wanted assistance bathing, too. He dragged me into the shower with him, his focus on learning more of my body instead of freshening up his own.

But this time it didn't feel like sex.

It was something different. Something that started off voracious and passionate, then petered into a slower connection that was far more intense. He lavished me in slow kisses, one hand cradling my chin, the other between my thighs. He murmured his dreamy Italian promises between strokes of tongue and grinds of hips.

He made love to me, and it made me realize I'd been a virgin to the experience up until this point.

By the time I dried, dressed, then redid my makeup, it was after eight.

He held my hand as we walked into the rooftop restaurant, letting everyone know I was his and he was mine. The waitstaff greeted him by name, with smiles and enthusiasm, before escorting us to a table in the corner with an unfettered view of the Washington Monument alight in the clear night sky. And the whole time, I couldn't wipe the smile off my face.

"Is that happiness ebbing from you, *amore mio*?" He eyes me with contentment across the table. "You seem in good spirits."

I sip my wine, willing my rampant heartbeat under control. "I am, despite being locked in your penthouse all day."

He frowns. "Why? Didn't Bishop tell you about the spare key?"

To hell with Bishop.

"No." I return my gaze out the window. "That must have slipped his mind."

That asshole deliberately kept me caged. He wanted to have the last word, and it came in the form of my isolation.

I continue to feel Matthew's stare from my periphery, the slight gleam of white announcing a building grin.

"What?" I ask. "Do you like knowing I was trapped in your penthouse like a damsel in distress?"

"No, but I'm beginning to understand why you were so excited to see me when I returned home." The grin lessens, the subtle lift falling flat. "Bishop told me the two of you had an intense conversation this afternoon."

"Intense is one word for it."

His brows knit with curiosity. "How would you describe it?"

An ambush.

An assault.

I shrug. "I guess intense is accurate enough. I'm surprised he told you, though."

"It's the bonus that comes from working with someone who always thinks they're right. They never have anything to hide." He relaxes into his chair. "But just to be clear, I didn't appreciate what he said."

I take another sip of wine, biting back how much I didn't appreciate it either.

"Why didn't you call me to tell me what he'd done?" he asks. "Or tell me once I got home?"

"For the exact reason I argued with him in the first place. I'm not here to cause trouble."

"Bishop being a prick isn't you causing trouble."

I hold his gaze, wanting him to understand my sincerity as I say, "He's one of the few people you have in your life, so even if he's an absolute asshole—which he most definitely is—" I smirk. "—I'm not going to bring that up with you. I can understand him being protective."

Matthew raises a brow and inclines his head, his mouth set in an understated smile as he falls silent.

It's unnerving. The way he admires me with quiet fascination. It's energizing, too.

"What?" My cheeks heat the longer he looks at me.

"I'm just adding more attributes to the list of what I find entirely endearing about you." His voice is a murmur of underlying seduction. "Along with picturing how many times, and in what positions, I can have you once we finish dinner."

My cheeks flame hotter, the inferno creeping down my neck.

I've been picturing that, too.

I can't stop.

His touch haunts my skin, the possessive grip of desire keeping me chained to memory. Problem is, it's also distracting me from the other important motivation for flying across the country.

"We should really discuss the Costas before we become sidetracked again." I lick the dryness from my lips. "I'm not going to lie. Our common interest in them is another reason why I'm here."

"I figured as much." He leans back in his chair, the confident seduction leaving his expression. "But they're not going anywhere. Why not enjoy getting to know each other first?"

Why not? Because I don't deserve the pleasure.

Because I need to focus on my mistakes.

His lips curve, the wickedness returning to his eyes. "Let's make a deal—once you think the chemistry between us is fading, we can divert our focus to scheming."

"Once *I* think…? What about you?"

He grins, sly and handsome. "It won't fade for me."

That has to be a lie.

Before I can question him on it, a muffled beep sounds from his suit jacket.

He drags in a long breath and retrieves his cell. "I need to take this call." His brows pinch in apology. "I won't be long."

I nod and grab for my own device on the table, reluctantly turning it over to read the screen as Matthew walks away.

Five missed calls.

Two texts.

My chest tightens. Every notification will be from my family. More regrettably, my brother.

I open my inbox, the preview of the most recent message hitting my eyes.

Answer your fucking…

I shouldn't open it. The time away from them has been a wonder drug of positivity. Unfortunately, curiosity gets the better of me.

Answer your fucking phone and help sort this out like a fucking adult. The least you can do is let us know you're all right. Your sister is worried sick.

My sister… but not him.

Do you think this is a joke, Layla? We still have enemies. You still need to tell me where the fuck you are so I can make sure you're safe.

He doesn't care about my safety. His concerns lie with the chess pieces that will topple if anyone successfully targets me. It would make him look bad. Weak.

But he's right about Keira. I don't want her to worry.

I dial my sister's number, my ribs tightening with the dial tone, my breath halting when she answers.

"Layla?" There's panic in her voice. "Are you okay?"

"I'm fine. I just need some space."

"Where are you? Hunter found your car at the airport."

Of course he did.

"It doesn't matter." I reach for my wine, needing the alcoholic calm. "I'm safe. That's all you need to know."

"Lay, please, you're freaking me out. Why are you acting this way? I know it's been hard on you since Stella moved away, but it doesn't mean you're alone. I'm here for—"

"Don't say you're here for me, Keira." I cut her off. "We both know that's not true."

"W-what do you mean? You're my sister. I'm always here if you need me."

I shake my head, pained by the lies. "I haven't been your sister since the night Benji died and you know it."

She gasps. "Is that how you really feel?"

"It's two years later and you can barely look at me after what I did."

"No," she pleads. "I'm sorry if you think I haven't forgiven you—"

"You haven't. None of you have."

"That's not the case, Layla. It's just different now. Things changed. *Everything* changed. There was my relationship with Sebastian, then the news of what our father had been doing. Then what happened to Richard. It was an avalanche of adjustment even before Dad died. Then Tobias entered our lives and everything became chaos. And Benji..." She sighs. "I guess in the aftermath, I inched away from everyone and hid in the comfortable world I'd built with Sebastian because it was easier."

She might like to believe that story, but it's a lie.

She pulled away from me. From what I did. Just like Cole, Sarah, Hunter, Decker, and even Luca, too. They made me a pariah. And although it was initially deserved, I didn't earn a lifetime of this suffering.

"I haven't held it against you," she whispers. "I want you to be happy."

"You want me to be happy—you just have such a low opinion of me that you think I'm weak enough to be with a man who would hit me."

"Jesus Christ. You can't blame us for making assumptions when you're deliberately being secretive. You keep escaping out of town without letting anyone know and not using your credit cards to make yourself untraceable. Even now, you took off after withdrawing a whole heap of cash. What are we supposed to think?"

I glance out the window, heartbroken and needing to diffuse the conversation, while being angry and itching to blow it up at the same time. "Forgive me for not wanting to be stalked like a fugitive. Two years ago, my husband was taken from me. Now my daughter has been shipped away. I had to find something to distract myself from a house that has become hauntingly quiet. It's goddamn lonely, Keira."

"But why hide where you're going?" she asks softly. "You had to know your actions would spark Cole's paranoia."

"Maybe I want to be free from our family for a little while... Maybe I want to pretend I'm someone else." Someone who doesn't have skeletons to hide and mistakes to resolve.

"I can understand that. I've thought the same thing many times. It's the—"

"I don't want to talk about this anymore," I interrupt as Matthew returns to the table, his raised brow questioning whether I'm okay. "I only called to check in and now I've gotta go. Tell our brother to stop contacting me. I want to be left alone."

"Layla—"

I disconnect, not waiting for her response, and place the cell face down on the table.

Matthew takes his seat, his jaw tight. "What happened?"

"It's nothing. Just family drama." I grab my cloth napkin and place it over my lap, unable to maintain eye contact.

"Want to talk about it?"

I can't share those parts of my life with him, no matter how much I want to. "Honestly, it's nothing."

"Honestly, *amore mio,* I can tell that's not true." He reaches over the table, sliding his hand out for me to take.

I stare at the offering. The lifeline.

I want nothing more than to take it. To latch on. Cling tight.

"That was my sister on the phone." I raise my gaze and paste on a fake smile. "My family don't appreciate me disappearing to places unknown. Apparently, they can't stop me from making careless mistakes if they don't know where I am."

"Are you prone to making mistakes?"

"Yes," I admit. "I've made a few. I've trusted people I shouldn't and paid the price."

He appraises me for a moment, his weighty consideration stripping me bare. "Trust is a favorable quality to most. Would we be here together without it?"

No. But my husband would be alive and my daughter would live without nightmares if I'd been more hesitant when offering my faith.

"My family is different." I slide my hand to meet his, our fingertips kissing on top of the table. "We usually function in our own little utopia, so it's hard when things go wrong."

"I'm sure they'll forgive you."

I scoff a laugh. "It's been two years."

"Damn." His eyes narrow. "Well, I'm glad you're here with me instead. Did you tell them where you are?"

"No. And I've been using cash so they can't track my whereabouts through the bank, but my brother will find another way eventually."

He pulls his arm back, sitting straighter. "He's trying to track you?"

Shit. I've said too much. "It's not that extreme."

His chin raises, his posture growing tense. "I should speak to him."

"*No.*" God, no. I press my lips tight to suppress a delirious laugh. Cole would kill him on sight. "It's not as bad as it seems. We have joint accounts. Any purchase I made through a credit card would announce my location."

"You don't need to worry about money while you're here. I'll take care of it."

This time I'm the one to reach farther across the table, my fingers seeking his. "I appreciate the offer, but I withdrew enough before I left to tide me over until I return home. I can look after myself."

"Believe me, you've demonstrated that without fault." His hand finds mine again, the calloused palm skating over my knuckles. "The thought of taking care of you brings me pleasure."

I blush, my mind sliding into the gutter. "You're doing that just fine without any financial contribution."

He laughs, the utterly brilliant sound tickling every sensitive part of me. "Why don't we get our dinner to go and take this conversation back to the penthouse?"

My pulse increases, the fluttering wings of arrhythmia swooping through my limbs. "Will we be merely conversing, Mr. Langston?"

He grins, smooth and flawlessly seductive. "No, *amore mio*, but a lot of my plans involve what I can do with my mouth."

21

____

LAYLA

One night swoons into another, each romantic evening meal distracting me from the reason why we met.

Sometimes Matthew is gone when I wake. At other times he remains in bed, his arm wrapped possessively around my waist like I'm a priceless treasure. And no matter how much he's at work, he always makes me his priority.

His out-of-town trips never last overnight. We either spend hours together in the morning or the evening, and it's never enough. Not with the way he listens intently whenever I speak, or how he continues to offer exaggerated, outlandish promises for our future that make me ponder if they could actually become reality.

Could we forge a life together even though we're still yet to talk about the common goal that made our paths cross in the first place?

The days have passed with the Costas not being more than a passing word. Neither of us seem ready to fizzle the sparks between us by bringing up the elephant in the room, even though it needs to be discussed sooner rather than later.

We've kept our truce in place regarding personal information. He gives me space when I call Stella. He doesn't ask questions. Doesn't demand insight I'm not willing to give. But every day my walls grow fragile, tiny fissures forming to allow slips of my life to spill free.

"Get dressed, *amore mio*." Matthew walks into the bedroom from his private bathroom, a towel wrapped around his waist, his muscles glistening from the shower. "You're coming to work with me today."

I sit taller in his bed, the tray loaded with my empty breakfast plate rattling on my lap. "I am?"

"Yes. My commitments won't take long." He discards the towel and pulls on a fresh pair of boxer briefs from the chest of drawers. "Then we can do whatever you like afterward. I'll arrange a hotel room for the night. You just need to pack a change of clothes and your toothbrush."

I pull back the covers and glide to my feet, not showing a hint of curiosity at learning more about his life while trying to hide my fear of what he wants from me in return. "When are we leaving?"

"As soon as you're dressed."

"I guess that's my cue to hustle."

I shower quickly, brush my teeth, and paint on a subtle layer of makeup in record time. Then I shimmy into a long ruby sundress and fill the remaining space in the small suitcase Matthew left open for me on the bed.

"Ready?" He stands at the bedroom door, one shoulder cocked against the frame, a subtle smirk of appreciation tweaking his lips as he takes in the loose material dancing over my legs and the low neckline that cradles my breasts.

"Ready." My heart beats a dull throb, my eyes eagerly eating up my view of him dressed head to toe in black—suit, shirt, tie.

He's a dark prince, the stubble covering his jaw making him appear all the more devilish.

He pushes from the doorframe and prowls toward me, slow and sleek.

My body melts like it always does. My nerves flutter. I stand still, wondering if his predatory approach means we're about to delay our departure.

He stops beside me, the grin continuing to linger as he leans around me to zip the suitcase closed and drag it to the carpet. "We don't have time, *amore mio*."

"Time for what?" I purr.

"For that look in your eye."

He kisses my temple and takes my hand, leading me from the room, from the penthouse, then into the elevator, our mini suitcase trailing along at his side. When we reach the underground parking lot, Bishop is there to steal my buzz. He waits in his idling Lincoln, the window lowered, his arm resting on the frame.

"Morning." He scowls at me.

"Morning." I hold his gaze, refusing to cower under the intimidation.

"Get in." Matthew releases my hand. "I'll put the suitcase in the back."

I nod, bathing in Bishop's death glower with every step toward the rear door, then slide inside. I've been lucky not to have seen him since our confrontation almost a week ago. He hasn't been to the penthouse. There's been no talk of him at all.

Too bad it didn't last.

"It's so lovely to see you again," I drawl. "What have you been up to?"

"Just the same ol' same ol'—preparing for when my buddy's latest conquest is going to blow shit up and make my life a living hell."

I glare at him through the rearview mirror as Matthew opens the cargo space to store our suitcase. I wait until the trunk door is closed moments later before I say, "Well, if you're the cleanup crew, I guess I should make sure it's a worthwhile explosion."

Matthew climbs in the opposite side of the Lincoln, and I'm not sure whether it's his presence or my spite that keeps Bishop quiet. But that's how things remain as the car exits the parking lot into the midmorning sunshine.

We drive through the city traffic, Matthew's hand gliding over mine on the middle seat as we pass block after block, then head onto a freeway to take us toward the suburbs. I relax, expecting a long journey ahead when twenty minutes later, Bishop slows into the turn to send us to Dulles Airport.

We bypass the parking area, driving away from the main buildings and alongside the boundary fence, then come to a temporary stop before metal gates that are opened for us by a young man. Bishop inches the car into the airport yard, slowly passing one metal hangar, then another.

"What are we doing?" I ask.

"It's time for a change of transport." Matthew caresses my fingers as Bishop breaks and shifts the car to park.

A whisper of something unwanted slips through me, the life-long teaching of a paranoid and overly protective brother ringing in my ears.

You're being careless. You're putting us all in danger.

No. I know Matthew.

I might not have intimate knowledge of the events that make up his life, but I know *him*. I know his unwavering commitment. His building affection.

That's why I didn't ask how far we were travelling. Or who was coming with us.

I've learned to trust him—with my body, and now, also, my safety.

"I'll get the luggage." Bishop climbs from the driver's seat, the engine idling as he lobs the fob at the young man who opened the gates.

All I can do is watch in silence while I force Cole's voice from my mind.

"You're nervous." Matthew's hand slides from mine. "Are you questioning my intentions again? You don't have to accompany me, Layla. I can have you taken back to the penthouse."

"I'm not questioning you." My heart hurts at the disappointment in his features.

"You're apprehensive."

I could claim a fear of flying. Hell, it wouldn't be difficult to make up any number of reasons to explain the devil on my shoulder.

Instead, I give him what he deserves. "I've told you my brother doesn't appreciate my current secrecy. If he was aware I was about to jet set to places unknown with someone he's unfamiliar with, he'd judge me harshly."

Matthew's jaw ticks. "It sounds like he judges you harshly regardless."

I don't deny it. I want him to understand that part of me. The part that may affect him the most. "He does."

"He's controlling," he adds.

I don't deny that either.

The trunk door opens and Bishop steals my focus as he removes not one but two suitcases from the cargo area. Of course the asshole is still coming with us.

"Do you want me to arrange a driver?" Matthew asks as the trunk door closes. "The last thing I want to do is—"

"No, I'm excited to go with you. I promise. I just hadn't anticipated your meeting to be far enough away to require a plane." I unclasp my belt and smile. "You're not taking me to Paris, are you?"

He huffs a breath of lifeless laughter. "No. We'll have to do that trip another day. And we're not taking a plane either."

I'm about to ask for clarification when he swings his door wide and escapes the car to round the hood.

I follow, climbing from the back seat as a loud mechanical whir fills the rustling fall breeze, the sound coming from the other side of the hangar to my left.

"We're taking a helicopter?" I meet Matthew at the hood of the car but fall quiet, not wanting to interrupt the younger man who's relaying departure and arrival details as the unmistakable *whoop, whoop* floods my ears, the rush of energy growing around us.

I bite my lip, struggling from the whiplash of flipping from apprehension to exhilaration.

"I hope you're not scared of heights." Matthew steps away from the chatter to wrap an arm around my waist.

"I'm not. But how far are we going?"

"Virginia Beach. Is that a problem?"

I wince, wishing I hadn't shown my temporary slip of confidence in the car, the hesitation now gone as if it never existed. "I'm sorry." My voice barely carries over the air chopping around us. "I…"

I'm not sure what to say. I can't tell him I was brought up in a family who doesn't believe in trust. Or relay the justifiable reasons for them being that way. He'd never understand and I wouldn't want him to.

"You don't have to explain." He leads me toward the hangar, the wind growing more fierce the closer we get to the corner of the building.

Once we reach the edge, elation takes hold, sending blood rushing through my veins.

A sleek black metal bird sits yards away, the glossy paint gleaming in the sunlight. It's beautiful. All polished curves and extravagant masculinity with the pilot under the propellers, standing in wait.

I'm breathless.

Speechless.

"It's not too late to change your mind." Matthew tightens his arm around me.

"I won't. I want this more than anything."

I do.

I want the new memories with him.

I want a new life.

He leans in, kissing my temple like he has so many times before. "Then let's do this."

He holds me close as we approach the helicopter, and exchanges shouted greetings with the pilot. Matthew guides me inside, the back cabin lusciously appointed with leather seats and pristine carpet. He encourages me to take the far window seat before he climbs in after me to hand over a headset from a hook on the wall adjoining the cockpit, guiding the restrictive weight over my loose hair to settle against my ears.

The deafening sound gentles but the rush in my veins doesn't slow. Matthew leans against me, his arm tight around my waist as I stare out the window, preparing for my fascination to increase. I'm rabid with rapture, my limbs thrumming, my pulse a giddy staccato.

My heart flutters with excitement while Bishop and the pilot settle into the cockpit. They talk, their mouths moving without the words filtering through the headphones.

"We can hear each other. They can't hear us." Matthew's voice glides into my ears. "It shouldn't take long for us to be off the ground."

He's right. Within moments, the gleaming monstrosity is wobbling off the tarmac, hovering for a second before it glides forward, taking my breath with it.

I'm not new to luxury travel. My family have been boarding jets without a thought to cost or environmental damage since I was a toddler. But this is a first for me.

I've never traveled with a man's arms wrapped possessively around me, the potent devotion sending my head into the clouds.

Lightness overwhelms me the farther we ascend. Buildings become tiny blocks. Cars turn into ants gliding along black curving trails that stretch as far as the eye can see. A cluster of suburban homes transform into an ocean of green trees and sun-burned fields, all while Matthew guides me to rest against his chest, the side of my head nestling into his neck.

I'm Cinderella. Once, I was dirty and corrupted by my family's choices. Now, I'm swept off my feet by a devilish prince who only seeks to earn more of my trust.

"Stella would love this." I picture the surprise in her beautiful eyes. Her smile. The awe. "She'll be entirely jealous."

"We can bring her along whenever you like." His hand splays on my hip, no hint of hesitation in his actions or words.

My child doesn't daunt him. Not like she did Benji.

I know it's different. One was a paternal parent conscripted into fatherhood. The other is an outsider who can easily walk away. But Matthew has no fear. No doubt.

He's all in on this insane fairy tale, eager and enthusiastic to keep me from the darkness I'm meant to return to.

"You're such a good guy." I keep my attention on the patch-work fields. The tiny puffs of trees.

His mouth brushes just below the base of my neck, planting the softest, sweetest kiss. "You wouldn't say that if you knew what I was thinking."

My chest blazes with heat, the naked skin on my back prickling with goose bumps.

That's all it takes. A few words. A strategically placed glide of lips.

I fight against the need to glance over my shoulder to see the expression that matches the wicked words, but I visualize it in my mind, all sinful and sly.

His touch teases my shoulder, his fingers straying to the thin spaghetti strap. "Have I told you how gorgeous you are in this dress?"

"You don't need to," I whisper. "I always feel beautiful when you look at me."

A rumble in his throat is his only response as his mouth continues to lead me astray, the sweet kisses turning into erotic flicks of tongue and rugged scrapes of teeth.

I bite my lip against the tingles in my breasts, the hitch of my pulse. I succumb to the need to see him and turn, my gaze finding his, his mischievous grin sending the flames inside me far lower.

I stare for several punctuated heartbeats, each thump an exclamation of need.

He's such a phenomenally handsome man. Sensuous eyes dark as night. A jawline chiseled from stone and covered in masculine stubble. Then the smoothest lips a woman would sell her soul to kiss.

God, do I want to kiss them.

But not now. Not when a taste of him will make me want to devour.

"You're missing the view." His arm around my waist descends, his hand on my hip falling to the top of my thigh.

I look back to the window, attempting to break the trance, and freeze when his fingers slowly hitch the material of my sundress, creeping higher and higher.

"Matthew…" His name is a barely heard entreaty.

"Mmm?" He keeps hitching, not stopping until the hem is raised to my crotch, the gentle breeze of filtered air sweeping against my panties. He nudges closer to me, his body turning into mine, shielding me. "Keep admiring the view, *amore mio*, and I'll keep doing the same with mine."

I shudder, unable to control my body's reaction, helpless against the moisture dampening my sex.

"Let me play." His fingers skim the waistband of my underwear, his entire hand sneaking beneath to cover my mound.

"*Matthew.*" This time it's a plea. A gasped warning.

I shoot a frantic glance toward the cockpit. One glimpse over Bishop's shoulder and he'd see. Everything.

"He won't look," the devil taunts through my headphones. "It's just the two of us."

His touch slides lower, grazing my clit, parting my folds.

Nerves tingle. Limbs throb.

An inner voice is aghast at what I'm doing. How tawdry I've become. Yet, my blood boils for more. My pulse thunders to an erotic rhythm.

"We can't do this here." I grasp his wrist, the hold lackluster at best.

"Why not? We did it in a hotel bathtub with a stranger present. This time nobody is watching." A finger teases my entrance, the digit effortlessly sliding through my slickness. "I'm the only one to admire your beauty. It seems like such a waste."

"Bishop is *right* there." I shake my head accidentally bumping our headphones. "Do you like being watched?"

"I like *you* being watched. Being *wanted*." He leans tighter against my side, his fingers plunging deep.

I hold in a gasp, the air tightening my lungs.

"I enjoy the look men get when they see you," he murmurs against my neck, slaying me. "When they admire how fucking gorgeous you are. How perfect. How compliant."

I wish I could argue otherwise. That I'm not quick to obey or easily malleable. But in his arms, I'm all those things and more.

A puppet.

A servant.

A slave.

He curls his digits inside me, his entire body pressed to mine, his other hand sliding into my panties to find my clit. "Fuck my fingers, *amore mio*."

I'm helpless to deny him.

I want to do this. For him. For me. For happiness that is usually stretched thin and far between.

I close my eyes, grinding into his touch, becoming one with pleasure.

I can't breathe.

There's too much… everything.

Bliss. Lust. Lies.

I want him to strip me bare. Not merely of clothes and underwear, but of secrecy and deception. I want him to know me. The real me. The person my family don't see. The woman my husband never noticed.

"I'm so fucking hard for you, Layla," he murmurs into my headphones. "I promise you'll be sore and sated before the day is through."

I don't doubt it.

Not for a second.

"I want to taste you," he growls. "To plant my face between your thighs until you're lost for breath."

I picture him doing exactly that. On his knees. My dress raised. My hands in his hair with Bishop a few feet away, able to catch us at any moment.

Oh, God.

My core flutters with an approaching orgasm. "I'm so close."

"And so sensual." His touch becomes more firm against my clit, wiggling back and forth, faster and faster. "So tempting. So fucking perfect."

I pant. Gasp. Wheeze.

"Non ne avrò mai un altra."

His softly murmured Italian is my undoing. I latch tight to his wrist with my nails, holding him deep inside me as I grind and thrust and shatter.

My pussy convulses, the spasms building and morphing.

"See?" His appreciative growl hums in my ears, the viciousness tattooing my soul. "Perfect."

I whimper, climbing the crest, riding the wave.

I want to scream for him. Cry. Vow.

I could give him everything in this moment. My promises for the future. My commitment to togetherness even though I told myself this would be temporary.

How can I ever walk away from this? I never want to be without him.

I come down from the peak with clawed fingers and heaving breaths. "You have too much power over me."

"You have it all wrong, *amore mio.*" His voice grows somber, his lips once again finding my shoulder for a gentle brush of affection. *"Sei quella con tutto il potere."*

22

———

LAYLA

WE LAND AT A HELIPORT FAR FROM THE CITY BUILDINGS, MY HAIR scattering from the *whoop* of the helicopter blades as Matthew leads us to an awaiting town car.

Our driver doesn't say a word as we glide toward the coast, the sea breeze filling my lungs from Bishop's open front-seat window, before we pull into a beachside hotel.

"I'll get us checked in." Bishop shoves open his door. "I'll meet you in the restaurant."

Matthew follows, holding out a hand to assist me in sliding along the back seat to step into the warm sun as a young male bellhop rushes toward us.

"Mr. Langston, it's a pleasure to see you again." The boy beams. "Do you have any bags I can help you with?"

"The trunk." Matthew jerks his chin toward the rear of the vehicle and discreetly slips the man a tip. "Has Lorenzo arrived?"

"Yes, sir. He's waiting inside."

It doesn't surprise me that Matthew is recognized on sight, or that the man he's meeting is familiar to staff. What concerns me is the slight hint of tension that enters Matthew's shoulders as he turns to face me, his dark eyes tight with hesitation.

"What's wrong?" I scrutinize his expression, trying to understand the change in him.

"Come with me." He grabs both my hands, entwining our fingers. "Come to my meeting."

I hold my surprise in check, unsure if I should be concerned or appreciative.

This is a far bigger step than I anticipated. A massive switch from the information injunction we've had in place. And as much as I want to learn everything there is about him, I know I'm not ready to reciprocate at this level. Not yet.

"Who is it with?"

"An old friend. He's a mentor of sorts. At least, he used to be."

"You want me to meet your mentor?" That's big. *Huge.*

"I'd be honored, and so would he." He raises one of our joined hands and kisses my knuckles. "And if you haven't figured me out by now, the request was a courtesy, but your attendance is compulsory." He grins and tugs me toward the hotel doors. "You'll be joining us, Layla. You've got two minutes to prepare."

Two minutes? To prepare to meet his mentor?

"Are you kidding?" I scope my disheveled appearance in the glass windows as we approach. "I look a treat."

"You better fucking believe it." He shoves past the doors and leads the way into the reception area. "You always look edible."

I ignore the heat rushing to my cheeks. The tingle in my belly.

I'm not succumbing to lust right now. Nope. Not again.

"Can we just stop for a minute." I plant my feet and squeeze his hand, forcing him to comply. "Please."

He turns to me with a frown. "What's wrong?"

"What's wrong?" I huff a laugh. "This is a big moment for me. And I think it is for you, too."

The frown deepens, but he doesn't deny my statement.

"This man is important to you." It's not a question. The evidence was his tightening posture when he realized Lorenzo was already here. That he was about to dictate for me to meet someone he cared about. "I don't want to make a bad first impression."

He steps forward, wrapping a rough arm around my shoulders to drag me into him, his face finding my hair, his aftershave filling my lungs. "I thought giving you no notice would be easier." There's forgiveness in his tone. "He will adore you, Layla. Just as much as I do."

"And if he doesn't?" I close my eyes, relaxing into him for the briefest respite.

"Then he's out of my life," he murmurs into my hair. "Gone. Done. I won't spare him another thought."

"I'd never let you do that." No woman of worth would. "If you were considering getting rid of Bishop, on the other hand…"

"That's different." He snickers, pulling away to guide my hair back behind my ear. "What you get from him isn't personal. It's personality."

"Well, his personality sucks."

"I don't disagree." His fingers trail my jaw, my chin. "You'll like Lorenzo."

I have to trust him. Trust that this meeting will go well. That these new steps toward full disclosure are the right ones to make.

"The two of you will get along fine." He places a kiss to my hairline, then reclaims my hand and continues toward the entry of the restaurant, the maître d' watching us approaches with familiarity in her gaze.

"Welcome, Mr. Langston. I think you'll find Mr.—"

"It's okay, Sophie." He interrupts her speech and guides me to stride past her. "I can already see him."

I scope the open dining area, seeing couples and families, none of them sparking interest until I reach the three men standing together at the bar. Two are younger, bulky and tall. The other is older, grey-haired with a shorter build. All of them wear dark suits, stylish and formal.

I'm underdressed.

The older man catches sight of us as he places his scotch glass before him on the polished wood, his grin quick to form. He strides toward us, spreading his arms, his light blue eyes beaming with pride. "*Figlio mio.*"

"Lorenzo." Matthew squeezes my fingers before releasing my hand and accepting the offered hug. "It's good to see you."

They embrace with strong arms and claps on the back, all masculine in their affection as the two other men turn to witness the show from a few feet behind.

Matthew's mentor isn't what I expected. He's far older, maybe in his sixties, with sun-kissed skin gentled by a myriad of deeply etched laugh lines. The only thing I anticipated correctly is his air of success. He oozes triumph, exactly like his mentee, the confidence in his expression bordering on arrogance.

"It's been too long." Lorenzo retreats to look him up and down. "You seem different. Overly carefree and alive."

"I'm not sure I'm carefree, but I definitely feel alive." Matthew returns to my side, placing a protective palm on the curve of my back. "This is Layla, the cause of my new lease on life and *quella che possiede il mio cuore*."

I tense at the words spoken in a foreign language, slightly unnerved at being kept from part of the conversation.

"The one who owns your heart?" Lorenzo's brows rise as he steps forward to grab my hands in his. "I can see why. It's such a pleasure to meet someone whose beauty is profound enough to ensnare my Matthew. I've heard so much about you."

I glance to the man by my side. What the hell has he said about me? And why the hell has he said it? Is he really entrenched in this connection enough to have already told his mentor about me?

The slight raise of his chin, as if steeling himself against my response, makes me wonder even more.

"I assure you her beauty is merely part of the allure." Matthew winks. "She's captured me on every level."

I can't respond.

Not in words.

Instead, I blush. Cheeks to neck. Inside and out.

Compliments from strangers aren't new. People who want to get close to my brother often attempt to get there through me or Keira first, with most using kind lies and false admiration. But this is different.

I'm not a potential asset.

I'm of no use to these men because they have no idea who I am.

"I see you both have the same remarkable skills of flattery." I smile at the older man, his grandfatherly face seeming oddly familiar with its warmth and kindness. "Is that something you taught Matthew?"

His laughter rumbles like rolling thunder. "I wish I could take the credit, but he's always had his own ways when it comes to women. After all these years, you're the first I've had the pleasure of meeting."

"And if I have anything to do with it, she'll be the last." Matthew shakes the hands of the men looming in Lorenzo's shadow, then walks farther into the restaurant. "I need coffee. Are we sitting inside or out?"

"Out. We can't remain inside when we have the ocean to stare at." Lorenzo links his arm with mine, leading me after Matthew who directs us toward the glass doors to the al fresco dining area, the two other men following behind. "I reserved the best table just for us."

I walk on numb feet as a crowd of emotions seeks attention inside my chest.

Jubilation dances with twists and dips of hope and possibility. The kindness I've been welcomed with by these men is a blessing. I'm overwhelmed with gratitude to be so freely accepted. But the bitter edge of my shady upbringing still itches from the scars it's left behind.

How darkly tainted is my life that this is the first time I've felt free from judgment?

With each passing minute, I want to settle more into Matthew's world. To plant roots in soil that wasn't made for me. But could it be?

Could I change who I am to remain with him?

Maybe I could be accepted for who I want to be if I'm willing to sever ties with my brother. With my entire family. With the crime and danger and lies.

Could I do that though?

Could I start over with Stella, placing her boarding school days in the rearview to live like a normal person?

"Tell me about yourself, Layla?" Lorenzo pats my hand as we step outside, the rush of waves crashing in the distance. "How did you meet my Matthew?"

I open my mouth, then pause, cautious at what to offer that won't incriminate me. "We met in Denver."

Lorenzo's fingers twitch on my arm. "Matthew has been to Denver?"

"Stop plying her for information, *zio*." Matthew continues to stride ahead, passing dining customers to enter a private cordoned off part of the seated area, making himself at home amongst the empty tables. "If you have questions for me, you know who to ask."

"He's always been touchy," Lorenzo murmurs near my ear, his accent thick. "I don't know how you put up with him."

I grin as we reach a table in the far corner next to a waist-high hedge blocking us from the public bike track that's busy with people exercising.

"Are more people joining us?" I take in the sea of emptiness around us, all the nearby tables bearing reserved signs just like ours.

"No, *bella*." Lorenzo jerks his chin at the two men who came with him, sending a silent message that has them taking sentry positions at the farthest corners of the cordoned area.

Not business partners. Bodyguards.

"It's for privacy," the older man continues. "I can't have everyone learning my secrets."

Even though his comment is tongue-in-cheek, I'm tempted to ask what type of secrets could warrant reserving such a large area of the restaurant.

"*Vecchio mio*," Bishop calls behind us, his stride long as he approaches to engulf Lorenzo in a hug with clapped backs and foreign greetings.

The two of them reunite like father and son, and for the first time, the man I've grown to despise doesn't seem entirely feral thanks to a generous smile and sincere affection.

"Sit." Lorenzo breaks the embrace and waves a hand toward the table. "Take the chair opposite me, Bella. Bishop and Matthew can protect us from the prying eyes of the world by sitting on the outside."

I'm certain he's more intent on keeping his prying eyes on me, but I comply, happy to have his attention.

"The room isn't ready." Bishop slides a plastic suite card across the table. "They said to give them half an hour."

Matthew pockets the offering and we all take our allotted seats, Bishop and Matthew against the hedge, while I settle in front of

Lorenzo, who clicks his finger in the air, gaining the attention of a waitress who hustles over.

Coffee is ordered. Cake and bagels and croissants, too.

Once the waitress is gone, Lorenzo sits back in his chair, his warm eyes fixed on me. "Tell me about yourself, *cara mia*. Spare no details. I want to know everything."

"Lorenzo," Matthew warns. "Don't push."

"I'm not pushing. Merely getting to know the woman of your heart, *figlio*."

"It's okay," I lie, wishing I knew how to defuse this conversation respectfully. I don't want to offend Lorenzo by staying silent. I also don't want Matthew to think I'm willing to open up to a stranger when I've spent the duration of our relationship hiding. "I guess the thing that defines me most is that I'm a single mother." I pause, hoping the usually disparaged label will end my time in the spotlight. "My daughter is eleven going on twenty-three."

The older man laughs. "They're all the same at that age."

"You have children?" I latch on to the information, hoping to divert the conversation from me.

"Many. Some by birth. Others by fate." He glances to Matthew and Bishop.

"You must be very proud."

"I am. Now tell me more." He flares his eyes with exaggerated excitement. "I want to know everything. I'm in awe of the way you've ensnared such a stubborn bachelor."

"*Zio*," Matthew growls. "You're making her uncomfortable."

"*Se la metto a disagio, sicuramente me lo può dire.*" Lorenzo frowns. "Isn't that right, Layla?"

I balk, his words going completely over my head.

"I'm sorry." He reaches across the table to touch my hand. "Do you not speak Italian?"

"No." I wince, physically pained at the thought of disappointing him—a stranger—someone I shouldn't care about. And yet, I do. I want his approval more than anything. "I enjoy listening to your beautiful language, though, so please don't stop on my account."

"Matthew will have to teach you."

I glance to the man in question, my heart warming with the ease of the smile staring back at me.

"I agree." There's a teasing hum to his tone. "All I need is for her to commit to the long process."

He's not talking about a commitment to a language. His intent is on a pledge of another kind, and right now, I'm mindless to think of one reason to deny him.

"We can talk about this later." I force my attention back to Lorenzo. "Is it my turn to learn more about you? Matthew told me you're his mentor."

"He did, did he?"

"You know it's true," Matthew mutters. "Stop fishing for compliments, old man."

Lorenzo laughs, carefree and bold. "Okay, okay. I know it's true. I taught Matthew everything I know about business."

"And arrogance. You taught him that, too." Bishop shoots me a glower, as if pissed I'm taking over the conversation.

"I assume you were there for that lesson, too." I quirk a brow at him.

Matthew snickers. "Without a doubt."

"So you're in the club business?" I ask Lorenzo.

There's an awkward pause as the fatherly figure holds his smile, his focus moving to Matthew. Nobody speaks. Or acknowledges the question as the two stare at each other.

I've said something wrong.

Bishop shifts in his seat, placing his arm against the hedge to watch the bike riders as they pass.

My question has made things awkward. And with the necessity for guards and a private seating area, I should've been less forthright in asking for information.

"I'm sorry… I didn't mean to be—"

"Don't apologize." Lorenzo returns his gaze to mine. "Yes, *bella*, I own clubs. Many clubs. I only hesitate to discuss the topic because it's become somewhat of a point of contention lately. Especially with Matthew."

The awkwardness continues, prickling my skin.

Bishop glowers at the passing bike riders while the gorgeous man beside me turns impassive, his expression not giving a hint of emotion.

Footsteps approach behind me as the quiet stretches, the chatter from pedestrians filling the awkward void.

"Who ordered the latte?" The waitress stops beside our table with a tray filled with food and drinks, her smile beaming into the discomfort.

"That would be me." I focus on the cream tablecloth, wishing I hadn't siphoned the enthusiasm from our heartwarming arrival.

"Don't worry." Matthew leans into me, whispering in my hair. "We've been destined to have this unwanted conversation for a while." He inches away to refocus on Lorenzo. "I guess it's time we discussed your retirement."

"It's been time for months." Lorenzo juts his chin. "Have either of you considered my offer?"

Matthew doesn't move. Not even a flinch.

Bishop continues to stare at the bike track, or maybe even farther to the street traffic.

"Your offer is something that should be reserved for your sons. Your *real* sons." Matthew reaches for his piccolo, calm and controlled as he takes a sip.

"You already know they've received the same offer. You're also well aware that hard work never suited them."

"It's not the hard work they're opposed to," Bishop mutters. "They're already successful in their own right, and so are we."

"*Il tuo successo non è niente in confronto alle profondità dell'impero familiare.*" An edge creeps into Lorenzo's tone. "*Saresti uno sciocco a rifiutare l'offerta.*"

"Then call me a fool." Bishop returns his attention to the conversation. "As tempting as the offer is, I have no plans to return here."

"*Questo è un insulto alla famiglia.*" Lorenzo glares. "You both know this."

"It's not meant as an insult." Matthew sighs. "Don't take your frustration out on us. It's your sons you should be speaking to."

"*Fanculo i miei figli.*" Lorenzo slaps a hand down on the table, startling me. "They don't deserve to be part of this."

"*Calmati,*" Matthew says, a warning in his tone. "If I'd known you were going to push the issue, I wouldn't have brought Layla here to sit awkwardly through the exchange."

I press my lips tight at his protection. Appreciating it. Loving it.

I've always hated when my brother did the same.

Lorenzo's shoulders loosen, his face losing the harsh lines of irritation. "My apologies." He drags in a long breath, regaining composure. "Forgive me, *bella*. As you can see I've grown frustrated at my children for turning their back on the family business. I didn't raise them to be ungrateful."

"Families are tough. I know that better than most." I pull my cell from my dress pocket. "But please don't censor the conversation on my account. I've got messages and emails to return. Pretend I'm not here."

He holds my gaze, admiring me in silence for long moments before he says, *"Non lasciarla andare. È una da tenere stretta."*

"Lo so." Matthew shifts his chair closer to mine, sliding his arm over the back of my seat, the heat from his suit jacket sinking into my shoulders, the strength of his body settling in against me.

I glance at him, hoping for a translation. Our eyes lock, and without words, I understand the silent message he conveys.

Lorenzo approves.

I'm considered worthy.

The realization is enough to make my stupid throat dry.

He leans in, placing a kiss to my temple, a whisper to my ear. "You're amazing."

I flush, so much more than cheeks and chest. I feel the heat everywhere. Arms. Legs. Stomach. No place more potent than my heart.

"Enough of the PDA bullshit," Bishop mutters. "I'm not here to watch soft porn."

"If whispering in my ear is considered soft porn, I truly feel sorry for your lovers." I give him a smug smile.

"Who says I'm talking about a whisper?" He gives me the same look in return. "Maybe I meant the helicopter flight."

I stiffen, my temper flaring.

"Watch it," Matthew threatens him while he squeezes my shoulder.

"It's jealousy, *bella*." Lorenzo claps my nemesis on the chest, a gesture that's harshly shoved away. "I doubt poor Bishop has experienced love."

Love?

I ignore the implication. "Nonetheless, I think I'm becoming a distraction. I should go for a walk on the beach—"

"No, stay." Matthew's hand remains firm on my shoulder. "Eat. Enjoy your coffee. Our conversation won't take long."

Bishop keeps his feral stare on me as I concede with a nod, clinging to the cell in my hand.

They continue talking without me, the Italian more heavily spoken than words of English. I sit there and stare at my locked screen as the sea breeze dances in my hair and Matthew's accent plays havoc with my libido.

What if this is love?

We barely know each other... yet what I feel for Matthew holds a romanticism and tightly woven affection far more potent than anything I've experienced.

I yearn for him. All the time.

Even with him by my side, his arm around me, his voice in my ears, it's not enough.

I want more.

Birds chirp, people ride past, waitresses clean tables, and all I can do is simmer in infatuation, my life shifting to revolve around the man beside me as if nothing else exists.

He's becoming my world.

I swallow, attempting to alleviate my parched throat, and unlock my cell to swipe through numerous unread messages from my siblings. I make sure to keep the screen tilted from view as I scan Cole's condemning texts, and those from Keira that are equally accusatory but cleverly intoned with concern.

Would either of them care that I'm at peace here?

Would they deny me this happiness?

I reach for my latte and take a sip, wishing I had someone to talk to, but my sister is the only confidant I've ever had.

I haven't risked the luxury of friends since childhood. My family's reputation has kiboshed the ability to trust anyone outside our inner circle.

There's only Keira. A sibling who usually forgives but never forgets.

Matthew's fingers brush reassuring strokes against my shoulder as I contemplate reaching out to her. I breathe deeper of his scent, sink further into the confidence in his tone. I become bolder in his embrace. Stronger.

My pulse pounds as I hover my fingers above a new text, Keira's cell number the recipient.

If I tell her, there's no going back.

I won't be able to pretend this is a temporary fling. Our relationship will be real. Undeniable. I'll have to commit to telling him who I am in the future and face the possibility of him walking away.

My heart plunges. My stomach, too.

I tilt my face to look at him, watching intently as he speaks flawless Italian, trying to hide my lust when he shoots me a knowing smirk before returning his attention to Lorenzo.

He leans in again, his heated breath tickling my neck as he murmurs, "Don't look at me like that or I'll be forced to fuck you on this table."

I sit taller. Clear my throat. Pretend my sex isn't already preparing for the actions of his threat, and start typing—*Keira, I think I'm in love.*

23

———

LAYLA

Her response comes thick and fast.

What?!

Where are you?

Who is he?

How long have you known him?

I could've maintained my elation if it weren't for the last text.

Goddamnit, Layla, don't do anything stupid.

Those six words hit hard, her judgment threatening to convince me I'm not worthy of happiness.

I fight against the potential downfall. Glare at the screen. Cling to the last vestiges of my pride until my self-respect slowly returns.

I'm tempted to reply. To tell her exactly how I feel about my despised position in the family with far more clarity than I did in our last conversation. I'm even inclined to answer the call she puts through seconds later just so she can hear the renewed confidence in my voice as I tell her about the possibility of me never returning to Portland.

But the allure isn't worth instigating another fight. Or disrupting Matthew's conversation.

I'm in love, not a masochist.

"You okay?" he whispers in my ear. "What happened?"

I lock my cell and shake my head. "Nothing."

"It's something."

Lorenzo and Bishop continue their conversation as Matthew leans closer. "Is it your family again?"

I hate how he hits the bull's-eye easily. I'm grateful for it, too.

My family has always been my destruction.

I never would've been painted a traitor if it weren't for my despicable father using me in the first place. I wouldn't have had the chance to drag my husband through the mud with me if we weren't forced to marry. And I wouldn't be here, ignoring the vibration of my sister's continued calls, if my siblings didn't make me feel like a leper.

But I guess that's the silver lining.

Him.

Matthew.

They may be my ruin, but he'll be my rise.

I won't retreat from what we have because of Keira. I won't continue to be conditioned to believe I'm unworthy of even a second of the heaven I feel when I'm with him.

"Talk to me, Layla. Tell me what's going on."

I turn into him, our lips a breath apart when I whisper, "You're special to me."

He inches back, his brows furrowing.

I've shocked him, and I guess it's to be expected.

He's spent all our shared time calling me *amore mio,* promising me his devotion, showing me his commitment. And this is the first I've given it in return.

"You're going to do this to me *now?*" He places a hand on my upper thigh, his palm possessively sliding higher. "Here?"

Hunger ebbs off him, the fire beaming in his eyes.

I blush, my cheeks undoubtedly stained crimson as I turn away. "We'll talk about this later."

His fingers pause at the crotch of my panties. "We're going to do a hell of a lot more than talk."

"Stop it." I shoot him a playful glare. "Pay attention to the conversation." I jerk my chin at Lorenzo who talks to Bishop, the older man giving me a brief smile before asking Matthew something in Italian.

The three of them continue chatting while I ignore another call from Keira then turn off my cell. I won't speak to her again. Not until I'm stronger. More immune.

Instead, I focus on the foreign debate around me, attempting to decipher the topic. *"Ricchezza"* and *"Cruciale"* are spoken numerous times. Matthew repeats *"la mia risposta è no,"* more than once.

Sometimes they converse in English, the sentences holding just as much insight as those spoken in Italian when there's no prior context.

And through it all, Matthew's hand remains on my thigh, no longer a sexual taunt, but a companionable reminder that I'm not alone.

I sip my coffee between their laughter and hostility. The ups and downs come thick and fast until Lorenzo heaves a heavy sigh to focus on me with fatherly kindness.

"Alas, *bella*, I fear my boys aren't to be convinced." He clucks his tongue. "Who raised such stubborn fools?"

I grin. "I could make a wry comment about all men and their stereotypical stubbornness, but now probably isn't the time."

He chuckles. "I think we would all appreciate your restraint."

Matthew squeezes my thigh again and I take the gesture as encouragement. His appreciation settles in the air between us, our building bond tightening around me.

"You've barely eaten." Lorenzo frowns at all the untouched food spread across the table. "None of us have."

"It doesn't help when you're trying to tear us a new one." Bishop reaches for a pastry and takes a bite. "I'm fucking starving."

Matthew grabs a croissant. "Me, too."

I admire his strong hands, eager to find out how they'll be put to use later as the roar of a motorbike rumbles in the nearby intersection behind me, loud enough to momentarily deafen.

I wince, sipping the last of my latte, but hesitate in placing it back on the table.

Bishop sits taller, his attention cutting toward the sound. He stiffens as the thunder continues, the roaring muffler coming closer.

"What is it?" Matthew places the croissant on his plate and turns to look.

There's no response. Nothing other than a poised hardening of Bishop's stare.

I glance over my shoulder to the traffic lights, my gaze catching on the red that turns to green, but it's the motorcycle cutting away from the street to mount the bicycle lane that raises my hackles.

"We've got trouble." Bishop shoves to his feet.

Matthew's quick to do the same.

I'm unsure whether I should follow, the latte glass now frozen in my hand.

I glance between the men surrounding me, all of them on edge. All now standing, including the two bodyguards at the farthest corners of our secluded area. Both of them rush forward as the leather-covered biker howls toward us, face unseen below the darkened visor.

"What's going on?" I brace to stand, only to be stopped by Matthew's steely grip clasping my shoulder to hold me in place.

"Stay down," he barks.

I scramble to figure out what's going on, glancing from one man to the next, then back to the biker who reaches around his back to swing an automatic weapon toward the hotel.

Screams ring out. Chairs scrape and scatter.

"Get down." Matthew slams into me seconds before the *ratta-tat-tat* of gunfire rings out.

I topple backward to the cement. My elbow takes the brunt of the fall. The latte glass shatters on impact, splintering around me.

I cry out as he smothers his body over mine, covering me head to toe. But the reverberation in my throat doesn't make a dent on the nearby sounds seeking supremacy.

Women scream. Footsteps scramble. Glass smashes. More gunfire blasts the air. Closer. Louder. More threatening. Someone is returning fire.

Lorenzo is taken to the ground by his men. Shouts ping-pong around me.

"Lay flat," Matthew demands. "Straight against the ground."

I don't comply. I can't. I cling to him instead, wrapping my arms around his neck, burrowing my head against his shoulder as splinters of glass dig into me from all angles.

The bike grows louder. So close I feel the vibrations in every nerve.

I'm going to die.

I'm going to be shot while plastered to the cement, and my daughter doesn't even know where I am. I'll never get to speak to her again.

"I've got you." Matthew keeps me pinned, every inch of him holding me in place as the gunfire recedes, the hacking rumble of the engine speeding into the distance.

Then silence.

There's only the rasp of my fractured inhales against the ringing in my ears.

"Are you okay?" Matthew inches off me, his gaze frenzied as he scans my face.

"Yeah… I think so."

"I'm getting you out of here." He raises to his haunches. "Don't get up until I tell you."

I nod, but nothing fully penetrates the shock.

Men snarl and snap above me, the Italian words attacking with none of the beauty they held before.

I turn onto my side and hiss from the broken glass poking through my dress to my ribs, quickly discarding the hazard only for it to be replaced by ten more. I brush my arms, the shouts and screams from strangers rising above the bell tolling in my ears.

Diners slowly drag themselves to their feet in the distance. Others peer over the waist-high hedge from the bike track to take in the destruction. There are offers for help. Calls for the police.

Matthew. Is he okay?

I rake my gaze over him as he snaps words in Italian, scrutinizing the way he stands, how he holds himself, the way he moves his arms, needing to make sure he's uninjured. Then I focus on Bishop who clutches a gun at his side, and Lorenzo's guards who do the same, their weapons at home in their grasp as they shield their employer.

The show of defense brings another wave of apprehension.

I assumed they were armed. It's their job to protect.

But the air of calm under pressure is far too familiar, enough to inspire déjà vu. This snapshot is like so many others in my life. The shattered glass. The screaming women. The men with guns poised to retaliate on an unseen enemy.

"Were you shot?" Matthew demands of his mentor.

My attention snaps to the parting guards who expose Lorenzo sitting on the ground behind them, his hands clutching at his chest.

"No," he wheezes. "I'm good."

I push onto shaky hands and knees, needing to see for myself.

"Stay down." Matthew steps closer, towering over me as he plasters his phone to his ear then barks foreign garble.

"I'm fine, *bella*." Lorenzo gives an unconvincing smile, his face starkly pale. "It's nothing more than the temperamental heart of an old man."

"We need to leave." Bishop shoves chairs aside to squat before Lorenzo, helping to pull him to his feet. "That fucker could come back."

"Who was that?" Questions slam into me. "Who were they targeting?" I look to Matthew, the man who previously told me he had enemies.

He glances away, shoving a hand through his hair as he sneers more Italian into his phone.

My scrambled thoughts turn inward, the need for answers overwhelming.

What if I was the target?

I choke on an inhale, struggling to breathe.

Emmanuel has to know my family don't forget an injustice.

What if he found out I'd been in Denver? What if news got back to him that a stolen purse had been discovered with my ID and a vial of cyanide that all but had his name on it?

"Who the fuck knows? This could be anything from terrorism, to attempted assassination, to sabotage against the hotel chain." Bishop jerks his chin toward the restaurant. "But from the look of those bullet holes, it was either a warning or the person taking aim reads braille."

I follow the direction of his chin to see the shattered windows and the pockmarked facia above the frames. All the holes are well above head level. Too high to be life-threatening.

"Get Lorenzo out of here." Matthew pockets his cell and leans down to glide his fingers over the back of my arm, gently coaxing me to my feet.

"No," the old man growls. "I'm not leaving until I have answers."

"Don't be a stubborn fool." Matthew keeps me close at his side as he narrows his eyes on Bishop. "Go with him. Take him home to see his doctor. Make sure he's okay."

One of Lorenzo's guards holsters his weapon beneath his jacket. "Or at least wait inside."

"You'll take him home," Matthew demands, his face contorting with aggression. "*Now*."

He's barely recognizable. The sophistication is gone, replaced with lethal authority. Feral fury. I don't know this man.

"I dare you to defy me," he warns. "You may gain his anger for dragging him out of here, but I'll kill you if he gets hurt."

I stiffen.

He walks into me, hustling us from the outdoor dining area by the crook of my arm, not allowing them a rebuttal or me a chance to think.

I'm hurried through the restaurant and into the hotel reception, my feet numb, my ears still ringing, my panic making thoughts unclear.

"Where are we going?" I struggle to keep up as he increases our pace, dragging me past staff who run in the opposite direction, their blurring faces rushing toward those yelling for help from the restaurant. "Matthew?"

"It's best if we get to our room. You'll be safe there."

I stop, needing the stillness to settle my foggy mind.

If the attack was targeting me, I'd be more safe at home. With my family. Where security is part of our genes.

With siblings already sick of your complications.

What's more important is that I need to get to Stella. To make sure she's all right. To ensure I haven't put her in harm's way.

"Layla, we need to keep moving." He pulls me toward the bank of elevators.

"No. Wait." I tug my arm from his grip. "I can't stay here. I have to get to my daughter."

"Your daughter is fine. *You're* fine." He leans close, his

beseeching eyes demanding me to understand. "Once we get to the room, the quiet will help."

The confidence he exudes makes it easy to believe him. To at least trust mindlessly while my thoughts remain scrabbled.

He reclaims my hand and drags me to the elevators, my fear making me pliable. I blink in a daze as he presses the call button. I breathe shallow while more shouts reverberate off the walls and the blare of sirens approach.

We just walked out of there. A crime scene. A possible attempt on my life. Or was it his? Or Lorenzo's? Maybe the target was the hotel and its owners.

So why does it feel like it was all me?

My mistakes.

My problems.

My life on the line.

The metal doors open and Matthew closes in behind me, guiding me forward with heavy hands on my hips.

The air around us grows thicker in the confined space. My chest tightens. I can't get enough oxygen. I can't fill my lungs.

"You're okay." Matthew presses a button to close the doors, then moves in front of me. Foot to foot. Eye to eye. "It's over. You don't need to worry."

He has no clue.

This profoundly protective man has no idea I might have been the cause of this. That I would bring more untold danger into his life if we remained together.

"You're in shock." He presses a kiss to my forehead, the caress barely felt through my turmoil.

His affection is sweet... and caring... and something I'm entirely unworthy of.

I put him in harm's way. If not today, then with my actions in Denver.

The elevator jolts as it starts to ascend, the whir of movement increasing my turmoil. "I don't want to go to the room, Matthew. I want to go home. I need you to take me back to the helicopter."

"It's over, *amore mio*."

I shake my head. "You don't understand."

Even though I've been careful—covering my tracks, using cash for every payment—Emmanuel still could've found me.

He may have got his hands on airport passenger lists... or tracked my phone somehow... or... *Fuck.* Could the Costas be watching Matthew like he's been watching them?

"Breathe." He cups my cheeks, his hard eyes demanding compliance. "I understand just fine. Trust me. I looked after you in Denver, right? And I've given you no reason to doubt me ever since. I'll take care of you, Layla. I promise."

His assurance crumples me. Sickens.

This is the exact drama I promised not to bring into his life. It has to be far worse than Bishop could've anticipated. My existence could ruin them both.

The elevator bumps to a stop, the doors open, and nausea overwhelms me when Matthew strides for the hall.

I can't follow.

"I need to go home." I inch toward the button panel. "I'll find my own way to the airport."

I don't care about my belongings. They're replaceable.

What I can't handle is another death on my hands.

"I won't let you leave on your own." His voice is barely contained frustration.

"I'll call my brother."

I'll tell him everything—my plans to take down the Costas, my stolen purse, the vial of cyanide. I'll beg for understanding...

And then what?

I'll become a bigger burden. A more despised part of the family.

A sob clogs my throat. "I have to go."

"I said no." Matthew storms into the elevator, hauls me off my feet, and lobs me over his shoulder. "I swore to protect you, and if that means from your own bad decisions, then so be it."

"Put me down." I wiggle with his booming steps, only resulting in him tightening his hold around my waist. "Matthew, I'm serious. Put me down."

"And *I'm* fucking serious," he growls. "You're not leaving. I need you with me."

I need you.

I. Need. You.

Each word slices at my skin, the unfamiliar sentiment tearing a sob from my scorched throat.

Nobody ever needs me. Not my family. Not my husband. Not even my daughter, who left for boarding school without a backward glance. The only person who ever claimed to need anything from me was my father, who used those words against me.

Matthew doesn't stop his vicious pace until we reach an open suite door. I push against his back, moving high enough to see around his waist to the housekeeping trolley standing idle a few feet inside the darkened hall.

"Is someone in our room?" His question is a commanding boom.

"Oh," a female replies, a scuffle of noise following. "Yes, sir. It's housekeeping." A petite brunette pokes her head around the corner, her face in flickering shadow. "I'm sorry, I haven't finished preparing what was request—"

"We need privacy." He storms forward, carrying me like a sack of potatoes.

I should fight. Run. Leave him to a life that would be less dramatic without me, but… *I need you.*

That declaration. That honesty.

God, I need him, too.

I need the assurance. The protection. The authority that quietens the screaming within.

"Please put me down." I soften against him. "Please, Matthew."

He trudges ahead, the scent of candle wax hitting my nose sweet seconds before we reach the open living area where he places me on my feet next to the sofa.

I pause in confusion, the sight not computing.

The housekeeper stands before the kitchenette, a silver wine bucket on the counter, a lighter in her hand. The room is emblazoned with dozens of flickering tea lights. The beauty steals my breath, the glow emanating from every horizontal surface.

Rose petals are scattered over the carpet, the sofa, the television stand.

Matthew requested this?

"It will only take me a moment to finish." The woman's gaze shifts between us. "The bathroom just needs—"

"Leave." Matthew shoves a hand through his hair.

The woman winces, nods in apology, then rushes to a dark corner of the kitchen to retrieve a box of rattling candles. "The food you requested is already in the fridge. Again, I apologize." She scampers for her trolley in the hall, the rattle of shampoo bottles and cleaning supplies filling the room before she pulls the door shut behind her.

Then, more silence.

Thick, painful quiet which contrasts with the beauty of the dancing flames around me. Hell consumes my thoughts, yet heaven fills my vision. The opposites add to my instability.

I need something to make sense.

Anything.

"Do you want a glass of water?" Matthew begins to pace, both hands raking into his hair, his fingers clawing against his scalp. "Maybe wine is best. Or food? Do you need something to eat?"

His questions are fast and emotionless. Spoken without thought or follow-through.

I watch him, noting the sweat beading his brow, the rapid rise and fall of his chest. He's spiraling. Descending into shock as he trudges back and forth along the carpet.

"Matthew…" Guilt consumes me. "I need to leave." It's harder to say this time. Harder to admit the truth in the face of his torment. "This has to end."

He stops abruptly, his hands falling to his sides as he scowls. "What did you say?"

I cringe against the surprise in his eyes. The rejection.

But I made a promise. I said I wouldn't cause drama.

"I never should have come here." My heart squeezes with the admission. With the lies and secrecy and unending mistakes. "I think I caused this."

He straightens. "Why would you think that?"

I don't want to tell him specifics. To ruin the fairy tale. To witness his opinion of me disintegrate like so many others have before.

"Layla, why would you think that?" His eyes narrow in confusion.

"I'm not who or what you think I am…" I backtrack toward the door, each syllable pulled from me like a deeply rooted tooth. "I'm not a good person."

"Hey." He prowls toward me, eating up the space, reclaiming my cheeks in his palms. "Stop it. This wasn't about you."

"You don't know that." The truth sits like bile at the back of my throat, needing to be expelled. "I've put you in danger with what I've done with the Costas."

His eyes scan me. Scrutinize. "Tell me everything."

"I can't." I'm too ashamed.

"Layla." His voice drops in warning. "Emmanuel has nothing to do with this. Neither do you. So whatever it is you're worried about, don't."

He's in denial. About me. About Emmanuel. I step back, needing to leave. To end this before I drown in him any further. But he holds me captive with his palms, matching my retreat with a bigger advance. He keeps us toe-to-toe, hip to hip, almost heart to heart, weakening me with his savior complex.

"The purse that was stolen from me in Denver had cyanide in it," I blurt, needing him to let me go. "If it got into the wrong hands, along with my ID, and the Costas caught wind of it…" I cringe, hating the shocked scowl peering back at me. "They'd know they were my target. They'd want to strike first."

He doesn't speak. Doesn't move.

It's only harsh eyes and harsher energy bearing down on me.

"Now will you let me go?"

"No," he repeats with steadfast conviction. "Downstairs had nothing to do with you. Lorenzo was the target. He's *always* the target. So if anyone is to blame, it's me for placing you in danger."

24

MATTHEW

This moment has been destined. It's only ever been a matter of time. And even though I've known it's been approaching since the moment we met, I'm far less prepared than I was the night she walked into my life all confident and magnificently mysterious.

"How do you know?" She blinks back at me, confused.

"He's a powerful man." I release her cheeks and retreat, needing a break from her scrutiny.

"How powerful?"

I wipe a rough hand down my face, becoming less ready for what's to come with each passing second.

I don't want her to deal with this now. I was meant to tell her in my own time. In my own way.

I huff a deep breath. "Powerful enough to—"

A pounding knock sounds at the door. She startles, gasping at the noise, exposing just how fragile my decisions have made her.

"Who is it?" I bark.

"Bishop," comes the mumbled reply. "Open the fucking door."

I stalk for the entry only to be stopped by Layla scrambling in front of me, her eyes stark with determination.

"Tell me." She splays her hands on my chest, her heavy palms feeble at best against my strength. "Who is he?"

I stiffen against the pent-up air in my lungs, the pressure of a lifetime's worth of bad decisions caging me behind tightening ribs. "Let me get rid of Bishop first."

Stall. Stall. Stall.

That's all I've fucking done with her.

Delayed the truth.

Delayed her disgust.

Delayed the end of us.

I step around her and stalk for the hall, checking the peephole to find Bishop's scowl before I yank the door open. "You're meant to be taking Lorenzo home to see his doctor. Why—"

"The old prick is still downstairs. He told me to take a hike. I'm not going to baby him."

I clench my teeth, battling against rage. They're both as prideful as each other. Both pains in my fucking ass. "He needs a doctor."

"He needs a lot of things, but mothering ain't my strong suit." Bishop juts his chin toward the inside of my suite and lowers his voice. "Nice mood lighting. It's almost as if you anticipated needing the romantic seduction to stop her from running."

I lash out, grabbing him by the throat.

I don't know if it's his audacity or the reaffirmation of her leaving that makes me snap.

He doesn't flinch. Not even when I shove him backward, walking us down the hall, away from her listening ears. The door clicks shut seconds later.

"Watch your goddamn mouth," I snarl.

He tilts his chin higher in defiance. "You need to get rid of her."

"I'm not doing that." My voice is barely a whisper as I keep stalking us farther from the suite, my fingers digging into his neck, my aggression impatient for him to retaliate so we can take this exchange to the next level. The one where I get to dispense all my anger through a mindless pummeling of fists and decimating impact.

"Then at least tell her the truth so she can see herself out."

"She won't leave me." I release him with a shove and step back, needing space from his smug grin.

We both know I'm full of shit.

She'll leave. She'll fucking sprint.

"We need to get back to D.C." He yanks at his lapels to straighten his jacket. "I'll get the helicopter organized—"

"No." I stand tall, denying him the most logical response to a targeted shooting. Now, more than ever, I need this isolation with Layla. These hours are necessary to explain everything she's going to demand to know. To convince her to remain at my side. "I'm not changing our plans. We're staying the night."

He scoffs. "And I'm supposed to what? Sit in the hall like a guard dog?"

"We don't need protection. We won't leave the room."

His eyes harden to conniving slits. "You're losing it, you know that, right? Everything we've worked for is going straight out the fucking window because of a piece of ass."

"You're wrong. She makes me better."

"Better?" He raises a taunting brow. "Is that what you call threatening to kill Lorenzo's guards if they don't listen to you over him? If I didn't know you better, I'd say you were gearing up to take the helm."

"Fuck you." My words thrash against clenched teeth.

"Touchy subject? Have you been thinking about it, BB?"

I see red, the hint to a forbidden nickname acting like a fire poker to my rage. "Do you want to die today?"

He grins. "There he is. The villain I know and love."

"Walk away," I warn.

"I'd fucking love to. Unfortunately, your dumb ass refuses to carry a gun. So I'm stuck protecting you. Protecting *her*." He steps forward, getting in my face. "You need to tell her the truth. Tell her what she's getting herself into. Tell her all the things you've hidden just so you can keep her like a fucking pet."

I'd been trying to. I'd had the confession on the tip of my tongue. I never envisaged misleading her this long. I just didn't plan on wanting her this much when I exposed the truth.

The tiniest squeak of a door filters down the hall. I turn to see Layla inching out of our suite, her wary eyes finding mine.

I step back from Bishop and cringe at my instinct to shield things from her. She deserves transparency—honesty—even though she hasn't offered it in return.

"Go back inside." I leash the aggression in my tone. "I'll be there in a minute."

The wariness grows in her stare as she glances from me to Bishop then back again.

"It's okay, *amore mio*. I won't be long."

Her chest rises with a deep breath beneath the tempting red sundress before she silently slips back inside, the door closing with a barely heard click.

"She may have a pretty face, but don't forget she's as fucked up as you are," Bishop mutters. "We don't need that shit in our lives."

A storm rages inside me. The energy batters my veins. Sneering. Demanding.

I close my eyes, reining it in, mastering the aggression.

He chuckles, the briefest breath of sound. "Look at you, trying to battle the inevitable. This is a waste—"

I lunge, grabbing his shirt in my fist. "Shut your fucking mouth." I struggle not to lose myself to the insanity. Fight not to shove my knuckles into my best friend's throat.

He doesn't retaliate. He's the only one armed, and all he does is raise his chin as if reiterating his point.

Fuck.

I retreat, releasing his shirt. "I'll fucking tell her." I turn my back on him before I do something I'll regret, and start for the suite. "Check on Lorenzo. I don't want to see your face again until he's been looked over by his doctor."

I reach the door and grab the key card from my jacket to swipe over the lock. I stalk into the shadowed room flickering in candle-light, the fury following me.

"What's going on, Matthew?"

Layla's voice increases my struggle, her trepidation creating guilt that whirlpools with my anger.

She stands in front of the sofa, her cell in her hand, the screen lighting up her face in the darkness. "What's Lorenzo's surname?"

Shit. She's searching for him online?

I stalk to her, stepping around the coffee table, making her stiffen as I get within reach.

Jesus fucking Christ.

She's questioning me again. Judging. Fearing.

Rightly so.

"What are you doing?" I slow my approach, cautiously reaching for her hand to tilt the cell screen my way.

Lorenzo Virginia Beach is typed into the search bar with a page of irrelevant results about some specialist doctor listed below.

"I want to know what's going on." She pulls the phone back toward her and locks the screen, the snuffed glow making her face shadowed. "I tried googling him but there are too many results in Virginia Beach."

I nod, teeth clenched, limbs thrumming.

Her gaze weighs heavily on me. Every blink of her lashes acts like a physical blow. "There's a lot to explain." But the explanation doesn't come. The truth refuses to slither from the darkest depths of my soul.

And this room isn't helping.

With the closed curtains and the mass of flickering candlelight, it feels like I'm in Satan's dungeon. And I've already spent too much time there to want to return.

I march to the window and yank back the heavy drapes, the burst of sunlight searing my eyes. Yet it's not enough to assuage my darkness. Not the beach or the sun or the sand.

I lunge for the closest candles and snuff them out. One after another, after another, after another. The scent of smoke wafts in the air, the threat of the fire alarm merely adding to the shitstorm inside me.

"Matthew…"

I pause with my back to her. Straighten. Succumb.

"Please tell me."

Her plea undoes me, my knotted threads unraveling.

I turn, finding her chin raised. She already knows the impending increase of seriousness in this already fucked up situation, and she's preparing to take it head on.

I wish I could laugh at the naivety of her conviction, but there's nothing funny here. Things between us never should've gone this far. I wasn't meant to get entangled.

Bishop knew she would be my undoing. He even explained the psychology behind why I'm drawn to her. *Obsessed* with her. And yet I still can't push past the mental trickery to let her go.

"Matthew?" Her eyes beg for me to ease her suffering. To break the torturous suspense.

She's such a fucking maze, some paths leading to dead ends, others harboring threats and misdeeds. I applaud her strength. Her tenacity. Her viciousness. But the cyanide admission threw me for a loop.

I guess we've both got bigger secrets than either of us led the other to believe.

"Please, Matthew. Tell me what's going on."

I release the toxic air eating at my lungs and slump my ass onto the coffee table, letting her tower above me. Rule over me.

"Before I met Lorenzo, I was homeless."

Her lips part at my admission, her stunning eyes widening.

"Through mistakes of my own, and sabotage from others, I lost everything. I had nobody. Not a penny to my name. Only the clothes on my back and a shitload of emotional baggage."

"How old were you?"

I scoff. Too young to be without a family and too old to be a sorry son of a bitch. "A few months from my eighteenth birthday."

Pity floods her expression. "Matthew, I—"

"Don't say anything. Just let me speak." *Let me explain all the things you're going to hate about me.* "Lorenzo took me in. Gave me a home. A purpose. An income. He provided an outlet for my teenage anger. Introduced me to Bishop. And helped me get where I am today."

She shuffles closer as if drawn by my pathetic story, her sandals bumping my shoes, her eyes filled with compassion.

"Everything I have is because of him," I continue. "Without his intervention, I have no doubt I would've died on the streets."

She remains quiet, letting me bleed parts of my truth, her hands reaching out to slide through my hair in delicate strokes.

"He became my father figure and treated me like another one of his sons—harsh when I needed it, but equally supportive when necessary. He invited me into his success and I helped him achieve more." I lower my gaze, focusing on the carpet, running my palms around her waist to stop her from escaping when the truth hits. "There's nothing I wouldn't have done for him."

"He sounds like a wonderful man," she whispers.

"He is," I say with conviction. "And he isn't."

Slowly she stands taller, her spine straightening in caution.

"To me, he's a savior. A lifeline." I look up at her. "He's the reason I still have air in my lungs. But he's not what most would call a wonderful man."

Her hands stop sweeping my hair. Trepidation ebbs from her.

Quiet seeps in, curling around us with tight arms and sharp claws. Her breathing slows, long and pained. She knows where this is going. She can sense it.

"You said you're not a good person, Layla. But in my past, I've done things in the name of survival that would chill you to the core. And I've done them all for Lorenzo."

Her hands slowly withdraw from my hair to rest at her sides, the retreat emotional as well as physical.

She doesn't ask the questions I know must be eating at her. She lets the silence fester between us, its thorny spikes digging into my skin, her panicked thoughts flashing in her wild eyes.

Maybe she no longer wants clarity.

Maybe she'd prefer to remain ignorant and leave my life without the darkness of the truth haunting her.

But it's too late for that.

I refuse to let her go.

"My mentor is Lorenzo Cappelletti," I admit, taking in the stark recognition that now stares back at me. "He's Italian mafia."

25

───────

LAYLA

I WAIT FOR THE PUNCHLINE. FOR THE CRUEL PRANK TO BE LAUGHED away so I can shed this second skin of shock and confusion.

But no humor gleams in his expression. There's not even the slightest sign of banter.

Instead, his expression begs for understanding. For forgiveness.

"You're in the Italian mafia?" The question is wrenched from my drying throat.

"No. I got out."

A mindless scoff escapes me before I can stop it. "You got out?"

"Yes." His shoulders slump, his handsome face losing the mask of confidence.

"I may not know a lot about the mafia," I lie. "But I'm pretty sure it's not something you can simply walk away from."

"There was nothing simple about it. I earned my freedom. Bishop did, too. We've been out for years."

That's not how it works. Is it?

Could other parts of the underworld let their members walk free? Are there ways to safeguard family secrets once someone defects? A strategy to stop competitors from targeting turncoats?

No, otherwise I would've fled long ago.

I step back, only to be kept close by the cage of Matthew's hands.

He strengthens his hold on my waist, firmly imprisoning me. "Don't walk out on me, *amore mio*. Give me time to explain."

"Stop calling me that." I push him away and stumble backward, bumping into the sofa, almost falling into the cushions before I can right myself to stagger farther.

He has no idea what he's done.

Being with him—an enemy—will singlehandedly destroy the already tattered relationship I have with my family.

They'll never forgive me for this.

"Why?" He stares at me through harsh hooded lashes, each bat of his eyes slaying me. "You *are* my love. My past doesn't change that."

"Your past changes everything," I whisper as madness overwhelms me. The questions. The stupidity. The shame.

How could I have made more mistakes? Created more complications for my brother? More and more mess that continues to compile, stealing the air from my lungs? And yet through the gasps for respite, some sickeningly, stupid part of me latches onto the tiniest glimmer of hope in his story—he got out.

He left the underworld.

He created a new life.

I walk on numb feet to the window, my gaze seeking the calm of the ocean. But the deep blue doesn't soothe me. My mind is in chaos. The sharp claws of panic shred the inside of my skull.

"I have more to tell you," he murmurs. "So much more. I want you to know everything. I want—"

"Why?" I beg, mostly of myself. "Why me? Why now? Why any of this?"

How could he make me fall in love with him when we can never be together?

How cruel can fate be?

"We're alike." He slowly rises to his feet, seeming even more handsome and commanding now that I have to walk away. "We have common enemies. We've contemplated similar crimes."

I frown.

"The cyanide," he clarifies. "Were you really going to use it?"

I snap my attention back to the ocean, wishing I hadn't made the confession. Realizing he could easily use the information against me. Against my family.

"Could you have killed someone, Layla?"

I keep my mouth shut. My lips fused.

He approaches, sidestepping the edge of the sofa in my periphery.

"Stop." I turn to face him, glaring. This is serious. I need to rewind time and remember all the things I've told him. All the clues I've given. All the insight I've shared. "Stay where you are."

His face falls. Plummets. And in the split-second of this powerful man's pained rejection, I see myself reflected in him.

I see the woman forsaken for the mistakes of her past. I see the person turned pariah due to circumstances out of their control.

"Just…" I attempt to shake my head free from the emotional onslaught. "Just give me a second."

I need to think. To understand. To do damage control.

"Layla, you're bleeding." His attention narrows on my hip, his expression transforming from devastation to concern. He strides forward, forcing me to scamper backward. "Don't fight me on this," he warns with an edge of malice. "Let me make sure you're okay. You mean so much to me. I—"

"You don't even know me."

He stops a foot away, his nostrils flaring. "*Yes*, I do."

I shake my head and glance at my dress, trying to see where the hell I'm bleeding from. "No, you don't." I twist, finding blood splotches that match the red fabric, the material nicked with tiny cuts along my side. "You have no idea."

"So everything between us was fake? Was it all for sex? For the lifestyle? For attention?"

I gape. "No, I never—"

"Then I know you. I know how I feel when I'm with you. I know how good we are together. How we fit. How we're perfectly matched. How we can hold a conversation for hours. And fuck until we're exhausted, but far from sated, because being with you means I'll never get enough." He bridges the space between us in an adamant step. "*That's* how I know you. And it's the only knowledge that matters."

His admission shakes me. Grabs me by the arms and rattles me to my bones.

I'd thought I'd known him, too.

I'd thought the knowledge I had was all that mattered. Now I'm painfully aware that's simply not true.

What he kept from me changes everything. It bends and twists the already stretched limbs I'd stepped out on to have this secret relationship in the first place. It makes the already unattainable nauseatingly impossible.

"Let me see why you're bleeding." He doesn't quit holding my gaze as he reaches out, fingering the material at my waist, bundling it in his hands.

My heart clenches, beating harder at his affection. At the weeks of deception.

"Why did you bring me here?" I blurt, unable to contain the mania.

His brows knit. "To Virginia Beach?"

"To the meeting. To the hotel. Why introduce me to Lorenzo? Why risk my life?"

"I didn't think there was any risk. Nobody has dared to target him in years. I never would've brought you otherwise." He keeps my dress bundled in his hands, his chin lifting. "I'm sick of the secrets, Layla. I wanted him to get to know you. I want you to know who I am."

My pulse weakens, my entire body withering.

I return my attention to the ocean, unable to voice a protest when he bundles more of my dress in his grip. Unwilling to deny his cautious affection. Powerless to walk away even though I know I have to.

I thought he was my safety vest in the midst of the pummeling waves of my life. Instead, he was nothing more than a mirage. Yet I still hunger to cling to the illusion. I continue to hope he'll save me from drowning despite him being just another shark in the water.

The hem of my dress rises from my ankles to my calves, then my thighs.

I hold my breath against the exposure. I clench every muscle against the judgment of my family snipping in my ears. Their recrimination. The fury.

But Matthew hasn't lost the calming touch. He soothes me. Provides solace.

How?

How can his proximity dilute the devastation of my situation? How can he—a man now exposed as having underworld ties —comfort me?

Because despite the darkness of his admission, he's the only support I've got.

The fabric creeps higher, exposing my lace panties, my bra. He keeps pulling the dress farther until it's over my shoulders and head, then lets the clothing fall into a pool of crimson on the carpet.

I close my eyes as he steps around me, his fingertips gently gliding from my shoulder to the ribs at my back, every inch of nurtured skin awakening in a blanket of goose bumps until his touch stops at my waist.

"You're covered in scratches," he murmurs. "None deep enough to require stitches, but too many for me to escape more guilt over bringing you here."

I battle inner turmoil as his fingertips trail intricate circles along the sensitive flesh at the small of my back, the beauty of his soothing contact tearing me to shreds.

"Forgive me." He closes in behind me, one hand still learning my injuries, the other arm taking liberties to skim around my waist to my stomach, holding me to him. "I've made mistakes." He speaks against my shoulder, his breath sending a shiver down my spine. "I'm not that person anymore."

A whimper tightens my throat.

I'm not the person I used to be either.

"Start a new life with me, Layla," he whispers my wishes into existence. My dreams. My hopes. "Be with me for who I am now. Not where I came from."

"Where you came from just had us ducking for cover." I turn to face him, finally able to ignore all the parts of me that want to disappear into the shelter of his arms. "You haven't moved on, Matthew. That life is still a part of you."

"No. I walked away from their—"

"How can you say that when Lorenzo was asking you to take over right in front of me? He was begging you to come back."

His jaw ticks with tension. "I'm next in line because his sons declined the offer. He's growing desperate. But I'll never go back."

"It seems to me that you're going back every time you meet with him."

"I've been out for years," he enunciates with slow adamance. "Bishop and I—"

"Yes, tell me about Bishop." I've never trusted that asshole. "If you wanted distance from your old life, why keep him with you?"

For a moment he's silent, perhaps biding his time.

"Matthew?" I raise a brow and snatch my dress from the floor, huddling it against my chest.

"He's with me out of misguided obligation. He thinks he owes me for getting him out."

"And how did you do that?"

"I did whatever I had to. I wasn't leaving without him."

His words say nothing, but I understand regardless. I know the sins. The darkness. The bloodshed.

The duties of underworld men aren't unfamiliar to me. I'm aware of the atrocities my brother inflicts on our enemies. Hunter, Decker, and Luca, too. And all the underlings that follow.

I was raised to believe an eye for an eye is for the nine-to-five crowd.

My family is different. If someone betrays the Torian name, the cost is high and lifelong. Not merely an eye, but the breaking of one's spirit. The shredding of their soul.

I don't want to see Matthew like that. I can't picture blood on his hands and hate in his heart.

I wrap my arms around my waist, unable to deny it any longer. "You've killed people."

His jaw ticks again. "I can admit I'm not without sin. Can you?"

"Excuse me?"

"What were you planning on doing with the Costas, Layla? Why were you carrying poison?"

"This isn't about me. We're—"

"Why not?" He cocks a brow. "We're one and the same. You might not want to tell me who you are, but the fact you haven't run a million times already says we're from similar worlds. We understand each other. We can make this work."

"Our similarities are what I'm trying to get away from."

"Me too." He runs a hand through his hair. "Me fucking too."

I hate this side of him. The frustration and suffering. It awakens a weakness in me I never knew existed.

"I wish we were different people." I drag my dress back over my head. "I wish for so many things, Matthew. A lot of them involving you. But—"

"Then stop right there." He decimates the space between us to grab my wrists, the red fabric falling to huddle at my hips as he tugs me into his chest. "We'll start fresh together. You, me, Stella." He inches forward, and I'm not sure if it's his words or his proximity that sends me into a tailspin. "I've never—"

"No. *You* stop." I splay a hand against his sternum in warning. "Don't—"

"I care too much to let you walk out on me, Layla."

I shake my head. Over and over and over.

These reactions. This craziness. None of it can go on.

"I didn't grow up planning to take a path toward a man like Lorenzo," he continues. "But every decision and every fucking mistake led me to the night we met. Every crime. Every unforgivable action brought me to you."

My veins hum with fear and anticipation. Panic and power.

I'm torn. Severed in two.

"It doesn't matter." I have to get home. To monotony and misery. Solitude and sadness.

Another knock sounds at the door, rattling the wood against the frame. I snap rigid at the intrusion as Matthew growls a curse.

"Who is it?" he barks.

"*Me,*" Bishop yells from the hall. "Who the fuck else are you expecting?"

Matthew doesn't move. Doesn't even loosen his hold. The only change is the flare of his nostrils as he glares at the entry. "I'll get rid of him."

26

LAYLA

I scramble to right my dress as Matthew stalks for the entry, the whoosh of the door soon following.

"I told you I didn't want to see you until Lorenzo was taken to the doctor," he growls.

"Relax," comes the arrogant reply. "He's on his way there now."

I hustle across the room, taking in the sight of Matthew at the door and Bishop scowling over his shoulder at me from the hall.

"Why didn't you go with him?" Matthew asks.

Bishop drags his gaze from me, his focus tight when he says, "Because I've got news."

There's a beat of silence. Of non-verbal communication.

"What news?" I interrupt. "I want to know what's going on."

The quiet continues, their silent communication lasting a muted microsecond before Matthew steps back, allowing his friend access to the suite.

My nemesis strides inside, his chin arrogantly high, his lips thin. He stops before the sofa and turns away from me to take off his suit jacket, exposing the gun buried in the back of his pants before he throws the item of clothing over the armrest.

It's a show. A deliberately theatrical intimidation.

I'm not buying tickets.

When he pivots to face me, I want to roll my eyes. To roll them so far in the back of my head I gag, but he doesn't need to know men like him are a dime a dozen where I'm from.

He descends to the sofa, spreading his arms along the headrest, crossing an ankle over his knee. He's attempting to appear superior and relaxed while I'm expected to cower and hide.

Not going to happen.

I want answers.

Matthew follows after him, his presence both comforting and daunting depending on whether I listen to my heart or my head.

"So…" Bishop drawls. "What's going on?"

"I told her." Matthew makes his way to the kitchenette, distancing himself as he scoots his ass onto the counter. He sits there, frustrated and remorseful, entirely focused on me while he leans forward in his immaculate suit, his elbows on his knees.

"Told her what exactly?" Bishop remains imperious as he watches me. Both of them attempting to slither their way under my skin for different reasons.

"That you're in the mafia." I cross my arms over my chest.

His eyes narrow. "We *were*," he growls. "That shit is ancient history."

Relief sparks a tiny flickering flame inside me. "You *were* in the mafia," I correct. "You earned your way out of that life somehow, but decided to stay together afterward. Why?"

"You didn't tell her the reason I stick around?" Bishop glances over his shoulder to the kitchen, but my lover's daunting attention doesn't leave me for a second.

"No, he didn't," I answer. Not really.

Bishop scoffs a laugh. "It's because Matty boy wants to receive his very own martyrdom status. I need to stay close so he doesn't obtain his title."

I frown, glancing from Bishop's smug expression to Matthew's cold one. "What does that mean?"

Are we talking about suicide?

"That's enough dramatics," Matthew mutters. "He's here for protection."

Bishop clears his throat louder than necessary. "If you were concerned about protection, you'd carry a gun."

"I said, that's enough."

The questions in my head multiply. There are so many more now than the millions I had before.

"Quit the look of defeat, darlin'." Bishop uncrosses his legs to kick his shoes onto the coffee table. "Your bad boy fix isn't going to end anytime soon. Not unless you finally start listening to my warnings. You should've walked when I pushed."

What? Had his aggression been for my benefit? To scare me away from all this?

"I didn't plan on dragging you into my life, *amore mio*." Matthew pinches the bridge of his nose. "You're the last thing I expected to find in Denver."

"I can attest to that," Bishop agrees. "Which brings us to the topic of the Costas and your association with them."

I cinch my arms tighter around my middle. "I think we have more pressing things to discuss, don't you? Like being shot at?"

"If you'd prefer to discuss blatant dangers first instead of those that are far more sinister in their subtlety, then that's fine with me." He shrugs. "Lorenzo sends his apologies. He understands the complications he must have caused between you and Matthew, and begs forgiveness."

"So he knew the attack was coming?" Matthew asks.

"No. He underestimated how hungry the local biker gangs are for power. There's a turf war over distribution, and Lorenzo refused to get involved. He wanted them to sort it out amongst themselves. Now he assumes this morning was a little nudge to let him know they'd prefer his involvement."

He relays the information as if it's week-old news. As if we hadn't just been in a life-threatening situation moments ago due to the drug trade.

I see through the tough-guy act, though. He'd been the first to shove to his feet when the threat arrived. He'd feared for Lorenzo and Matthew's lives, if not his own.

"He wanted you to know he's taken care of the police." He talks over his shoulder. "He spoke to them while I was downstairs and promised he was leaving to go see his doctor."

"Bullshit," Matthew mutters. "You know he won't."

"You might be right, but I'm not going to cup his balls while he takes a piss. If he goes, he goes. If he doesn't, that's not my fault. He's not our responsibility anymore."

Matthew takes the remark like a blow, his face momentarily sharpening as our eyes meet.

He's not *out*, no matter what he says. Maybe physically, but not emotionally.

"I still care for his well-being, Layla." He holds my gaze as he answers my unspoken thoughts. "That will never change."

"My boy has daddy issues." Bishop winks at me. "But who doesn't, right?"

My heart thuds a painful beat at how right he is. At how Matthew and I continue to have more things in common.

"Are you done?" Matthew pushes from the counter. "As much as I'm enjoying this provoking mood, if you've got no more information, it's time to fuck off."

"Touchy much?" Bishop shoves from the sofa to pull on his jacket. "Am I calling in the helicopter?"

"No. We're staying."

"Are we?" I scowl, making it obvious I don't appreciate the dictatorship.

"We're staying," he repeats. "You still have questions and we're not going anywhere until they're answered. If you want to walk out on me, you're going to do it with crystal clarity."

"I'm surprised she hasn't walked already." Bishop fixes his lapels and smirks at me. "Slow learner."

"Go to hell," I snap.

He snickers, breathing in my anger like a fine wine. Consuming it. "You're far too lippy for a woman who's just found herself in the middle of a gangland drug war." He starts for the hall, his gaze turning to Matthew. "Make sure you ask some questions of your own. If she's learning my secrets, I sure as hell want hers in return."

I fight against the need to stiffen as he continues for the door, leaving the suite without another word.

I should follow. Escape. Cut ties with the thin threads of hopeful possibility that have me pondering whether I could start over, fresh and renewed.

Matthew won't want me when he finds out who I really am.

Despite the instinctive connection between us, an enemy is still an enemy.

"Ask, Layla." Matthew approaches. "Whatever's on your mind, let it out."

"Whatever's on my mind?" I counter his steps, keeping the coffee table between us. "I can barely think straight."

He stops behind the sofa, clenching the headrest in both hands. "You've gotta start somewhere."

No, I don't. I shouldn't start at all.

I should walk. He knows it. I know it.

Lord knows my family would know it if they were privy to my latest phase of stupidity.

But curiosity and yearning tag team inside my chest, demanding answers.

I have to find out how far Matthew has distanced himself from his past. How he could've escaped the inescapable. And if he's truly sincere about a future between us.

If he's asking me not to judge, then maybe he won't judge in return.

He might not despise me for who I am and what I've done.

Then there's Lorenzo. If I'm going to return to Cole with my tail between my legs, the best option is to go back with information. Insight on the Italian mafia might soften my latest blow of shitty decisions.

The Cappellettis are a force.

Holy fucking shit.

The *Cappellettis.*

"What is it?" Matthew frowns. "What's wrong?"

All the blood drains from my face.

"Layla," he demands. "Fucking ask. Talk to me."

"Your mentor is Emmanuel Costa's brother-in-law." My voice is barely audible as a tremor takes over my limbs. How could I forget? How could he not have told me? After all this time, he kept his connection to the Costas a secret. "Is this a setup? Have you been playing me since the moment we met?"

"Stop. *No.*" His upper lip sneers. "My mentor is Emmanuel's enemy. They despise each other. Lorenzo can't stand the man his sister married. None of his brothers can."

I shake my head. This is too much.

Too many secrets.

Too heavy a reliance on trust that I never should've given.

Warning bells and calls for calm poison my blood, the warring toxicity increasing. I'd been happy with him. At home. I'd been empowered and invigorated and blissed.

And all this time, we'd both been lying. To ourselves. To each other.

He has no idea who he's introduced to his infamous mentor.

"I'm leaving." The words are a pained whisper over the bile at the back of my throat.

"Not like this you're not." He stalks toward the entry, preempting my escape. "Once I've answered all your questions and you have the information to make an informed—"

"This isn't merely about making an informed decision. No matter what you tell me, it won't change the fact I have secrets of my own. Secrets that make this situation worse than the hell it already is."

His face loses the tense edge. "I know you, Layla."

"You keep saying that, but you have no clue."

"You're wrong." His voice lowers, the edge of hostility replaced with a tone I can't describe. Pity? Regret? "I know who you are."

There's something different in his conviction this time. Something more pointed in his confidence over my character. Something capable of twisting mercilessly at my stomach.

My pulse increases. My panic, too.

I shake my head, ignoring his faith. Needing to brush it off.

"I know your name," he continues. "Your family. Your legacy."

I hold my breath.

He's bluffing. He has to be.

Only nothing but fortitude stares back at me.

A spike of panicked nausea rolls through me. "No."

If he knew, he never would've brought me here. Never would've introduced me to Lorenzo. Never would've said all those dreamy, optimistic things.

"Yes." He gives a somber smile. "You showed your ID to one of my bouncers. That was after Bishop had instructed them to take notes if someone matching your name and description showed up."

No. I keep shaking my head, denying my secrets have been his for what... days? Weeks? He knew all this time and didn't say anything?

"You're Layla Hart," he continues. "Sister to Cole Torian. Daughter to the infamous Luther Torian. And part of the notorious crime family that rules over Portland."

My shoulders hunch with the verbal blows that punch like a physical assault, but this time, it's not shock that overwhelms me. It's shame.

I didn't want him to find out about the sinister shadow cloaking me.

Bile sears the back of my throat, scarring, choking.

He'd known this whole time. During the lovemaking. Through the conversations and seduction.

"How could you?" The contents of my stomach surge for attention.

I stagger around the coffee table, dashing for the far hall, needing the bathroom. I shove open the closest door finding more candlelight in a room of darkness, the flames dancing from tea lights along a vanity and reflecting in the wall-to-wall mirror.

I scamper toward the faint hint of the toilet in the corner, falling to my knees beside the shower as coffee and croissants desert my body in rolling waves of dread.

I submit to the devastation. The loss of hope. The failure.

Each purge claws at me, scratching away parts of the fairy tale I never should've believed in but couldn't stop myself from falling for.

How could I have been so oblivious to the truth?

I continue purging until nothing but acid escapes. That's when I hear him entering the room, his footsteps approaching before he clatters something to the vanity beside me.

I want to scream for privacy. To yell at him to leave me to my destruction. But he moves closer, his hands finding my hair with gentle authority, pulling the errant strands away from my cheeks as more bile floods my lips.

"We'll work this out." He speaks with confidence.

I spit, clearing the dredge from my mouth. "Get out."

"I'm not going anywhere, *amore mio*. You're stuck with me."

His vow makes this worse. The caring hands. The affectionate determination.

I shrink away from him and reach over my head to flush the toilet. First shame, now humiliation. Add to that the stupidity and danger. The naivety and gullibility.

I've created a Molotov cocktail of mistakes. All I need now is to strike a match and let the flames take hold.

I pull myself to my feet, appreciating how he keeps his distance as I approach the sink that now holds company with my toiletry bag. I close my eyes briefly, thankful for his thoughtfulness and desperately despising the sensation at the same time.

How could he do this to me? How could he keep both secrets— his and mine—when alone they're problematic, but together they're catastrophic?

I retrieve my toothbrush without a word, cleansing my mouth of the humiliation while his gaze taunts the back of my neck.

I rinse and spit, rinse and spit, scrubbing the enamel from my teeth as if I were dislodging my mistakes. But no matter how hard I scour, he doesn't disappear, and neither does the romantic flickering firelight.

He remains quiet behind me until I turn to face him, broken, hollow, and defeated.

"How?" I croak. "How could you keep this from me?"

"It was no secret to either of us that we had things to hide. You wanted your privacy and I needed to keep mine until I figured out who you were."

"But you figured it out," I accuse. "You learned who I was days ago and never breathed a word of it. You never even acted differently."

He stares into my eyes, hard and strong and powerful. "I never acted differently because where you come from doesn't matter to me. It doesn't change a thing."

I scoff.

"And I didn't say anything," he continues, "because I held out hope you'd tell me yourself. I wanted you to trust me."

"Yet you knew exactly why I couldn't. There's a reason you

never gave me your truth either. I'm only learning it now because you were forced to confess."

"I wasn't forced to do anything. You don't think I could've convinced you your original assumption was right? That you were the target of the shooting? That the Costas were behind this?" He lowers to sit on the edge of the bathtub, his penetrating eyes all the more commanding in the candlelight. "I could've hidden for a lot longer. I could've hidden forever if I wanted. But I brought you here because I was done with the secrecy. Shooting or not, I would've told you who Lorenzo is before we returned to D.C."

Pain radiates beneath my sternum.

Burning, branding pain.

"Did you do it for information?" The question sears my throat. "To get insight on my family?"

"Fuck your family," he spits. "I said I was out, Layla. And despite knowing how much you love to question me, it's the fucking truth."

I want to deny him. To deny all of this.

I sink against the vanity, then slide to the floor, my ass planting on the cold tile.

"We both had our reasons to keep quiet, *amore mio*. There's nothing wrong with that. It doesn't mean what we have isn't real. I fell for you long before I found out who you are."

I swallow over the mint taste dominating my tongue, wishing I was somewhere else. *Anywhere* else... Yet somehow I still want to be here with him. To remain where attraction rules and affection flows.

"Well..." I lick the dryness from my lower lip, committing the sight of him to memory. "It was fun while it lasted, I guess."

He presses his mouth closed, the tilt of his chin swift as he narrows his stare.

"My family can't find out about this. I need you to let me walk out of here and pretend we never met." My heart squeezes with every word, hating their necessity.

"They can and they will. And I'll be right by your side when they do."

I whisper a pained laugh.

He continues to believe we have a future, and my heart wants to believe it, too. If only it were possible.

"No." I shake my head. "I'm begging you. You have no idea how my brother will treat me if he learns I've been sleeping with someone who worked for the Cappellettis."

"Lorenzo and Cole aren't enemies." He slides from the edge of the tub to sit on the tiled floor opposite me, bolstering my naivety with statements that simply aren't true. "As far as I know, they've never had anything to do with one another."

"Doesn't matter. Competition is competition. And stupidity is still stupidity."

"You say that as if either one of us had any control over this." He stretches one suit-covered leg toward me. I'm sure it's to test how jittery I am at the proximity. "Do you think I'd be here if I had the ability to walk away?"

"We're not star-crossed lovers, Matthew."

"Aren't we?" He raises a brow.

I'm not sure if he's being derisive or insane.

I glance away, hating how he makes me feel warm through the icy chill of reality. We're not star-crossed anything. No matter how much I crave the opposite.

"You're mine." He leans over, grabbing my ankles to slide me forward between his open legs, my dress bunching beneath me. "I'm yours."

"Don't." I plaster my hands to the tile. His thighs cage me. His chest is within reach. "I'm not doing this with you."

"You have no choice. You walk, I follow. We won't be apart."

I glare. "How predatory."

"It would be if you didn't crave me, too, Layla. If you didn't want this, I'd let you leave. But you do. And I won't allow you to give up on something we both want just because of what your brother may say or do."

"My brother may say or do something that puts you six feet under. Do you understand that?"

"I have no issue with Cole and he has no need to have one with me. If he wants his sister to be happy, he'll give us his blessing."

I scoff. "It's not that simple."

"It can be."

"No. I let down my guard when I shouldn't have. He doesn't even know I was in Denver. That I was watching the Costas. He'll think you're trying to get information through me. That you could be—"

"I could be doing a lot of things, but I'm not." He cups my cheeks in his heated palms, demanding I believe him with an expression that bleeds sincerity. "I don't want to be anywhere near that lifestyle anymore. I don't need money. The only thing I want from your family is you."

No. This isn't how it works.

I make mistakes and I pay for them. I don't win prizes. I don't come out in front. I bleed and burn and ache. I suffer and agonize and endure.

This misplaced longing and hope has no right to be inside my chest.

"I didn't want to become distracted by you." His thumb strokes my cheek. "I didn't want any of this. But I'll be damned if I give it up."

I wince, believing him with every ragged beat in my chest. Succumbing. Yet I still know so little. I need more information. "How long had you been homeless?"

His face falls. In a blink, he's defensive and inching away to rest back against the tub, his palms falling from my face. "Not long. A few months. Maybe more."

"You don't remember?

"I remember enough... It's—" He huffs a sigh. "Give me a minute."

He shoves to his feet and stalks for the hall, his loud footsteps echoing into the living room momentarily before returning. This time, he enters the bathroom with the contents of the hotel minibar in his hands. "This conversation requires alcohol."

He reclaims his position a breath in front of me, dumping the liquor bottles to then grab my waist and deposit me on his lap.

"Matthew." My protest is weak as I clutch his shoulder. If I had any chance of leaving it was before proximity set in. It needed to be prior to the chemistry shift and the attraction deluge.

"What?" He taunts me with a raised brow and snatches the tiny scotch bottle from the tile, unscrews the lid then takes a gulp. "In answer to your question—" He takes another mouthful. "—I'm not sure exactly how long I was homeless because I try my best to forget."

I steel myself against the empathy. Against agony.

"I spent frozen nights under bridges and inside dumpsters. Then I started breaking into cars to have somewhere clean to sleep. It didn't take long to start cashing them in for drugs and booze, which is how Lorenzo found me." He finishes the remainder of the scotch and drops the bottle, the plastic bouncing against the tile. "Apparently, I'd built a name for myself for being the sorry son of a bitch who was smart enough to hot-wire a car, but too self-destructive to find himself a safe place to stay."

My muscles tense, every inch. "Are you still using?"

"Hell no. Back then I was a stupid teenage kid, and I was suffering." He holds my gaze, his face tense. "Prior to losing everything, I had a girlfriend, Layla. A beautiful, happy, and motivated girl who made my shitty family life livable. We had plans to skip town together. To start fresh."

Dread creeps into my veins, the horrible sense of foreboding suffusing me.

"But she..." He pauses, scrunching his nose in anger, his brows slicing in vicious strokes. "She died."

My heart creeps into my throat, the tightness cutting off air. "I'm sorry."

He grabs for another liquor bottle and cracks the lid. "It was a long time ago. But in the moment, she was all I had. I adored everything about her. Her smile. Her laugh. Her light... then that light was gone and my grief became rage."

I have no words. And I've suffered through enough unwanted placations and anecdotes about loss since Benji's death to know silence is a far kinder response. All I can do is blink at him through burning eyes and hope he understands my support.

"So Lorenzo's generosity wasn't only a home for the homeless," he continues. "It was a distraction for the crazed. Not to mention stability and power for someone obsessed with revenge."

"Revenge?"

His lips flatten in a tight line, his free hand tangling in the material of my dress. "Grace was murdered."

I close my eyes, his pained journey hitting too close to home.

I always knew we were one and the same. Two people from different parts of the country living such similar lives it hurt. Now it's so much more than that.

We've traveled an identical path. Climbed equivalent mountains. Battled the same enemies.

His indoctrination into the mafia seems understandable now. Acceptable. And the fact he got out... I shake my head, overwhelmed with admiration. Burning from it. Blistering with the need to whisper my support.

I reach for the liquor bottle. His strong fingers let go of the prize to allow me to take a gulp. The burn of vodka hits my tongue, my throat, then sears its way into my empty stomach.

I want to tell him I understand. That I *know* how he must have felt. But instead, a question seeks supremacy, bubbling from my lips. "Do you know who killed her?"

"I do." He nods. Succinct. "I'll give you one guess."

27

———

LAYLA

"EMMANUEL KILLED HER?" THE QUESTION TEARS UP MY THROAT.

Matthew nods.

His revelation only makes our paths more entwined. It's him and me. There's not a soul in the world who could understand what we've both been through. Only us.

"Does Lorenzo know?" I ask.

"Yes. My hatred wasn't something I could hide."

"But you've never..." I let the sentence fall short.

He's been in the same room with his girlfriend's murderer. He watches him. Stalks him. How can he not react?

"There isn't a day when I don't think about ending his life," he confesses. "But as you know, there are rules. Lorenzo might despise his brother-in-law, but the man is still his sister's husband. He's not to be touched."

"So you keep an eye on him instead."

"I snoop to find things I can sabotage." He reclaims the vodka and finishes the bottle. "Being unable to physically hurt him doesn't mean I don't do it financially."

I lower my gaze to his chest, attempting to relive every moment we've had together in the hopes of understanding. Not only the implication, but what this all means for me and my plans.

"What are you thinking?" The alcohol on his breath brushes my lips, filling my lungs, intoxicating me. "What did I say this time?"

Is it wrong to still be here? To still want to make this work despite the strangling complications?

God.

My head screams with indecision. My heart yearns to salvage the unsalvageable.

"Layla?" He drops the second bottle to the tiles, his fingers finding the sensitive skin below my chin to gently lift my face to his. "Talk."

"Explain how this all started," I whisper. "How we met. What was going through your head. Were you trying to manage the threat I posed toward the Costas? Have you kept me close because I can achieve the things you can't? Or because you've needed to distract me from my plans?"

Because I've been distracted.

Entirely.

Completely.

I inch back, needing space, only to be fastened in place against his lap by strong hands clutching my waist. "Are you with me for a purpose?"

"Would you consider greed a purpose? Indulgence? I'm with you for no other reason than my own selfish desire." He stares at me, unblinking. "You intrigued me from the first night we met. You became *my* distraction. Then an obsession. And even after I found out you were a complication, and a potential threat, I still wanted more."

He leans closer, the heat of his mouth breaching my own as he reclaims my cheeks with his palms. "I haven't fallen for anyone since Grace, Layla. I've fucked, but never fallen. Not even close, until you."

His spiel sinks under my skin, the tendrils of hunger and longing infusing me with more delicious hope.

"I want you," he murmurs, harsh and low. "I need you."

He speaks to my weaknesses. My insecurities.

I've never been wanted. Not by lovers. Not even my late husband.

Being needed is just as foreign. My daughter doesn't require her mother anymore. She moved on effortlessly, already growing independent at such a young age.

There's only Matthew.

Only the man I shouldn't desire, but do with a level of force that's beyond my control.

"I had to agree Emmanuel would remain untouched if I wanted to leave my previous life behind. The same goes for his wife and children." He adds pressure to my waist, slowly dragging me closer into him. "Those rules will always remain in place, hanging like a noose if I break them."

"What happens if you defy the rules?"

"Then I'd owe Lorenzo a debt. I'd be his again. With no way out this time."

"And if I break the rules while we're together?" I whisper.

"I don't know." He holds my gaze, unblinking. "It's a grey area. Especially when I don't understand your connection to the Costas."

I'm not willing to give him that insight.

Not yet.

"You should've left me alone, Matthew. I would've done your dirty work for you. We both could've got what we wanted."

"I have what I want," he growls. "Don't you?"

He can't ask me that.

He can't possibly understand what it would mean to choose him, not only forsaking revenge, but my family, too.

I lower my attention to his shirt buttons, itching to unfasten them and press my skin to his. I've grown tired of words. I need more. Something to tether this wildness inside me. Something to dissolve the doubt.

"Do you really want them dead?" he murmurs. "Was that the plan?"

I don't know anymore. I don't know anything.

The loss of Grace should cement my bloodlust. Instead, I'm fearful of the cost my actions might inflict upon the man I'm growing to admire.

A sinner with the control of a saint.

"Which one of them hurt you?" He runs his thumbs along my hips, gently coaxing. "What did they do?"

"You didn't dig that deep into my life?"

"Bishop tried. He couldn't find a connection."

He uncovered my name. My reputation. My family's sins, but not the circumstances surrounding my husband's death or my child's abduction. *Good.* That means Cole's cover-up is tight. Not that I ever had any doubts.

I slide a fingertip over his top button, my gaze trekking the movement. "I'm not ready to share."

But I have to make a choice.

I've reached the peak of this mountain. There are only two courses of action to take. I can return to the protection of where I came from, living a life where I'm judged and loathed. Or I can take the last step off the cliff, plunging myself into an abyss of recklessness and potential bliss.

Safety and sadness.

Or risk and the possibility of emotional reward.

"I need to think first." My heart thunders a frantic beat.

I have to decide if I'm going to choose Matthew over my family.

To pick him instead of revenge. Can I choose this gloriously secretive man, with his adamance and determination, in place of everything I've ever known and relied on? Can I step toward something that scares the absolute hell out of me?

I glance up at him, desperate to read his thoughts as those dark eyes hold mine.

He drags me closer, forcing my knees to spread around his waist, the material of my dress hitching to the top of my thighs. "We need to discuss it, *amore mio.*"

"I know."

"Soon."

I nod. "But not now."

His palms add pressure, pressing my crotch into the hard length hidden beneath his zipper. I gasp at the contact, hypersensitive and hungry.

Things are different now. Cautious. Intense.

Yet the underlying energy between us is stronger. The attraction more fierce.

Every inch of me vibrates for him. It hurts to breathe. To refrain from all the luscious thoughts that shouldn't fester at a time like this.

It's as if one spark against the kindling of our magnetism will ignite an inferno I'll never control. A passionate explosion of lips and hands and spirit.

Flames flicker in his eyes, the hellish severity enough to cause arrhythmia.

"You'll learn to trust me, Layla." He grinds into me, the friction grazing my clit. "Give it time." He leans closer, his stubble brushing my cheek as he speaks near my ear. "Until then, let me atone for the secrecy." A hand slides to my thigh, his calloused palm delving beneath the pool of material at my crotch. "Let me show you how much I need you."

There he goes again with the need.

The want.

The necessity.

I may willingly succumb to him, but his yearning for me makes me soar. Fly. Free fall.

He slides his fingers beneath the elastic of my panties, skimming my clit before moving farther to part my folds.

"I won't lose you," he grates into my hair. "Not over issues that are out of our control." His lips find my neck. "There are too many things I want to do to you."

"Then do them."

"My pleasure." In a jerk of movement, his hand leaves my flesh. He shoves off the tiles, holding me in his arms to take me with him.

I clutch his shoulders, my legs tight around his waist as he takes three steps and plants my back against the freezing tiled wall. Our lips meet. Our teeth. Our tongues.

He turns rabid, devouring me. His hands on my body. His breath in my lungs.

I gasp. Cling. Claw.

I fight to unfasten his buttons only to be stopped when he hefts my dress over my shoulders. He throws the material to the floor, his hips strong and adamant against mine, his lips finding my neck.

He licks. Sucks. Bites.

One hand circles my nape. The other finds my hip. Both dig deep into flesh, possessing, demanding, while his cock teases my clit through my panties.

"We've got more to discuss." His voice vibrates against my skin. "It won't be easy."

I nod.

I know.

From his life *and* mine.

But the world can wait.

I need respite from the revelations. To have him against me, on top of me, inside me. Each moment is a reminder of why I took this risk in the first place. "For now, all I need to know is that this is real."

"It's fucking real." He digs his fingers harder into my skin. Pleasure and pain. Animal and man. "It always has been."

I ignore Cole's disagreement whispering through my mind.

Keira's denials, too.

The voices have to stop.

"Fuck me." I grind into him, whimpering as clit meets cock. "Hurry."

He pulls back, his eyes narrow, as if noting my first significant instance of sexual confidence.

I shove the jacket from his shoulders and rip at his shirt. Rabid. Starved for more.

He keeps watching, keeps stalking me with his gaze.

"What?" My cheeks heat under his scrutiny. "Why did you stop?"

"Because hearing those words is beyond a fucking turn-on," he growls. "Keep going, *amore mio*. Tell me exactly what you want."

Heat blazes down my neck. "Jesus Christ." I fist the hair at his nape and yank his face to mine. "Just fuck me."

He grins. "Don't worry. I will." He licks my lower lip, following it with a bite of teeth. "Within an inch of your life."

My pussy flutters, tingling and tight.

He smothers his mouth against mine and undoes his zipper while leveraging me against the cold tiles.

He doesn't take off his pants. Doesn't remove my underwear.

One minute, he's consuming me with kisses—the next, he's ripping the lace apart at my crotch and shoving his dick home.

I cry out as I'm filled, the walls of my pussy exquisitely stretching to accommodate his girth.

Fuck.

He's brilliant.

Perfect.

He pulls back, pressing our foreheads together as he thrusts into me. "You're mine."

"I'm yours."

He growls in approval, the vibration thrumming into my chest. "I'll never lose you."

My heart pangs.

I can't reciprocate. Not this time. Not without lying.

"Say it." He keeps plunging his cock into me. Harder. Faster. More punishing. "Tell me I'll never lose you."

"Matthew…"

"Tell me," he demands.

I'm on the cliff's ledge, arms hesitantly open, heart painfully fragile.

I can't leap. Can I?

"All that I have is yours, *amore mio*. The money. The assets." He steals my lips, punishing me with a rough kiss. "But you're mine. I won't lose you."

I cup his cheeks, my closed eyes burning as I nod.

I don't have a chance to contemplate the severity of my capitulation before he drags me from the wall with strong hands on my hips, his dick remaining inside me as he walks us to the bedroom across the hall.

The space is bathed in darkness, the only light coming from more candles on the nightstands.

He places me on the bed, decimating our connection when he descends to his knees, grabs my ankles, and drags me in one rough slide to the edge of the mattress.

I struggle to catch my breath as those forceful hands yank at the waistband of my shredded panties, dragging the elastic to fall to the floor. My legs are plastered wide, my sex on full display when he swoops in to plant his mouth directly over my pussy.

I jolt with the contact, the sudden rush of lips and tongue not merely kissing, but utterly ravaging.

His fingers dig into my thighs, the appreciative rumble from his throat vibrating deep in my core.

I grasp the bed coverings, wiggling my ass for more. "Matthew…"

I want to tell him how I feel. How I hurt and yearn and crave for this to be real. *Truly* real.

For the possibility of living without recrimination to be something other than a fairy tale. For this paradise to be more than an illusion.

"I need you, too," I admit. "I need you too much."

His growl turns to an animalistic snarl, his mouth rising to latch on to my clit. He sucks, flicking the sensitive nerves with his tongue while two fingers plunge inside me, curling into my G-spot.

I struggle for breath, my core snapping tight around his digits, the pleasure infusing me all the way to my toes.

But he's too far away.

I need skin to skin. To touch instead of being touched. To give pleasure instead of merely receiving it.

"I want you inside me." I strangle the bed coverings, my legs squeezing around him.

"I'm not even close to being done here."

"Matthew." His name is panted from my drying lips. "Don't deny me."

He pauses, edging backward, his stubble scratching my inner thighs. "I'd never fucking deny you." He rises to his feet, roughly shucks his pants, then crawls on top of me. "My mouth not good enough for you, *amore mio*?"

"Your mouth is divine." I grab him around the nape and drag him closer, licking his lips in a quick tease, tasting my own arousal. "But I want to be close. I don't want space between us."

He grinds his hips as his nostrils flare, the tip of his cock edging into me. "No space. No lies. No secrets."

I nod, not knowing what I'm agreeing to as my teeth dig into my lower lip.

All I understand is hunger. Desire. Demand.

He nudges farther, sinking deeper. My core clamps around him as soon as he's fully seated inside me. I'm already so close. The heat in his eyes undoes me.

I could come.

From his gaze alone, I could splinter.

"You're ready." He grins, backing out gradually, before sinking in equally slowly. "*Amore mio* wants to come."

I mewl, raising my hips to meet his, silently pleading for him to move faster.

"Tell me what you want."

"You," I pant.

He clucks his tongue. "You know that's not what I meant."

I whimper, my cheeks regaining the heat of unease. "Fuck me."

He increases his pace a fraction. "How?"

"Hard," I beg, kicking off my sandals. "Fuck me hard... Please... Hurry."

"All you had to do is ask." He slams into me, jolting me farther along the bed. "I'll fuck you as hard as you want." He thrusts into me, over and over. Stronger and more ruthless. "I'll fuck you until you can't see straight and neither of us can walk."

Again and again he plunges, each slam pushing me closer to the edge of no return.

"And I'll still want more," he pledges. "I'll never get enough."

I come undone, every inch of me pulsing, the waves of my orgasm consuming me.

I sink my nails into his shoulders, command his mouth to mine.

We kiss as the pleasure sets my chest on fire and gives my heart wings. Over and over he bucks into me, our legs knocking, my pussy throbbing.

I don't breathe until the tide recedes. Don't acknowledge consciousness until he stops moving and leans up on one arm to stare down at me with cocky arrogance.

"Are we done?" I tease.

He raises a brow. "I thought I made it clear we'll never be done." His free hand slides around my neck, holding me in a possessive grip. "Not today or tomorrow. You're stuck with me."

I want to be stuck.

Unequivocally. Emphatically.

His hips retreat, moving back until only the head of his cock breaches me. "This tight little pussy is mine." He slams home, harsh and unyielding, sinking to the hilt.

My back arches with renewed pleasure, my chest rising to brush against his.

"These tits…" He pays my breasts homage. Rough, ferocious kisses. Harsh, punishing sucks. "All mine."

He plunges harder. Unrelenting.

More.

And more.

And so much *more*.

"That's not all." His hand releases my neck, his palm sliding down my body and around my hip. "This fucking ass is mine, too."

I shudder with the words. Pulse with the deep dig of his fingers into my meaty flesh.

I wrap my legs around his waist. Lick my lips. Fight against the burn in my nipples.

"I'm going to fuck you there, *amore mio*," he promises, carnal and severe. "I'm going to stretch that perfect little ass and make it hurt so damn good."

Oh… My… God.

I come undone again. My imagination succumbs to his filth. My pussy enjoys the ever-loving fuck out of it.

I moan with bliss. Close my eyes. Clamp my core.

"*Fuck.*" He pistons inside me, following me into mindlessness. "Fuck this perfect little cunt."

I whimper. Exhausted. Tired. And entirely helpless against the shudders still wracking me.

He pumps harder, his fingers digging.

The pain is intense. The pleasure is incredible.

"Goddamn you, Layla," he roars.

Those hips buck once. Twice. His seed fills me until finally, he crashes down upon me, deftly dragging me to my side so his weight rests into the mattress.

We stare, breathing each other's liquor-tainted air, our bodies joined, the candlelight dancing over our skin.

I wait for morality to nip at my heels. To bite and punish and scar.

Nothing comes.

I remain shrouded in bliss, my gaze entranced by the man who owns my heart, my head free from criticism—at least for now.

I run my fingertips along the scratch marks I left on his chest. "When did you organize the candles and food?"

"This morning, while you were in the shower." His lips curve. "But I wasn't entirely responsible."

I raise a questioning brow.

"I texted Bishop. He called the hotel to make arrangements."

"Bishop?" His name leaves my mouth with incredulity.

"Yeah, Bishop." He grabs my wrist with a gentle hand and raises my knuckles to his lips. "He's cooperative when he wants to be."

"And a bastard the rest of the time," I mutter.

"Not always. He actually likes you."

I scoff. "We're both good at lying, Matthew, but you didn't come close to pulling that one off."

"No more lies, *amore mio*. I promise his caustic exterior is just for show. He didn't want you getting messed up in our world. Then, when he found out you were already in the thick of it, he tried to convince me to cut you loose to save you from complications."

"I'm still not buying it." I inch closer, snuggling into his side, sliding my thigh between his. "But I don't need to. I'm here for you, not him."

"Just as long as you know he's no threat." He places a kiss to my forehead. "He's all talk when it comes to you."

I stew on his words, unsure what they mean yet unwilling to ask.

We lie there for long moments, his arm sliding around my shoulders to keep me close, my fingers drawing invisible pictures on the muscles of his chest.

My mind drifts to our earlier conversation, the revelations slowly creeping back in. "Why don't you carry a gun?"

He stiffens. It's only slight—the mere tweak of corded sinew. "I've got my reasons."

Matty boy wants to earn his very own martyrdom status.

"Tell me one," I urge.

Just one. Any one. Even the briefest glimpse of the unknown will tide me over until we're both comfortable enough to discuss this further.

"Normal people don't carry guns," he mutters.

"But normal people don't have a past they need to be protected from."

He doesn't respond. There's only thickening silence between us.

"Didn't people come after you?" I pull back and raise onto my elbow, needing to see his face. "I assume you would've been a target for anyone wanting intel on the Cappellettis."

"Nobody came after me." He rolls onto his back to stare at the ceiling, shutting me out.

"Nobody? Not even one person? Not an enemy or a competitor? Not even someone who felt you abandoned your position?"

His eyes harden, his nose wrinkling at my heartlessness.

"I'm sorry," I whisper. "I didn't mean to say—"

"No, you're right." He sits, my hand falling from his chest, his back turning so I can no longer read his face. "I did abandon Lorenzo. But just like Emmanuel, I'm off-limits. Nobody would dare to touch me unless they wanted a fast-track ticket to death's door."

I grab at the bed coverings, dragging them to my chest in a makeshift shield against his sterility. "People always dare. Aren't you worried about the one in a million who's willing to cross the line?"

"No. I don't like guns and I don't need one. I don't know what else to tell you."

I cling to the covers.

The floodgates on information are going to be harder to open than I'd thought. "What about the suicide comment from Bishop? What did he mean?"

He huffs a sigh. "He was being a dick."

"I don't think so. He said it for a reason."

"He's jealous." He pushes from the bed, gloriously naked, his ass perfectly defined. "We worked hard to build a new life. One without violence. And then you came along."

"And I brought violence?" I follow him to my feet, standing tall at the edge of the bed. "I thought we weren't lying to each other anymore?"

His nostrils flare. Fingers twitch.

"Matthew?"

"Jesus Christ." He shoves a hand through his hair. "He's pissed, okay? Pissed at me. Not you."

"Why?"

Muscles flicker under his stubbled jaw.

"Why?" I demand.

"Because he knows I'd give my life to make sure you don't end up like Grace."

I straighten. Stiffen.

"He knows I would die for you." His eyes harden with the admission. "Either by Emmanuel's actions or by going back to work for Lorenzo, and he fucking hates it. But if that's the price I have to pay, so be it. I won't lose you."

28

LAYLA

"Did you grow up in D.C?" I stare at Matthew sitting behind the wheel of our luxurious rental, his sunglasses hiding his eyes.

"No. I moved there to start over."

"Once you stopped working for Lorenzo?"

He nods, keeping his gaze on the road.

Yesterday came and went in a blur of emotional overload. After the shooting, then the sex, we spent the rest of the day in a weird state of hesitant conversation.

Although the embargo on information has been trampled, it's clear we both find it hard to open up. I'd share a tidbit about my life, something insignificant and trivial, then he'd do the same.

He told me he had good grades in school. Lost his virginity to Grace. Played football. And planned to buy another club next month in Philadelphia. But I still don't really *know* his past, and the same has to be said for him with me.

I haven't told him why I hate the Costas. He hasn't divulged the work he did for Lorenzo. Secrets still linger between us. The only thing we successfully achieved was a strengthened physical bond.

We laid in bed for hours, naked and sweaty, doing with our bodies what we couldn't with our minds.

He touched me everywhere, learning every curve, committing all my sensitive spots to memory. And I did the same with him. We showered and ate, then repeated the loop all over again, adding glimpses of insight when quiet sank in, and contemplating the future when the truth became too hard.

Full disclosure will take time. And until that happens, there's chemistry to rely on.

I can't even look at him without tingling between my thighs.

That mouth has tasted every part of me. Those strong fingers have delved into parts I never knew existed.

This morning, we left the hotel without police intervention.

As Lorenzo promised, nobody questioned us about the shooting. Hotel staff didn't mention the events, either. The only telltale sign that anything happened were the contractors working on the damage.

It was Matthew's idea to arrange the rental car and drive to D.C. without Bishop as a third wheel. And I've spent the long hours on the road staring at my lover's profile, our fingers entwined on the gearstick, my heart fully owned by a man I know wholeheartedly and don't have the slightest understanding of at the same time.

"You're always checking your phone," he murmurs. "Have you spoken to your brother about us yet?"

I slide the cell under my leg and glance out the windscreen. "You know I haven't."

"Will you tell me before you do? I'd like to know when I should be pulling the Kevlar from the dresser."

I whisper a laugh, but pain stabs through me.

Cole won't understand what I have with Matthew. Not even when he fell for someone equally problematic.

"I'll call him tomorrow and feed him whatever information necessary to keep him off my back. But I won't be telling him about us for a while."

He squeezes my fingers, giving me support in the most subtle of ways.

"I want to keep you to myself for a little longer." I drag our entwined hands into my lap. "Is that okay?"

"It's not only okay, it's a preference. We should figure ourselves out before anyone else gets involved."

Figuring ourselves out means full disclosure.

That could take days. Maybe weeks.

I'm not sure I can ignore my brother that long. I'll try though.

As it is, Cole calls three times on the journey back to D.C. and texts twice. But the only person I reply to is Stella. I check in to make sure she's doing her homework and eating properly. Then I ask about her nightmares and the latest visit with her counselor, because here I am, living wild and free, while she continues to suffer for my mistakes.

When we arrive at the penthouse, Matthew drags our suitcase into his bedroom, discarding it at the door to his walk-in robe before pulling me against his chest. "You're quiet."

"I'm contemplative." I paste on a smile. "There's a lot to think about."

"And we still need to talk." He guides an errant strand of hair behind my ear. "We should've done it in the car, but you've been so damn quiet. One word from me and I expect you to run."

"I don't have my running shoes on."

He flashes a grin at my lame humor, the expression quickly fading. "When are we going to do this, *amore mio*?"

I don't know.

I don't want to start counting down the minutes before he starts to look at me with judgment for my role in the Costas' actions instead of the constant admiration I'm used to.

He knows what our world demands of us. He, more than normal people, will understand how low I stooped to help my father.

"Tonight?" I hedge.

His brows pull tight. "I have to work. There are loose ends from the shooting that I have to chase up."

"What loose ends?"

"I haven't heard from Lorenzo. I need to make sure everything is under control."

"You can't do that here?" I don't want to be alone tonight. Tomorrow, maybe. But not now.

"This isn't like you." His eyes narrow. "What's going on?"

"Nothing." I step back, pasting on a smile. "I just assumed you'd be home, that's all. We can talk tomorrow."

I ignore the hollowness growing beneath my sternum.

I already understand the types of things Matthew would've done for Lorenzo. The intimidation. The threats. The violence. We both have a past that's unkind. But will my sins outweigh his? What I did was personal. In comparison, his brutality would've been sterile and strategic. A necessity instead of self-fulfilling.

"You're worried." His attention doesn't soften. He stares, reading me, his intense observation sinking under my skin.

"I'm tired."

"Whose fault is that?" He grabs my wrist and drags me back into his chest. "You do nothing to discourage my hunger. But you're also lying because you still don't want to talk, do you?"

I contemplate another lie.

"What part of it is the problem?" He holds me close. "You don't want to discuss your family or your connection to the Costas?"

I don't want to discuss any of it. Not one single part of my existence before he entered my life.

I keep my mouth shut, unsure how to respond when his cell vibrates in his jacket.

"Shit." He releases me and pulls out the device. "It's Lorenzo. I need to take this."

A hard kiss is plastered to my lips before he strides across the room, answering the call as he shoves open the balcony door to step outside. He greets his mentor in pristine Italian, the words turning to murmurs once he closes the door behind him.

I watch him pace, the late afternoon sun gleaming in his dark hair, the glow kissing his tanned skin while I unpack the suitcase. Every minute of conversation adds a new notch to his stiffened posture. An increased hike to the confident set of his chin.

When he walks back inside, the placating smile he gives me is pitiful. "I need to get to Trend earlier than anticipated."

"Is something wrong?"

"Just loose ends."

"I thought you didn't work for him anymore."

"I don't," he grates. "Lorenzo heard there was footage of the shooting. Someone uploaded it to social media. It's already been taken down, but I want to make sure there isn't a trace left behind."

My pulse kicks. "What kind of footage?"

"A blurry twenty-second snapshot. It isn't a big deal."

"You're pacifying me." I can see it in his eyes. He isn't giving me the full story.

"No, I'm not. It's been taken down. It didn't gain traction and wasn't picked up by journalists."

"But we were in it, weren't we? You can see our faces." There's evidence I was with my family's competition when a shooting happened. "I need to call Cole."

"What you need to do is be rational. Involving him will only cause complications." He walks up to me, gliding an arm around my waist. "Let me handle it. If things escalate, which they won't, then you can call him."

"If word gets back to him—"

"Word won't get back. Lorenzo handled the cops. He's had the video taken down. People don't care about another drive-by shooting, especially when nobody got hurt. It's not big news." He leans in, his lips close to mine. "I just want to make sure it remains that way. Okay? It's only a precaution."

I close my eyes, letting his mouth ease my concerns as he kisses me possessively.

"I'll be home late. I'll try not to wake you." He walks from the room, leaving me in a silent penthouse that grows more desolate by the hour.

I order takeout for an early dinner. Shower. Stalk my phone.

When night falls, I help myself to Matthew's liquor cabinet to ease the constant simmer of apprehension.

I text him for an update before I go to bed. He placates me immediately, pretending everything is peachy when I'm certain nothing could be further from the truth.

But when he arrives home after midnight, his naked body finding mine under the covers, the reconnection of our bodies makes the worries disappear.

We make love in the dark. Slow. Silent. Sensual. There's only heated eye contact through the shadows and possessive touches beneath the sheets.

I don't question the new depth of our passion, or how it feels like we're both clinging to something destined to end.

I fall back asleep with his body spooned behind mine like a

perfect puzzle piece, his lips on my shoulder, his arm around my waist.

The mattress doesn't jostle again until the morning sun beams around the edge of the drapes.

"Matthew?" I roll toward his side of the bed, finding him already dressed in another impeccable suit as he kneels to tie his shoes near the door.

"I didn't mean to wake you." His focus remains on his laces. "I'm going to walk to the cafe on the corner and get breakfast."

"I'll come." I fling back the sheet.

"No." He stands with a frown, still not meeting my gaze as he fixes his lapels. "I've got calls to make. Stay here until I get back."

There's no offer of clarification. No apology. Just dictatorship that doesn't have the same appeal as it does when spoken sexually.

"Is everything all right?" I cling to the sheets, wanting to give him space while instinct demands I pry. "Has something happened?"

"We'll talk when I get back." His gaze finally meets mine. "It's time we laid everything on the table."

He doesn't glance at me with admiration. Doesn't rake his attention over my body with his usual predatory hunger. He barely registers me at all before he pulls his cell from his jacket pocket to concentrate on the device. "I won't be long."

"Wait." I push to my feet, dragging the sheet along with me. "Tell me what's going on."

"I'm paranoid," he grates. "Word has spread about the shooting, and I want the two of us to be straight with each other before the world starts firing complications our way."

"The world or my brother?"

"Either. Both. It doesn't matter." His jaw ticks. "Yesterday we said no lies and no secrets. We need to start living up to that promise."

There's more to his change in demeanor. Something that sits heavy on my chest. Has he already figured out what the Costas have done to me? To Stella?

"Okay." I nod, my throat drying. "We'll talk."

"Good." He strides for the hall with no kiss in farewell, no heated promises. "Bishop will be here soon. You might want to get dressed before he arrives."

"Why is he coming?" I ask the empty doorway.

"I'll explain when I get back."

His footsteps don't pause along the hall. They grow distant, the front door slapping closed moments later.

I'm tempted to spy on him from the balcony. Just for the slightest hint of understanding at his temperamental mood. But I shower instead, quickly scrubbing the remnants of last night's eroticism from my body while wondering if I'm doing it for the last time.

It can't be more than ten minutes later, when I'm drying myself in front of the wall-to-wall mirror, that a knock sounds at the front door. My stomach twists.

I don't want Bishop here. Not for this.

I refuse to discuss my daughter's abduction in front of his smug face.

"*Hold on a sec.*" I pad into Matthew's bedroom and steal his robe from the chair in the corner, shoving my arms through the silk as I continue down the hall. "*I'm coming.*"

The knock sounds again when I reach the living room, my feet slapping against the cold tiles. "Have a little patience."

I reach the entry and check the peephole, holding out hope it's Matthew with arms full of food. Only the shoulder of the shadowed suit I glimpse isn't his. The size and shape are too damn familiar to Bishop's frame.

"I'm here." I fight with the dead bolt, then twist the handle.

When I fling the heavy wood wide, it's not Bishop who swings around to face me.

The man standing in the dimly lit hall turns my way in a tailored suit, dark thick stubble hugging a tight jawline, his posture holding an air of bulletproof confidence.

He says something. *Asks* something. Yet the words don't register. Nothing sinks past the panic rendering me speechless.

It's *Remy Costa*—Emmanuel's youngest son.

My heart sprints, my veins flooding with adrenaline.

They *did* find the cyanide. They found me, too.

Is that why Matthew was on edge?

"Did you hear me, sugar?" He smirks, his gaze raking up and down my body.

Our first meeting wasn't meant to be like this. It was supposed to be planned. Strategic. Powerful. Being a few sharp breaths away from hyperventilating wasn't in the manifesto.

I white-knuckle the handle to slam the door closed only for the momentum to stop as he lunges forward to shove his hands against the wood.

"Whoa, there. I didn't expect a welcome party, but this is a bit dramatic, don't you think?" He shoves harder against the barrier between us, overpowering me. "Where is he?"

"Where is who?" I shake my head, my voice hoarse.

He stalks forward, nudging me out of the way to continue into the living room. "Nice try. But he sent me a colorful text a few minutes ago, so I know he's awake."

My pulse stutters, ricocheting through my chest with the force of jagged shrapnel. "You're in contact with Matthew?"

He stops in the middle of the open area and swings around to face me, continuing to walk backward into the penthouse. "Look, there's no need to freak out. I'll do you a solid and make sure he doesn't blame you for letting me in. Okay?"

I drag in a ragged breath, realizing the extent of what I've done. Not only am I face-to-face with my enemy while completely unprepared, I've also let the son of the man who murdered Grace into Matthew's home.

"Get out." Venom enters my voice. "Get *the fuck* out."

"Not going to happen." He swings toward the hall leading to the bedrooms. "Dante, where are you?"

The name snaps me rigid, every ounce of blood in my body siphoning to my feet.

The asshole shoots a glance over his shoulder, levelling me with a demeaning smirk. "Sorry, you referred to him as someone else, didn't you? What name is my brother going by these days?"

I turn cold. Blood. Heart. Breath. "You've got the wrong apartment."

This has to be a mistake.

A coincidence.

Dante Costa must live in this building. Matthew has to be watching him, too.

I inch toward the kitchen, destined for the knife block calling to me from the middle of the counter.

"*Dante,*" he raises his voice. "Get out here."

"Leave." My tone sounds like a beg as I reach the marble counter, my ears thunderous with my frantic pulse. "Before I call the police."

I'm ignored. Entirely dismissed as he strolls toward the dining table, picking up last week's mail. "Matthew Langston." The name rolls off his tongue with heavy criticism. "I guess it's no surprise he chose a variant of his middle name. He never liked Mateo." He swings back to face me. "So where…"

His question falls short as I slide the knife from the wooden block, his gaze narrowing on the sharp blade. "Planning on stabbing me, sugar?"

"I plan on doing whatever necessary to get you out of here." I cinch the robe tighter around my middle with my free hand, my nakedness beneath the silk making me feel far too vulnerable.

"How long has he been playing you?" His expression turns into mock sympathy.

Black dots assail my vision.

Matthew isn't playing me. He can't be. Not for weeks. Not after *he* demanded *my* honesty.

I would've sensed the treachery. Felt the deceit.

Wouldn't I?

"Get out." I thrust the knife toward the entry. "*Now.*"

"Damn." His brows rise. "He's been doing this for a while, hasn't he? You poor, sweet thing."

His derision undoes me, unraveling the binds of loyalty that tie me to the man I'd fallen for.

"*Dante,*" he calls toward the hall. "*Get the fuck out here.*"

"*He's not here,*" I scream. "It's just me. And if you dare to do anything to me, I swear my family will return the favor tenfold."

"Dare to do to you?" He frowns. "Why the fuck would I want to do anything to you?" He looks me up and down again, the frown deepening. "For starters, you're out of my usual age bracket.

No offence. And I'd never lower myself to stick my dick where my brother has already been. Especially if that brother is Dante."

He doesn't know who I am?

I cling tighter to the knife, my palm beginning to sweat.

This son of a bitch doesn't recognize me? He dared abduct my daughter. Was vicious enough to participate in the death of my husband. But didn't bother to learn the faces of the lives he'd torn apart?

Fuck him.

"Look, I'm sorry he's been playing games." He crosses his arms over his chest with a look of chagrin. "But I need to speak to him about the shooting. I assume you were the one with him."

No.

I shake my head, refusing to understand the reality taking shape around me.

"I get that you're pissed." He ignores the knife as if it doesn't exist. "But don't women usually snoop for shit like this? Aren't those tactics in your DNA?"

My DNA is currently made up of rage and ruin. Devastation and destruction.

And I *had* snooped.

I'd checked the mail minutes after first walking into the penthouse. I spoke to people Matthew works with. People he knows. Not a single soul addressed him as anything other than the name he gave me. Not helicopter pilots. Not waitresses. Not one single motherfucker on the face of the Earth.

I'd also done a thorough check on his clubs. All are owned by Matthew Langston. All of them legitimately structured without shell companies or dodgy dealings.

There'd been no indication. No inkling I'd been played the entire time my heart and soul had succumbed.

"Obviously his bills aren't anything to go by." Remy shrugs. "But surely you would've thought to go through his wallet. Or his drawers. He'd have something lying around."

He's right.

If Matthew isn't who he says he is, there has to be evidence.

I drop the knife, the metal clinking against the marble as

violence floods my veins. I reach for the nearest drawer, scavenging for anything to ease the sickness in my stomach.

I go through cupboards, below the marble counter and above. I search for anything with a name on it. With a hint. With a clue. And come up empty.

"Maybe try the bedroom," Remy drawls. "Go on. I'll wait."

I glare and snatch for the knife.

Admissions bubble in my chest. The confessions of where I plan to drive my blade and why, all begging to be heard.

I could kill him and claim self-defense. But the pain of possible betrayal by a man I love punishes me far more than my need to decimate Remy Costa.

I trek his every move while I stalk across the room. Then keep one eye on my back as I enter the hall.

When I reach the bedroom, where pleasure and bliss had been awakened after years of drought, I pause, hating myself with or without evidence.

If Remy's claims are true, I'll never recover.

There's no going back from this type of mistake. Not after the ones I've already made.

God, please don't let it be true.

I step inside, slam the door behind me, throw the knife to the bed, and fall to my knees at the closest bedside table.

I yank the top drawer from its holding and dump the contents on the carpet.

There are coins and buttons. Receipts and innocuous tidbits, too. Normal things. *Innocent* things.

I pull out the second and the third drawer. Socks and underwear fall to the floor. Stupid typical items that deny me the proof of Remy's claims.

I scan under the bed. Nothing.

I scramble to the adjoining bathroom, checking the cupboards and drawers to no avail.

I run for his wardrobe, shoving aside hanging shirts. Kicking away shoes. Throwing and heaving sweaters. I move from one row of shelves to the next, yanking everything from its neatly folded place. The jeans. The gym tanks.

Row after row.

Shelf after shelf.

I don't stop until a pile of clothes lay strewn on the floor. Then I climb, reaching for the stack of blankets lying dormant on the top ledge. They sail through the air behind me, one after another until my fingers no longer feel material and instead skim cardboard.

I stretch higher, struggling on the tips of my toes, my robe gaping, my sanity failing.

My fingertips brush the corner of a box and I hold my breath as I strain to inch it into sight. Shift by incremental shift, I edge it toward me, my arms straining over my head, my body aching from the uncomfortable pull of muscle.

Once it's close enough, I wiggle it, the light weight sliding onto my palm. I descend, dragging it with me until one foot slips its perch on the shelf and I jostle to remain upright.

I lose my hold on the shoe box, the lid slipping free before the items inside topple to the pile of clothes on the floor.

"Shit." I jump down, determined to find what I'm looking for when my gaze catches hold of the contents scattered before me.

My pulse thunders in my ears. My throat. My stomach.

I feel it everywhere, the booming beat pounding through every inch of me.

But it's not evidence of Remy's accusation that litters the carpet around me.

It's worse.

My ID.

My credit cards.

My lipstick and pens and hair ties.

All the things that had been in my purse when I'd been mugged in Denver. Even the small vial of cyanide.

29

MATTHEW

I JUGGLE TO HOLD THE TRAY OF TAKEAWAY COFFEE CUPS AND THE oversized bag of food as I shove into the penthouse. "I'm back."

I should've stayed outside longer. Should've taken more time to chill the fuck out and strategize my next move. But Layla had already been suspicious when I left, her eyes reading the mood I couldn't hide.

I kick the door closed behind me and start for the kitchen, stopping dead in my tracks at the sight of the asshole sitting on my sofa, one leg crossed over his knee in relaxation, his arms spread along the headrest.

Fuck.

I scan the room, looking for her, praying she fell back asleep while he somehow broke inside.

"Where is she?" I force calm as I continue to the counter, dumping my haul from the cafe.

He raises a brow, smug. "You mean the woman you've been playing?" He jerks his head back toward the hall. "I assume it's your bedroom she escaped into, *Matthew*."

I snarl, my worst fears realized, but it's his choice of words that give me pause.

He doesn't use her name. Doesn't address her as if they have history.

Why?

"I sincerely apologize for ruining the fun." His voice drips with sarcasm. "If I'd known you were pretending to be someone else I wouldn't have used your real name."

"Matthew *is* my real name." I stalk across the room, needing to get eyes on her.

"Matthew is who you wish you were. Unfortunately, you'll never be anyone other than Dante to those who know you best."

Anger stabs through my skull, blinding in its efficiency.

I stop my progression to the hall, unable to escape the rage fighting for control.

"What is it, brother?" Remy drawls. "Does the truth hurt?"

One second, I'm determined to find Layla. The next, I'm cocking my fist as I reach the sofa and launch my knuckles at his face.

My punch connects with his chin, the impact screaming through my bones.

I launch again and again, pounding, pummeling. Seeing blood and tasting fraudulent victory.

But he's already won. I know he's ruined everything as he uses both feet to kick me backward, sending me tumbling over the coffee table, my head hitting the tiles.

"That was a fucking cheap shot." He shoves to his feet to tower above me, that smug expression now wiped from his face. "You may be older than me, but I'm no longer a kid you can push around."

I shove to my elbows, then rise to stand in front of him. "I bet you're still your daddy's little snitch, though, riding his dirty coat-tails all the way to the bank."

His eyes flare. Nostrils, too.

I tense for retaliation and don't have to wait long for his fist to swing for my face.

I block the strike with my forearm. It's the swift kick to my ankle I don't expect. I stumble sideways, grabbing his shoulders in the process, then punch him in the gut.

We grapple and shove. Swing and charge.

I ram him into the sofa. He pummels my head with his knuckles.

The little fucker is right. He isn't easily pushed around

anymore. It takes a good two minutes to pin him beneath me before I grab him in a choke hold.

"I told you not to come here." I spit blood to the tiles.

"And I told you we needed to talk." He bares his teeth, the vicious smile covered in crimson.

"It's been fifteen years." I add pressure to his throat, clamping down on his carotid. "There's nothing we could possibly discuss."

"You were fucking shot at. Excuse me for caring."

Caring?

My hold loosens without my consent, my intuition searching for the real reason he's entered my life after more than a decade apart.

The swoosh of an opening door steals my attention. Footsteps patter toward us.

I raise my gaze to the hall, finding Layla standing there in my thin silk robe, knife in hand, face pale, eyes wild.

I release Remy and scramble to my feet. "Let me explain."

She storms toward me, blade raised in threat, while her other hand reaches into the robe pocket. "Explain this." She throws something at me, the small projectile hitting my chest before rico-cheting to the floor. "And this." She grabs something else, throwing that, too.

I drag my gaze from the pain I created, the anger I deserve, and take in the items she continues to launch at me.

Lipstick.

Concealer.

A packet of tissues.

"Explain, you fucking son of a bitch." She holds up her ID. "How did you get this?"

I close my eyes, stealing the briefest second of respite from her suffering before I return my gaze to hers. "It's not what you think. I didn't—"

"You didn't what?" Her eyes spark like the devil. "You didn't play me from the moment we met, *Dante*?"

I clench my fists, wanting to slaughter Remy for what he's caused.

"Oh, shit." The fucker snickers. "The cat's really out of the bag."

"Listen to me." I step closer, needing her to understand. To think clearly. "This is what I wanted to discuss." I grab her wrist, hoping touch will help her remember our connection.

"Let me go." She fights my hold. Twisting. Tugging.

Fuck.

I loosen my grip.

She yanks to free herself, her hand sliding through mine. The ID gets caught as she tussles, falling to the floor.

"Goddamnit." She stabs the knife toward my face with a glare and bends to pick it up.

Remy's closer. He rolls onto his stomach and snatches at the flimsy plastic.

"No," she warns. *"Don't."*

I step between them, ignoring her weapon, willing to endure a stab wound if it means keeping that prick away from her.

"Stop." She barges into me.

"Layla Hart… Portland, Oregon," he murmurs to himself. "Why do I feel like I should recognize that name?"

I'd like to know, too.

"Give it back," she screams. *"Now."*

For weeks, Bishop has attempted to discover the connection between them, every turn coming up empty. There was no lead toward a romantic relationship with either of my brothers. No evidence of business ties, either.

"Layla Hart," Remy repeats, his scrutinizing gaze rising to her as he lumbers to his feet. "Layla from Portland, Oregon."

She stiffens. Swallows.

"Jesus Christ. You're a Torian." He stalks forward, his shoulders straightening in menace. "You fucking bitch."

"I'm a fucking bitch?" She lunges forward with the knife. "How dare you?"

I turn my back toward her blade, certain she wants to embed it between my ribs, and shove at Remy's shoulders. "Get the fuck away from her."

He glowers at me, then her, his fury finally settling on my face. "How could you be with her after what she's done?"

"What I've done?" she screeches. "What *I've* done?"

"Tell me what this is about." I shove him again. "How do you two know each other?"

"It's none of your business." Layla attempts to move around me, the knife slicing the air.

"As if you don't know." Remy's eyes narrow, then he scoffs a laugh. "Or do you really not know?"

"Know what, asshole?"

"Don't," Layla snaps.

"You're fucking her." Remy laughs with spite. "And you have no clue?"

Pressure bears down on my chest, punishing me.

"Stop it." This time her request is a plea.

"Looks like she wasn't the only one being played." His eyes gleam. "This bitch is using you to get to us."

"She isn't using me. I've known of her hatred all along. I just haven't known why."

"Well, brother, let me provide you with the insight—"

Layla charges around me, slashing the knife toward him. "I'll kill you."

Shit.

I grab her around the waist, hauling her off the ground, the robe gaping, the knife slicing.

"Will you kill me like we killed your husband?" Remy smirks.

Fuck. Me.

I hold her tighter, feeling the second his words make an impact. She stops fighting, her inhales vicious as she pants, the slightest whimper accompanying each breath.

"We abducted her daughter, too." He meets my gaze. "It was two years ago, but as you can see, our family made a lasting impression."

She screams, reinvigorating her fight, kicking, thrashing.

"Stop it," I snarl in her ear, ready to kill him myself. "Calm the fuck down."

She doesn't listen. Doesn't settle. She's all rage and pain and frenzy.

"Nice tits," he adds, focusing on the space where the robe gapes across her chest.

"Shut your fucking mouth." I swing her toward the hall, dumping her on her feet at the start of the carpet. "Get back in the bedroom," I demand of her, seconds away from reverting to the man I promised myself was dead and buried.

The past reignites in my veins.

The dark savagery begs to be freed.

"Go to hell." She stumbles away, then turns on me, her knife held at the ready.

"Now, Layla," I warn. "I need to speak to him alone."

"Listen to him, bitch," Remy sneers. "Because if I get my hands on you before he does, it's going to take more than a knife to save your life."

I fight against the animalistic need to defend her. To lash out and strike him down for daring to even glare in her direction.

"*Go,*" I grate through clenched teeth. "I'll be there in a minute."

"Fuck you." She straightens to her full height, her chin regally high, her shoulders broad. "You'll pay for this." She backtracks toward the bedroom. "You'll wish we'd never met."

I've already had many of those moments. Too many times to count where I regretted getting involved—for her sake, not mine.

"*Go.*" I stare her down.

She sucks in a strangled breath, belying her strength, and it fucking kills me.

If only we'd cleared the air sooner.

She retreats into the bedroom, slamming the door in her wake, the deafening vibration crashing through the entire penthouse as I stand staring into the darkened hall.

"That's a pretty impressive mess you've made for yourself, brother. I guess the grass ain't greener after all."

I curl my lip, determined not to be distracted by violence. "Why are you really here? Why contact me after so long?"

"Because of her. Because of *them*. I came when I heard you were shot at because I thought you deserved to know her fucking family have been shooting at us, too. But evidently, I got it wrong if that bitch was with you yesterday."

It's hard to decipher what he says. Hard to hear anything other than him cutting her down.

"You've betrayed the family by sleeping with that whore, Dante. Uncle Lorenzo is going to be pissed when he finds out."

"He already knows." I stalk toward him, menacing and ready

to slaughter, jabbing a finger at his chest. "And if you call her that again, or refer to me by that name, I'll make you see stars. You hear me?"

He glowers, his lips pressed tight.

"Do you fucking hear me?" I repeat.

"Yeah, I fucking hear you." He slaps my hand away. "But does he know you kept quiet, not telling us they were going to declare war after two years of radio silence?"

"I don't know what you're talking about."

"No?" He raises a defiant brow. "I call bullshit."

"You can call whatever the fuck you want. But up until a few seconds ago, I had no clue about your connection to her. Let alone the depth of how low you could stoop by abducting a fucking child."

"Wasn't my decision, asshole. The point is—they shot Dad."

I don't respond.

There's nothing more than a flinch at the memory of a man I despise.

"How can you have no loyalty?" He starts to pace, his face stark apart from the hatred in his eyes. "You're sleeping with the enemy."

"She's no enemy of mine." I grind my teeth, refusing to take the bait, refusing to care one iota about Emmanuel's health just because my youngest brother demands it of me. "And I'm surprised you think your actions don't justify their response."

For the love of God. Abduction? They involved a child?

And to think Layla would've suffered every time I asked about her connection to the Costas. Each and every moment I attempted to find out if she was in a relationship with Remy or Salvatore.

Not once did she expose her past.

That beautiful, fucking unfathomably strong woman faked her way through continuous bluffs.

But he's right. Lorenzo will be pissed if Emmanuel was shot and her family were to blame. I'll need to prove I wasn't involved, and do whatever possible to make it seem like she wasn't either.

"That was two goddamn years in the past," he argues. "The situation was dead and buried. Yet, they shot Dad three weeks ago."

"It's my turn to call bullshit. He was in Italy three weeks ago."

"Was he? Or were those the rumors we had to start to hide our weakened position?" He mocks. "He's currently in a makeshift hospital room at home, struggling to ditch a chest infection that stemmed from the bullet wound in his shoulder."

"What a shame." I pull my cell from my pocket and open a new text to Bishop. "I guess you learned the hard way that the only thing that gets dead and buried in the lifestyle you've chosen are the bodies. The need for revenge lives longer than any of us."

"You're judging me?" He raises a brow. "Your sins are far greater than mine."

I type *Get here now* before pressing send. "I never abducted a child."

"If the whispers are true, it's the only thing you haven't done."

I huff a derisive laugh. "I guess you'll never know, because I'm not explaining shit to you. Now get the fuck out."

"I can't believe you." He starts for the hall, walking away from me. "We were brothers once. But you're right on one thing—revenge lives longer than any of us. And I'm sure Dad will agree once I tell him she's fucking you to get back at us."

"You're threatening her?" I shove my cell into my pocket and stalk after him. "You'd tell him?" I grab his shoulder and haul him around to face me.

"I'd take pleasure in it. Why wouldn't I when you abandoned us? You fucking walked and left us with him. Now look where we are." He throws his arms wide. "You caused this. You caused *all* of it—that kid's abduction, her husband's death. If you hadn't left, he wouldn't have spiraled."

The accusations are sharply embedded into my chest, stabbing me with guilt. With truth. "I couldn't stay—"

"Because you were humiliated that Grace left you?" he asks with incredulity. "I don't know how you became the man you did, because the brother I knew was a fucking pussy. I overheard your plans to ditch town with her. But she didn't wait for you, did she? She didn't want to stick around to finish senior year because her dad was an abusive drunk and her mom was a junkie, so she took off, not giving a shit that you weren't—"

I launch, striking my forearm into his throat, slamming him backward against the door. Not seeing. Only feeling.

I press harder, ignoring his rasped breath, not flinching as he claws at my arm. "She didn't go missing, you pathetic piece of shit." I lean close, sinking all my weight against his neck, so there's nothing between us. Nothing apart from my ignorant baby brother and the facts. "*He* killed her. He slit her from throat to gut and showed me the pictures to make sure it sank in."

Remy's eyes bug as he continues to fight me off, his breath wheezing.

"He murdered her because he knew I'd made plans to move out," I seethe in his face. "He slaughtered the girl I cared about, someone who was still a fucking child, because I wasn't dedicated to becoming his perfect little minion like you were."

Remy's mouth works like a fish as I press and press. Open. Closed. Open.

"He took the one thing that was mine and made sure it no longer existed, because he wanted my attention all to himself." I watch the panic build in his eyes, enjoying the victory through the devastation. "So yes, I fucking left. I ran away from money and prestige. I hitchhiked across this godforsaken country to put as much distance between us as I could." Spittle bubbles from my lips, my fury uncontainable. "I lived on the streets. I stole to survive. And you have the fucking audacity to think you know what went down?"

I glare.

I glare so hard I sense an impending aneurism.

"Fuck you, Remy." I pull my arm away, not giving a shit that his grown ass crumples to the floor before me. "You always were a naive little prick."

I kick his shoes and step over him, pulling the door wide to find Bishop poised with his key in the air.

"Perfect timing?" He takes me in with caution, no doubt seeing the monster I've become—the clenched fists, the heaving chest. "What the hell is going on?"

"Get him out of here." I turn for the living room. "Before I fucking kill him."

30

LAYLA

I close myself in the bedroom, snatch my hair into a vicious ponytail, then dress in jeans, Chucks, and a white blouse. Everything else is shoved into my suitcase and zipped tight.

I spend minutes poised at the door, overhearing muffled shouts and heavy thuds.

They're fighting again, and I don't know who I'd prefer to suffer more pain—Remy or Matthew.

No, not Matthew. *Dante.*

A goddamn Costa.

I will the sickening disgust to the back of my mind, trying not to acknowledge how I fell for a man who shares the same DNA as my daughter's abductors. My husband's murderers.

There'll be enough time to hate myself for it later.

Right now, there's too much adrenaline to think, the hormone acting like venom in my veins.

I want to hurt him. To drag the vial of cyanide hidden in my jeans pocket and throw the powder in his face. But whenever I picture his death, the only sensation to consume me is regret. *Suffering.*

I'd loved him.

I'd adored and admired every part of that man and now every memory is tainted and twisted by lies.

I open the door a crack as another one slams on the other side of the penthouse.

More shouting follows, but this time the voices aren't raised in anger. Matthew's tone holds frustration. Panic. And it's Bishop's responding aggression that brushes my ears as I inch the door wider.

"That little asshole is running back to Emmanuel as we speak," Matthew yells. "They're going to come after her."

I take the news with a sharp breath.

I need to get out of here. To grab my cell from the coffee table and leave.

"What did you expect?" Bishop mutters. "And isn't that why you got involved? You couldn't let her be a target on her own, you had to pin a bull's-eye on our backs, too."

Matthew growls a reply too low to understand. A threat? A warning?

I pull the door wide enough to slip into the hall, cautiously wheeling my suitcase in delicately slow increments along the carpet behind me, the knife in my free hand.

I hold my breath with each step toward the conversation, the growing thunder of my pulse in my ears making it harder to hear.

Lorenzo's name is spoken. Others', too. Men I'm not familiar with.

"What are the options?" Bishop asks. "How confident are you of an outcome?"

"My only confidence comes from knowing Emmanuel won't let this slide. He'll do to her what he did to Grace. And not just Layla, but Stella, too."

I gasp.

"Layla?" Matthew calls out.

Shit. Shit. *Shit.*

"Layla."

This time my name is a command. An impatient warning.

I straighten my shoulders and raise my chin as I continue into view.

The two men stand at the dining table. Tall. Commanding. Aggressive.

Matthew has the sense to look somewhat apologetic beneath

the frustration tightening his features. But Bishop, like always, isn't welcoming.

He gives me a dismissive glance before returning his attention to the man who deceived me. "What are we going to do?"

Matthew ignores him and starts toward me. "Good, you're dressed. We've got a big day ahead." He speaks as if things between us are normal. As if he hasn't pummeled the walls of our relationship and left the bricks to fall upon me.

"Don't," I warn. "Don't you dare come near me."

He complies, rooting his feet in place and raising his chin while I stride toward my cell on the coffee table.

"Your breakfast is on the counter. You need to eat."

I maneuver the suitcase around the sofa, bumping into the armrest, and release the handle to snatch for my phone.

One call and Cole will make this right. Him, Hunter, Decker and Luca. They'll fix this mess with blood and broken bones… and hate me more while doing it.

I shove the device in my pocket, the knife still at the ready, and wheel my suitcase out from where I came to make for the entry hall.

"You can't leave." Matthew's gaze haunts me from my periphery.

I keep walking, striding out the distance to freedom.

"Layla, stop."

My body wants to obey. There's no rhyme or reason, but every muscle tenses at his command, including my heart.

"Let me explain what's going on."

He continues toward me, the dwindling space between us causing me to panic. Not from fear of physical pain, but from that of pure emotional torture.

I can't be near him. Can't let him get within reach.

I run, my black Converse Chucks squeaking against the tiles, my suitcase wheels clicking.

He gives chase, his heavy footfalls thunderous behind me as I reach the door and drop the knife to wrench at the dead bolt.

The metal clatters at my feet while I snatch at the handle. Twist. Pull.

The crack of freedom brings hope, the euphoria snatched away when his heavy palm slaps against the wood, slamming the door closed, his body caging me from behind.

"Let me leave." I cling to the handle, twisting and tugging.

"I'm not that person," he growls near my ear. "I'm not one of them."

The words whisper over my neck, poking infected wounds. Memories of him speaking against my neck in better times haunt me, crawling under my skin like torturous bugs.

"You're a monster." I pull and yank and thrash at the handle, willing it to open.

He doesn't move. Doesn't lift his splayed hand from against the wood.

"I'll explain everything later," he vows. "Once it's just the two of us."

"Later?" I swing around to face him only to jerk back at the stifling proximity.

He's there. Right there. Dark eyes manic. Stubble harsh. Face severe.

"You want to talk to me *later*?" I seethe. "Because it's easier for you to lie when we're alone?"

"I haven't lied."

"Not once have you told the whole truth," I shriek.

We stare each other down, my chest rising and falling from a body demanding punishment, his warm breath taunting my lips.

He doesn't move. Doesn't free me from the cage of his arms. All he does is look at me as if he'll tear the world to shreds if I escape. Like he'll lose his mind if I walk from his life, never to return.

It hurts.

His confusing suffering. His unsettling battle.

I want to soothe him and stab him all at once.

"Leave the suitcase." He straightens, his order blanketed with a subtle level of control. "Go eat breakfast."

I rage, wanting to yell at the top of my lungs. To claw at the severity in his eyes. To steal the oxygen from the air to dispel his intoxicating aftershave while suffocating us both.

"I'm not staying." I swing back to the door and snatch at the handle, turning the metal toward freedom, erupting with relief when it opens.

He steps into me, the wall of pressure smothering my spine as he slams the wood shut with a chest-rattling snarl.

"I'll scream," I warn.

"You don't want to do that." He presses into me, his hard body grazing my ass.

The threat is clear in his voice. The pure conviction. But my blood doesn't react in fear.

It warms.

My pulse throbs.

My body still reacts to our chemistry. Succumbing. Yearning.

"You're threatening me?" I turn again, this time concentrating on my hatred when I look him in the eye.

He's even closer now, our noses almost brushing as he intimidates me in the cage of his arms.

"I'll do whatever it takes," he purrs. "We're not done, Layla."

So be it.

I force a smile. Bat my lashes. Pray to God I'm not making another mistake. Then launch my knee at his groin, making direct impact.

Shock splashes his face. Eyes wide. Mouth, too.

He grunts.

Crumples.

My regret hits just as fast, the remorse heavy enough to suffocate.

I don't let it consume me. I scramble for the door, swinging it wide, leaving the suitcase behind. I'm one step over the threshold when I'm viciously yanked backward by a painful grip on my upper arm, then dragged into an entirely different body.

"My turn," Bishop seethes. "And let me warn you, I'm far less patient."

31

LAYLA

I'M SHOVED ONTO THE SOFA, MY SUITCASE LEFT AT THE DOOR, MY CELL confiscated.

Bishop scowls at me from a few feet away, the minutes passing in silence until Matthew limps into the living room. His shoulders hunch as he makes his way to the kitchen to lean heavily into the island counter.

"I knew we had secrets, but I underestimated just how many." His voice is graveled as he clings to the marble, his face now a paler shade of sun-kissed beauty. "You should've told me your grievance with the Costas had nothing to do with dating Remy or Salvatore."

I remain quiet, my hands in my lap, my eyes glaring in rage.

"What reason did you have to keep the details of your daughter's abduction and husband's murder from me?"

I flinch at the ease with which he relays my nightmares. The simplicity. The lack of emotion.

"Why didn't you tell me?"

I scoff, finding him sickeningly self-righteous for asking about my skeletons when his pile far higher.

"Why pretend you'd had a love affair?" he continues. "Why allude to being a past lover?"

"I didn't allude to anything. You assumed."

His eyes narrow with impatience. "I could've done something. I could've—"

"You couldn't even tell me your real name."

"Matthew *is* my real name." He straightens, wincing with the movement. "They're not my family."

"No?" I raise a brow. "I think your DNA would argue."

"My DNA doesn't make them family."

"That's exactly what it does."

His jaw ticks as Bishop takes one retreating step after another until he's leaning against the far wall, arms crossed over his chest, watching us like a soap opera.

"I was born a Costa." Matthew hobbles to the fridge, pulling out a bag of vegetables from the freezer drawer to hold against his crotch. "I didn't stay one."

"That doesn't change a thing."

"No?" He raises a brow as he settles back against the counter. "So you loved your father? You loved a man rumored to traffic sex slaves?"

I press my lips tight, refusing to answer.

"Families aren't so clear cut are they, *amore mio*?"

I grind my teeth, scowl my fury, my jaw aching from the tension.

He's undaunted by my hatred, not batting an eye while he repositions the makeshift ice pack against his crotch. "You could've at least told me your family had Emmanuel shot. Especially when I told you yesterday what would happen if I was associated with him being hurt."

My mouth opens in protest. My heart races.

Is that what Cole had been hiding the last time I was home? Had he instigated war without warning me?

Jesus.

I force my chin high. "Turns out we both had secrets that could hurt the other."

His gaze assaults me, scrutinizing, a cruel smile curving his lips. "You didn't know." He scoffs a laugh. "Your fucking brother didn't have the sense to tell you."

"Jesus Christ," Bishop mutters. "She's clueless."

My fingers twist in my lap, my loathing skyrocketing.

Matthew stands taller. "That settles it then. You're staying with me until this is sorted."

"That settles it?" I dig my nails into my palms. "How does *that* settle anything?"

"You still want to run home to a brother who put you in danger?"

Cole's frantic texts make more sense now. How he wouldn't quit demanding to know my whereabouts and who I was with. If only he'd told me what was going on.

"You hate your brother," Matthew states.

"No, I don't."

I despise him at times. Am sickened and beside myself with fury occasionally. But I've never hated him. Instead, it will be Cole who detests me for the complications I've created.

"No? He treats you like shit. Are you really in a hurry to get back to that?"

"As if you've treated me any bett—"

"I've treated you like a queen. Like *my* queen. Cole's actions are the reason you found it so fucking easy to move in with a stranger."

My stomach twists, the pain spreading.

"You don't want to return to Portland, Layla." He gentles his tone. "Once we sort out our differences, you'll want to stay here."

"Of course," I drawl. "I'd much prefer to remain with someone who makes it their job to hide the truth. You even had the balls to introduce Lorenzo as your mentor."

"He is my mentor."

"He's your *uncle*."

He inclines his head. "He's that, too."

I growl in frustration, my nails embedded in my palms. I need to hurt him like he's hurting me, but shooting or stabbing would never be enough. I have to reach inside his chest and wring the life from his beating heart, just like he's done to mine.

I cut my gaze away, unable to withstand those deep, dark eyes anymore, and whisper, "My brother will kill you."

"In that case, I better make the most of our time together." He places the ice pack on the marble and rounds the counter. "Bishop, can you give us a minute?"

"Need me to do anything?" Bishop pushes from the wall, his arms falling to his sides.

"Call the charter. Have a jet placed on standby."

"Destination?"

"To be determined."

I keep my face cast in the opposite direction as Bishop strides for the entry, the front door closing seconds later.

The tension increases tenfold. My suffering, too.

I wish I still had the knife. Death by cyanide won't be gruesome enough.

"Layla, listen to me." Matthew hobbles closer. "Everything between us is real—I promise you that. But I understand I hurt you." He reaches the sofa and continues to hesitantly sit on the coffee table before me. Knee to knee. "If it's any solace, I can assure you my balls ache like a motherfucker."

I keep my mouth shut, not finding solace at all.

The quiet stretches, his gaze haunting my periphery, his body entirely too close.

"The silent treatment isn't an option either, *amore mio*. You're going to have to find a way to push your animosity aside. Remy may have already told Emmanuel about us."

I snap my head around to glare at him, wordlessly letting him know there is no *us*.

"Do you understand what's happening?" His gaze leisurely rakes mine. Unfazed. In command. "Your brother's shooting would be considered retaliation. An attempt at murder in response to your husband's death. But this?" He waves a lazy hand between us. "This is personal. Depending on what information Remy shares, you might be held accountable for taking things further. For you, *personally*, levelling up the war all on your own."

My throat turns dry.

"I don't know if they have men in D.C.," he continues, "or if Emmanuel is capable of arranging retaliation from his hospital bed. But do you want to risk leaving here and finding out how quickly they can strike a helpless woman on her own?"

"I'm not helpless," I snarl.

"No?" He sinks to his knees before me, the show of submission in conflict with the sickening severity in his eyes. "Do you really think you can protect yourself?" He places his hands on my knees, the heat of his palms seeping through my jeans. "That you'd stand a chance?"

"Don't touch me." My voice shakes with the demand. With the disgusting thrill his contact provides.

He slides his fingers farther along my thighs and leans against my shins. "You're in danger, Layla."

I know. And not only from Emmanuel.

The man before me is my biggest threat.

His touch is impending doom. His gaze promises suffering of the most wicked kind.

"Get. Your hands. Off me." I enunciate the words slowly. Violently.

"Admit it," he murmurs. "You still want to fuck me."

I raise a hand to slap him only to have my wrist captured in a vise grip. I try with the other and he steals that, too, dragging me forward by my forearms until we're face-to-face, our breath mingling.

"What we have is real whether you like it or not," he snarls against my lips. "I can see it in your eyes. You're still hungry for me."

"I'm hungry for blood." I struggle to free my wrists, wriggling, tugging, hating not only the hold he has on my arms, but the one he has on my heart. "You're going to regret what you've done."

"No, I won't. Because what I did brought us together."

His confidence sparks insanity. I thrash, scream, attempt to kick at his thighs.

"*Enough.*" He stands, dragging my arms above my head. "Want me to prove how much you want me?" He swings me sideways, stretching me across the sofa.

I buck and twist and struggle, fighting and fighting while he climbs on top of me.

"*No,*" I scream. "Don't you fucking dare."

I stop breathing, stop moving as the heavy weight of him sinks against my hips, my hands trapped above my head, his eyes never leaving mine.

I hate this.

I hate *him.*

But he's right. I want him, too.

I need him. Crave him. Can't stop my nerves tingling from the lust-drunk memories of what it means for our bodies to be joined.

And his dick—*oh, God*—is erect, hard and adamant against my pubic bone, sending me into a world of tingles.

I despise him. I love him. I loathe him. I'm lost.

He leans in, attempting to kiss me, my mouth watering in response.

"Don't." I turn my face away, not willing to capitulate. I'm stronger than this.

"*Amore mio*," he murmurs against my cheek. "You're all that matters to me."

I squeeze my eyes shut, forcing down the pained cry that demands to be heard.

He nuzzles my jaw, my neck, his lips leaving gentle kisses along my carotid. "I will earn your trust."

"Impossible," I whisper. "I'll never believe a word you say."

The kisses stop. The nuzzling, too.

"We will see." He rests his forehead against my shoulder, a defeated sigh brushing my ear. "But for now, you need to stay with me."

"No."

"Think of Stella. Think of what they'll do to her."

My fragile pulse becomes frantic. "She's safe."

Nobody knows where she is. Who she is. Stella was enrolled in boarding school under a different surname, her tuition paid from an account that has no correlation to my family.

"Are you willing to stake her life on that? Because I'm not." He shifts on top of me, pulling back until I meet his gaze. "You don't know enough about my past. Or what I mean to Emmanuel. I may be estranged, but that bastard will always consider me his successor. I'm his golden child. Your presence in my life won't be ignored."

"Which means I should get as far away from you as possible."

"Distance won't matter. He'll find you. He won't stop looking— not when his hatred for you will be more than what he holds for your brother. You infiltrated his family. You targeted a son who wasn't involved."

Goddamnit.

What have I done?

What has *he* done?

"This is your fault." I wiggle beneath him, only endeavoring to tease my pussy against his shaft. "*You* did this."

"So let me fix it."

"How?"

The front door opens with a whoosh of air, footsteps following straight after.

I scramble, reigniting my fight to get this bastard off me. Unwilling to be seen as a victim. Especially a sexual one.

"Get off." I buck. "*Now.*"

Matthew growls and releases my wrists, removing his weight from my body. "Have breakfast, *amore mio*. We leave for Denver in ten minutes."

32

MATTHEW

Her eyes flash in fear at the mention of Denver. But she doesn't protest. Instead, she sits up, straightening to her full height to accept her fate.

She doesn't argue about leaving her suitcase in the penthouse.

Doesn't fight getting on the jet.

She comes of her own volition, taking the lone seat on the far side of the aisle while I sit across the polished compact table from Bishop, scrutinizing her.

"I don't have a good feeling about this." He taps his fingers against the arm of his chair. "I'm assuming you have a plan."

"I do."

He raises a brow, waiting for clarification while I attempt to figure out why Layla came so willingly. Why didn't I have to drag her alongside me, kicking and screaming?

"Well?" Bishop asks. "Do you mind telling me what it is, seeing as though I'm following you into the lion's den?"

"Emmanuel is no lion." I return my attention to the only friend I've had in ten years. The only man I've trusted apart from my uncle. "He's a fucking hyena. An opportunistic scavenger and a coward. But the strategy is simple. I'm going to talk to him and get him to leave Layla and her daughter out of the war with her brother."

He raises a brow. "*Talk* to him?"

"Yes. *Talk.*" I grind my teeth, hating the vow that keeps Emmanuel alive. "I won't betray Lorenzo."

"Do you plan on taking her with you?"

"Yes." I can't do this any other way. The man who spawned me won't have her killed if I'm standing in the line of fire.

At least, he never would've in the past.

Emmanuel Costa has, and probably always will, see me as the one rightfully meant to take over the family business even though I walked away.

There's a reason that fucker hasn't retired despite the money piled in his bank, and I'm sure it has everything to do with him still wanting me at the helm.

Problem is, it's risky to assume he hasn't changed.

I don't know him anymore.

Before today, I'd tried to kid myself about the lengths he would go to for success. For *power*. I'd prayed for the sake of my siblings that the rumors of blood on their hands hadn't been true. But today, Remy alerted me to a callousness I'd been oblivious to. One Layla had painstakingly survived and her family kept hidden.

Emmanuel is more inhuman than I wanted to believe. More sick and twisted.

That's where I get it from.

But as long as I stand between her and his vengeance, she'll survive.

She has to.

Bishop clears his throat, subtly regaining my attention. "You're going to take her right to your father's door?"

The description punctures my chest, wielding a vicious blow.

I slam my fist against the table and glare. "He's not my father."

Layla startles in my periphery, her fear punching me with guilt.

"Biology disagrees," she snips under her breath, settling back into her haughty posture of hostility, bratty even in the face of what's to come.

"My apologies." Bishop lowers his voice, the deep rumble of the jet giving us a modicum of privacy from her prying ears. "Are you sure you want to drag her into the heart of this? You're not worried they'll slit her throat in front of you?"

"Remy and Salvatore wouldn't dare. And Emmanuel is supposed to be laid flat from complications of a bullet wound."

"That part could be a trap. Nobody has heard a word about his injury."

"Nobody heard a word about him abducting Cole fucking Torian's niece and killing his brother-in-law either," I snarl.

"True. But still…"

He's right. This could be a setup. Emmanuel might have concocted the entire plan—a fake instigation of war, a pretend vulnerability.

Layla knew nothing about Emmanuel being targeted. Lorenzo hasn't said a word about his brother-in-law being shot.

The fucker might have even paid the Virginia Beach gang-bangers to do the hotel drive-by so Remy had an excuse to find me after all these years and claim to give a shit about my well-being.

"If they attempt to harm her in any way, I'll break the vow to my uncle without a thought." It's a pledge. A fucking promise. "And if you're forced to do the same, I'll pay the price. I'll take the blame."

"Neither one of us are going back to that life. Not now. Not when—"

"I'll deal with it," I grate. "I just need to know you'll protect her if I can't." I hold his gaze, conveying the importance of what I'm about to say with a hard look. "I have no right to ask you to guard her with your life, but—"

"Consider it done." His face tightens, obligation and loyalty staring back at me.

"You know you don't owe me. You don't need to be here. Whatever happened in the past has been repaid over the years—"

"I haven't paid for shit. My debt is still owed. And even if it wasn't, I'd be here. I have your back. I'll protect her." He drags his gaze away to stare out the window.

If I wasn't a selfish prick, I'd force him to walk. To get the fuck away from all of this.

Too bad I'm the most self-centered bastard he's ever met.

I can't risk losing her.

Not to a family I despise or because of the deceit I spun.

She's mine. Has been from the night we met.

I show my appreciation with a nod, and retrieve folded pieces of paper from my jacket pocket. "These are the house plans for the property. I need you to commit them to memory."

I slide the pages across the table and wait in silence as he scans the mansion, his concentration heavy as he frowns his way along the multitude of halls and rooms on the multi-level building.

"It's fucking big."

"I've heard that a time or two," I drawl. "But it could potentially be bigger. These plans are what I had drawn up after I left Denver. God knows what renovations have been done since."

He swipes a hand over his mouth as he continues to scan the pages, his focus gradually tracking from one side to the other, over and over until finally, he slides the architectural drawings back toward me. "How many men should we expect to be guarding the property?"

"I don't know." The admission annoys me. Weakens. "Emmanuel used to be protective of his solitude, so best-case scenario—none. Worst? God only knows."

"And you don't want to bring some of our own?"

"I've already made the arrangements. De Marco and two of his team will be waiting. But this isn't a show of force. It's a negotiation. A conversation."

He relaxes back into his seat, unconvinced. "Should I be worried about you reverting to your old ways while holding said conversation?"

The question stings. "I don't know."

He nods, unfazed by the complication. "I've got one last question, then I'm done." I brace for impact as he turns his attention to Layla, his eyes callously narrowing. "We protect her with our lives —that much is clear. But who the fuck protects them from her? She's out for blood just as much as they are."

"You don't." She tilts her head to face us. "You stay out of my way, because I'm more than happy to take you down at the same time."

Normally, I'd admire her strength. But now, instead of pride, I'm agitated by her tenacity. If she's here for a misguided chance at revenge, she could get us all killed.

"See?" Bishop drawls. "She's fucking crazy."

"She wouldn't be stupid enough to make a move." I hold her gaze. "Would you, *amore mio?*"

Her eyes harden.

"This isn't a game, Layla. We can't risk messing this up."

She rolls her eyes and returns her focus out the jet window, her arms clamping over her chest. But there's something else I see in her expression before she hides her face from me. Something I hope isn't pained resignation.

She can't be willing to give her life to end those of the Costas. Can she?

Fuck.

The rest of the flight is spent relaying tactics for different scenarios, none of which are likely to come true. We land in Denver below a clear blue sky, the fall breeze rushing into the cabin with an icy edge of warning as soon as the door opens.

Bishop is the first to make for the aisle with Layla following.

"Wait." I push from my seat.

She doesn't listen.

"Layla, I said wait." I start after her, lunging forward to grab her arm. "We have to talk. As much as I understand your enthusiasm for destruction, you need to be on your best behavior."

She swings around to face me, yanking her arm from my grip. "No, I need to do what's best for my family."

Her brattiness chafes. The resolute conviction, too.

I'd love to splay her over my knees and belt her ass. "You're letting your anger at me cloud your judgment. You know full well you'll get yourself killed if you start shit today."

She makes an exaggerated attempt to bat her lashes and pout her bottom lip. "But you said you'd protect me."

"I can only do so much," I growl.

"Well, you should've thought about that before you brought me here." She turns for the door.

"So you're happy to make your daughter an orphan?"

She swings back around so violently, I stiffen on instinct. "I'm going to *save* my daughter. I'm going to take advantage of this opportunity and do whatever it takes to make sure your family doesn't get anywhere near her. Now *and* in the future."

"Layla—"

"Don't *Layla* me." She holds my gaze, her big blue eyes cutting to my ashen heart. "Don't look at me in pity or reprimand. You have no right to do that anymore. You wanted me here, so I'm here—"

"I wanted you here because by my side is the safest place to be."

"No, you did it to control me. To confine me. And I didn't protest because it works in my favor. If I don't end this, at least I'll gain information."

"You won't end it, *amore mio*."

"Oh ye of little faith."

I itch to shake some sense into her. To kiss it. *Fuck* it.

"Let me call my brother." There's more demand in her voice than request. "Give me the chance to explain what's going on. To warn him, for Stella's sake."

"Soon."

She squares her shoulders, her throat working over a swallow. "*Please*." Her forehead creases as if the taste of surrender is vile on her tongue. "I waited until we arrived to ask so you'd know there was nothing he could do to interfere. But if this is..." Her brows pinch, her eyes gaining a gleam of vulnerability.

"If this is what?"

"The end." She regains her composure, the words snapped with a retreating step. "If I don't make it home, I need to have spoken to my family first."

She undoes me. Fucking kills me.

"You'll speak to them again, my love. I can promise you that."

She smiles, vindictive and cruel, yet still so fucking inviting. "Thanks for the vote of confidence, *Dante*. However, despite your extremely comforting reassurance, I want that phone call. Now."

My hackles rise at the name. But I understand the reason for the barb.

Amore mio, she can reluctantly stomach. *My love*, she can't.

"One phone call right now." She crosses her arms over her chest, plumping her breasts beneath the thin blouse. "You owe me that much."

I owe her everything. I'll give it to her, too. Just not yet.

I step toward her, my predatory side enjoying her continued

retreat a little more than I care to admit as we make our way down the slim aisle, neither one of us stopping until her back bumps into the cockpit door.

She steels herself as I close in. Squares her shoulders. Clenches her teeth.

My limbs thrum with the desire to connect. To command. To fist her fucking hair and drag her forward until our lips mash and tongues tangle.

She wants it, too. I can tell by the way her gaze darts to my mouth, heated and hungry, her chest rising and falling with shallow breaths.

I inch closer, walking into her, my thigh parting hers.

Then, nothing.

I simply stand there, letting the chemistry between us do its thing. Allowing her to see without words or action that there's no end to the attraction we've created.

We're meant to be together. We won't be separated.

She blinks back at me, stunned yet steadfast. Panicked and panting.

I ignore the pulse of my dick and lean closer, a bare few inches from those captivating lips. "This isn't the time or place."

Her eyes flare. "There will *never* be a time and place. Never again. Do you hear me?"

I smirk. "I was talking about the phone call."

She thumps my chest, pushes and pummels, her cheeks turning red. "You're a bastard. Of course I assumed wrong when you're all over me."

"I *am* a bastard." I sober in agreement, remaining in her space as her attack dwindles. "But I'll give you everything you need, Layla. I promise. I just can't risk a phone call right now. Not with what I've learned of your brother's reputation."

She snarls and shoves past me to escape toward the stairs, mumbling, "Well, I can't wait to learn the truth about yours."

33

MATTHEW

"It's only a few miles up the road." I sit behind the wheel of a rental Lincoln Navigator, driving through the outer reaches of Denver.

I've come to this hellhole of a city too many times over the past ten years and not once have I returned to the home I fled as a teenager.

We pass farming houses and million-dollar estates with masses of cropped land in between. But everything is different now. The trees lining the streets tower higher. More homes scatter the countryside. The road has been widened and marked.

"De Marco is leaving it until the last minute to show," Bishop mutters. "Where is he?"

I slow as I reach the last intersection before Emmanuel's property, making sure there are no cars in sight when I veer onto the gravel at the side of the road. "We should see him any second now."

I bring the vehicle to a stop, scrutinizing the nearby trees and bushes along the fence line, searching for the guys I've worked with on multiple sabotage tasks in the past.

"There are men running around the corner." Layla shifts in the back seat. "I hope they're yours."

I check the rearview, recognizing De Marco's bald head, Goodin's neck tattoo, and the intimidatingly wide build of Whitby jogging toward us, all of them in long-sleeve camo shirts and pants.

"Yeah, they're ours." I press a button on the key fob, opening the door to the cargo area, the back row of seats already folded in preparation to stow the men inside.

Layla bristles when they climb in, their labored breathing filling the air as I press the button to close them into their cramped hiding place.

"I was beginning to think you weren't going to show." De Marco wipes the sweat from his brow. "How's things, Langston?"

"They've been better." I hold his gaze in the mirror. "Are you guys ready?"

"Always." Whitby settles his back against the side of the interior. "We're locked and loaded."

"But this is only a conversation," Bishop mutters.

"It *is* only a conversation," I reiterate. "Do you all understand what we're doing here?"

"You've sent more than enough messages to make it clear." De Marco mimics Whitby's seated position on the opposite side of the cargo area, Goodin doing the same at his side. "We keep our mouths shut. Back you up if necessary. And get the woman out if shit happens."

I nod, my gaze flicking to Layla who stares at me through the mirror. "You can trust them."

She scoffs. "Just like I can trust you?"

I'm not fighting with her again. The last thing I need is to battle my dick when her bratty attitude takes hold.

"We scoped the place while we were waiting," Goodin adds. "Caught sight of two armed guards outside, but nothing else. There might be more in the house."

"Doubtful." I shake my head. "Emmanuel likes privacy."

"Then it's safe to assume there's two." Goodin shrugs. "But there could be fifty on standby at a moment's notice just in case you're thinking of getting cocky."

"Nobody is getting cocky. If bullets start flying the battle won't end until both parties are dead, and I have no intention of dying today." I shoot a glance to Bishop. "You good now?"

"I'll be good once it's over." He focuses out the windscreen, resting his arm on the window ledge. "Let's get this done."

I pull onto the road, increasing the pace to eat up the distance between us and imminent hostility.

"There's to be no complications. Are we all clear?" Bishop reiterates louder than necessary. "This is a conversation. Nothing more."

I don't reaffirm it. He's been given enough assurances on how this has to play out. His issue is that he knows me too well. Knows the *old* me and what that animal is capable of when cornered.

"This is it." I jerk my chin toward the upcoming property with its head-high brick-wall perimeter stretching more than a quarter mile in the distance. Large decorative spikes line the top ledge, the glossy metal maybe intended as a decorative feature, but also offering intimidation and security. "You guys in the back need to get down. Stay out of sight until we're through the gates."

They do as instructed, slinking from view as I drive by the first security camera affixed to the boundary wall. The round black devices are positioned every ten yards leading up to the thick barred gates that never existed in my childhood.

"Nothing gets said or done without my say so." I stop in front of the barrier separating me from assholes I despise, the intercom a foot outside my closed window, and shoot a glance to Layla through the rearview. "No comments. No actions. Nothing. You hear me?"

She smiles, batting her lashes in an innocent taunt.

"Don't test me, Layla."

"Don't worry," Bishop snarls. "If she fucks this up, they won't be the only ones preparing to kill her."

Her smile remains in place. "I'd like to see you try."

"Enough," I grate. "We're on the same side."

"You sure about that?" Goodin mumbles in the back. "You guys aren't giving off a fuzzy sense of comradery."

"We'll be fine," I force the misguided optimism into existence. "We're only here for a fucking conversation."

Layla rolls her eyes, crossing her arms over her chest. "We'll see."

"Yeah, we'll fucking see," Bishop mutters.

"Enough," I repeat. "None of us are stupid enough to fuck this up, right? So show some goddamn restraint." I lower my window and reach for the intercom to press the call button.

The inside of the car falls silent. There's nothing but the rumble from the engine and the rustle of wind as we wait.

I'm sure our presence is already known. Either Emmanuel, my siblings, or a battalion-sized security team are hiding in the wings watching. Waiting.

"Hello?" A fragile female voice breaks the quiet, the fake innocence nudging my agitation.

Adena—the woman who birthed me.

I clench my teeth against my disdain. "I need to see Emmanuel."

"I'm sorry but he's currently in Italy. If you'd like to leave your name and number I can arrange for him to get in contact on his return."

They don't know it's me. They weren't expecting a visit. Why?

"Maybe Remy didn't say anything," Bishop whispers. "You might have been wrong about him."

Bullshit. That fucker was beyond hostile. He would've told someone.

"I know he's inside." I speak to the intercom. "He's going to want to see me."

There's a pause, the briefest blip in time where I picture her squinting at the live feed from the security camera pointing my way.

"Who is this?" she asks.

My anger rises at having to use the only name she's familiar with. "It's Dante. Now open the damn gate."

The silence returns, creating a cavernous void where Layla's loathing grows. I can feel her judgment from the back seat even though those five fucking letters were put behind me when I disowned this godforsaken family.

"Dante?" Adena's voice fractures. "Is that really you?"

I glare at the security camera, reliving the last conversation we had and hating her more for it as the seconds pass. How she denied what Emmanuel had done to Grace. How she took his side over that of her innocent teenage son.

The gates rattle, the intimidating metal bouncing a moment before they begin to part.

I don't answer her question. Don't acknowledge her offensive excitement. I wait until the gate opening is wide enough, then drive into the heart of hell, pebbles crunching under my tires, disgust settling in my gut.

The gardens are different. The shrubs and flowers once littered in the front yard no longer exist. It's now all perfectly manicured grass. Nothing but unobstructed view to ensure intruders are seen.

"Fucking big house," Bishop murmurs. "More than enough room to confine our dumb asses for the rest of our lives."

I ignore him and stalk my gaze along the two-story mansion as we approach, checking for signs of life behind the sheer curtains, both upstairs and below.

The balcony is empty. No potted plants to block the view. No siblings to welcome me home from the wrought-iron railing.

The only sign of life comes from the two guards Whitby spoke of, both of them wearing dark uniforms as they stand at the front steps of the mansion, each of them with a hand at the ready near their holstered sidepiece.

"De Marco, it's time for you guys to shine." I pull to a stop a few yards from the front of the house and cut the engine. "Everyone else, stay in the car. Let me get a read on things first." I unfasten my belt and climb out, slamming the door behind me before Bishop can protest.

The cargo area opens as I walk to the hood, Whitby, Goodin, and De Marco all piling out to take different positions around the vehicle.

Emmanuel's guards don't show surprise. They don't talk or scowl or move. They're prepared. On alert. Adena might not have anticipated my arrival, but someone did.

I stalk toward them, jaw stiff, lips snarled, and poised to demand a meeting with Emmanuel when Salvatore opens the front door.

"Brother," he sneers in greeting. "You shouldn't be here."

"Believe me, I wish I wasn't."

"Then leave." He approaches, passing his two guards to eye the

Lincoln. "Is that *her*? You brought her here?" His hard eyes cut to mine. "Are you fucking insane?"

"Are you?" I counter. "Stealing a kid? Killing a major player in the Portland underworld? Who the fuck have you become?"

"Someone loyal to my family. Which is more than I can say for you."

I smile, all teeth and anger. "I want to see him. So either wheel him out here if he's in as bad shape as Remy claims, or we're going in."

"You don't want to do that."

"I agree. But I'm still going to." It's been a lifetime since we were face-to-face. Now, there's a mere few feet of space between me and my closest sibling, who stands at the top of the three stairs leading to damnation. But the prankster kid I grew up with is nowhere in sight. The man who stares back at me is cold and calculating. "I won't let Remy twist the situation and make her more of a target."

"He hasn't twisted anything." Salvatore keeps his tone level, exuding a calm I can't reciprocate. "Nobody knows. Neither me or Remy want to continue this war with her psychotic family. So the last thing we're going to do is tell Dad you've hooked up with the enemy."

"That's not the impression he gave earlier today." I slide my hands into my pants pockets, hiding the way my fingers twitch for a gun I no longer own. "Remy made it clear he wanted her dead."

He scoffs a laugh and descends the stairs, the guards following a few steps behind him. He doesn't stop until he's squared up with me, shoulders broad and proud, chin arrogantly high.

As a teen, I towered over him, my growth spurt coming well before his, but now we're equally matched in physical appearance as well as disdain.

"He's always been more of a slave to his emotions than either of us," he drawls. "So it's only natural he reacted to yet another layer of your betrayal when he was the one who took the longest to understand why the fuck you would abandon us in the first place."

I bristle.

I hadn't wanted to leave them behind. I'd been a kid when I made those plans with Grace. I'd been young and dumb and stupid. I'd thought things would change once I was gone. That Emmanuel would wake up to himself instead of doubling down on criminal decisions.

"Don't resent me for getting out. You could've done the same a hundred times over."

He laughs with derision. "Ignorance is bliss, brother. You have no idea what our lives are like."

"Spare me the multimillion-dollar sob story. I'm not here to reminisce. Either bring him out here or tell your dogs to stand down so we can go inside."

"Do you really want to make that mistake?" He steps closer, getting in my face, the shuffle of feet closing in behind me, Salvatore's guards following suit. "Remy may have been driven by emotion if he spoke of killing her, but our father will be entirely collected when he gives the order for her death. You're shortening her already precarious lifespan."

"I'll shorten yours if you don't get out of my way."

We stare each other down, neither one of us budging until the front door opens, the slight creak of a well-worn hinge dragging my attention to Adena paused in the entry.

"Dante?" She scrutinizes me with a cautious approach. "Is that really my boy?"

Salvatore steps back, his face bitter as she breaks into a run.

Fuck.

I brace for impact as she descends the stairs and throws her arms wide, barreling into me for a hug that snaps my muscles rigid.

I don't remove my hands from my pockets. Don't reciprocate.

Guilt is a punishing motherfucker as I imagine Layla's thoughts as her enemy embraces me like the long-lost child I am.

"My son." Adena's face snuggles into my neck, the affection pathetic. "I've missed you more than you could imagine. I always knew you'd come back."

"I haven't." I retreat, breaking the connection. "Once I speak to your husband, I'm gone."

She blinks, her face falling as Salvatore comes to stand at her side. "Why? What is this about?"

"Business," my brother answers. "It's not a reunion."

Another body enters the doorway, the feminine greeting of, "Hi, brother," brushing my ears before I turn my attention to Abri.

She's in perfect costume, accentuated makeup, figure-hugging clothes, immaculately styled hair. It's the smile curving her lips that places a fault in the facade, the jubilation not matching the sadness she can't hide in her eyes.

"Abri," I grate.

I remember her as the heart and happiness of this family when I was growing up. Too pure and sweet to survive Emmanuel. Too young and innocent to be taken with me when I left.

I was wrong, though. From what I've heard, she's adapted to the changing environment, transforming into a snake who seduces wealthy married men only to blackmail them with their transgressions.

"What's going on?" She glides her attention over De Marco and his men, then focuses on the car before stiffening. "What is she doing here?"

"We're here to see Emmanuel. Who's going to—" My words fall short as the front gates rattle open behind me.

I glance over my shoulder, watching the heavy metal move as Bishop disobeys instruction and climbs from the car, his large frame moving to stand in front of Layla's window, protecting her from the view of the approaching Maserati.

"Good," Salvatore murmurs. "Remy's here to join the fun."

The vehicle accelerates, kicking up pebbles and dust to abruptly skid to a stop next to the Lincoln. In seconds, my youngest brother is shoving from the sports car, the engine still purring as he storms toward Layla's door.

"You brought that bitch here?" he accuses. "Didn't I warn you?"

"Back off." Bishop braces for attack, arms tense, knuckles locked.

De Marco does the same, closing in at his side.

I remain in place, my demons screaming for action even though I know it would be a sign of weakness. "I'll kill you myself, Remy. You know I will."

They need to see I'm in control. That I'm not mindless in my need to protect her, even though that's far from the truth.

I'd slaughter for her.

And I'd do it too damn easily.

Remy stops a few feet in front of Bishop. "Get her out of here."

"I will as soon as I see Emmanuel. Until then, keep your thoughts about her to yourself or risk becoming a folktale."

His eyes cut to mine. "She won't make it out of here alive."

The hair at my nape prickles. "You kill her, I kill you, Salvo kills me, Bishop kills him. The list goes on until a generation is slaughtered. Not to mention the aftermath from Lorenzo if anyone survives. Is that what you want?" I glare. "Because I didn't come here for violence."

Nobody answers.

"I *will* kill for her." I meet everyone's gaze in turn—Salvo, Remy, Abri, Adena, then their guards. "Without pause or guilt. So if anyone has that on their mind, start preparing to meet your maker."

"You're such a piece of shit," Remy mutters. "Lorenzo really did a number on you."

"And look what your father did to you. Clearly, you're not the pinnacle of virtue."

"He's your father, too," Adena corrects.

"No." I look at her in earnest. "Both of you gave up parental rights when you had Grace killed."

"What?" Abri stiffens, her mask of perfection slipping as her lips part in shock. "Is that true? Is that why he left?"

"No. He's stirring up lies from the past." Adena crosses her arms over her chest, every wrinkle on her tired face growing deeper as she scowls at me. "Why are you being like this? You've become just like her family." She turns her daggered stare toward Layla in the back seat. "Breaking the peace after years of silence."

"Peace?" I smirk. "You abduct a child of the Portland underworld and expect peace?"

"Two children," Abri murmurs. "There were two."

"For fuck's sake," Bishop mutters.

I shake my head, scowling at Salvatore. How the hell could he let that happen?

"Don't judge me." His jaw ticks. "You don't know me."

"Evidently… and murder?" I raise a brow. "And still, you expected there to be peace?"

"Nobody else was meant to be there," he growls. "Everything ran smoothly until that asshole spooked us."

"Everything ran smoothly?" Abri's hand tentatively climbs to her throat. "I disagree."

Salvo ignores her. Everyone does as silence falls, the hum of the Maserati the only sound.

I knew they never had the picture-perfect relationship they projected on social media. The overheard conversations at Perfezione are proof of that. But seeing them like this shows the cuts run deeper.

None of them are proud of their lives. They're miserable here.

Yet they still don't leave.

"I'm not here to recap your mistakes." I pull my hands from my pockets, raising my palms to show I'm not here to fight. "I only came to make sure Emmanuel doesn't repeat them in the future. So are you escorting me inside or am I entering by force?"

Remy sneers. Their guards grip the handle of their holstered weapons.

"Fine. Be my guest." Salvatore smirks and turns to the house, swinging an arm toward the front door. "But it's her funeral."

34

MATTHEW

I open Layla's door, offering a hand to help her climb out only to fight frustration when she pushes away my hospitality.

I make sure she stays at my side as we're led into the house, Salvatore climbing the curved entry staircase, a guard marching close at his back when he enters the upper-level hall.

We become a long line of temperamental fuckery as we stride into a wing of the mansion that didn't exist when I was a child. Bishop and De Marco remain in my shadow, followed by Adena, Remy, Abri and their second guard, then Goodin and Whitby at the rear.

"You sure you want to do this?" Salvo stops at a closed door at the end of the hall, his hand poised on the handle. "Times may change, Dante, but he hasn't learned to listen."

I glower. "Open the fucking door."

He shrugs and does as requested, pushing the painted wood wide to continue inside, the guard on his tail. He exposes a sunlit room full of medical equipment, Emmanuel seated in the middle on an inclined hospital bed. The grey-haired bastard's legs are covered by sheets and a knitted blanket, his torso draped in an oversized grey shirt with heart monitor cables snaking out from one of the short sleeves and neck hole.

He's lost weight since the last time I saw him at Perfezione, his cheeks now gaunt, his skin a pale shade of grey.

"Son." He greets me without surprise, the Italian accent lingering in his voice while he repositions himself to sit taller. "I was beginning to wonder when you would come inside. It's good to see you again."

"Stay behind me," I mutter to Layla and continue forward, looking down my nose at him with blatant scorn as the peanut gallery enter behind me to suffocate the space. "I heard you were shot. Too bad they didn't have better aim."

Emmanuel chuckles, the sound morphing into a wheezing hack of a cough. "It was merely a scratch to the shoulder." The hacking continues, his struggle growing. "Unfortunately, complications came with the recovery. Sepsis hasn't been kind."

"What a shame," Layla mutters.

Emmanuel's eyes narrow on her as he reaches to the side of the bed, retrieving an oxygen mask to place over his mouth. "Ahh, yes. The woman I saw on the security feed. Let her come closer so I can take a better look."

"She's fine where she is." I raise an arm at my side, making sure Layla isn't tempted to oblige. "I'm sure you recognize her."

"I do." He nods into the mask, dragging in breaths. "And I appreciate you bringing me such a gift."

I straighten to my full height, fuming at the taunt.

Bishop clears his throat, hard, as if warning me to keep my rage under control.

I struggle to comply. I fucking battle not to reach for his mask and wrap the rubber cord around his neck until the smug superiority vanishes from his face.

"She's no gift," I snarl. "I suggest you treat her with respect if you don't plan on giving more strength to your enemies."

"You'll never be an enemy, son." He waves me away, lowering the mask. "But I know you've been sleeping with her. That you lied about your name and withheld your legacy to win her over. The news actually brought a proud tear to my eye."

Layla mutters a curse.

"And how do you know?" I turn my attention to Salvo, the asshole who promised Remy hadn't spilled.

"I didn't say a damn thing." He glances to his father. "We were going to tell you once Remy returned."

"Of course you were, son. But I have faster ways to gain information."

Faster?

Emmanuel could only have learned the news from Remy. Bishop wouldn't betray me. And Layla hasn't left my sight.

Unless… "You have someone listening in on their calls." I grin at Salvatore. "I bet that's comforting."

The muscles in his jaw tic.

"I watch my children more than most." Emmanuel drags in a deep breath and lowers the mask. "You're never too old to need guidance."

"I bet. But the guidance you offered two years ago has placed your ass in a hospital bed with the Grim Reaper stalking your shadow. So maybe your leadership skills need a tweak or two. Don't you think?"

"I'm not scared of Cole Torian. Enemies are the price you pay for power and money. And he's merely a pup. Nowhere near the type of cutthroat businessman his father was."

"My father was a sex trafficker," Layla snaps. "Cole would never aspire to be anything like him."

"And that's why he's weak. Are you as pathetic, my sweet?"

"I'll show you how pathetic I can be." She storms closer, but I block her path.

"Don't let him provoke you," I growl under my breath. "You're smarter than that."

"How smart can she be?" Emmanuel wheezes another chuckle. "She didn't even know your real identity until this morning."

I grab her wrist as she takes another thunderous step, willing her to ignore him with my strong grip.

"I can promise you, your daughter showed far more tenacity in the face of adversity than you are," he continues.

"*Dad*," Abri warns.

"She was a real little spitfire when we first got hold of her. We had a great time, though. In fact, I'd really love to see her again. I should—"

Layla screams, yanking her arm from my grip to barge past me like wildfire. She charges for Emmanuel, her face turning red, her hand shoving into her jeans pocket in search of something.

Shit. The fucking cyanide.

I lunge for her, grabbing her upper arms from behind as guns are drawn by the guards, Salvo, and Remy. My men follow suit in opposition.

"I'll kill you, you fucking prick." Layla thrashes and bucks against my hold. "I'll kill every single one of you."

"I'd like to see you try." Remy levels his barrel on her.

"Come on now." Bishop holds up a hand in placation, his weapon pointed at Emmanuel. "Nobody wants to lose blood over this."

She continues to thrash and scramble, rampant and manic. "Let me go, you bastard."

"Stop it." I smother her against my chest. "Calm down."

I stalk her from the room, Bishop hot on my trail as he walks backward to cover his ass. My anger is barely bottled as I guide her into the far wall, pressing her chest into the plaster before closing in behind her.

"What the fuck were you thinking?" I clamp both her wrists in one hand and use the other to delve into her pocket, retrieving the vial of fucking cyanide. "What was the plan?" I growl in her ear. "You'd sprinkle some magic fairy dust and try to kill us all?"

"Yes." She bucks. "At least then this would have been over."

"You would've been dead before you unscrewed the lid." I release my hold, allowing her to swing around to face me, her eyes stark, her cheeks flushed.

"You said it yourself—if they kill me, you kill them, and so on and so forth. At the very least, some of them would die."

I lean closer, glaring as our noses almost brush. "And you would've been the first."

"So be it." Moisture wells in her eyes, the liquid born of rage. "He needs to pay for what he's done."

"What about Stella? Do you think she deserves to lose another parent?"

She recoils, her gaze shooting daggers, each blink sending a scathing wave of hatred my way. "Did you hear him? He's going to go after her. I know he is."

I remain in her face, her mouth a breath away. "I'll fucking kill him before I let anything happen to either of you. Do you understand? Love me or hate me, Layla, I'll still keep you safe."

She bares her teeth, vicious and pained as footsteps approach from Emmanuel's room.

"Dante?" Abri murmurs.

I flinch at the name and glare over my shoulder to see her blocked from the hall by Bishop's large frame.

"It might be best for her to wait in the room across the hall." She glowers at the man guarding me as she pushes past. "You can keep the doors open. You'll be able to see her at any time."

"No." Layla rasps. "I want to hear every word that motherfucker has to say."

"And I want to get us all out of here alive," I murmur under my breath, leaning into her, taking liberties with her personal space. "Get yourself under control, *amore mio*. Or I'll do it for you."

She squares her shoulders, her rage smoldering.

"That's right. Keep that anger directed at me. Not him." I press my hips into hers, our cheeks brushing as I guide my mouth to her ear. "Hate *me*. Loathe *me*. Curse my fucking name for playing you the way I did, because I will never hurt you, Layla. But he will."

I'm so fucking tempted to kiss her. To steal a gasp and make her moan, just in case this is the last chance I get.

"Now move your ass into the other room." I force myself to pull back, my restraint threadbare, my gaze brooking no argument as our eyes meet. "And make sure you stay there."

She continues to glower, the only sign of fragility coming from her heavy swallow.

"I'd die for you, *amore mio*." I retreat and turn for Emmanuel's room. "But for the love of God, I'd prefer not to do it today."

35

LAYLA

I REMAIN PROPPED AGAINST THE WALL, HUMILIATED AT BEING BARRED from a conversation I deserve to be in.

"Stay with her," Matthew instructs Bishop, then returns to Emmanuel's room, leaving me to fight against crumpling to the floor.

I should've tried harder.

Should've stolen a gun and pulled the trigger without a second thought.

Maybe I would've died. Who's to say I won't anyway?

Emmanuel has it out for me. I could see it in his eyes.

He'll go after Stella. He'll destroy my family.

"Come on." Abri gives me a sad smile and opens the door to the adjacent room, allowing more light to spill into the hall. "Let them talk. It's clear you're a weakness where my brother is concerned, and that's the last thing he needs when facing off with our father."

I don't understand her sympathy.

I don't appreciate it either.

She saunters inside, walking out of view.

"That was a dick move." Bishop closes in, intimidating me into following her with his evil glare. "Now he doesn't have me in there to watch his back."

I reject the twinge of guilt sparking in my chest.

"Get moving." The aggression in his voice is next level. "I swear to God, if he does something he'll regret, I'll hold you responsible."

I clench my teeth, refusing to let Bishop daunt me and walk into the unfamiliar room to stop a few feet inside. I keep my lips fused as I take in the cherry-stained wooden bed in the middle of the expansive area, a matching dresser along the closest wall, and sheer curtains covering French doors leading to what I assume is the balcony.

I remain still as I search for weapon potential—the lamp on the nightstand, the ceramic female figurine on the dresser, the chair in the corner—while Abri watches my inspection from the open doorway of the adjoining private bathroom.

"Are you okay?" She frowns at me as Bishop comes to lean against the closest bedpost, the conversation reigniting across the hall, the words skirting the edges of my consciousness. "You don't seem to be here by choice."

"I've never had a choice when it comes to your family. I didn't when you stole my daughter. And I had just as much when you killed my husband."

Her eyes soften. "I'm sorry for your loss. I didn't—"

"Save it." I continue toward the French doors and inch the curtain aside, wishing I was anywhere but here.

Time passes with the rise and fall of voices. Matthew makes threats. Emmanuel chuckles. His bitch of a mother chastises every now and again.

"Can I speak to her for a moment?" Abri asks Bishop. "In private. There's a few things I have—"

"No way in hell, darlin'. I'm not letting her out of my sight."

"Beside the fact I'm not interested," I add, "I've got nothing to say to you."

"Please." Her brows pull tight. "It's important."

The vulnerability is an act. The politeness, too.

But I'm curious to know why.

She's not armed. Not with a gun at least. Her clothes are too tight to conceal a firearm. There's potential for a knife, though.

"We can talk on the balcony." She starts toward me. "We'll remain in sight at all times."

Bishop frowns, his gaze trekking her with agitation.

"*Please*. It will only take a minute." Her arm brushes mine as she opens the French doors, her long blonde hair dancing in the breeze. "I wouldn't beg if it wasn't important."

"I never knew Costas could beg," Bishop mutters.

She glares at him, then gives a brittle smile when her attention returns to mine. "He's right. We don't usually stoop this low. But like I said, it's important."

I have no idea what she's up to.

Is she going to haul me over the railing? Does a weapon lie in wait outside the door?

"You'll be fine." Bishop pushes from the bed to stand tall. "I'll be watching."

I nod and follow her past the threshold, stopping two feet outside as she stands out of view of the room.

"*Listen to me,*" she mouths. "*I can help you.*"

I frown and glance back at Bishop in confusion.

"Don't look at him," she whispers. "Do you want to get out of here or not?"

I balk. "Excuse me?"

"Do you want to leave?" Her voice is barely heard over the breeze, her pretty face pinched in apprehension.

My heart kicks up a gear, my pulse increasing. "What are you trying to do?"

She inches closer, her voice dropping further. "Despite the estrangement, I love Dante. But I don't think you want to be here…" She pauses, waiting for me to fill the silence.

"So you'd help me escape?"

"Normally, no." There's no apology in her tone. "But I owe your brother, and I want the debt off my shoulders."

"Why would you owe him?"

"You don't need specifics."

"If there's any way I'm going to trust your help, I'm going to need them."

She sucks in a tired breath. "He showed me kindness the night your husband died. He could've hurt me, but he didn't."

"You're lying." Cole wouldn't have shown anything other than hostility toward the people who stole my daughter.

"Believe what you want. I'm not here to convince you. The question is whether or not you want to get away from Dante."

I disregard the name she uses while my stomach sinks.

Do I want to get away from him? Do I want to distance myself from heartbreak and betrayal at the cost of vulnerability?

"How?" I whisper.

"There's a window in the bathroom. The screen can be removed. If you climb through, there's an old trellis that will get you to the ground."

She's serious.

Holy shit.

"To what end?" I frown, keeping my voice low. "How am I meant to outrun nine grown men when stuck behind towering walls that are miles from civilization?"

"Once you reach the lawn, move around the back of the house to the garage. The roller doors should already be open. My car is the Bentley. The keys are in the center console along with the remote for the gate."

I stare at her, trying to find a hint of deception. "Why are you doing this?"

"I already told you. I owe Cole. This is me repaying the debt." She reaches for my arm, her fingers cautiously touching my wrist. "I'm not your enemy, Layla. I never have been. What happened with your husband was a horrible tragedy. And your daughter..." She winces. "Me and my brothers had no idea what was going on until we were in the middle of a war. It never should've—"

"Are you two finished out there?" Bishop growls, his footsteps approaching.

Abri retreats to stand at her full height, her face transforming into a mask of innocence.

Are we finished?

It seems like she's merely scratched the surface of withheld information. And none of it makes sense.

Cole showed her kindness? My husband's death was a tragedy?

"What's going on?" Bishop comes to stand at the threshold.

"Nothing." I clear my throat and swallow to alleviate the dryness. "I was just about to come inside."

I maneuver past him, hiding my face from his scrutiny as I reenter the room.

Indecision claws its way into my skull, awakening a thousand questions, stirring up more trouble. It's too much to think through. I can't concentrate to make a plan.

My instincts boil down to Matthew and whether I should trust his offer of safety or flee to find my own. The thought of escaping his manipulative protection fills me with dread. And my damn heart still clings to the hope of him making amends.

But he can't. How could he?

He lied. Had me mugged. Made me fall for him under false pretenses.

He duped me better than my father ever did, the resulting emotional scars capable of outweighing those already in existence.

I'd loved him.

Wholeheartedly.

With optimism and passion.

He made me believe in a future without darkness. A life without recrimination. He had me planning a fresh start, one that I never deserved.

My gaze treks to his across the hall, our eyes briefly locking for a pained moment while he addresses someone in the other room.

There's possession in his stare. Hunger even in the depth of this darkness.

The sight of it breaks me. Cuts me down at the knees in humiliation. In sorrow.

I'd wanted an entwined future. I'd never craved anything more.

Now our time together boils down to one question—do I stay or do I go?

I hold onto the sight of him as Abri closes the French doors. I take in the parts of him that inflicted betrayal—the hands that brought me pleasure, the lips that lied to me, and eyes that deceived.

I breathe it all in, dragging the pain deep into my lungs, and release the last lingering threads of hope with the exhale. Then I turn to Bishop, hating him for the role he played as I announce, "I need to use the bathroom."

36

MATTHEW

"You're caught in a temperamental position, son." Emmanuel holds my gaze, his eyes gleaming with superiority. "Yet again you've fallen for someone who weakens you. Someone who has you begging."

I glance across the hall, watching Layla walk out of sight, a door closing shortly after.

Where the fuck is she going?

"*Bathroom*," Bishop mouths, reading my mind as he gestures to his dick.

Good. At least she can't cause trouble in there.

"You've got me wrong, old man." I turn back to Emmanuel and prowl closer to his bed. "I'm not begging. I'm telling you to leave her out of this. Her *and* her daughter. Otherwise I'll make good on all the things I've wanted to do to you in the last fifteen years."

He smiles. "All the things you wanted to do but were too loyal to instigate…"

"I'm loyal, yes. But not to you. Lorenzo is the only reason you still have air in your lungs."

"*Dante*," Adena snaps. "Don't say such things."

"It's okay, my sweet." Emmanuel doesn't break our stare. "What our son doesn't realize is that his threats are a blessing. Every decision I made in his childhood was to shape the brilliant man standing before me. My actions placed fire in his belly and strength in his soul."

Venom in my veins.

Hate in my heart.

"You're exactly what I aspired to create." He grins. "I couldn't be more proud."

My nostrils flare.

"We need to endure to evolve, my son. You never could understand that. But what I did in your teenage years was a favor. A gift."

Grace's murder was a gift?

Slicing her open was a fucking favor?

I laugh, otherwise I'd roar.

I picture ripping out his throat. Watching him suffer. Hearing his cries for mercy.

"That girl from your senior year was beneath you, anyway." He continues digging his grave. "Can you believe she offered to spread her legs if I promised to get her out of town?"

My body detonates. Rage and hatred collide.

I lunge for him. Two steps is all it takes to have my hand around his throat, my eyes venomous as they will death upon him. "Your actions didn't make me strong." I seethe, spittle coating my lips. "They turned me into a monster."

My mother screams. He doesn't look at me in fear. Only in satisfaction. "I'm honored," he wheezes.

Motherfucker.

I gave him what he wanted. I turned into the man he'd wished for. Someone callous and cruel. Vicious and brutal.

Goddamnit.

Cold metal presses into my temple, the barrel of a gun hard and unyielding against my skin as Emmanuel rasps for breath.

"Let him go," Salvatore demands. "Get your hands off him."

I can't.

I want to end this. To squeeze the breath from the asshole's lungs. To watch the life drain from his eyes.

I've pictured it a million times. Felt the euphoria. Tasted the victory.

"*Langston*," Bishop shouts across the hall. "We're not here for this."

But I want to be.

I need it.

The brutality calls to me. Fucking sings.

Every wheeze invigorates me. Each stuttered breath appeases.

"He dies, we all die," De Marco mutters behind me. "Come on, man. This isn't the plan."

Fuck.

I can justify my own death, but not those who followed me here. Not my siblings, either. Not yet, anyway.

And not Layla.

Never Layla.

"Fuck you." I shove Emmanuel into the bed before releasing him. "You *will* stay away from her. You *will* leave her the fuck alone." I backtrack from the gun and glare at Salvatore, then Remy. "Fuck over whoever else you like. Ruin lives. Start wars. But she stays out of it."

"I applaud the vicious show," Remy drawls, "however, I'm deducting points for the fear in your eyes. I can see right through you."

"I don't fear you." I march to him, not stopping until we're toe-to-toe. "And I don't fear death. I fucking welcome it, because staying alive means I'll spend every waking moment wasting my time thinking of ways to torture you if you dare to touch her."

"*Stop.*" Adena rushes to Emmanuel's side, helping to place the oxygen mask to his face as he barks and chokes. "Please just stop. Don't you see how much we love you? We always have. We just want you home."

"He never left," Emmanuel rasps. "He's always remained close, still wanting to be a part of what he left behind."

"I haven't been anywhere near this house since I left years ago. This is—"

"You come back to Denver," he corrects, his voice weak beneath the mask but the intent strong. "You come back and watch us share our family meal almost every month. You listen to our conversations from afar. Soak in the nostalgia."

He's known.

All this time.

"Spying, big brother?" Salvatore lowers the gun to his side. "That's a little pitiful, don't you think?"

"It's fucking pathetic," Remy seethes. "Why weren't we told?"

"Because he's a piece of shit." I throw my arms wide with a maniacal laugh. "If he's known, that means he's let me sabotage your warehouse shipments and rat out your distributions channels. Every problem you've had in the last ten years has been my doing, and he knew the whole time."

"It's the price I paid to keep you close."

No. He did it because he's insane.

Fucking psychotic.

"Enough of this back-and-forth bullshit." I run a rough hand over my mouth, pulling myself in check. "I want your word you'll leave her alone."

"Agree to return home and I'll give you whatever you want," he counters.

I smile, all teeth, no charm. "How about this?" I step closer and Salvatore follows, his gun raising again. "I promise the next time I come back, I'll burn this place to the ground. With or without you in it."

"Dante," my mother sobs. "*Please.*"

I don't drag my attention from Emmanuel. Don't blink. Don't breathe.

I stare into those godforsaken eyes and let him know I'm not bluffing. I make it clear I'd love to watch him burn. And that damn twinkle in his eye tells me he's only growing more proud.

Jesus. Fuck.

"It's time to go," I address my team, still staring at my maker, waiting for him to say something I can't ignore.

A knock from the adjacent room breeches my ears, the subtle sound rising above the hiss of oxygen and whir of strangled breath.

"Layla." Bishop's voice travels from across the hall. "Hurry up."

I tense at her name. At the vision it provides. At the fucking yearning. But I don't move. Don't quit staring even though every-thing in my soul wants to focus on what's happening across the hall.

"Just like Grace, she distracts you." Emmanuel removes the oxygen mask. "How can you not see that?"

"Because a distraction from what you created is exactly what I need." I backtrack toward the door, passing Goodin, De Marco, and Whitby. "I'll do anything to protect her. Remember that if you're stupid enough to test me."

"I'm definitely going to test you, son. It's what makes you stronger."

I smirk, pretending I'm calling his bluff when I know he speaks the truth. I'm going to have to find a way to kill him without getting pinned for the blame.

I'll pay someone. Bribe. Threaten.

I'll do whatever it takes.

"Those are adamant fighting words coming from someone in a hospital bed." I turn on my heel and stride for the threshold, telling De Marco to, "Block the door," as I pass and continue into the adjoining bedroom where Bishop faces off with Abri who stands before a closed door.

"We're getting out of here." I stalk toward them. "Where's Layla?"

"Still in the bathroom." Bishop flings a hand in Abri's direction. "She's been in there for over ten minutes with no flushed toilet or running faucet. And no goddamn response when I call her fucking name."

I shoulder my sister out of the way and slam my fist against the door. "Layla. Open up. We're leaving."

There's no reply.

No sound. No shift of movement from inside.

I glare at my sister. "What have you done?"

She raises her chin, defiant.

Fuck. What the hell has she done?

I step back, panic consuming me, rage inspiring me. "Layla, move away from the door." I plant my heel next to the handle, sending the door flying and wood splintering from around the jamb.

I don't have to step inside to know she's not there.

The window is open, the white lace curtain dancing in the breeze.

I race forward, my hands sweating as I grip the ledge and shove my head outside.

A screen frame lays dormant on the grass below in an otherwise still garden.

There's no sign of her.

"Where is she?" I swing around and charge for Abri. Her eyes widen. "What the fuck did you do?'

She braces her feet apart and squares her shoulders. "Nothing."

The crunch of pebbles carries from outside. Loud and urgent. Bishop shoots me a glance, then makes for the French doors.

I'm right behind him.

"What's going on?" Salvatore yells from the other room.

Bishop and I step onto the balcony to see a Bentley fishtail around the drive, the brake lights glaring as the gates begin to open.

"It's her." Bishop shoves his hands through his hair. *"Jesus goddamn Christ."*

I fight the compulsion to jump the balcony and chase after her the fastest way possible, knowing I'll break my fucking legs in the process.

"What are we doing, Langston?" Bishop turns to me. "What the fuck do we do?"

How could she leave?

Does she hate me that much? Enough to risk running without protection?

"Wake the fuck up, bitch." Bishop thumps my chest, the blow hard enough to jar bone. "What's the plan?"

"Is something wrong?" Emmanuel calls from the adjacent room, his derision sparking insanity.

He'll give an order for her to be chased.

He'll command my brothers. Their guards.

I've got no chance of finding her first.

"Hey." Bishop grabs my shoulders. "I know that look in your eye, asshole." He gets in my face, friend to friend, monster to monster. "We didn't come here for this. No bloodshed, remember? Just a fucking conversation."

"I can't do it." I shake my head. "I can't let him go after her."

"He's bedridden, for fuck's sake. He's not going anywhere."

"And what about Salvo and Remy? One order from him and they're out the door."

He leans closer, grabbing me behind the back of the neck. "They're pussies. They—"

"They won't hurt her," Abri whispers from the balcony threshold. "I promise, Dante. They'd never do that."

"See?" Bishop digs his fingers into my neck. "Pussies. Emmanuel's the only one heartless enough to kill in cold blood and he's too decrepit to do it."

"No." I shove him away. "They'll find her and bring her back here."

"If that happens, we'll have De Marco and the guys waiting."

"Abri, what's going on in there?" Salvo snarls with impatience. "If this guard dog doesn't move, he's not going to appreciate my lack of warning shot."

I claw my fingers into my palm, unsure which path to take as De Marco mutters something in reply.

"We'll be there in a minute." Abri cuddles her waist, the picture of sophistication and class now marred by eyes filled with regret. "I'm sorry," she whispers.

"For what? Betraying me or putting her in more danger?"

She cringes and casts a cautious glance toward the hall. "I was *helping* her."

"Why?" Bishop grates.

"She didn't want to be here. You were forcing her—"

I step up to my sister. "I was *protecting* her."

"I know what forced proximity with a man looks like." Her response is barely heard. "I know what it feels like, too."

"We don't have time for this," Bishop warns.

I fucking know we don't. But Abri's unchecked show of emotion raises my hackles. "What does that mean? Are you looking to get out of here?"

She straightens, her lips parting a crack, her eyes widening. She surprises me by not shooting down the offer. By hesitating for long seconds.

"Abri?" Emmanuel yells. "What's going on? Where's Torian's sister?"

"We don't have seconds to spare." Bishop glares at me.

"Abri?" I warn. "What's—"

"Go." She steps back from the threshold. "We'll talk later."

I keep looking at her, keep trying to read what she's withholding while my pulse beats for Layla's safety. "Let's get out of here."

"About fucking time." Bishop storms for the hall.

I follow, De Marco stepping aside as I continue into Emmanuel's room, fists clenched, pulse rocketing.

"Problems, son?" Emmanuel wheezes, clasping his oxygen mask as he smirks. "Did your pretty little thing run?"

I can't bite.

I won't.

A future with Layla can't exist if I return to the Cappellettis. I won't drag her into that. I need to find her before Emmanuel does.

I focus on Adena, glaring my hatred. "You betrayed me when I was a boy. You let him run loose, destroying the only happiness I had. You won't go unpunished if you allow it to happen again."

She stands taller, frowning.

"He's your husband to control," I sneer. "Your problem to solve. From now on, any action he takes will also be yours to absolve, and I don't punish in halves."

Emmanuel chuckles, the humming, wheezing noise growing.

I turn to my brothers, the muscles in my jaw aching from tension, my head pounding as I fight to ignore their father. "My hatred has always been for him. *Never* either of you. But so help me God, if you do anything to put her in harm's way I'll start a war you won't survive."

They don't react.

Neither in spite or understanding.

Their faces remain emotionless. Impassive and detached.

"Let the race begin." Emmanuel chokes as he laughs. "I'm sure we'll see each other again as soon as we catch her."

37

LAYLA

I force myself not to think of how Matthew will retaliate as I monkey climb down the trellis, my feet getting stuck in the thick vine weaving its way through the wooden slats.

I pretend he doesn't exist as I run around the house to find the garage. And I focus on how the inside information on the Costas' home will help my family as I scramble into the Bentley and drive my ass out of there.

I don't think about how I'll get home.

How I'll survive.

I don't contemplate anything more than the broad strokes of my escape plan until now when the desolate road is stretched before me, and I have nowhere to go.

I should've thought about how the hell I was going to get to Portland without a cell, money, and identification.

I should've focused on the issues that would arise if I attempted to escape in a car that had less than half a tank of gas.

"*Shit.*" I press my foot harder against the accelerator, eyeballing the rearview mirror, waiting for the first sign that someone is giving chase.

I need to find a phone. More importantly, I need to figure out how I'm going to tell Cole what I've done.

He'll disown me. They all will.

I take deserted back road after deserted back road, using the car's GPS to navigate an indirect route around the city.

I circle the outskirts of Denver, not knowing exactly where I am once farm road turns into suburban streets. All I can see are dilapidated homes with junk in the yard and old vehicles that make my current ride look like a carjacker's dream come true.

I keep off the main thoroughfares, searching for a sign of life, finally slowing when I see three teenage girls walking along the street footpath, one of them scrolling on her cell.

I pull to the curb, slowing as I come up beside them, and lower the passenger window.

"Excuse me." I raise my voice. "I need your help."

The girls glance at me in unison, each of the teenagers sporting raised brows and expressions of disdain toward the Bentley.

"How could we possibly help you?" the closest asks, glancing from my face to the car and back again.

"There are men chasing me, and I have no phone or money. Can I borrow your cell to make a call?"

The one on the far end snorts, flicking her bleached hair behind her shoulder while she continues to walk ahead.

"*Please*." I crawl the vehicle along beside them. "It's only one phone call."

"Get fucked, bitch." The closest curls her lip, then turns to her friends, all of them breaking into laughter.

Goddamn teenagers.

I pull away from the curb and plant my foot, speeding farther along the street. I need to ditch the car, and fast, but I need security first.

I zigzag my way through the suburb, eventually coming to a four-lane street with heavy traffic, fast-food outlets on either side, and a hotel sign looming ahead that sparks hope.

I keep one eye on the road, the other getting a brief glimpse of the dark tan four-level building as I drive past, then take the next turn in the opposite direction. I continue down another street, then turn and accelerate along another, not pulling to a stop until I'm at least a few blocks from where I want to be. Then I ditch the car and start running.

I take shady back alleys and cut across house yards. I don't stop looking over my shoulder or scrutinizing every car that passes, but none come close to the extravagance I found in the Costa family garage.

I make my way back to the main road, then continue into the hotel parking lot, my stomach bottoming at the full-frontal view.

What my split-second, drive-by glance didn't ascertain is that this place is something out of a horror movie.

Windows are cracked with grey electrical tape holding them together. The cheap blinds inside are broken and disheveled. The balconies to the three upper levels are nothing more than a red metal fire escape, the staircase exposed to the elements and rusted in parts.

But it's the man eagle-eying me from the third-floor railing, his wifebeater dirty and boxers loose that concerns me the most.

I recognize that opportunistic expression, and I have no intention of being a part of it.

I glower, letting him know I'm not in the mood to be fucked with, and keep jogging to reception, my skin prickling the closer I get to the chipped paint of the front door.

Inside is worse.

The scent of stale beer and urine hits my nose as I walk into the small room to find a middle-aged man sitting behind a counter, the sound of porn coming from his computer, his scuffed buttoned shirt crinkled, his hair thinning and skin pale.

He looks up at me, his blue eyes narrowing. "Lost?"

I contemplate retreat, but I have nowhere else to go.

"Can I use your phone?" I keep my voice strong. "It's an emergency."

He sighs and turns his attention back to the computer. "Five bucks."

"I don't have any money." I raise my empty hands. "Not on me, anyway. But if you let me make a call I promise I'll be able to repay you with more than spare change."

"Promises come easily around here, Gucci belt." He relaxes back into his chair, his gaze remaining on the screen. "Find someone else to buy your bullshit."

"*Please.*" I cringe through the plea. "It's one phone call. It won't take long."

"It's always just one phone call. One extra pillow. One more towel." He shoots me a two-second glare. "So unless you've got money, I'm busy."

I bite the inside of my cheek, holding in aggression.

"Well? Get goin'." He jerks his chin to the door. "If you hang around I'm going to assume you want to participate in the finale." His eyes meet mine as his mouth curves. "That'll get you a free phone call."

Fuck him. And every other motherfucker in this godforsaken city.

I start for the door, majorly pissed and equally helpless, until my palms press against the wood. "What about a Bentley?" I glance at him over my shoulder. "There's one parked a few blocks from here."

"And?"

"And you can have it."

"A Bentley?" He looks at me as if I'm deranged. "You're offering a car for a phone call?"

"I'm offering someone else's car for a phone call."

He raises a brow. "Stolen?"

"Borrowed."

He crosses his arms over his chest, scrutinizing me. "And the person you borrowed it from?"

"Can afford to replace it without batting an eye." I pull the car fob from my pocket and lob it toward him. "Just don't get caught."

He seizes the projectile with a grin and reaches beneath the counter to place a cell on the scuffed laminate. "I guess we have a deal."

I wish I could slump with relief, but as necessary as a phone is, the resulting call with Cole isn't something I'm looking forward to. If only I had the luxury to put it off.

I walk for the counter, about to reach for the cell when the man stands and recaptures the device.

"Hold up, Gucci belt. Where is this borrowed Bentley of yours?"

"A few blocks from here. Maybe a ten-minute walk. I can draw you a map."

He flashes a mouth full of yellow teeth. "You can walk along with me."

"That's not going to happen. Just give me the goddamn phone."

"Why would I? I already have the car key."

"You also have a death wish if you plan to fuck me over. Up until this point I've been more than civil. I promise that won't continue if you don't hand over the cell."

"They're big words from a teeny, tiny woman."

"A teeny, tiny woman who has family in some pretty dark places." I smile, hoping the curve of my lips exudes equal threat and confidence. "Have you ever pissed off the underworld before, little man?"

His eyes narrow, the squint deepening before he finally pushes to his feet. "Fine. A Bentley for a phone call."

"A Bentley for a phone call *and* a room to stay in for a few hours."

He scoffs. "She comes in here a panting, skittish mouse, and now thinks she's a ball-busting hustler."

"Deal or no deal?"

He reaches beneath the counter, the clink of metal sounding before he slaps a key with a large wooden keychain on the laminate. "Take room 102. Ground floor. Two doors down. But if I walk away from here and there's no Bentley—"

"There's a Bentley. Now give me a pen and paper so I can draw the damn map."

He complies, hovering close as I sketch the streets from memory. Once I'm done he snatches the scribbled paper and skirts the counter to stride across the small reception.

"One phone call," he warns, pulling the front door open. "And there better not be no international charges on my account when I get back."

I don't wait for the door to close behind him. I grab the device and dial Cole's most recent burner number, hoping I've remembered the digits correctly. My heart beats a rampant staccato as the chirping rings in my ear. Once. Twice. Three times. Then the message service kicks in.

Shit.

"It's me," I start as soon as the beep sounds. "I'm in trouble... I need you to call me back."

Fuck. What if this cell number isn't visible?

"Hold on a sec." I scramble for a brochure. A business card. Anything that might have the contact number of this hellhole.

Goddamnit. What's the name of this place?

"I'll have to call you back in a minute. *Please* answer when I do." I keep clinging to the cell, keep wishing for some spark of brilliance to blindside me until I concede defeat. "Please, Cole. I need you."

I disconnect the call and pace through the panic, my Chucks trekking over threadbare carpet.

I don't know if I've waited five minutes or mere seconds when I redial, but the line connects straight away. "Cole?"

"Yes," his response is gruff.

I close my eyes, the regret and gratitude hitting instantly. "I'm sorry."

"What have you done?"

I want to laugh. To scoff. To arrogantly inform him of his misconception that I'm responsible for anything. Only I can't.

"The guy I met… he wasn't who he said he was." I wait for a reply that doesn't come. "I need help getting home, and I need it in a hurry. I've got no money. No cell. No ID. I'm stuck here."

"Where?" he growls.

I drag in a long breath and square my shoulders. "Denver."

"Give me two seconds."

There's a rustle over the line, then muffled words. I hear biting anger. Snapped responses. Then the rustling clears.

"The jet is being arranged. Tell me your exact location."

"A hotel. Some seedy, rundown place on the outskirts of the city. I don't think I'm far from the airport." I maneuver around the reception desk and crouch to look beneath the counter. There are crumpled magazines, discarded rubbish, and a filthy bong.

"I need a name, Layla."

"I'm trying. Hold on." I open a drawer finding tissues, a half-used bottle of lube, and condoms. "Jesus Christ. I'm going to have to take a look outside."

"Is that a problem? Tell me what's going on." The annoyed edge remains in his voice, but this time concern lingers. "You said you're in trouble. Are you in danger?"

I wince, my stomach twisting in knots. "Yes." I move out from behind the desk and stride for the door.

"Explain. *Everything.*"

"I don't know how much time I have." I pull the handle and poke my head outside, making sure there are no fancy cars or men in suits nearby. "This isn't my phone."

"Fucking tell me. I need to know who to bring with me."

My stomach bottoms.

Normally he travels with his wife, Anissa. Unless there's a threat. Then there's Decker or Luca who can provide a show of muscle when necessary.

But there's one man who accompanies him when blood needs to be spilled.

"Bring Hunter." The request burns my throat.

"If I'm dragging him out of state and away from Sarah you better tell me why."

I jog a few steps into the parking lot to stare across the street at the motel sign. "I'm at the Flamingo Inn."

There's a pause of silence. A beat that I'm sure is filled with animosity, not frantic notation.

"*Tell. Me,*" he growls.

"*Okay.*" I run back to the security of the reception area, closing the door behind me. "I met a guy here months ago. We hit it off, and I've been staying with him in his D.C. penthouse for the last few weeks—"

"I don't give a shit about how you met, Layla. Tell me what I need to know."

My palms sweat. My stomach twists. "He told me his name was Matthew Langston. He owns nightclubs. Popular ones. I checked them out and they're legit. Successful. By the book—"

"*Layla,*" he warns. "I'm not going to ask again."

This is it. This is where he vows to disown me.

"He said his name was Matthew," I repeat, needing to ease my way into the admission. "But that's not his real name." I swallow, not allowing the emotion to take hold. "Cole, I'm so sorry, but the man I've been with is Dante Costa, and him and his family are currently searching Denver to find me."

38

———————

MATTHEW

I RUN FROM THE HOUSE, NOT STOPPING UNTIL I'M AT THE DRIVER'S door of the Lincoln, unwilling to give Bishop control of setting the pace on our search.

He climbs into shotgun. I slide behind the wheel while De Marco, Goodin, and Whitby sprint for the gates, already instructed to hide at the front of the property and use any force necessary if someone arrives with Layla.

"I was certain you were going to kill him." Bishop snatches for his belt as I start the engine and hammer the car into drive.

"I should've." I accelerate hard, kicking up pebbles and dirt to escape through the gates Layla left open.

I jet down the road, the farmhouses and tall trees passing in a blur, any chance of levelheaded thought left behind.

"Where are we going?" Bishop grasps the hand rail above his head.

"I don't know."

"But you know we have to get there like a bat out of hell?"

I clench the steering wheel tighter. "This isn't the time to goad me, motherfucker." I ease my foot off the pedal. Breathe. Try to think. "You realize they'd be able to track the Bentley, right?"

"Yeah. But she's smart. She wouldn't stick with a stolen car for long. I'm sure she's already ditched it by now."

"But they'll still know her last location and we won't. How far can she get without money or a fucking cell?"

"She doesn't need to get far. She just has to hide. And she's good at that, seeing as though she hid the shit with Emmanuel for so fucking long."

I rerun his argument, focusing on the logic. The reliability. "She'd hide and wait for someone to get her." I shoot him a glance. "We need to get in contact with her brother."

He judges me harshly with a raised brow. "You're going to call Cole Torian?"

"Just find the fucking number. Reach out to one of his restaurants."

I press my foot back down on the accelerator and head toward the highway, creating a mental list of all the places Layla might turn to—airports, hotels—while Bishop raises his cell to his ear, the subdued ringtone trilling before a woman answers.

"Hey Alesha, I'm trying to get a hold of Cole Torian but I've lost his number."

He pauses, the responding chatter mumbling through the line. "Yeah, I understand. But it's urgent. There's been a serious complication with a contact we share. I need to speak to him straight away."

The response is short and sharp.

"It's a business matter," he clarifies. "I can't give specifics. But I will warn you someone will be held accountable if the message arrives late. I'd hate for that to be you."

I take the ramp onto the multi-lane highway, one eye on Bishop, the other on the road.

"Okay. Fine," he mutters. "Pass on the message that the situation in Denver is critical. If he doesn't call Matthew Langston straight away it will be too late."

I scowl, knowing Cole will interpret the information as a threat.

"Thanks, Alesha. I appreciate the help." Bishop disconnects and lowers the phone. "Now we wait."

"We wait?" I contemplate reaching over and slamming his head against the window. "Did you have to be so fucking dramatic? You could've paved the way for a more amiable introduction. This asshole doesn't know me."

"It was a call to action." He shrugs. "I bet he reaches out in minutes."

I bet he does, too.

I bet he dials my number with rage in his veins and death on his mind.

Bishop scans the cars around us. "Where are we headed?"

"Centennial Airport. Her brother won't get a jet near the international tarmac." I coast us down the inside lane, gliding in and out of traffic.

No call comes through though.

Not in five minutes. Or ten.

I take the turn to Centennial with increasing pessimism, haunted by the last picture I saw of Grace and wondering if it's already too late to save Layla when my cell vibrates in my jacket. The incoming call connects to the car's Bluetooth, *Private Number* flashing across the dash display screen.

"Here goes nothin'." Bishop sits taller.

I answer the call. "This is Matthew."

"Is it though?" A superior drawl carries through the speakers. I don't need to confirm it's Cole. "I've heard you go by another name."

"Not anymore I don't. But that's a conversation for a time when your sister's life isn't on the line." I pull over to concentrate, letting the car idle on a random curb while I fight the need to rub at the pressure building beneath my temples. "I need you to help me find Layla."

He scoffs a laugh. "You made the wrong choice, getting involved with her."

"I didn't know who she was when we first met."

"But you stuck around to fuck with her once you did."

I don't answer. I bite my fucking tongue until I taste blood.

"What was the aim, *Matthew Langston*?" he asks with censure. "Did you want to get to me through her? To finish what your father started?"

"He hasn't been my father for a long time, asshole. I want nothing to do with Emmanuel. Or you, for that matter. I don't know what Layla told you, but I only want to protect her."

"And are you usually this incompetent at the things you set out to achieve?"

"I'm incompetent?" I seethe. "I'm not the son of a bitch who shot a motherfucking psychopath after two years radio silence, then didn't tell my goddamn sister about it to ensure her safety. None of this would've fucking happened if—"

The line disconnects, the barely heard hum of the radio kicking back in.

What the *fuck* did I just do? What the absolute fuck?

"Well… that could've gone better," Bishop mutters. "I'm sure he'll call back."

I slam my palm against the steering wheel. Over and over. Harder and harder.

That heartless prick *won't* call back.

I sure as hell wouldn't.

He doesn't know me. Need me. Trust me.

Layla, where the fuck are you?

"Calm your shit, Langston. We'll figure this out." Bishop thumps my chest. "Either we find her and everything is apples. Or your brothers do, then De Marco will retrieve her before she gets to Emmanuel. Or fucking Torian will get his ass here and pick her up."

Maybe.

Or maybe my brothers aren't the men Abri thinks they are.

Maybe they'll kill her on sight. Or hand her off to someone who will do it for them.

"Come on." Bishop taps the dash. "Let's get to the airport and check the parking lot for the Bentley."

"And if it's not there?"

"We hustle and figure out another fucking plan. You can call your snake of a sister and figure out a way to convince her to relay the last known location of her car." He bangs his fist against the dash this time. "We've got options, Langston. But for now you need to fucking move."

"Since when have you cared so much about Layla?" I pull back into traffic, breaking the speed limit with my acceleration.

"I don't. Abri made a fool out of me back there. It's pride I'm fighting for."

Sure it is.

He gives a shit about Layla. At the very least, he gives a shit about *me* giving a shit about her.

"Message our pilot." I focus on the cars ahead. "Make sure we're refueled and able to take flight at a moment's notice."

If Layla's at Centennial, I'll make sure we're in the air within minutes. Willingly or not.

He does as requested, swiping at his device while mine begins to shudder against my chest, the incoming call reconnecting to Bluetooth.

Bishop glances my way. "Want me to talk this time?"

"If you open your mouth, I'll fucking kill you." I answer the call. "It took you long enough to wake up to yourself, Torian."

"I suggest you check the tone and the attitude, you arrogant piece of shit."

Not Torian.

Not a man at all.

The voice is female. Confident. Merciless.

"Forgive my assumption." I frown at Bishop. "Who am I speaking to?"

"Keira. Layla's sister. And I don't have the patience to deal with self-serving motherfuckers right now, so shut up and listen."

I raise a brow, grated by the attitude, yet fucking grateful for the contact.

"My sister told me she loved you," she states simply.

The blindside hits me like a bus, the tension in my ribs exploding.

"She texted me," she continues. "It was a few simple words, but she's never sent me anything like that before. Not in reference to her husband. Not when she was dating in high school. Unless she's talking about her daughter, those words haven't existed in her vocabulary until a few days ago. So why did I just overhear my brother say you were playing her?"

"I didn't play her." My chest takes the onslaught of her accusations, the L-word knocking me down more pegs than I can stand to fall.

"So you didn't hide your identity? You didn't pretend to be someone she could trust instead of someone she would despise?"

The car falls silent, my ears ringing with my mistakes.

"I'm waiting," she snips. "Explain what the hell you were thinking in targeting my sister."

"I wasn't," I admit. "I was spying on Emmanuel the night we met. She was, too. And I wanted to know why. There was no malice or ill intent. I only wanted answers."

"And?"

"And once I got them, I needed more."

The line falls quiet, the silence making me focus on the dash display to see if she's hung up.

"Do you love her?" Her voice softens.

"I've told her as much since the day we met."

It's a cop-out. My endearments have never been spoken in anything but playful banter. But *do I love her*?

I'd kill for her.

Die for her.

Keira sighs. "I don't believe you."

"Then believe this—the last time I saw her she'd stolen my sister's car. One that's sophisticated enough to have GPS tracking. She has no money. No phone. No identification. And your brother doesn't seem to give a shit."

"He gives a shit, you ignorant prick. We all do. Cole walked out of here as soon as he knew the jet was ready. He's already on his way to Denver."

"Has he brought a body bag? Or is he stupid enough to expect her to still be alive in a few hours?"

"Fuck," Bishop mutters under his breath. "Bees and honey, champ. Bees and fucking honey."

I close my eyes. Breathe deep. Force a patient swallow. "Look, I'm beside myself trying to get to her before they do, but I've got no clue where to start looking. Do you know where she is or not?"

The quiet returns.

I'm forced to stalk the display screen again. "Keira?"

"A hotel." She sighs. "I don't know which one or where exactly. Cole told Hunter it's on the outskirts of the city. She was advised to stay there until he arrives."

"Can you get me a name?"

"No. I already stole your number and am blindly trusting that my sister saw something in you that was real... At least, real enough to save her life. You're going to have to do the rest on your own."

"*We'll find the hotel*," Bishop mouths.

"Okay. Fine." I wipe a hand down my face. "I'll figure it out."

"Good," Keira responds. "Because if you don't, I'm sure you know what will happen."

39

LAYLA

I PACE THE CARPET OF THE DIRTY HOTEL ROOM FOR HOURS, ONLY taking short intermission breaks to inch the cheap plastic blinds apart to see what's going on outside.

Cars come and go on the busy street, the frantic traffic driving by like a thousand and one potential threats.

I'm hungry.

Tired.

And although it's hard to admit, I'm scared, too.

Fear didn't eat me like this when I was under Emmanuel's roof. I'd felt protected. Stupidly immune because Matthew was by my side.

Now he's not here, and I'm unsure what will happen if the Costas find me.

"Hey. Open up." The reception guy knocks on my door. "I found that car of yours."

I remain quiet, my heart trembling, my feet cautiously creeping me toward the entry.

"I said, I found that stolen car of yours," he says louder. "Are you going to open up or not?"

"Keep your voice down." I double check the security chain and open the door a crack, finding him an inch away, his acrid breath turning my stomach. "What do you want?"

He eyes me from face to feet and back again. "I hope you're not bringing trouble my way."

"I'm not." I try to close the door only to have him lean his hip and shoulder into it.

"Well, you might like to know someone was calling about a woman fitting your description earlier. Said it was important they got in contact with you."

My pulse skips a beat. "Who was it? What did you say?"

"They didn't give a name." He runs his tongue over a rotting front tooth. "And I told 'em nothin', but that payment of yours is only going to go so far if I'm getting caught up in something that's not my business."

"You won't." I pull the door a smidge wider to chance a peek outside, then begin to close it again. "I'll be gone soon."

He thumps the wood with his hip. "How soon?"

"Any goddamn minute. Okay?"

I'm hoping Cole is already in Denver. If not, he has to be close.

"All right, Gucci belt. But just so you know, if I get another phone call, I might be tempted to sing like a little canary." He runs a hand down his chest to his stomach. My gaze isn't tempted to follow the path farther as he jerks his hips. "If you want we can come to an agreement on a cash-free transaction that will ensure my silence. What do you say?"

"Go to hell." I shove the door shut and secure the flimsy handle lock.

I return to pacing, my fluctuating adrenaline having me hyped one minute and heartbeats from being comatose the next. I'm starving, scared, and nauseated. Helpless, hopeless, and horrified at what's to come.

But it's the familiar tone calling out, "Hey" ten minutes later that has every hair on my body standing on end.

I tiptoe to the window to peek through the plastic blinds, finding a black Mercedes pulled into a nearby parking space with Salvatore standing at the open door.

"I said, hey." He focuses to the left of my room. Remy is nowhere in sight.

"What do you want?" the creep from reception calls back. "I'm busy."

Oh, shit.

I slowly glide the blind back into place and sidestep to the door, holding my ear close to the frame.

"Have you seen a girl?" Salvatore asks. "Dark hair. Jeans. Blouse."

"Pretty face?" the creep replies.

I backtrack toward the dilapidated kitchenette, my limbs heavy as I open the top drawer to find two plastic forks and a metal butter knife. There's nothing else. No potential weapon. No cause for hope.

I'm going to have to escape through the bathroom window into the alley. Then what? Run for my life? Hide around the corner until Cole comes face-to-face with a man responsible for his brother-in-law's murder?

They'll kill each other.

"I guess," Salvatore replies. "So, you've seen her?"

"No, but I'd like to." The creep snickers. "If you find her, do you think you can give her my number?"

I don't buy the act. Paranoia has me picturing the sleazy asshole blatantly pointing Salvatore toward my door.

"You sure you haven't seen her?" This time it's Remy's voice, closer than his brother's. "She isn't hiding in one of your rooms, is she?"

A car door slams. A shadow passes my window.

I blindly trek backward toward the bathroom, my limbs growing heavy. I'm about to step into the tiled area when a skitter of sound carries from the alley, the subtle rattle of my bathroom window following.

My throat burns. The pounding beat of my heart threatens to crack my fragile ribs.

Did Salvatore run to the back of the building?

Now there's nowhere to go.

I lunge toward the wall beside the open bathroom door, my back to the plaster covered in fingerprints, the butter knife clutched in my hand.

My head fills with visions of Stella, my eyes burning at the thought of never seeing her again.

I wipe my tingling nose with the back of my hand, measure my breathing, and raise the knife, preparing to strike. I won't go down without a fight. Butter knife or not, I'll cause injury.

Remy's voice continues to carry from the parking lot at the scrape of the window opening. A light footstep against the tiles follows.

Salvatore is inside. He's right there.

The ring of static grows in my ears.

I hold my breath, my raised arm throbbing, my heart frantic.

As soon as the suit-covered frame hits my periphery I lunge only to have the knife blocked, my wrist snatched, and my arm twisted behind my back before a rough hand clamps over my mouth.

"Quiet, *amore mio*." Matthew holds me against his chest. "Save your screams for later."

I hyperventilate, my breaths short and sharp as relief pummels me.

I hate him. But I hate even more that I love that he's here.

"If they find you, you're done," he whispers in my ear. "Do you understand?"

I nod, grateful and angry. Panicked and indebted. Hurting and so goddamn confused.

"Good." His palm falls from my mouth. "We need to get you out of here."

I turn to face him, retreating a step. "Cole's coming to get me."

"He's not here now, though, and my brothers are right outside your door." He grabs my wrist and drags me toward the bathroom. "Come on. The car's in the alley."

I attempt to pull my arm free, but he tightens his hold.

"Don't test me, *amore mio*." The endearment is growled. "My patience is dead."

"Please give me your phone." I implore him, no longer capable of fighting. "Let me call and see where he is."

"In the car."

I pause, barely recognizing him through the aggression. Sweat beads along his brow. His eyes are wild. And that hold of his is restrictive—tight and confounding, like he refuses to release the tether holding us together.

I shake my head, wishing I could depend on him but knowing I can't.

"You'd prefer to take your chances wasting time in here than trust me to save you?" He inches closer, his brows furrowing. "Do you hate me that much?"

My heart says no.

My head disagrees.

"Let me call him. It won't take long."

"I'll throw you over my shoulder, Layla. You know I will. Stop using my mistakes as an excuse to risk your life. You're smarter than that." He releases me, his chin rising at the loss of contact. "I'll make sure you see Cole, okay? I've already spoken to him once today. Your sister, too."

I flinch in confusion. "How? Why?"

"I knew you had no way of getting home."

I swallow, hating how useless and predictable I've become. "He knows what you did," I whisper. "And who you are."

"He told me as much."

"He'll kill you," I add, gaining face the only way I know how.

"Yeah, he made that clear, too."

"Can we get the fuck out of here?" Bishop mutters from the alley. "Save the foreplay for later."

I scowl at the interruption. At the bullshit Bishop always provides.

"Look." Matthew raises his hands in surrender. "I understand your hatred."

"No, you don't." He couldn't comprehend how my father did the exact same thing to me. How I was led to believe I was adored when I wasn't. That I was appreciated when instead I'd only been used.

"If I'd known about your connection with Emmanuel, I never would've—"

"Deceived me for every minute we were together?" I accuse. "You knew I deserved to be told they were your family."

"And you would've run."

"Exactly." I rub my wrist where his hand had just been, soothing the tingling skin. "If I'd been aware, I never would've been with you."

"What about the things I should've been aware of?" He grates through clenched teeth. "You didn't do me the courtesy of telling me I was fucking my way back into the underworld. I had to find out—"

A pounding knock sounds at a nearby room.

I freeze. Matthew straightens.

"Housekeeping," Remy shouts.

"They're going door to door," Bishop snarls. "Yet again, we don't have fucking time for this."

Where the hell is Cole?

He should've been here by now.

"I'll fight to the death to stop them from taking you." Matthew leans closer, his commanding face an inch from mine. "But I'm unarmed and Bishop's outnumbered. Do you despise me enough to risk them taking you back to Emmanuel?"

I wish I knew.

"Come on, *amore mio*." He reaches out. "Be smart about this. Do what's best for Stella."

I hate how he wields my daughter like a weapon even though his argument is valid.

"You'll take me to Cole?" I ask.

"You'll see him as soon as he arrives. I promise."

He holds out a hand as another booming knock sounds, this time closer.

I'm running out of time. Out of options, too.

"Okay." I ignore his offering and nod. "I'll go with you, but once I find Cole, I never want to see you again."

40

MATTHEW

I help Layla into the back of the Lincoln then climb into shotgun while Bishop takes the wheel.

She's safe for now. At least from herself. She can't escape again with the child lock on both doors. But my threat toward her is a different matter.

I want to throttle her. To shake and scold until she understands exactly how stupid it was to run from me.

"Ready?" Bishop shifts into drive. "I don't think we're going to leave the alley without being seen."

I know, and I have no clue what Salvo will do about it. Give chase? Give up? Who fucking knows with that asshole.

"Slam your foot down and don't stop until you lose him." I glance to Layla in the back seat. "Put your seatbelt on."

She does as instructed, her frantic eyes meeting mine. "What about the phone call?"

"Later."

"Later? That wasn't the deal."

"We're kinda busy here, *amore mio*." I turn my attention to the side mirror as Bishop inches forward, my focus on the closed window we climbed out of more than a few yards back. "If we're lucky, Salvatore and Remy will be searching one of the hotel rooms when we pass."

They know she's around here somewhere. In this suburb. Abri told me as much after the city search failed and I was forced to bribe my own damn sister.

"Evidently, we're shit out of luck." Bishop rolls the Lincoln to a stop.

"Why?" I raise my gaze to the alley, my pulse kicking at the sleek town car slowly approaching to block our exit.

"Want me to blow this pop stand in reverse?"

"That's Cole." Layla releases her belt and tugs at the door handle only to have it deny her freedom. "Let me out."

"I need to speak with him first." I shoot Bishop a hard look and shove from the car. "Keep her inside until I return and make sure you watch the back of those hotel rooms."

"No, take me with you," she demands. "He'll kill you."

I ignore her, unsure if her intent is to intimidate or warn, and close the door behind me to stride ahead. She shouts for me to stop, the muted calls trapped behind closed windows and smothered by heavy traffic, but her suffering punishes me all the same.

I'm sure I've got nothing to worry about, though.

Cole is smart enough to pause his trigger finger when his sister is still trapped in my car. I'm banking my fucking life on it as I continue forward, the two men seated in the car before me glowering, the driver lacking subtlety when he casually rests his gun on top of the steering wheel.

I stop a few yards from the hood, watching them talk, the conversation seeming relaxed as fuck.

I'd do the same—fake self-assurance in the face of my enemy. But from what I've learned about the infamous Cole Torian, we're different in almost every other aspect.

To me, death is a transaction—clinical and cold.

He sees it as a game—thrilling and ego-boosting.

I have confidence he won't shoot me before he has the chance to taunt me first.

He climbs from the passenger seat and strolls casually toward me, his equally well-known enforcer stepping out from the driver's side to remain behind the open door, his weapon coming to rest on the roof.

Cole doesn't speak as he approaches, his dark grey suit wrinkle-free, the slightly imperious set of his brows confirming he'll at least toy with me before I'm dead.

"I'm unarmed." I raise my hands at my sides before letting them fall.

"That's a mistake." He grins, the flash of teeth cocky. "You've got my sister."

"I do. She's safe and unharmed."

"But still being held against her will, otherwise she would've run to me by now."

I don't deny the obvious. There's no point.

"Let her go," he drawls. "And I'll let you live... for now."

I should scoff. Or at least mimic his arrogance, only this isn't about ego.

It's about *her*.

Layla.

Nothing more, nothing less.

"I can't do that. She doesn't want to return to Portland."

He raises a sardonic brow. "You can hear her yelling, right?"

"I can." And it fucking kills me. "But are those shouts for her freedom or my life?"

He pauses, contemplating me for long moments.

"She's been happy with me for weeks," I add. "She *loves* me— just ask Keira."

"Proof of her love wouldn't mean shit. You're not the first scam she's fallen for." He steps closer, losing the mask of delight. Now he glares. Hard eyes. Curled upper lip. "You're her MO. This is what she does—falls prey to predators. She's the walking, talking definition of gullibility."

My hackles rise. "And that right there is why I can't let her leave with you. She's told me all about her position in the family. How you make her feel worthless."

"Her *actions* make her feel worthless. She's her harshest critic."

"Are you sure about that?"

He scoffs a silent laugh. "That's some set of balls you've got, Costa."

"Don't call me that." I clench my jaw. "It's not my name."

"Sorry. I forgot Layla told me about the label change. But tell me, *Matthew*, have you informed her of your moniker yet? Has the man who wants to rescue her like a fucking hero told her what he's best known for?"

I clench my teeth harder, refusing to react.

"You didn't tell her that, either, did you?" His eyes narrow. "You're delusional if you think she could love someone with your reputation."

"Reputations are usually built on gossip and exaggeration. You and Hunter should know that better than most."

"I think we're both man enough to admit the worst of us is kept secret from the world because those who witness it die at the scene."

I fall quiet. Unresponsive.

He's right.

"I'm told you were once a monster, Matthew Langston," he drawls the name with censure. "And yet you expect me to what? Let you leave with my sister?"

"I *am* leaving with her. The only decision left to make is if it will be done with force."

"You're threatening me now?" He steps closer, less than a foot between us when he clenches a fist.

"I'm preparing you."

I don't attempt to block his punch. I take the blow to the gut as punishment and hunch with the impact, Layla's muted screams surpass the thunderous pulse in my ears.

He strikes again and again. My chin. My cheek. Each impact hitting without defense.

"That's enough," I warn.

Another blow hits my jaw. My temple. The pain rings through my skull.

"I said, that's enough." I charge, ramming my shoulder into his ribs, sending him backward in a grappling bear hug. Impatience consumes me as I hold him close and shove a hand beneath his jacket, snatching for his holster to unclasp his weapon.

The soothing familiarity of the gun is in my hand in seconds. The urge to pull the trigger calls to me.

"I deserve a few hits for the secrets I've kept from her." I place the barrel against his sternum. "But now you're done."

Rage flashes across his face. "We're done when I say we are."

"Give the order," Hunter growls beside their car. "One word and he's dead."

"If he's dead, she's dead, too," Bishop calls from behind me. "I don't have a fondness for the bitch like he does."

I smile, tasting blood. But it's Layla's silence that unsettles me.

There are no shouts.

No screams.

Bishop can threaten on my behalf all he likes, but if he's got her at gunpoint there's going to be trouble.

I glance over my shoulder, finding him behind the wheel, his upper body half out the window, while Layla's frantic eyes stare at me from the back of the Lincoln, her hands gripping the front seats.

"Interesting that you chose to threaten instead of negotiate or beg." Torian reclaims my attention. "I would've thought you'd be smarter than that."

"You wouldn't respect me if I did. And I wouldn't be a strong enough man for Layla either. I'd go to war for her. What I won't do is wither on my knees."

"So you choose death?"

"No." I shove him away and raise the gun, making a show of letting it fall limp in my fingers. "I'm the one who came unarmed, remember? I don't want you as an enemy." I lower the weapon to the asphalt and kick it aside. "Nobody needs to die today."

"Just be taken hostage?"

I expel a heavy sigh. "She's only a hostage to her own anger. We had a fight. She's pissed. But she still wants to be with me. And from what I'm told, you'd appreciate not having to deal with her anymore."

"Is that what she told you?" He frowns.

"That she's the outcast? The black sheep? Yeah. She hates her life in Portland, and loved the time she spent with me. Let me take her off your hands. I'll protect her. Provide for her. She'll never be left wanting."

"Except for the truth, right?"

My jaw ticks. "We don't have time for this. Salvatore and Remy are inside that shitty hotel looking for her. They're not going to unfurl the welcome mat if they find you here."

"I already placed a call to the owner. If he knows what's good for him, he would've gotten rid of them."

I fall silent.

Cole does, too. Both of us scrutinize each other through our animosity.

"So you think you're going to convince her you're a good guy?" He focuses on the car over my shoulder. "I say you're kidding yourself. Hunter has a sinister reputation, but even he's disgusted by some of the tales of your glory days."

"I'm not a good guy. But I'm not that man anymore either. I did everything I could to get out of the lifestyle and start over. You, of all people, should understand the dedication that required."

He continues dissecting me beneath his gaze, his thoughts loud but undecipherable. "She'll hate you before she ever attempts to love you again."

"I can live with that. But I won't live without her. I promise you I'll rain hell down on everyone until I get a chance to redeem myself. And I'm a man of my word, Torian."

"I'm beginning to see that." He grabs his lapels to straighten his jacket. "I'm assuming you love her back?"

I stiffen, every muscle, every limb.

I'm getting somewhere here. I'm winning him over. I'm not going to lie, though.

"No," I answer simply. "What I feel for her doesn't represent the whimsical bullshit people brag about."

"Then why the fuck would I—"

"Because she fucking consumes me," I snarl through clenched teeth. "She destroys me. Rips me apart and leaves me weak. Every thought I have is savaged by her. Every breath is tainted with her scent. What I feel for her is more than the bullshit of love. It's something you wouldn't understand and couldn't comprehend."

He raises a brow, mocking me. "Nice speech."

My anger spikes. I glance for the gun, itching to sweep it off the ground.

"I suggest you leave it where it is. Especially when I'm finally starting to not want you dead." He waves a lazy hand toward my face. "You're lucky I recognize the pussy-whipped expression. You're also fortunate I have plans for your family and no patience to babysit her while they unfold."

"With all due respect, don't you think it's a little late for babysitting? You should've told her before you made a move."

His left eye twitches, the seconds passing in reignited hostility before he states simply, "I was yet to make a move, *Langston*. Do I look like the type who would repay what Emmanuel has done with a friendly bullet wound?"

"Then who—"

"Who's to say he didn't do it to himself? It got us all here, didn't it? It gave him the attention I've learned he craves. It also fuels your siblings' hatred and makes them more inclined to follow Emmanuel's lead."

"Maybe you're right. But what does that mean for Layla?"

"It means I'll give you what you want. At least partially, anyway. You've got thirty days."

I pause, waiting for a catch.

The bait and switch.

"An entire month where you can do your best to win her back, because *yes*, I agree she deserves happiness, and it's been clear for a while that she won't find it with us in Portland." He steps threateningly close, causing Layla's screams to reignite. "But if you hurt her. If you fail to keep her safe—"

"I won't."

"Good." He strides for his gun and bends to pick it up before shoving the weapon inside his jacket. "Because no words can describe the fun things I'll do to you if you don't."

"What happens after thirty days?"

He shrugs. "If you win her over, she's yours. I won't get in the way. She'll be your responsibility and you'll get no trouble from me."

"And if I don't?"

"For your sake, I wouldn't let that be an option." He strolls back toward me, giving me a demeaning clap on the chest. "Make her happy, otherwise it'll be the last thing you fail at achieving. Hear me?"

I raise my chin. "I hear you."

He passes me, continuing toward the Lincoln. "Now, I think it's time you two were formally introduced, don't you? It's only fair that she learns she's going to be spending her days with the Butcher Boys of Baltimore."

Please consider leaving a review on your book retailer
website or Goodreads

Other Titles in the Hunting Her World

Hunter

Decker

Torian

Savior

Luca

Cole

Seeking Vengeance

Ruthless Redemption

**Information on Eden's other books can be found at
www.edensummers.com**

ABOUT THE AUTHOR

Eden Summers is a bestselling author of contemporary romance with a side of sizzle and sarcasm.

She lives in Australia with a young family who are well aware she's circling the drain of insanity.
Eden can't resist alpha dominance, dark features and sarcasm in her fictional heroes and loves a strong heroine who knows when to bite her tongue but also serves retribution with a feminine smile on her face.

If you'd like access to exclusive information and giveaways, join Eden Summers' newsletter via the link on her website.

For more information:
www.edensummers.com
eden@edensummers.com

www.ingramcontent.com/pod-product-compliance
Lightning Source LLC
Chambersburg PA
CBHW050747190726
48285CB00005B/1558

9 781925 512502